BLOOD
RIVER

Also by Tony Cavanaugh

Kingdom of the Strong
The Train Rider
Dead Girl Sing
Promise
The Soft Touch

BLOOD RIVER

TONY CAVANAUGH

hachette
AUSTRALIA

hachette
AUSTRALIA

Published in Australia and New Zealand in 2019
by Hachette Australia
(an imprint of Hachette Australia Pty Limited)
Level 17, 207 Kent Street, Sydney NSW 2000
www.hachette.com.au

A catalogue record for this book is available from the National Library of Australia

ISBN: 978 0 7336 4074 2 (paperback)

Cover design by Luke Causby, Blue Cork
Cover photograph courtesy of Luke Causby, Blue Cork
Author photograph courtesy of Jasin Boland
Text design by Kirby Jones
Typeset in Sabon LT Std by Kirby Jones
Printed and bound in Australia by McPherson's Printing Group

For Cassandra

HANGING WITH GLOOM AND SADNESS, THE SKY WAS FULL.

With dark clouds of silver blue, crackles of grey and black, black and grey, heavy across to the horizon, ripples of thunder getting closer, closer, closer, rolling across the ether towards me. Pulsating me, twining me, scaring me. And then –

Maybe dissipating. Maybe not. And the rain, deep in the desert. Coming towards me. To all of us. I see it now. I see it all. I didn't, not then, not back then, when I was seventeen. When I –

The city waited. We all did.

The flood was coming. A deluge. Brisbane had been cascaded with rain for almost three weeks. The sky, a low ceiling of pulsing bursts, ebbing grey and black, lifting its curtains to sheets of silver water. We haven't seen a blue sky in three weeks.

Like the city, I was about to go under.

We all were.

PART I

LARA

Oh Mary, don't you weep, don't you mourn
Oh Mary, don't you weep, don't you mourn
Pharaoh's army got drownded
Oh Mary don't you weep

If I could I surely would
Stand on the rock where Moses stood
Pharaoh's army got drownded
Oh Mary don't you weep

Wrong Girl

1999

IS THAT A POLICE CAR?

It's four in the afternoon and I'm upstairs, looking down through my bedroom window. We live on Ascot Hill and the corkscrew of our narrow street winds its way up to the top. Up to us.

The sky has fallen so low that the clouds are touching the surface of the streets and through this wall of shifting black, grey then white, I'm watching the pulse of a red light. Snap. Then blue. Snap.

From down at the base of the hill, the pulsing snap-snaps of an emergency vehicle's lights have been drawing closer. Towards us. Sometimes the lights, fuzzy through the veil of fog, vanish for a moment, as if the vehicle is lost, then they appear again, on another side of the hill. Making its slow, spiralling journey upwards.

Is that a police car?

Maybe someone has died, up here in the quiet suburb, so still and wet that there are no signs of life outside. We're all indoors, all waiting for more rain, for the flood and then for the skies to finally open once more returning the sight of a blue sky.

It's been raining all day. Again.

In the tendrils of mist, white, then grey then black, canopies of trees hang low, as if the rain is pushing them down. Some branches touch the broken concrete footpaths. Purple jacaranda flowers, shaken in the storm that sped across the hill, litter our street, so tight that only one car can edge up or down at a time.

Whatever the vehicle is, if inside are police officers or ambulance workers or maybe even firemen, it comes in silence. There is no siren. Just pulsing, flashing lights of brilliant red and ominous blue.

—

IT WAS A police car. Coming for me.

I heard mum open the front door, a guy saying he was a police officer. He and his partner wanted to ask me some questions and a moment later I heard: 'Jen!' being called up the stairs and I walked down, not at all sure why a police officer would want to talk to me.

All the school stuff, that'd been resolved; detentions, mea culpas and onwards we march and anyway – it was just school stuff. So, I was totally bewildered and nervous as I reached the bottom of the staircase.

There were two cops standing in the living room.

She wore tight black jeans and a black t-shirt and he wore a dark blue suit, pale yellow shirt with a blue paisley tie. She wore Doc Martens and he had shiny patent leather brown shoes. She was Asian, tall, at least one-eighty centimetres, with dyed platinum-blonde hair and a gun tucked into a holster tucked into her hip. I couldn't see his gun but there was a bulge under his jacket. He was a lot older than her. She must have been mid-to-late twenties. He was from that old-guy age which starts to become indefinable after a person turns forty, or so it seems to me at the age of seventeen. Maybe he was in his fifties or sixties. How do you tell? He looked as though he'd been in the navy. He looked weather-beaten. Kind blue eyes but he could smash your head in. Without warning; that's the impression he gave. He was short, quite a bit shorter than her and wind-swept and had a 1960s crew cut. Barrel chested and massive biceps. They were smiling as if we were all about to go on a picnic. She was pretty, with dark eyes. She had the brisk and efficient thing going on. She looked dangerous. Dangerous-smart, not dangerous-smash-your-head-in. They were trying to lull me with their smiles, disarm me, make me think that there was nothing wrong.

There was a rising fear. I knew I was in trouble, big trouble. My head began to spin in a kaleidoscope of colliding, possible scenarios, me wanting to grab onto a wedge of *Oh, this is what it's about* so I could quickly place myself in this sudden and unexpected twist to the thus-far banal journey of me, Jen White, seventeen years old. What are they doing here, staring at me?

Stay in control Jen. Stay on the life raft. It's a misunderstanding.

'Hi Jen. It's Jen, right?' asked the woman.

Yes.

'Hi. I'm Detective Constable Lara Ocean, and this is my colleague, his name is Billy Waterson, and we just want to ask you a few questions.'

Okay. I kept staring at the gun tucked into her black leather holster. How heavy is it? I wondered. Has she ever shot it?

'You want to sit down? Hi, you're Jen's mum, right?' she asked.

Yeah. The woman cop Lara Ocean pointed to the Balinese couches, over-stuffed with white cushions.

Mum just nodded as she went to sit. She was doing her wobbling thing. It's what me and Anthea call the VX effect. Vodka and Xanax. Breakfast of champions.

'Great. Good. Do you want to sit next to Jen as we ask her some questions?'

Mum fell backwards into the couch. Turned to me as I sat next to her and smiled, a smile from Jupiter because it's not Earth.

Lara Ocean and the older cop sat next to one another on the couch opposite. Between us lay a long wooden coffee table, also from Bali. Dad's art magazines piled up on one side. Mum's travel magazines on the other.

'Are you okay for us to ask Jen a couple of questions, Missus White?'

No, I thought.

'Yes,' said mum, haltingly.

I sat with my hands clasped in my lap, staring at the Moroccan carpet beneath the coffee table. Dad trades in crafts from the Maghreb but mostly in Aboriginal art. He's never at home. He used to tell me stories, made-up stories, to get me to sleep. He stopped doing that a long time ago. After I begged him to.

Stay in control Jen, stay on the life raft.

—

'NO-ONE REMEMBERS WHERE they were on certain days or nights – I mean, who travels with a diary and cross-references that stuff?' She smiled and laughed. The man cop, Billy, also laughed.

Me too. Funny joke. Anything to make them like me.

'But Jen, can you tell us where you were on the night of Thursday, November eighteenth?'

No …

Hang on. What's happening? Why are they here, staring at me? What have I done? I haven't done anything, have I?

Everything suddenly went very still, like a freeze-frame in a movie. I turned to look outside, at a swift new torrent of rain and I thought that life needed to go into rewind now – press the button Jen – so the rain would be sucked back up into the sky and I would be transported back to my bedroom window, looking down, into the black, grey and white mist, tendrils and gloom, watching as the lights of the police car were receding, that the press-reverse button had worked and life was returning to normal. There. See. The red blue snap-snap of silent warnings going backwards, sucked down into the clouds hovering on the hill of narrow roads, backwards they retreat, into a darkness. There. See. They have gone. The lights, they have returned to another world. Not mine. They came from darkness and that's where they have returned.

'Jen?'

I turned back to face them, smiling, like we were all going on that picnic together.

'Jen, we're going to ask you to come with us to the station where we can do a formal interview. Missus White, you'll come down with us. Your daughter is under-age and she needs to have a parent or guardian present as we question her.'

'What is this about?' asked mum. Finally.

I was quivering. I thought I was going to pee my pants.

Anthea, who is sixteen going on seventeen, appeared at the crevice of the door to the kitchen. She'd been listening.

She was shaking. More than me. She was staring into me with a: *What is happening? There are cops in the house?*

I try to give her a reassuring smile – it's okay, it's just a weird fuck-up. There were tears rolling down her face because she knew that we were in an alternative universe and it is bad, bad, bad. I dragged my gaze away from her after sending what I hoped was a (but I don't think it was) look of reassurance; *Hey, it's going to be fine, it's going to be okay.*

She didn't buy it; she knew I was lying. Because she saw the fear in my face. As I felt the fear in my stomach.

'Jen is a person of interest in an investigation; aside from that, we can't really say anything until we get to the station,' said the old guy, Billy. Speaking for the first time.

Why was it her who'd been doing all the talking? Because she's not a man and three times my age, I figured. I figured they, the cops, had agreed on a game plan before they walked in. You do the kid because you're a girl and you're not that much older than her. She'll like you, she'll reach out to you and want to tell you stuff. You and her, Lara and Jen, you'll connect.

He leaned forward. Billy Waterson. He smelled of something ridiculously sweet. He said in a British accent that reminded me of the actor Michael Caine:

'Now, Jen, Missus White: there is nought to be alarmed about.'

Which is when I categorically knew for sure that my life would never be the same again.

—

I WAS TAKEN, along with mum, out through the front door and down to the police car at the bottom of the driveway. It had stopped raining. But the sky was still dark with deep blue–grey clouds. The trees in our front garden dripping, the street gleaming wet silver and covered with fallen flowers. Water running down driveways and into the gutters. We lived on the top of Ascot Hill, one of the wealthiest suburbs in the city, where all the houses were big, old wooden Queenslanders with wraparound verandas.

They say the Brisbane River, down at the bottom of the hill, will burst its banks. They say the city will flood.

My new best friend, Detective Constable Lara Ocean, was gripping my arm, guiding me, staring straight ahead like a robocop. I'd almost rather she had her gun stuck into my back; the grip of her tensile fingers was like an animal's claw. Maybe she was anxious about leading an underage girl to their waiting car. I still had no idea what was going on.

But I knew it was a fucked-up mistake, that I was in big trouble. I was starting to get pissed off.

I've been told I need to work on this. Anger. My anger which seems to roll inside me any time I lose control of a situation. Focus Jen. If something happens which is outside of what you've planned – and it will Jen, it will; the unexpected happens to us every day, all the time – then do not resort to anger, lashing out. Take it easy and let it roll.

I imagined the neighbours, in all the old houses around us, up here on the hill, were staring at me, through windows, reminding themselves how odd I was, how Goth I was, how I went out at midnight with a skateboard, how violent I was towards their stuck-up daughters at school, how the devil had cursed me with one blue eye and one green, like David Bowie but not like David Bowie because I was a catastrophe, an aberration in the cloistered streets of boring-town. Well, fuck them, I hope they all die, get swept away in the coming flood, down the Brisbane River and out into the ocean.

Lara put her hand on the top of my head and pushed me into the back of the car.

Take it easy Jen and let it roll.

She didn't speak, Miss Lara. Didn't say a word. I sat on the back seat. It was an unmarked police car, which looked totally obvious because they are brand new, totally clean and have a clutch of aerials on the back window, like something from *My Favorite Martian*, an old black and white TV show I used to watch, along with *Mr Ed*, the talking horse and mum crawled in after me and the door closed on both of us. I reached for mum's hand but it was soft and damp like a noodle and I took a deep breath as Lara slid into the driver's seat and Mister Billy with the shiny-shoes slid into the passenger seat and she glanced up at me through the rear-vision mirror and, for the merest of moments, we just stared at one another and I wondered if she really believed I was somehow involved in something to do with the police or had I stumbled down Alice's hole, into another world.

'Sorry,' I said to her, 'What department are you from? I don't think you mentioned it.'

'We're from Homicide,' she said, then turned her gaze to the road ahead, put the car into gear and buckled her seat belt.

I thought I could see Anthea standing by the front door.

Wet leaves and purple flowers had stuck to their windscreen. Lara turned on the wipers and they swished, this way and that, as we began to drive off.

The Odd Couple

THE TWO CONSTABLES WERE SHUFFLING NERVOUSLY ON THE dark street, looking anywhere but at the body. A woman – Rachael – had almost tripped over the corpse while jogging late through Kangaroo Point, along River Terrace, which traverses a sheer drop of a cliff down to the fast-flowing, swollen Brisbane River below. She was sitting on the ground, cross-legged. Dazed, with a my-life-will-never-be-the-same-again (in-a-very-fucking-bad-way) look in her eyes. A Walkman, clipped to her waist, was still playing *Scar Tissue* by Red Hot Chili Peppers. She was holding back tears, taking in gulps of air. Not hearing the music. On the other side of the wide and serpentine river, the city with its ribbon lanes of traffic and faraway sirens, lights reflecting onto the black water.

The body was nestled under a towering pink bougainvillea on a grass verge that spanned the length of the street and the cliffs. The heat was intense. Even past midnight, it was over thirty degrees. That, along with the sub-tropical Brisbane humidity, made them all sweat. Beads on their foreheads, droplets coming off their cheeks and wet pools on their chests and backs. Rachael asked one of the cops if either of them had a smoke, and the female constable – Belinda – did, even though she wasn't meant to because the Force frowned on smoking. She reached into a pocket and pulled out a packet of Marlboro Red and, with shaking hands, lit the cigarette for the woman on the ground and then decided to have one herself and then her partner – Geoff – who had only been in uniform for a couple of months, shipped across from Toowoomba, asked if he could have one as well and she just handed him the packet, which he took with shaking hands and they puffed, all three of them, deep and long, hearing in the far distance the faint sounds of sirens approaching and just get here already and none of them looking at the body of the man, dressed in a charcoal-grey suit, maybe in his fifties – hard to say because his head had been neatly sliced away from the neck but not entirely and then folded sideways, so it was resting on his left shoulder. A thin piece of flesh was all that remained between head and neck. As if he was a gory toy where you could pop his head back on then lift it off again. Adding to the toy analogy, thought the constables, was his mouth.

The killer had cut from the edges of his mouth to the base of his cheek bones, creating an upwards curl of the dead man's lips. His eyes were wide open, staring at them, his mouth frozen in a smile.

That was all they had seen. That was enough.

There was more.

—

BELINDA, SHE FELT as if she were in a chimera. Rachael didn't move, sitting on the edge of the footpath, staring at the reflections of the bright city lights on the surface of the swollen river. She wondered how deep it was. How far before you reach the bottom. After a moment, she realised the Chili Peppers were still playing and she pressed stop.

The sirens were getting louder now, a little closer. They smoked in silence, Belinda, her back to the others and the body. She watched as, off to the east, out past where the river mouth spews into the sea, about thirty kilometres away, sheets of lightning ricocheted across the sky, defining the edges of the massive storm clouds at the river's mouth, flashing with white light, then vanishing. No thunder. Not yet.

Geoff, his eyes closed, was looking back, down the calm streets of Toowoomba watching a kid riding a bike to school, laughing, with Vegemite sangos in his bag, slung around his neck at a time when life had not yet become confusing.

A sheet of drizzle began to wash over them. The lightest of rain. The weather bureau had predicted more storms. A flood was beginning to look inevitable.

'So,' Geoff said to Belinda in a contrived effort at making conversation (but look, he's freaking out, so give him a free pass) 'what do you reckon about the Y2K bug? You reckon that, like they say, all computers around the world are going to shut down on New Year's Eve?'

It was November 18, 1999, and there was panic that, at the end of the year, every computer on the planet was going to kill itself because only very recently did programmers consider that there was the next century, the one that starts with 20, and every computer on the planet could only note, see and think about years starting with the prefix 19. Doomsayers were thinking the world was going to end.

Belinda stared at him for a moment. Okay, yep, she thought, he's just seen his first murder victim, and it's very gory, and we weren't told about this shit at the Academy. The Virgin Death was how one of the instructors had referred to the rite of passage of seeing your first homicide. *Not every cop gets to see a murder victim but, just in case, be prepared for how your guts will freeze, and the countless hours you will spend wondering about the victim, what their life was all about, their close-to-last moment of realisation, knowing they were about to die. Because that's what they do to you, the dead, that's what they make you do – think about their last beat of breath, about your last beat of breath.* What the instructor didn't mention was that The Virgin Death might be so horrific, so hideous and grotesque, that it would be as if the killer wanted not just to kill his victim but to fuck with *you*, so that you might never erase the image from your mind.

As if the killer had just won a game, and the prize was to remain in your head for the rest of your life.

I have no opinion on Y2K, thought Belinda, I just want to go home.

As the first of the police cars turned the corner and screamed towards them – an unmarked, sirens and lights – she and Geoff quickly crushed out their smokes. They watched as the car pulled up and two cops stepped out.

They knew who the two cops were. Everyone in the Force knew who they were. Even if they hadn't met them. Homicide's Odd Couple. Lara, the youngest detective in the Squad, ever, a twenty-something Asian woman with dyed blonde hair and Billy, the oldest detective in the Squad, with the fiercest reputation in the state of Queensland, ever, an old school copper who would smash a suspect over the head, dangle him from a balcony or just forge a confession from him. In the old days. But the old days were long gone, so they said. Not that anyone, least of all Billy, believed that. So they said. And Lara was meant to be one of the new breed. Super smart, a woman, not Anglo. She was meant to have a huge career ahead of her. So they said. She could even be a commissioner one day, one day when people wouldn't scoff with disbelief and horror at the notion of an Asian woman in that role. So they whispered.

How on earth did these two get paired up and who's going to kill who first and how come it hasn't happened already?

—

DRIZZLE WAS TURNING into hard rain. A bolt of sharp lightning, like a dagger, pierced the horizon and then thunder rolled in. The storm was in the east, but closer now. Approaching.

'Can we put a fucking umbrella over the vic so we don't lose the crime scene? You!' Billy shouted to Belinda. 'Get a fucking umbrella now; it's about to fucking pour.'

He was wearing a dark green suit and his shoes were shiny black patent-leather; the phosphorus from the streetlight above reflected off his shoes as he sidestepped the puddles.

Every constable was nervous about Billy and hoped never to cross paths with him. Billy would smash you if you got in his way. The word was that Billy had grown up in the East End of London and his hello trademark was a slash across the face with a razor-blade-embedded bicycle chain. Billy was a bad guy, Billy was a good guy – it all depended on who you talked to. He'd been one of the top homicide cops when constables like Belinda and Geoff were still in the womb.

No-one knew very much about Lara, except for the obvious and that she was meant to be really smart. No-one even knew if she was of Chinese descent or Japanese or Korean. Someone said her parents were boat people from Vietnam but that was the extent of the word on Lara, on the street, in the world of police-constable-gossip-land.

As Belinda rushed to get an umbrella, Geoff took a few steps back and watched as Lara moved close to the victim.

'This is a serial killer,' she said to Billy.

'Have there been any other killings like this?' he shot back as if talking to a student who might have just failed a test.

Geoff watched as Lara turned to the older man and, like a student would talk back to a teacher, said, 'No.'

Ignoring Geoff, the two Homicide cops spoke to one another, the torn body of the victim on the ground next to them.

'What did you just do wrong then?'

'Not think,' she replied.

Neither one of the Odd Couple seemed to care that this was playing out in front of a rookie constable and a freaked-out witness. They were living in their own world.

Billy moved in close and lowered his voice and spoke in whispers. Geoff could still hear them, just, if he craned in to eavesdrop, so intrigued was he by this odd dynamic and certain a little bit of intel about the Odd Couple would elevate him in the eyes of others. He noticed they were staring intently at one another and, for the first time, he realised that Lara towered over Billy. She must have been about six foot and Billy must have been about five-six. He just carried the gravitas and threat of a giant.

'How long have you been in Homicide?'

'Seven months.'

'And this poor bloke, lyin' here on the ground, murdered in the most foul of ways, what number murder victim would he be for you, in your seven months?'

'Number four.'

'Don't fuck it up by ...'

'... by starting with a conclusion.'

'Good. You will get to the top of the class, one day girlie. 'Specially with Billy Waterson being your teacher. Right then, what do you see?'

—

I MUST HAVE been six or seven when I thought to myself: I'm going to be a cop. It had more resonance than being a firefighter or an archaeologist, probably because my mum had been one herself, back in Hong Kong.

It was the uniform that had first caught my attention. Mum, standing in a row of fellow officers, men and women. Staring straight ahead. Looking so serious. A dark blue suit of pants and a four-pocket safari jacket with polished silver buttons over a white shirt and black tie with a wide black leather belt and two-pronged silver buckle. She looked important.

I wanted to be important.

But the thing about being a cop is that people shoot at you. *You might go to work and you might get killed.* That's what dad had said. Before he had died. That's what mum had said. That's what my little brother who used to blow popcorn at me from out of his mouth, disgusting little prick, that's what he had said, in a rare moment of thought and care.

'Your dad is correct. You're going to put yourself in situations that will, inevitably, put you in the firing line of a crook's gun,' said mum.

'What's a crook, mum?'

'A gangster. We used to call them 'crooks' in Hong Kong. Lots of English policemen call them crooks. You do not want to be in the firing line, Lara. Listen to what your mother says. A crook is a person who might kill you.'

Oh no, not me, mum. Not me.

As I got older, the more they discouraged me the more I thought: this is my calling. I *am* going to be a cop and I *am* going to rise up through the ranks and join the Homicide Squad. Because I knew, even then, that Homicide was the most revered squad, and every time I read about someone being murdered I had an inner shudder of revulsion and kept thinking about who the killer was, and whether the victim would ever find justice.

By the time I was nineteen, after I had clawed out of an inferno of two catastrophically dangerous relationships and a spiral of self-hate, when things finally got clean and twenty/twenty vision returned, I said: Lara, become a cop. Do it. Stop thinking about it, just *do* it. Make your way from grunt, up the ranks, get to Homicide. It's where you need to be. In Homicide you will be in control and ruin will no longer be your friend. Duty, responsibility, the search for a killer and the fight for justice, these will be your life jackets.

Billy told me it would pass and I would become inured but it was the banality of murder that got me. People killing people like they were cooking a steak; hey, do you want it rare, medium or well done? That was what I battled, where my darkness lived. I had already seen some bad stuff, but justice or retribution, call it what you will, drove me every day, every night.

I didn't believe in God and I still don't but I do believe in the divinity of my job. I am honoured to avenge those who have been murdered.

Seven months in, my experience of murder had been: one, gang-related; two, a jealous husband; and three, a guy who thought killing his wife would lead to financial gain. All three with clean, clear motivations. An easy ride.

Now all of that was about to change.

Cry Me A River

'THIS IS WHAT I SEE,' I SAID AS I LEANED DOWN, UNDER THE dripping bougainvillea, its pink petals scattered on the ground, crouching on all fours, ignoring the damp grass, ignoring the dead man's grin, focusing on the separation of his head from his body.

I shone my small Maglite onto the wound.

'An extremely sharp-bladed knife. Not serrated or else we'd see jagged flesh. Victim has almost been decapitated. Head folded sideways, onto the left shoulder. There is deliberation here. The killer has created a pose. As if he's creating a sculpture.'

I moved in closer. I could smell the blood and the slow-rising putridity of the open wound. Staring hard at where the side of the man's neck was still attached to his shoulder, I thought that a snip from a small pair of scissors would finish the job.

'Further deliberation in that the head has been cut but not entirely removed. This would eliminate a strike while the victim was standing. Such a strike would be impossible to control and decapitation would almost certainly be the result. It wouldn't have taken long, cutting most of his head off. The victim is lying on his back. It is extremely unlikely, given the position on the grass here, that the killer made the incision from behind. Most likely cutting from the side, straddling him, looking into his eyes. No signs of a fight, so I'm going to suggest that the killer incapacitated our victim before he proceeded to cut into his neck.'

Billy was walking around the body, listening intently. He and I were in our zone. The two constables and the witness off to one side, watching.

I leaned over the victim. 'There seems to be another pool of blood under his head. We'll wait until forensics arrive before we touch or move him, but I'm going to suggest there will be another wound. The incapacitating blow.'

I then stared at the mouth. 'The killer has incised either side of the mouth with an upwards cut of approximately three centimetres. To make it look like a ... a smile?' I looked up at Billy. 'It reminds me of the villian character in the old Batman series.'

'The Joker,' he said.

'Yeah. Him.' I looked back to the face. 'Who knows what the psychology is behind the mouth-cuts and the horrible-looking grimace, but the killer would appear to have spent some time with the victim. This was not a rapid-fire killing. Once he demobilised the victim, he arranged him.'

I moved in closer.

'One of his teeth is missing. Third from the middle. I think it's called a canine something.' Shining my Maglite around the wide-open mouth, I added, 'It's a fresh wound. It's been pulled out.'

Billy said nothing as he watched me crouching over the dead man without touching him. As I stood, we both looked at my jeans, which from the knees down were soaked in blood. 'He's wealthy,' I said, moving on. 'Wearing an Italian suit.'

'How do you know it's Italian?'

'I caught a glimpse of a tag on the inside jacket pocket. His shoes also appear to be expensive and ...' I leaned down to his left hand without touching it. 'He has a Rolex. So,' I said, turning back to Billy, 'I guess we can eliminate robbery as a motive.'

'Do you want to roll him over and see if he has a wallet? Find out his name and address?'

'I don't want to touch him,' I replied. 'Do you?'

He nodded, as if I had passed a test, not that it was a hard one, even for a rookie in Homicide.

Billy turned and looked in the direction of the main road, about three hundred metres away. 'Where the fuck are forensics and the science teams? And the Coroner?'

Him

WHEN I WAS A KID, DAD TOOK ME TO THE EKKA.

You go to the showgrounds and eat fairy floss and ride on big rides and get scared in the crappy ghost train ride and eat those revolting hot dogs which are deep fried in batter, a bit like the revolting deep fried Mars Bars, which I once tried when I was in Glasgow.

I love my dad.

He did lots of things for me. When I was a kid.

I guess he would be upset with me if he knew I had just killed a fear, stabbed him in the back of the neck and nearly sliced off his head.

At the Ekka there were cows and horses and fresh strawberries and a massive hall where you'd buy your showbags, as many as you could carry. There were hot dogs or hot chips dripping with cheap tomato sauce which, if you weren't careful, would splodge onto your clothes. Lots of fairy floss and, even though I was a kid, the vague surety of being sick when you got home, clutching your tummy and spewing into the toilet bowl but, not for a second, with any sense of regret as I munched happily away.

My dad took me on a roller coaster. I was about seven but I was tall for my age. That's the criteria to take the ride. Not age. Height. Dad freaked out and gripped the edge of the seat and looked as though he was going to have a heart attack, which freaked *me* right out. But after, as he and I stepped back onto hard land, I felt an extraordinary surge of adrenalin. Later I learnt that it was an endorphin rush.

Rush, rush, rush. I felt as though I could fly. I felt invincible. My eyes were dazzling. A white burst of energy emanated from me, in every which way.

21

I felt the same when I killed the fear on the edge of the cliff tonight. A starburst of white energy. It felt good. The first fear kill, it felt great. Better than the first kill, the aoife kill.

Fear is His word for man. Aoife is His word for woman.

I am going to do it again. Another fear kill. I am going to do it again. Soon.

—

I WENT HOME and cleaned off the blood and put my clothes in the wash. I'm back now. Back at the crime scene. There is a bit of a crowd, even though it's the middle of the night. I guess word has spread around the neighbours.

The street is long and thin. It's a crest. On one side, a little stretch of park with a sheer and long drop of craggy rock face, down to the river. Mountaineers scale the rock face to practise before heading overseas to do the real thing. I've watched them. On the other side of the street is another long stretch of grass and stunted trees and bushes; hidden behind them, stepped back in darkness, are old wooden houses that look as though they've been there for over a hundred years. Big trees in the front yards. Most likely it's the people who live in these houses who have come out to gawk. Most of them are wearing pyjamas and holding umbrellas. It's hot.

I had a shower after I threw my clothes in the washing machine. Well, not all of them because my black jeans were drenched in sticky crimson. Dead fear's blood congealing with bits of gristle from inside the stem of his neck. The jeans I wrapped in plastic and dumped in a wheelie bin around the corner, on my way back to the place.

To watch and admire. To admire me. I did this. This is my work. Me and Him. My body sculpture. The head fold. In His honour. He watches me. I will reach Him. I will get to Him. I am on the journey. Through the skies.

I returned to the crime scene also to watch the police. And to learn. I have killed before, but this is new.

I am standing deep in the shadows. I'm sweating. After midnight and it feels fucking hot with off-the-charts humidity. And what was drizzle is now turning into rain.

—

IN ONE HAND he carried a bow and in the other, a club.

He was dark-skinned. A gold chain pierced his tongue and behind him were his followers. Each of them staggering to keep up, the gold chain piercing their ears, a chain connected by their ears to his tongue.

They had listened to Him and had chosen to be led by Him, across the rocky height where the Dragon soared and the Phoenix flew aloft. They were searching for the god of thunder who lived in the skies. He was waiting for them. He could hear the footsteps of their slow trek up the mountain path.

The followers gave Him their ears willingly, allowing them to be sliced off with a golden blade so sharp that the softest touch on flesh would cause a deep and fatal wound. Each ear was folded back, hanging to the side of the head by a mere thread, but now part of the chain.

He was malevolent but wore a smile.

I was with Him. Ascending to where the waters joined the sky.

His name was Ogmios and we were searching for the god of thunder.

Taranis.

The First Circle

BEFORE WE ALLOW A BODY TO BE REMOVED AND TAKEN INTO the custody of the Coroner, we create a circle, one of many, and the first circle was around the victim. This was, for want of a better phrase, ground zero. Where the killer might have left hairs or a footprint or a fingerprint, where he had interacted with the victim, where he had taken away their life. Collapse, black, darkness falling and fallen. He had been there and we needed to find a trace, any trace, of who he was.

The first circle was three metres wide. We laid it out and no-one, unless they had jurisdiction and were gloved and suited up, could enter. That first circle was hallowed ground because the trace of a hair might lead us to the killer.

The killer hadn't just nose-dived onto the victim, from the sky. He had walked along the jogging track. He had come from somewhere and he had left a trail – maybe a cigarette butt, spit, dandruff – and so we were going to spread out in concentric circles, spiralling out into the streets and suburbs beyond, closing off the area, our people searching with careful eyes.

Forensics was there. Another crew from Homicide was there. Crime-scene support teams were there. Crowd-control constables were there; a small crowd had gathered. The entire crime scene, in the first circle, was under a tarpaulin. It was the formal management of a killing, after the emergency services had arrived, working to an established set of rules.

The body was photographed in situ. Floodlights had been brought in, the white light beamed into our concentric circles, and there was a man screaming through the wind and rain: 'This is really dangerous! Electricity and rain do not mix! I gotta turn these lights off or my men are going to get fried!'

24

There was thunder to the west and the east; all around us, closing in as lightning ripped across the night, charging across a brutal sky.

We all knew the river was rising. We all knew the city was going to flood, but when? How long could the dam hold its banks before they were breached, before a wave engulfed the city? We could hear the banshee sound of wind coming up the river from the ocean mouth, a harbinger sound of the arrival, the deluge of approaching water.

And then we found something.

Splash

AS WE HUDDLED UNDER THE TARP ON THE EDGE OF THE CLIFF-face overlooking the Brisbane River, the forensics team scoured the crime scene. Among the McDonald's wrappers and used condoms and bits of plastic, was an unusual-looking flower which was caught between shards of grass, flapping in the breeze, as if eager to fly away.

'What's that?' asked one of the forensic guys who was on all fours in the first circle.

'It looks like a daisy,' said his partner, 'but not like any daisy I've ever seen,' he said, pulling out his tweezers to bag it.

—

WE CALLED FOR an expert from the Botanic Gardens, and got a woman who called herself Splash. She arrived at the crime scene in the early hours of the morning in lime-green overalls and pink hair with a dog called Bling – she happily told us – which she tied up under a tree about a hundred metres away, well away from the first circle, and strolled towards us holding an umbrella.

She held the evidence bag with the flower close, staring at it for several seconds. With its pale yellow circle at the centre and long thin white fronds, each one a distance from the next, it resembled blades of a fan.

Surrounded by an audience of intrigued cops and forensic cops, Splash said, 'It's *olearia hygrophila*. A swamp daisy. It doesn't belong here, in Brisbane. In fact, it only grows in one place in the world: North Stradbroke Island.'

Which didn't mean the killer had come from the island or had even visited it. The rare flower might have had nothing to do with the murder; maybe it was dropped by a passing jogger or maybe it drifted on the wind to this resting place. But it was our first potential lead.

We had to check out every person who lived on the sleepy little island just off the mainland, and log everyone who might have visited it over the past few days – an almost impossible task because the only way to get there was by ferry, and while CCTV had been used as a crime tool since the late sixties, there weren't too many cameras in Queensland and I knew there wouldn't be any at the two ferry ports on the mainland or on the island. Nor would there be any record of who had travelled there or of number plates; you just rolled up, paid for the ticket and drove on board. Checking out the residents would be the easy bit. Checking out the visitors and tourists would be tricky.

—

BILLY HAD WANDERED away and was on the edge of the cliffs. Once part of an old stonemason's quarry, they were about twenty metres high and ran alongside the river's edge below. At night they were lit up from below creating an eerie bright yellow wall to this side of the city. Billy was gazing across the fast-flowing river. He'd left the cover of the tarpaulins over the crime scene and the body, crossed the closed-off street and stood in wet grass while rain fell on him. I joined him, followed his look upstream.

'You would have been a kid,' he said.

'I was sixteen,' I replied, knowing exactly what he was referring to. 'She scared the crap out of me.'

'You and all else. Especially us blokes in Homicide. Shivered us right out. At least she confessed. Saved the poor geezer's family all the details.'

Tracey Wigginton. She was twenty-five, close to the same age as me when, in a demented, drunken rage, she killed a middle-aged man she had picked up along with three other girls, in their car, cruising, looking for a target. Tracey stabbed him twenty-seven times and almost severed his head. She was later accused of drinking his blood. She was called the Lesbian Vampire Killer. It was 1989, on the other side of the river, in a West End park. The judge sentenced her to Life.

'Do you think it's a copy-cat?' I asked.

He shrugged. 'Anything is possible. No conclusions until we gather what we can.'

Like any teenage girl, Tracey's vampire killing had an indelible effect on me. One night, twenty-seven stabbings. She brought fear to the city. A fear that took a long time to dissipate.

Walk on the Wild Side

LARA'S FIRST MEMORY IS HARD TO FIND.

Was it when she and her dickhead brother and her mum and dad went to the beach? When she might have been four or five and they all lolled by the edge of the water, as baby waves washed on to the sand, before dad cooked chops on his barbecue, which he would proudly load and unload from the back of their sky-blue Holden station wagon as her mum floated in the shallows like a starfish, slowly drifting away from shore, carried by a gentle swell, her eyes closed, arms outstretched and fingers dappling into the surface of the warm water, no-one really paying much attention to her until Lara noticed she was being swept, slowly, away, as if lured to an unimaginable doom on the other side of the horizon.

Imagining wraith-like sea monsters, submerged, trailing along the ocean floor, carrying her mother to oblivion.

—

MY MOTHER, WANG Ouyang, originally came from Beijing, growing up in a hutong near the Drum Tower. She and her family left mainland China in 1949, for Taipei, the capital of Taiwan, the small island off the south-east coast of China and the subject of an identity crisis ever since, when the Nationalists, fighting Mao and the sweep of Communism, fled the mainland, slaughtered many of the island locals and set up a rebel country or, as they say, a new and free country.

Mum was twenty when her version of China collapsed, when Mao took over and *her* mum, in her forties, took flight from Beijing to Taiwan, to escape, among almost two million other fleeing Chinese. One suitcase, hurriedly packed, for a family of seven.

Soon after, mum went to Hong Kong, where she got a job as a police officer working in Missing Persons, which she didn't enjoy because most of the missing they searched for were rarely found and if they were, they were usually found dead and then Fraud, which she did enjoy because the crooks were charming, most of them anyway. While holidaying in Queensland she met a guy called Richard, who was a vet; they clicked, went on hikes together, fell in love and mum made another ocean crossing, this time from her beloved Hong Kong to Cairns, a quiet town in the far north of the state, where they lived in a tumble-down wooden Queenslander not far from the beach. There were palm trees in the back yard and a slow, warm breeze every afternoon.

Dad was a Catholic so, to mum's bemusement, every Friday night they would go to the local (dreadful) seafood restaurant overlooking the water and she would say: I hate it here. And he would say: I love it here.

And they would laugh, she told me, and she would lean across the table, she told me, as he also leaned across the table, careful not to spill his beer and they would kiss, she told me, and through all of this I was born.

———

I WAS NINETEEN when I made the application to join the police force; the wild years of running away, tatts, drugs, booze and bad boyfriends had ebbed into the not-so-distant past. Another country.

Being a cop was like a series of hills. You climb to the top of one and right in front of you, is another. And another. And on it went. As I figured out early on, and as I had been told by mum, after she had come to terms with my choice of career, it was hard for any woman who wanted to break into an historically masculine society.

You have to be alert, observant, smart, you have to follow the rules and be a 'team player'. That last bit was not my forte; I often whacked out my basketball teammates if they got in my way and would be reprimanded by the coach whose name was Lizzie, for being selfish, which I was and, according to my mum, still am and occasionally I trampled on those same teammates if they fell to the floor, my foot on their head or arm or leg, whatever, with a: 'Fuck you bitch,' which, afterwards, late at night, as I contemplated my actions, I would regret and, even though I was not religious, I would look out into the sky through the bedroom window, the dark, the stars and ask Him for atonement. It never came.

It never will. That's me, seeking a place of contentment, asking the Lord and the Stars for a place to be at one with the universe, knowing with every slice of the ask, that it is futile.

This, the ever-present threat of collapsing into futility, is one of the dangerous potholes I remind myself to avoid. In the dark, when it's just me. Me alone. After my two brutally destructive relationships, one after the other, an erasure of self-esteem and too many dark thoughts, I work on staying afloat.

—

ANOTHER BURDEN: SHE was, is, pretty. Part Asian, almost-black eyes with dyed platinum-blonde hair and, to make the statement just a little more strident, with a thin strip of original jet black in her part, tied back in a pony-tail, her hair colour being the last outward display from the rebel-yell of the past. She was, is, the type of woman who makes guys pause for a beat and do the stare. But you know, a long time ago, she thought to herself: that's their problem, not mine. I am who I am. Should I scar my face with acid? Would that make it easier? Her beauty made her self-conscious. Until she became a cop, she was downcast, her head bowed. Nils and Guido didn't help that journey. As she expected, putting on the uniform for the first time helped. Call it a disguise, call it a badge, call it a whatever.

Another burden: she was, is, tall. Lara stands over most men and, as she learned at the time, the lack of self-esteem kicks in like a horse, that most men or boys do not like to look up to a woman, a girl. Subsequently she did the hunched-shoulder thing, as if to compensate for her height. A walking apology, she would angrily berate herself at times of dark night. Putting on the uniform for the first time helped. Call it a disguise, call it a badge, call it a whatever.

Lara now holds herself with shoulders erect, walks as if the first footfall carries the purpose of her journey. The second carrying the remnants of self-doubt, the not-so-distant past. One step, two step, a cycle. Lara, in her moments of dark, wondering with which footfall the journey will end.

—

YET AGAIN LOOKING down at the grinning face, frozen on the dead body of a man in his fifties whose head has almost been sawn off.

By what? she wondered. A machete? A long carving knife?

And why?

Let's start with the why. Why do you want to kill this middle-aged man? In this way? Why, killer, did you do this? Questions.

—

TO WHICH:

The answer would remain frustratingly elusive for almost two decades.

To which:

Motivation, the cornerstone of almost every murder conviction, would be deemed of secondary importance in the case of The Slayer.

To which:

A journey of twenty years would be like a snap of a millisecond, a thousandth of a second, through time, guilt, remorse and revenge.

To which:

Lara, at the age of seventeen, adrift on a sea-green lake, surrounded by mists of doubt and uncertainty, would coalesce with another girl, also seventeen, also lost; one finding an anchor, one not, instead being dragged under the surface of the lake, as if tentacles had reached up to claim her, to take her into a morass of dark.

To which:

A killer was laughing.

Hi, Look, We Just Need to Come Inside and Talk to You

I DROVE. BILLY WAS NOT A BIG DRIVING GUY. HE WAS BIG ON directions, though.

He had said, all swagger and chest: 'I've done this a million times, so let me lead it, all right girlie?' Totally. Because I had only done it once; this was my second time and it scared me.

The haunting part of the job, was what mum would say from her memories of Hong Kong. The moment you are indelibly memorised, your face, your demeanour, your clothes, your choice of words, by the person you're breaking the news to, as their lives come apart in a sudden wreckage of grief.

You have destroyed their life and they will have forever freeze-framed you and every detail of you, down to a dimple on your cheek and the smell of your breath and the crease of your furrowed brow, forever. Right through, mum would say, right through to their last dying beat, as they clasped the journey to that loved one who died before them, as they recall, as they have done every day since you turned up on the doorstep, remembered, in way-too exquisite detail, your face. Face of doom.

Mum, the Missing Persons' messenger of death, before she fled to Fraud.

Billy, however, seemed to relish passing on tragedy, as if it emboldened him. I saw it the first time I accompanied him to an apartment in the Valley, where we had to inform a young woman that her gang boyfriend had just been killed.

Billy told me, though I'm not sure I believe him, that the first time he broke the news of a death to a family member was at the age of nine, back in the East End of London, where he grew up in squalor, grime and blood. 'I bang-shot a geezer by the name of Cricket McKinty and went around to his mum's place and said, "Your son is dead." And I walked off, leaving her on the door stoop, all boo-hoo in tears.'

Like I said, I wasn't sure I believed him.

—

WE CROSSED OVER the Story Bridge as the rain intensified, sheeting the car from my side. I glanced out through the window as we cruised through the Valley. The neon was off, the bars and strip joints closed, some deadbeats slumbering in door stoops. Then over the river at Breakfast Creek, the creek itself looking about to burst its banks, and up the hill.

Ascot: a wealthy suburb of quiet streets lined with jacarandas of purple riot and poinsettias with their leaves of vibrant red clinging to the edge of roads, tree trunks, old and gnarled, pulling up chunks of footpath. Massive old Queenslanders, houses built of wood and raised off the ground with thick round wooden poles painted white, had stood in these streets since the previous century, and it was in front of one of these we pulled up. A two-storey with a Lexus parked in the driveway and two bikes tossed easily by the front door.

—

BOOTS ON THE ground. It was raining hard now, harder, so we ran because neither Billy nor I had an umbrella.

'Hello!' Billy shouted as he rapped on the door, and I said to him: 'Actually, maybe not quite so loud; we're not here to arrest anyone.'

And he stopped and said: 'Yeah, sorry.'

—

ON MY FIRST day as a police officer, as I was heading off in my freshly ironed new uniform, as mum berated me for the thousandth time about my dyed hair, she passed on some advice:

Don't be presumptuous. Listen and learn. Smile in deference when they mention your height, your appearance and any part of your anatomy but never *be* deferential. Pee whenever you get the chance because sometimes you'll be in the middle of nowhere for eight hours straight. This was after she vainly tried to elicit from me an assurance that, despite being a police officer now, I would not forsake every Chinese girl's duty to get married by the age of thirty and provide her with a grandchild. In no way, ever, did she contemplate that I would end up in Homicide.

Billy's advice, on my first day with him, was simple: Always have a second and third change of clothes in the boot of your car. Just in case.

Just in case you have been kneeling on sodden ground, hovering over a dead man, soaking up his blood and gristle into your jeans.

There is a reason I wear only black.

I had changed before we left the crime scene.

—

WE ALREADY KNEW her name. Her name was Lynne Gibney and she was born in Ararat, in Victoria, in 1968 and she went to La Trobe University and majored in Sociology and then got married and had kids, and the man she married, James ... well, he was the man whose head I could have snipped free with a small pair of scissors. Now on his way to the morgue.

The door creaked open. It was just before nine am. Lynne was still in a dressing gown, silk and pink, expensive, and her nails were immaculate crimson but no make-up and her hair was a little unkempt. She wasn't expecting visitors. She held a bowl of corn flakes in one hand, a spoon in the other.

'Yes?' she asked.

'Hello. My name is Detective Inspector William Waterson and this here is Detective Constable Lara Ocean. Can we come in?'

'Yes,' she said in a very hesitant way. 'What's this about?'

'When did you last see your husband?' asked Billy as we walked into the house.

She began to cry. She knew it. He hadn't been answering his phone this morning. He hadn't come home last night, and when she'd called Nick, his mate, who James said he was going to have a few beers with, Nick told her that James had left before midnight. He'd been pretty drunk, is what Nick said, and so maybe he had crashed in one of the cheap motels on the side of the highway, just up the hill from the Gabba, the cricket and football oval, close to the Story Bridge, is what Nick had said.

And now there were police officers in the house. She had watched this scene in movies and on TV a hundred times. She just didn't think it would come to her and she'd have a starring role in real life.

We didn't need to say a word. We could do it all in silence. Lynne could look the question, Billy would nod, sadly. Lynne would cry. Billy and Lara would look apologetic and take on the undertaker's demeanour, shuffling out backwards, heads down.

Slow dissolve to black, credits up.

'Darlin'. We're here to help you. You got the kids in the house? There's Matt, yeah? And there is Diane, right? Where are they?'

He had reached out and taken her hand and was holding it tightly. At the same time, he had taken her bowl of corn flakes and passed it to me. And she was staring into his eyes, and his eyes were dark but they spoke the truth.

'Where are the kids?' he asked.

'They're at school.'

'Let's get 'em back home, eh?'

———

LYNNE CALLED THE school and told them there was a family emergency and that her next-door neighbour was on her way to pick up Matt and Diane.

The school wasn't far. They arrived about fifteen minutes later. By that time Lynne's mother and father had arrived and were consoling her. Other members of the family were also arriving.

There was a priest. He looked uncertain, not knowing what to do.

Because we had done our duty, there were looks of curiosity. Why were we still there?

Because Lynne had asked Billy to do it, because she didn't want to. Nor did her parents. Nor did the other family members or the priest. Only Billy. He was ready for it.

It was November 19. Five weeks before Christmas. Their house had a Santa Claus cut-out on the front window. Great present they're about to receive.

We were waiting out the front as the neighbour pulled up and two frightened teenagers climbed out. They didn't know what to make of us.

Billy reached out and took Diane's hand and held it like a vice, like he had her mother's. I saw her wince as she looked up into his eyes, then to me, then back to him. Her brother was shaking. He began to cry. Not Diane. She was steadfast, as if daring Billy to say what she already suspected. If dad didn't come home and mum had been on the phone before you went to school, frantically searching for him and then there were police at the house and grandpa's car in the driveway, you would know. She knew.

'Diane. Matt. I ain't gonna lie to you: dad is dead. He got killed last night. It wasn't a happy killing; as if there ever was. Matt, you hold my hand too, and grip it tight, all right?'

Yes, sir.

'You, Diane, you keep holding my other hand real tight, yeah?'

Yes, sir.

Into their eyes, he said:

'All I can do is find the cunt – 'scuse my French – and kill him. Trust me on that. Yeah?'

Yeah.

'And I will,' he says. 'I will find him. And then I will kill him.'

I Will

THAT WAS FRIDAY MORNING. BY THE END OF THE DAY WE had asked Lynne if there was anyone who might have had a grudge against her husband: no. We had spoken to his work colleagues to see if there was a problem at work: no. We had checked his bank accounts for any suspicious deposits or withdrawals: no. We had tracked down his movements from working late in the office, to calling his wife to say he was going to Nick's place for a few end-of-the-week drinks and not to wait up for him. At about ten-thirty p.m., he left Nick, telling him he wanted to walk along the cliff top, which was just around the corner, before hailing a cab on Main Street to take him back across the Story Bridge, through the Valley and up the hill, back to Ascot. Nick, a mid-forties primary-school headmaster who lived alone, thought James was a nut for going out into the night, which was about to be hit by yet another torrential outburst. But that was James, Nick told us, also shattered by the news; James loved to embrace the elements. Nick told us he gave James an umbrella. We didn't find it. There was no umbrella at the crime scene. Maybe it blew away.

We checked out Nick but he stood in line with everyone else we had already eliminated. As well as profiling the killer, Homicide Squads had also begun to profile the victim. It was called Victimology. James didn't fit the profile of a premeditated target.

He was fitting into the profile of a man who was randomly chosen in one of the great and unfortunate hurly-burlys of life that doesn't make sense or conform to a satisfying explanation. His death was, we were starting to think, random. Like a Los Angeles drive-by shooting. Wrong time, wrong place.

The 'meteor moment', as mum would say.

—

MIDNIGHT SATURDAY, TWENTY-FOUR hours after Billy and I had arrived at the crime scene, I got to sleep. In my little wooden house in working-class Hendra, at the edge of the Brisbane racecourse. I slept right through the rain and the noisy click-clack of the horses as their trainers led them down the street.

Sunday dawn brought a brief reprieve from the wet. And the discovery of a second body. Two in three days.

—

BRIAN WAS THIRTY-SEVEN and, as he did every morning before dawn, was jogging through the Botanic Gardens. He lived with his wife and kids on the edge of the city, not far away, in Spring Hill. His body was found on one of the pathways that spanned the edge of the river. He was discovered by an early-morning shift worker from the nearby Stamford Plaza hotel, on their way to the kitchen before the restaurant started serving breakfast at six. The hotel was directly across from where Brian lay, his neck sliced open with a deep cut, severing all but a thin flap at the side of his head, which had been folded onto his shoulder, his mouth slit and opened to create the grotesque smile. A tooth was missing, pulled out. By now we knew this tooth was called a maxillary canine, the longest in the mouth. It looked as though it belonged to a sabre-toothed cat.

Across the water, on the other side of the river, were the cliffs of Kangaroo Point. Where, on Friday, James Gibney had also met the sharp force of a killer's face.

As I walked briskly through the park towards the crime scene, my phone rang.

'Where are you?' Billy asked.

'Thirty seconds away.'

'Turn around. Meet me on the street at the main gate. The Coroner needs to see us.'

Taranis

THE FIRST TIME I STEPPED INTO THE MORGUE I TOLD MYSELF: You were the one who wanted Homicide, you better get used to the territory.

My brother, who had been making tons of money selling used cars, had already said: You will never survive an autopsy. He had been watching too much TV, the bane of a Homicide detective's life with friends and family.

I've yet to attend an actual autopsy and, frankly, the need to do so is limited. The Coroner determines the cause of death, and when there are blatantly suspicious elements, as there were with James and now Brian, the Coroner will give us a detailed brief which provides us with much of the science to plot our investigation.

We drove to the John Tonge Centre, the mortuary for all of Queensland, south of the city, passing close to the suburb of Sunnybank where mum lives, in a brick home with a lot of concrete instead of lawn but also, weirdly, a side garden of topiary. Sunnybank is the hub of the Chinese community in Queensland. Everyone thinks it's Fortitude Valley with its Chinese street signs and endless rows of yum cha restaurants, but that's surface glitter. Mandarin and Cantonese are as common as English on the streets of Sunnybank.

Memories returned. This was the landscape I ran away from. The flatlands of suburbia, strip malls, big malls, acres of brick houses built in the 1970s and few trees. The landscape of a tormented teenage girl.

Rainwater gushed along the edges of the footpaths, too much water, moving too fast. The drains were overflowing and pedestrians ran like they were tap dancing, in order to keep their shoes and clothes dry. The sky was dark. These days it's always

40

dark. We haven't seen blue sky since October. Most people were driving with their headlights on, even though it was morning.

As I was his rookie, the student for his knowledge and wisdom, from murder to how to survive on the streets of London's East End, Billy told me that the old morgue, which was built in the nineteenth century – 'Fucking draconian, "House of the Dead" they called it, with the worst stench ever, a fitting monument to Calvary and the echoes of the damned, girlie' – was situated on the Brisbane River and was flooded out in 1887 and then again in 1890. And then, in 1893, it was not only flooded a third time but washed away.

—

HOW MANY DEAD bodies have passed through this room? Thousands, each of their stories and closing moments clinging to the walls. If you believe in that sort of thing. Which I used to. But not anymore.

'You need to see this,' said the Coroner.

She removed the sheet covering James's body, and it was immediately obvious in all its ugly beauty: on his chest was a large circle, dug in, carved in, obviously post-mortem because it was pristine. Within the circle were eight spokes. Like a bicycle wheel. I tried to ignore the upward twist to both sides of his mouth, the frozen grimace.

'Strike me fuck; what *is* this?' asked Billy as he stared at the circle and its eight spokes.

'You tell me,' said the Coroner. 'I've got no idea.'

'I'll tell you,' I said as I stared at a part of my life I'd rather forget.

—

IN MY YOUNGER years, I did some crazy things, and one of those crazy things was to hang out with drug-induced Celtic Goths. I was, like, fourteen, fifteen, sixteen. Maybe it had something to do with finding my identity – am I Asian, am I Australian? Where do I fit? Because it didn't feel, back then, that I was fitting into one or the other. I was half here, half there, all nowhere.

I was thirteen when we moved from Cairns to Sunnybank, which was four months after I had come home from school to find mum and my brother sitting at the kitchen table crying. Mum couldn't answer me when I asked what had happened, with that rising horror kids get when they know that something is really, really wrong and life was possibly about to change forever. Mum wept. It was up to my brother to tell me that dad had died. Car accident. Sudden. Some guy had been drinking all night and smashed into dad when he was on his way home for lunch. The drunk guy died too.

I had always seen myself as a balloon in the sky, held to the ground by two strings. One was dad's – my Anglo half – and the other was mum's, my Chinese half. With his death, one of the strings came loose and I was adrift. Maybe I put too much stock in my kid's simple image of identity, but at the time that's how it felt.

Life was a bit hazy after that. I remember the funeral. Sort of. Then life started to skid. I hit a few kids at school. Kids who called me Chink. We packed up and drove down to Brisbane in a blur and my brother was stoic all the way through and mum put me into a new school and on my fourteenth birthday I ran away.

I guess in the wake of our collective trauma we all, individually, clung to something in order to survive: mum reached out to become more and more Chinese, and my brother embraced the notion of making a lot of money to keep him secure and me, I wallowed in the notion of being a rebel.

We're better now, me and mum, despite some Confucian issues. But back then, at that time, I was a fuck-up. Hanging with some dark, spooky Celtic-loving guys and girls. Spiking my identity crisis with grains of hate.

—

'THAT WHEEL IS identified with the Celtic thunder god, Taranis,' I said. And I swear I could feel a thousand dead souls, plastered into the walls of this room of death, breathe outwards at me.

There was silence. Broken by:

'All right, then,' said Billy. 'Tarnis.'

'Taranis,' I corrected him.

'God of thunder.'

'Yep.'

Silence. Broken by:

'All right. Okay. Thanks for that, Miss Coroner.'

'My name is Annette,' she corrected him.

'Yep. Annette. Thanks for that Annette. Sorry, I should have remembered. Ain't no good with remembering names and you've been here for a while now so sorry about that. You've got a second body making its way over to you, Annette. Geezer by the river. Same head and face mutilation so give us a call as soon as he gets here and let us know if he also has the tarnis thing on his chest. C'mon, girlie, let's get out of here.'

—

'WHAT DOES THIS fucking tarynas thing mean?' asked Billy as we hurried across the car park in the rain.

'Taranis,' I corrected him.

'Yeah, whatever. What does it mean? I saw *The Silence of the Lambs*, we've all seen *The Silence of the Lambs* where the geezer shoves a moth into the mouth of the vic. Is that what we have? Some deranged ritual thing?'

'Perhaps,' I replied cautiously, 'but at the very least, it's a form of identity. Taranis, god of thunder; identifying with him makes you feel powerful, invincible. This also explains, or I think it might, the slicing into the side of the victims' mouths.'

'How so?'

'There is another god in the Celtic tradition, connected to Taranis. His name is Ogmios and he is always smiling. His tongue is pierced with a chain, which is made up from the ears of his followers.'

'You kidding me?'

'Nope. I am not.'

'And the tooth thing?' he asked, as we climbed into the car.

'I don't know anything about Celtic relevance to missing teeth.'

'So, he draws on these mythological gods to give him strength and power?' he asked.

'Perhaps. The whole Celtic thing is complicated, not to mention being twisted to suit twentieth-century beliefs and fears. But ...'

I paused, thinking back to my days immersed in this world.

'What?' he asked. 'But what? You paused on a thought. What?'

'Well, according to today's beliefs, if you follow Taranis, you're also into sacrifice.'

'Human sacrifice?'

'Yep. Usually burnings, people tied up in wicker baskets and burnt alive but, you know, like everything violent, anything imaginative would work, as long as it causes death. It comes from old pagan stuff where people wanted to bring on rain for their crops to grow. Taranis, if he was happy, would blow his thunder and it would rain.'

Billy looked up at the sky, out through the car windows. 'Sure seems to be working,' he said.

Night Comes On

Billy and I drove in silence, towards HQ. I appreciated the think-space. For the duration of my time in Homicide, I was still learning and now I was in the heart of a case which, we both knew, was going to explode. I had to focus on the process, the work, and not on the adrenaline that I could feel building.

I had fortuitously lucked out into the rarest of murder investigations. Generally speaking, and this was what they had taught us at the Academy, in that brief class on repeat offenders and serial crimes, *Because, the chances of you guys* (guys) *coming across this sort of crook are very, very low*, we need three bodies before we can make the determination that we have in fact got a repeat offender; a serial killer. Two can be a coincidence and sometimes is, but three? No.

Billy and I didn't have to say a word to one another. Same killer.

And he was going to do it again. My first instinct had been correct: The ritualistic nature of the murder suggested an agenda of killing that needed to be sated. You don't fold back a guy's head unless you've got something specific to say. And to keep on saying.

Brisbane in 1999 was a small town. It wasn't prepared for something like this. It wasn't that long ago that sheep were mustered down the main streets of the city, when pepper was considered an exotic spice and garlic something too exotic to use at all. On Sundays the shops closed, the city was empty and people went to church. You would stand impatiently in the supermarket line while the customer at the front chatted to the person at the till. Most people knew one another by their first name. Brisbane in 1999 was not prepared for the shadowy creep of a serial killer. This was new. *The Silence of the Lambs* had only come out eight years before. The whole notion of a 'serial killer' was rare, confusing, unexplained. Panic. Fear. Freak-out. These feelings would permeate the city. The dreadful daily tabloid would rise up into the miasma of all this, as the water of the river kept rising and the rain kept coming oppressively down.

And this was not just normal rain: this was thunder and thick curtains of wet that greeted you every morning, every night, never letting up. Footpaths had become rivers and houses had started to leak and people were thinking: Am I going to survive this? And for the religious, and there are many of them in Brisbane, I could see it becoming a Noah End of Days thing. And then there was Y2K. Everyone around me was freaking out that their computer was going to shut down and go into outer space on January 1.

I looked out the car window – past the wipers going swish-swish – at the river and wondered: How far can it actually rise? Will it burst its banks, as it did back in the seventies? Will the city go under?

Will people drown?

Yes, I thought: people always die when the river floods.

———

'GIRLIE?'

It was some time ago when I had asked him to stop calling me that. 'How about you try Lara,' I said. 'My name?'

'Yeah, I'll give it a shot, girlie.'

He doesn't mean it as an insult; it's just how he is. I was going to put in a request to be partnered with another crew but, scanning the floor of desks and blokes, all full of testosterone, lunchtime schooners of XXXX beer at the pub accompanied by stories of banging up birds down at the Breakfast Creek Hotel, in the car park late at night or scoring a freebie from a pro in a city alleyway instead of busting her for solicitation, I decided I would stay with the dinosaur who grew up during the Second World War. At least he had a wealth of cunning and experience and was as dismissive of the young buck-boy detectives as I was.

And there was something else about Billy: he didn't seem to care that I was part Asian, had dyed blonde hair, towered over him and was a woman. Long after I had been accepted into the Force, mum admitted to me that when she came to live in Queensland, before I was born, she had tried to get a job as a police officer. Years of experience in Hong Kong and she got:

'We don't hire Chinks.'

She didn't tell me that when I announced I had been accepted; I don't know if that is a good or a bad thing.

'Yes?' I said to Billy, still looking out the window at the mass of brown river water, flowing under the Victoria Bridge on its journey downstream to the ocean like an impatient humbering flow of low beasts.

'This Celtic thing; is he part of a gang? Is that how it works?'

'No. Maybe, but my guess is he has appropriated it. The god of thunder. He sees himself in that respect.'

'You were into this world?'

'A long time ago.'

I turned and looked at him.

He stared at me a moment.

'It was a teenage thing,' I added.

'Yeah, well, we all got them, ain't we. Go back. Reach out to old mates and see if you can find a lead. Maybe our killer is big-noting himself, bragging about how clever he is.'

—

I'D RATHER NOT go back, a voyage to the heart of darkness of a teenage girl I had well and truly discarded into the ash-heap of forgotten memory.

But back I would go, and a little part of me was exhilarated, because I was a Homicide cop now and we don't get any tougher or better than that. If the little teenage girl, full of quake and tremble, self-hate and subjugation, if she re-emerges, the me of now will stomp on her hard.

'You want me to come with you?' he asked, as if reading my mind.

I shook my head and smiled thanks. No way, Billy. Totally no fucking way. But thanks.

The Tattooist

IT WAS IN THE VALLEY, OF COURSE. ALL THINGS DODGY IN Brisbane resided in Fortitude Valley, on the edge of the city. The strip joints, the girls on the prowl, the nightclubs, the Italian mafia, the Lebanese mafia, the Vietnamese mafia, the crooked cops, the guys just out of jail, the boys and girls scoring a little smack, the narrow laneways covered in graffiti, the cops and the drunks, the pools of blood and vomit and tufts of spit, Chinatown and two main one-way streets, both entwined by the Brisbane River which serpentined its way through the city.

Carrying an umbrella, I hurried down a narrow cobblestoned lane, stepping over a smashed-out junkie in a doorway, thankful that my Glock was on my hip.

Stepping back in time. Stepping into a tiny shop, out the front of which a sign said: Anu Tattoos.

Anu was the Celtic god of magic, the moon, air and fertility, and this shop was, and had been for years, the go-to place for Goths and Celts. This was Celt Central. Its owner, Lugos, named after the heroic god who smote Balor, the one-eyed chief of the Formorii tribe, was the 'guru', and had been for decades, in the Celt and Goth underworld of Brisbane. I walked inside.

It hadn't changed, hardly at all. A new poster of Jennifer Lopez had replaced the faded poster of Duran Duran. Lugos, with a bandana on his head, wrapping up his ponytail which was greyer now, in jeans that were always too tight and a singlet that stretched across his abs in a doomed attempt at making the girls swoon, was in the back of the small shop, reclining in the oversized barber's chair, which we had stolen one night a long time ago, all of us, me the meek who followed. I walked past a too-thin girl at the front counter, biting her fingernails nervously. She had tigers on one arm and lions on the other.

A thick-set guy with red hair and rosy cheeks hunched over the computer said to me while staring at the screen: 'Don't mind me, I'm saving the world from Y2K annihilation.'

'I smell cop,' said Lugos.

'Hey Lugos.'

His eyes were closed. 'I'm not good with cops. You should go.'

'It's Lara. Ocean.'

Eyes still closed. 'Yeah, I know the Pacific Ocean and the Atlantic Ocean but don't know any Lara Ocean.'

I pulled up the back of my T-shirt and turned away from him. 'Look,' I said.

And while I kept my gaze steady on the nail-biter at the front desk, I heard the rustle of the barber's chair and felt hot breath as he examined my back.

'I did this.'

'Yep.' I pulled the T-shirt back down.

'I remember you. You came in and we did the whole back. Bum to shoulders. Celtic stuff. Demons. I think I even wrote my signature in there. Pull it back up again.'

I did. With my back to him, staring at the girl by the counter again. She had sunken eyes and a sad face. She was shaking. Crack. Meth hadn't hit the streets yet; that would come in a few years' time. I felt the tip of his index finger cross over my back.

'There! Knew I did! *Lugos the slayer of Baylor!*'

I pulled my T-shirt back down a second time as he walked around and stood in front of me.

'I don't think you paid me for this,' he said, memory slowly returning as he creased his eyes and stared at me, a long, narrow face with a goatee hanging off his excuse for a chin.

'No, I didn't. I fucked you for it. Remember?'

'Oh, you were the under-age girl! Jeez, I almost went down for the tatt on your back *and* the sex. How come I didn't go down? I remember cops but the rest is hazy.'

'My mum bribed the investigating cop. She was good like that.'

But not afterwards, when I would have to deal with the wash

of my fuck-ups. Then it all came out, rivers of vitriol and curses in Mandarin about how I was dragging her world through a pall of rot and sludge. Then I would just run away again.

'Nice one,' he said. 'What do you want? You're a cop now, yeah?'

'You knew everyone in the Celtic world.'

'Still do. Hey, you wanna walk down memory lane and have a quickie, just for old time's sake?'

'Touch me again and I'll handcuff you. Understood?'

'Fuck me! Yep. Okay. Understood, Wyatt-fucking-Earp.'

'Look at this,' I said as I pulled out a piece of paper showing the symbol of the circle with the eight spokes.

'My old mate, Taranis. Doesn't he have a little place on your back?'

'Left shoulder blade. Who else, over the past year, has come in to get a Taranis tattoo? Or anyone who might have talked about Ogmios. Anyone you can think of who's making a noise in the Celtic scene? You know, all loud and look-at-me.'

'Oh Jesus, could you have, like, made an appointment and sent me a list of questions before you came in? I've been smoking weed since, like, three this morning and my head is not exactly in the place of certainty or exactitude in terms of past clients. Or anything, for that matter.'

'You keep a record of all your tatts, though, don't you?'

'Maybe.' His eyes were bloodshot and he was swaying. Standing up had never been his strong point.

I spun around to the nail biter. 'You!'

She almost jumped through the roof. 'You do the bookings and have the record of all the tatts, right?'

She nodded as I approached her. She watched me carefully, anxious she might get into trouble with the boss, who had returned to his chair.

'Go into your books, your records,' I said, pointing at her computer, 'and find me who has, over the past year, come in to get a tattoo with this Celtic design. Okay? Got it?'

Got it.

I walked out with the name I thought I had successfully buried.

Nils.

Spill

Away from the city, eighty kilometres up north, Wivenhoe Dam held almost two million mega-litres of water. Built to contain a flood, to ensure that the city was not deluged as it had been many times in the past, the dam had a shoreline of over four hundred kilometres. Even further north were rivers, creeks and another massive dam to which Wivenhoe was connected. These huge bodies of interlaced waters, swelling with the endless rain, hovered above the city.

Weeks of grey sky, rain and thunder and people were going stir-crazy. When will it end? And will it end with a flood? And will the flood, which is all that everyone talked about, people even having flood parties and comparing prices on rubber dinghies, will the flood surge through all those low-lying suburbs along the banks of the river? Home to tens of thousands of people. Yes, it will, was the wise person's view; it did back in 1974 or, even worse, the killer Great Flood of 1893, the infamous Black February Flood. Staring at the graphics of the dam and the river in the local newspaper, people were starting to bow to the inevitability of gravity: what is up, must come down.

Only one thing held back this growing body of water, lapping against its edge, like an animal craving release. Rising from its base at the most northern point of the Brisbane River, amid low-lying farmlands, was a sheer, massive concrete wall. The dam. And on its top, on its edge, was a walkway.

Ray and Liam were the two very edgy engineers staring at the rising swell of water, lapping against the edge of the spillway.

The purpose of the dam with its massive sluice gates, was to hold back the waters which have flooded the city in the past. Build a dam, put in sluice gates. Hold back the water.

Standing on the concrete walkway, Ray and Liam, recently graduated, thought this job would be stress-free-cruisy. They were staring uneasily at this gathering body of hard, cold water, its level slowly inching towards the top. A few more centimetres every day. It's not like there was a rush, there was just an undulation, a growth, and they knew that the swell would spill over the edge and fall down into the river below, the river which snaked through the city then out into the ocean. Unless it stopped raining.

'What do we do?' asked Liam.

'Call head office,' said Ray.

'I did.'

'And?'

'They said: *You guys deal with it*,' said Liam.

'Look, it's probably going to stop raining soon; you know, it's contained at the moment.'

Both of them leaned over to see how far the surface of the water had risen.

'What if it doesn't stop raining? They told us about nineteen seventy-four when the city was completely flooded.'

'At this rate, I reckon we have another five or six days before the water level reaches the top and starts to spill over,' said Ray.

'Or we could open the sluice gates and release some.'

'And *cause* a flood? No, let's wait a couple more days and see what happens.'

They continued to huddle under the rain and looked uneasily at the moving expanse of silver blue water in front of them. Corralled, for the moment, by the concrete edge of the dam.

Does It Hurt?

I'M NOT SURE HOW MUCH I WANT TO TELL YOU ABOUT MY teenage years, when I went a little wild ... okay, a lot wild and got smashed on gin and vermouth and dope, and there might have been some cocaine; actually, there was, Carmen bought it – and that night I stumbled into a Brisbane tatt place and stripped almost naked and said to this guy with the ridiculous name of Lugos, 'Do my back!' Which he did, not entirely on the first night but over a few nights, each night me being as shit-faced as the last. I might have been fifteen and I certainly wasn't going to school, and there was a guy, Nils. I must have fucked Lugos three times to get the complete back tatt.

I'm better now, of course. No Vs. I cleaned myself up, finished Year 12, crawled through a TAFE course in criminology and applied to the Police Force. I didn't have a record. They didn't ask about my past. I didn't tell them.

I haven't told Billy all that, but he knows ... well, he doesn't but he can tell. He started out as a gangster at the age of seven in London's East End, for God's sake.

Back in those hazy, hairy days when I spent most of my time on someone else's couch, there were guys, dark guys I would see through the corner of my eyes as they swaggered through the share-houses. And there was Nils. Charming. Funny. Clever. Sexy.

At first.

—

NILS. BUILDING YOUR *little house deep in the rainforest.* Abandoning me, and why? What did I do for that? Why did you leave me? I loved you and you left, like a flake of life, off into the gloom, there you went while I was asleep at the time, in the caravan.

Waking up into a silence and nothingness.

Stepping out into a jungle of strangler figs and mangroves and palms, thinking: Are you coming back? Where have you gone? And why?

You didn't come back, did you, Nils.

And after three days of silence and waiting, I finally packed my stuff into a green plastic bag and stepped outside, into the Sunshine Coast hinterland forest, shaded my eyes from the sun. Leaving you because, by then, I realised you had left me. A flake in your life and yours in mine. Determined, with every footstep, to erase you, my passion for you, my adoration – stop.

Stop. Stop. Deep breath. Beware the pothole of futility, Lara.

The second time, there was another long walk home but at the end of that walk, a determination to be me, not a parenthesis in someone else's life.

Living in the caravan and laughing and fucking and cooking and drinking. How old was I, Nils? Sixteen? Fifteen? Was it before or after I got the tattoo on my back? It was after. Before you left me, after that time I left you, before I left, finally, the next time around, after you found me and begged me to return, the second time, which I *so* much regret, leaving you with tears and bitterness and regret and a *crushing* sense of failure, slamming the door to our second caravan as you lay spread-eagled on the floor with a spike of smack in your arm with a –

Stop.

Stop. Stop. Lara, you have to erase this guy from your mind; you had an obsession with him and he abused you, subjugated your mind. You can't be a parenthesis to someone else's life.

Uh-huh.

Guido was easy. Nils was not.

—

BUT NOW HE has returned. Nils.

I got the full back but you were going for the total body, head to toe. Celtic. Every month, every year, you got more. You must be covered now, Nils, from your toes to your neck, a gesture to the

Celt world. Even your dick is tattooed. Because, beneath the smiles and the charm and the funny stories and the raft of knowledge, your world was no good.

And you had the knives.

And you had the anger.

And you had the desire to hurt.

And you told me one night, smacked out, as was I, about how cool it would be to saw off a person's head. Not a hard and fast Japanese-World-War-Two decapitation, but a saw. Like working your way through a tree branch, you said. This was before you confessed to me about what you did in Alotau, in Papua New Guinea. As I lolled naked, lying in the grass or maybe in our bed or maybe in the clouds and I think I might have laughed at your silliness.

But I don't laugh now.

You've been back to the tattooist recently, Nils, to do the soles of your feet, all that was left, and you're not only still alive, you're still into the violent side of the Celt thing, which is why I finally left you. Along with the smack and the stabbing.

Remember?

When you brought out long-bladed knives and stabbed me, just a bit, no more than a millimetre into my skin, here, there, all over my tattooed back and into my legs and my breasts, which I did for you because I loved you and you laughed and said: 'How does this feel?'

'It hurts, that's how it feels.'

And you reached down and wrapped me and kissed me and said: 'No, it feels good.'

—

I AM A cop now, Nils, and I need to find you.

Thunder

NONE OF US REALLY UNDERSTOOD THE CELT THING. NOT AT first. It was just a series of tattoo designs in a plastic-sleeved book on the counter of a parlour. But instead of the clichéd tatts of the past – the man with Popeye muscles and a big-breasted girl hanging off an anchor – the knots, crosses, runes and shamrocks were mysterious and offered the promise of a distant culture, one in which people were more in touch with the earth and the stars above, more in tune with the land around them, and that, too, was considered extra cool as we swigged on vermouth and shot up heroin and smoked our Camels or Gitanes if we could find them, and never washed our hair and drizzled spit into our lover's mouth as we fucked in a grimy sweat, in the dirt, on the sand, on the floor of a crash house with Burmese flags picked up for two dollars apiece at the local Salvo outlet as curtains to keep out the light because sun was the enemy. As were so many other things, fabrics of life we had forsaken with an arrogant show of disdain as we tried to pepper our flesh with as much ink as we could, to outdo the next person and, above all, to show that we could deal with the pain. If you could do the knees, you were in.

Then someone, maybe it was Nils, maybe it was that girl with red hair on the left and green on the right who later blew her brains out during a bad acid trip, started to tell us that the knots and crosses, runes – especially the runes – and shamrocks actually meant something. Which had something to do with a bunch of gods, and we all remembered Zeus from when we were kids but these gods, like Taranis, were super-cool and we should all access our souls and plug the Celtic god world into our astral lives.

And so we did.

—

AT THE SAME time, back in the early nineties, the Goth thing was bursting into the clubs and the pubs. Black. Satan. Vampires. Blood. Death. Sacrifice.

Sacrifice?

As in, Taranis, the god of thunder who needed people to be burnt in baskets hanging from the branches of trees in a desolate landscape as offerings to him to bring on the rain.

So we danced naked and invoked stuff we failed to remember the next morning. But it was fun and we didn't kill anyone, but laughed about the possibility, and used to play a game, pretending if that person or that person or him or her would be a good candidate for our god of thunder's sacrifice.

—

I WAS HUNTING Nils. I couldn't believe he could be the killer, but one of the first rules of Homicide is to embrace the clichés: *Appearances can be deceptive* and *Don't judge a book by its cover.* The Son of Sam looked like a hot-dog seller, Jeffrey Dahmer looked like a handsome travel agent and Ted Bundy looked like a college professor.

Nils, I thought, when I get to you, and I will, I will let my partner Billy do the interview because I certainly do not want your eyes piercing into mine. I will find you, Nils. Just wait.

The I-Tye

LONG-BLADED KNIVES CAN ONLY BE IN A PERSON'S POSSESSION with a government-issued licence. We downloaded every name on the list and searched their history for any red flags. None emerged. But, as Billy said, the murder weapon might have been used to carve up a roast chicken the previous Sunday afternoon.

The search across North Stradbroke was yielding nothing. No-one had seen anyone or anything. The daily newspaper was like a buzzard with a variation on *HOMICIDE SQUAD FAILURE?* every day. It had been days since the first kill and the second, the speed of which, after the first, was alarming.

The third was yet to come.

—

BILLY GREW UP in the 1940s, in London; migrated to Australia at the age of seventeen and became a cop at eighteen, in 1955, at a time when admission was solely reliant upon how much of a 'good bloke' you were and how many beers you could drink at the Breakfast Creek Hotel. He had been in Homicide since 1964, the year The Beatles came to Australia, and from day one he'd relied on what's called The Murder Book to keep track of an investigation and its leads. Billy's Murder Book was about four inches thick; or, for people like me born in the early seventies, ten centimetres. He had many of these books, each leather-bound, in which he scribbled notes with a fountain pen like a character from an old movie. He kept all of the books on the floor under his desk, occasionally going back to a dusty past crime to double-check a detail and see if it might be relevant to a current investigation. When he wrote in the book and when he read, he leant alarmingly close to the page as if sniffing out the words. He did that every day, like a normal person might read the newspaper.

And that was what he was doing, as I was updating the file on our swamp-daisy person search – essentially eliminating everyone on the island of North Stradbroke – when he sat up and said:

'Girlie!'

'What, Billy?'

'I think I've found someone. An old nefarious mate who lives on the Brisbane River in a boat. Moored on the water smack bang between Kangaroo Point and the Botanic Gardens.'

We looked him up, checked him out. His name was Miles and he'd been interviewed by Billy over a decade ago for two knife attacks that had occurred in the Roma Street Parkland, around the corner from police headquarters and one of the main railway stations. The victims were young men, both students, walking through the park after midnight. Miles, it was alleged but never proven, attacked them from behind with a sharp blow and then, as they lay on the ground, stabbed them in the neck, but not deeply, not enough for them to bleed out. He was known – and that was a jail name – as Jugular.

We logged onto the computer. They had been phased into the Force in the mid-nineties and we'd all been sent off to learn about them at night-school classes and told that they would change the policing world. That, one day in the future, we would be able to look up a suspect and check out their entire profile online. Nobody had contemplated Y2K.

Down below us, on the first floor, was a tribe of computer geeks, madly scrambling through the system in order to ensure we didn't all shut down into a deep blue on January 1. Rumour had it they were getting paid three times what the Commissioner was getting. 'Scam of the century,' said Billy.

I'd already got into computers in the late eighties, so I knew a bit about them, but Billy and his ilk had a bit of trouble.

Why innit called a fucking rat?

Billy grew up in the time of typewriters, when he and his fellow coppers had to produce eight copies of a crime, incident or accident form for distribution. Rather than do two lots of four (with the accursed carbon paper) they would do the eight in one hit to save time. And I mean hit, with fifteen pieces of paper they had to bang so hard, the first couple of copies had clean holes where the Os or zeros were supposed to be. And, of course, he said, there was always the time you put the carbon paper in backwards and had to do it all over again.

I just stared at him: what on earth was carbon paper?

'There he is: Miles. Look at that,' said Billy as we stared at the screen, reading that Miles was released from jail two months ago. He had been convicted three years earlier, after a savage knife attack in a Gold Coast pub during which he sliced a bartender's cheeks into ribbons, because, he later told the arresting constables, he was bored and needed some 'blood-thrill'.

And he had thought to himself, before he lunged at the victim with his knife: why not? Why not slice the bloke?

I thought about that. 'Bored.' Needed some 'blood-thrill'.

'Why not' as opposed to the more pressing question:

Why?

That was the empty darkness which scared me. I could understand jealousy and revenge and greed; all clean, simple motivations when it came to killing, the idea that slaughter is the best way to solve a problem, real or imagined. I read the Bible (or, I should say, I was forced to read the Bible) as a kid because dad was a bit that way, so I heard the burst, as kids do, when learning about unnatural death. Even though Adam and Eve's firstborn, Cain, kills his brother on like the first page of Genesis, for no specific reason, you can *assume* the motivation:

He was jealous of a rival.

But was he?

We don't know. I've wanted to kill my brother heaps of times. Why? Because he is annoying. So ... yeah? Kill?

If violence comes from a random, spontaneous place, with no forethought, that's when I become mystified.

Because what is really lurking inside the mind of people like that? Like Miles. Like, it would seem, our killer.

—

TRAVELLING ACROSS THE choppy water of the Brisbane River, with rain sheeting at us in an almost horizontal assault, to interview a person of interest on a yacht that looked as though it had been built in the 1950s was a new experience for me. Miles didn't have a phone and so we were forced to clamber aboard his yacht and knock on the little door that led down below.

There was no answer. The boat, his home ('Perfect getaway for a slag-turd like him,' remarked Billy) was empty. We chose not to leave a calling card, thinking it might lead to a hasty unmooring and a trip up north into the camouflage of islands. Standing on his boat, in the middle of the surging river, I looked across at the banks on either side. The shoreline had risen dramatically. If it kept raining, the footpaths on the edge of the Botanic Gardens would soon be underwater.

—

IN THE MEANTIME, there was life.

Although Billy and I spent almost all our waking hours in the office, occasionally we needed to go home. To eat, feed the cat, check the mail, water the pot plants, stare at the moon; do all the you-are-still-a-human stuff.

I had a shower, thrashed off the water, dried myself, put on my pj's and sat on the couch listening to U2's *Rattle and Hum* with a glass of wine until I fell asleep, and in my sleep I saw him. I did.

He comes to me. He mocks me. I couldn't see his face because of his head, swivelling so fast that all I can see is the back of his neck. But I could hear his laughter.

There was no solace in my sleep. This was the place where, as Billy had warned me, you stay vigilant and avoid valium and vodka.

The two destructive Vs.

—

MUM RANG AND said: 'Are you sure you still want to be a police officer? I see your name in the paper every day and they are saying, you know ...'

'That I am incompetent.'

'Yes, but I mean who are they to say that? Still, maybe now is the time to think about something else.'

Even though she had lived in Australia for decades, even though she had been a police officer in Hong Kong, mum had become increasingly imbued with Chinese values, and the overwhelming one was that if an adult daughter was not married, she was what's called 'leftover'.

This 'status' kicks in when the daughter reaches her mid-twenties with no husband in sight, usually because of a desire to pursue a career. But career was not how your Chinese mum sees it; she sees it as failure, not only of *your* filial duty but of *her* parenting.

If you don't have a husband by the time you are in your late twenties, she is going to lose face. You are shaming her. You have brought dishonour to the family name.

It was Australia in the last year of the twentieth century, so it was nuts, this ancient Confucian thought. Even though I was part Anglo, I was fully my mother's Chinese daughter who was disgracing her.

Mum, to her credit, was aware that next year would bring the dawn of the twenty-first century, so she, like about four hundred million other Chinese mothers across the globe, understood that a subtle approach was needed.

My Australian girlfriends, all three of them, stared at me in bafflement and horror when I mentioned the ongoing pressure – subtle or otherwise. It was alien to the Anglo white woman's experience, of which I also carry. They, untrammelled by *their* own mothers' hark, would never understand, not really, not viscerally.

So, I didn't see them anymore.

Mum, however, was a hark I could not ignore.

When he was trying to be funny, Nils had called me his schizo banana babe. Yellow on the outside, white on the inside and never the twain shall meet.

'Mum ...' I said, trying to steer her away.

'Okay! All right! I can hear it in your voice; I am not going to say another word. You just go off and find murderers and be the subject of editorials in the newspaper ... Oh! Did I tell you Damon is back? He got back from Canada last week. I saw his mum at Woolworths. She came up to me and said he really wants to see you again. He was such a great friend to you. He's got his PhD in chemical engineering. University of Vancouver, or maybe Toronto. Did you know that? No, of course you didn't because you are hunting down murderers. Hardly the job for a young woman. I told you not to go into Homicide. I told you that Fraud is where you find the charming crooks, where you can work nine-to-five but no, you want to wallow in blood.'

'Mum!'

'All right, all right. I'm just saying. Damon would love to catch up. He's been trying to make contact with you.'

'Mum. Let me just tell you: I'm too busy to get married. I have no plans to get married.'

'Of course you haven't. Because you haven't found the right man. You are too busy concentrating on the things that are not, at the end of the day, important.'

'It's my career,' I said.

'A good Chinese girl always obeys her mother.'

I had no answer to that. A good Chinese girl does always obey her mother. I didn't. We drew our conclusions on that one some time ago. Yet, still, mum kept trying in the hope that maybe one day in the future the Confucian switch would miraculously turn on and I would adhere to everything she said.

The irony is that she, some thirty years ago, turned *her* back on filial piety to become a cop in Hong Kong, against the wishes of *her* mother, my grandmother; this is totally lost on her. My mother has a delicious ability to erase any part of her life that is not convenient for whatever is relevant to the present.

'I told Damon's mother you'd go out to dinner with him on Tuesday night.'

'I'm working a homicide, mum.'

'He's going to meet you at that new I-Tye place just around the corner from where you live. Seven-thirty.'

'It is not called the I-Tye, and that is totally racist.'

'Just meet him there.'

'Mum, I'm –' (in the middle of a serial killer homicide investigation!)

But she had hung up. Great, Tuesday at seven-thirty with Damon. And you know what? I have to do it. Because Damon's mum looked after my mum when my mum had the cancer scare and I was too busy with the advancement of my career to go around and make her chicken soup or take her out for a walk in the sun or read her the newspaper.

Not the behaviour of a good Chinese daughter with her filial devotion. She never brought it up. My brother did. All the time. But between me and mum, it's that silent gulf, never spoken about.

The Outsider

It was Damon's choice.

He texted: *Do you like Indian?* (No, not really.)

And I replied: *Yep, great, love Indian.*

Fantastic, let's go to the Taj Mahal in the Valley. I know your mum said that new Italian place but it had a bad review in the paper. Indian okay?

Indian is great.

Okay, perfect. I'll make the booking. Meet you there at seven. Can't wait to see you again, after so long.

Me too.

No murder stories, okay?

Mum, I am doing this for you, to assuage my guilt. Your adherent daughter is doing what you desire.

—

Damon was the guy who wanted to save me.

Or was I the girl who wanted to be saved? He certainly thought so.

After dad died, after we left Cairns, travelling south with three lives in the family station wagon – the fourth in a blue ceramic urn that I clutched to my lap, staring at the cane fields from the back seat, we arrived in the Brisbane suburb of Sunnybank and moved into a modern brick house with a wide yard and next door, hanging off the fence to greet us, was this skinny short kid, buck teeth, big smile and slicked-back sandy-coloured hair. Damon. Who raced up to us with hellos and a thousand questions shot rapid fire at us, as he grabbed our cases and bags and boxes and moved us in. He'd been waiting, he told us, for days, ever since the house had been sold and his mum told him the real estate agent said a family with two kids – one a girl his age – were moving down from up north. He reminded me of Charlie Brown from the Peanuts comic books.

He was the kid with endless questions, rarely waiting for an answer. He was the kid of energy and enthusiasm impossible to deny. He was the kid who'd wait out the front of my house on his bike with a couple of Nutella sandwiches, to ride with me along the baking hot footpaths to school. He was the kid who'd do my homework if I needed help. He was the kid who lured me into an abandoned caravan on the vacant block at the end of the dead-end street, really a cul-de-sac, when I was fourteen and sneaked a kiss on my cheek and gave me my first present from a person other than my family: a bottle of 4711 perfume. He was the only boy in our year who didn't care that I towered above him.

He was the guy who'd be there when I crept back after one of my rages, after I had run away from home. He was the guy who smiled and gave me a thumbs-up and a vapid but loving affirmation like, 'No rain for the rest of the month! You wanna go fishing down the creek, Lars?' those times I had slinked home after the beatings and the stabbings from Nils or Guido, after I'd done yet another trip to my second home during my teen age, the home called Wreck & Ruin on that slow journey to the distant but not too-distant world called Self & Destruct.

Living in the flat suburb, house after house the same, with an endless blue sky above and baking hot footpaths, sounds of lawnmowers on Sundays and the thwack of cricket balls batted into the sky, Damon was the sweet and innocent kid, the Sunshine Kid. And sometimes, I told myself, as I crawled back out of those dark, fetid places I'd rolled into, you just need a Sunshine Kid in your life.

But, after a while, I got to think that maybe my fuck-ups were bringing him too much contentment. He liked to save me. He liked it when I was lost. Or so I thought. Maybe I just needed to shut him out.

We drifted. We all drift. I got serious, enrolled in TAFE and became a cop. He lost his buck teeth, became obsessed with String Theory and Schrödinger and went to Canada to study one of those courses that take a lifetime and none of your family or friends know what the fuck you're talking about, although it's got something to do with maths.

And now he was back. Slotting into my mother's idea of what a potential husband could be like. Anyone with a penis and a gold credit card. Preferably Anglo and tall. (Because Chinese men are unreliable and take concubines.) With a BMW and his own house.

—

'HEY, LARS,' HE said as I walked into the restaurant, shaking my umbrella. He was sitting at the table and didn't bother to get up as I approached him, but he reached up, bent me down and kissed my cheek. I could smell beer on his breath as he said, yet again: 'Hey, Lars.'

'Hi Damon.'

'Hey.' His hair had thinned and he'd obviously spent some time in the gym. He was buffed and would, a little alarmingly I thought, flex his hands as if gripping a tennis ball, every few minutes.

'Been some time, yeah?'

'Certainly has,' I said as I sat, as the waiter took my wet umbrella with a scowl, glancing at the trail of drops I had left through the restaurant which was obviously, until quite recently, a Mexican cantina. The new owners hadn't bothered to remove the sombreros from the walls or the paintings of desert cactus or even the blackboard listing the margaritas. Sitar music played and an elderly Indian lady wearing a purple sari sat behind the bar counting money. Young waiters scurried across the polished wooden floors with hot plates of tandoori meat.

'You're in Homicide?'

'I am.'

'When was the last time we saw each other?'

And on it went, as these things do. We laughed about the sombreros, ordered white wine, which was easy, fumbled over what to eat, which was awkward, full of 'Whatever you feel like,' and it got worse when I accidentally let slip that I was tending, in life, towards a vegetarian diet. We settled on North Indian style chickpeas and the cottage-cheese-and-spinach palak paneer and vegetable kofta dumplings and too much rice and a cheese-and-chilli naan, and I felt a mild wave of relief when that part of the night was over, had another mouthful of wine and wished Billy would call me with news of a third murder.

I'm not really a social person.

I had friends. Or I used to. The three aforementioned girlfriends. They would call to check up on me. I would tell them I'm in Homicide. Best excuse ever, much better than the headache or the crowded schedule.

'You're on a murder investigation now?' he asked after the waiter took our order.

I nodded.

'The big one?'

'Yeah, the big one,' I said.

'Yeah, I saw your name in the paper.'

'I try to avoid that,' I said with a self-effacing smile.

'How's it going? The investigation. Do you think you'll find him?'

I shrugged. Not eager to talk about work. Now that I was here, I wanted to eat and go. 'Hope so,' I replied, glancing again at my phone.

'But it's hard catching a serial killer, isn't it? Like trying to find a ghost. Unless he trips up and makes a mistake.'

I nodded and tried to look interested. 'Tell me about you,' I said.

'Does it ever get too much for you?'

I didn't say anything.

'I reckon I'd get completely stressed out. And you work twenty-four-seven, right?'

I nodded. I didn't. Work twenty-four-seven but I nodded.

'You ever get time off? I mean, you must do a shift-rotation thing? Even if you're on a murder case. How many are working the case? Is it just you and the other man, the old English guy?'

There had been a very small side-bar article on us. The Old and the New: Billy, the oldest in Homicide; Lara, the youngest. It had been organised by Media Liaison; they always enjoy trotting out Ms Diversity. I never had a choice.

'Yeah. We get time off and we have shifts and even though there's a lot of us, I'm on call,' I indicated my phone, sitting next to the wine glass, willing it to ring, 'If ever something happens.'

After a moment I could see a gear-shift in conversation as he frowned.

'I thought we could go to the movies. Go see *The Sixth Sense*. It's meant to have the most amazing ending. What do you think? You know, any time you're free.'

'Maybe after this case is over. If it's still on,' I replied diplomatically, wondering if, now in our late-twenties, Damon actually had feelings for me. A few steps up from the kid in the caravan with the kiss on the cheek. Not that he knew me. Not now. He knew the dark girl who'd told him about Nils and Guido, but she had died about eight years ago.

'Even though we don't know each other that well these days, not since we used to hang out together, perhaps, you know, we could spend some together. Maybe you get a bit lonely.'

I must have looked horrified because he quickly followed up with:

'I don't mean to freak you out or anything. I'm not good at this.' He laughed. 'Better with my mathematical formulas. I'm having a paper published in *Science* magazine next month.'

'I'm gay, I've got a girlfriend,' I blurted, without thinking. Anything to halt the flow of talking about me and my feelings. But as soon as I said it, I regretted it. So childish. Wasn't it easier to just tell him you're not looking for a partner and if you were, it wouldn't be you, Damon. You're sweet and nice and we grew up together, but I cannot and do not want to imagine you in my bed, waking up to you in the morning. Any morning.

But thanks, Damon, thanks, for wanting to save me again. From what? I'm not sure; from Homicide? From being alone and independent? From being me?

'Oh,' he said with a smile. 'Really?' he added in a slightly disbelieving tone. Flexing his hands again.

'Yes,' I said, starting to feel that dinner was as much a mistake as I knew it would be. But Damon was beginning to creep me out.

'How does your mum feel about that?' he asked.

Jesus Christ, Lara, what have you gone and done, you stupid girl. 'No,' I said back to him. 'She doesn't know.'

'What's her name?' he asked.

'Who?'

'Your girlfriend.'

'Splash.' The first name that came to mind. 'Funny name, huh?'

The food came and I moved the subject away from me, to him. And then we talked about the kids we had gone to school with and what they might be doing now and who still lived in the suburb; all the things that normal people talk about when they get together after a time apart.

I felt an outsider, peering in through a window to a real world.

As he kept talking, now about our school friend Jo who was last heard from trying to save trees in the Cape Tribulation wilderness, I felt I was being dragged out through the window, from the real world of the Indian-restaurant which was a Mexican cantina, to my other world. The past.

Which, I have come to realise, is not going away.

—

NILS: THE MOMENT I saw Taranis etched into the body of our first victim, it was you I thought of. I've been unable to entirely forget you – how can anyone forget the first love who broke their heart – but now, now you are walking alongside me with every step I take.

Broke your heart. What a stupid phrase. You fucking hurt me and crushed me, made me doubt myself, my worth, my sense of being. Before I crawled back to reclaim a girl named Lara who still, even as a Homicide detective in control of her life, remains a little broken. You did that; I let you.

Your smile, your charm, your dance moves. When you were good, you were so good. So loving. Remember when you danced naked in the caravan, swinging your dick like a flag as you cooked up a triumph for the both of us to eat outside, later, under the moon, as you played Miles Davis, whom I'd never heard of, and me thinking you were only into that crazy Celtic Goth-inspired dark metal music I secretly hated but said I loved because I loved you and what was it, that night, that you cooked?

Chicken tikka masala.

—

AND AT THAT point I was swept back, as if in a reversing tornado, through the window, back to the cantina. Damon was laughing about the time he had kissed me in the caravan as he sprayed 4711 onto my neck.

'So, anyway, I think your killer will strike again, don't you?'

I didn't say anything. Why was he bringing up the killer again?

'Part of his thing is to taunt you, don't you think? I bet he's convinced he's cleverer than you and the entire police department.' He laughed again. 'Maybe he is,' he said with a grin.

It Bit Me Back

You spend more time sleeping with your phone than you do with a lover.

It went off at 4.13 a.m.

'Another,' was all he said.

I scrambled out of bed and doused my face with cold water – no time for a shower – and threw on a T-shirt and my jeans and boots, which I leave by the side of my bed for times like this. Within minutes I was out of the house and in the car, windscreen wipers flicked on.

I drove as fast as I could, too fast, towards the city, rain lashing the side of my car and gutters overflowing into the middle of the streets.

Fuck. Was dinner with Damon last night? It felt like a year ago. It had thrown me, not just Damon being all weird, but stepping out of the murder-world. Into the other world, the so-called real world.

'We chose this life,' Billy had said to me one day as we were driving. 'Civilians, they go to the office, to the supermarket or to the mall and have a latte and walk footpaths, and think about their issues – rent, mortgage, girl or boy, affairs, kids and what fucking school to send 'em to, bullying, smashers and grabbers, it goes on. We all know it, you know it, I know it, and when we have to rise to the surface we gotta pretend that we are part of their life. Normal life, life that most people go through. The footpath part of life. But we ain't. And we never will be, not even after we retire. Seen too much chaos, too much darkness. That's what Homicide does to you, girlie.'

I had, after last night with Damon, touched the outer life, the footpath, and it bit me back. Time, Lara, to refocus: on murderers.

That's what keeps you sane and centred, the person you are now. Not then. Not the time of harm and hate.

I am, I have to admit, an impatient person. So, when I pulled up behind a Lexus and the guy was texting at the wheel as the light turned from red to green and he didn't move, I leaned out the front window and shouted: 'It doesn't get any fucking greener!'

When was Brian? *Two* nights ago. James, *five* nights ago. This was becoming rampant, out of control. Our forensics and science teams were stretched; they still haven't finished up from the first crime scene, let alone the second and now we had a third. The press was screaming and the city was already wrapped in fear, just to add to the endless rain and skies of grey and black.

—

IN 1974, BEFORE they built the Wivenhoe Dam, it took three weeks of rainfall until the river broke its banks and submerged parts of the city. Sixteen people killed. Three hundred injured and taken to hospital. Eight thousand homes destroyed. Water in the main streets of the CBD. Deluge. Twenty-five years ago. Now the city had a dam to hold back a flood and it had been raining for almost five weeks.

Our third victim was Fabio. Mid-thirties, like the other two. He'd been out to dinner at a restaurant near the Quay West, a five-star hotel across the road from the Botanic Gardens and, according to the waiter who served him, he ate alone while reading a book (Tony Robbins, self-help). Then, apparently, he decided to take a stroll through the park on his way home.

The press were on to it. All five networks had choppers in the air, buzzing us with beams of light and I could see, in circle number three, about a hundred metres away, uniformed policemen and women holding back a horde, even in the rain. I closed my eyes to see tomorrow's headlines: *HOW MANY MORE MURDERS? CAN WE TRUST OUR POLICE?*

Fabio's almost-decapitated body was lying under a massive strangler fig tree in the Gardens, by the edge of the river, the tree branches reaching far and down to the ground, so old and heavy, some had come to rest on the grass. Fabio was lying about eighty metres away from Brian's crime scene. And directly across the river from James's crime scene.

Brian's body had the Taranis carving on his chest and I was sure that Fabio's would too. Same killer, same sculptured work.

I kept my gaze firmly on the river as Billy finally arrived, panting from having jogged through the Gardens. 'Fucking traffic, even at this hour,' he muttered as he stepped under the cover of the tarpaulins stretched over the first three circles of the crime scene. He saw my look.

He didn't even bother to glance at our third victim with the grinning face and missing tooth. He followed my gaze, across the river, to the rusting hulk of Miles' yacht, moored about forty metres away from us.

Inside, down below, in the cabin, was a light.

Someone was home.

L-Plater

'HELLO MILES. THANKS FOR COMING IN.'

'As if I had a choice. What's this all about?'

'Just for the record, if you could lean into the microphone ... Yeah, actually that's a bit too close, we'll get distortion. Just back a bit. Okay, perfect. Thanks Miles. Don't move. I'm Detective Inspector William Waterson and this is Detective Constable Lara Ocean. And we're here on Wednesday, the twenty-fourth of November, nineteen ninety-nine, in the offices of the Brisbane Homicide department. Correct?'

He said nothing. We were in one of the three interview rooms in a corridor on our floor. On the other side was the Officer-In-Charge's glass-booth office alongside the rest of the crews in an open-plan space, four to each desk, which were actually two desks pushed together to make one.

'You have to respond, Miles. Just say yes. If you believe you are here with Detective Constable Ocean and me in this interview room.'

'What if I say no?'

'Well, you *are* here. We are video recording this interview and it will be clear to one and all who watch this, that you *are* here.'

'But, Detective Inspector, what is *here*? You see, I did a philosophy course through TAFE last year and one of the things they talk about is meaning. Am I really here? Are you real? I can touch you but does that mean you exist? For instance, is this a table? You call it a table, I call it a table, we all call it a table. But why? Why can't it be a clarinet? Who says it's a table?'

To his credit, Billy just rolled back and took a few deep breaths. Me, I wanted to lean across the *table* and throttle him.

Billy leaned back in. Gave Miles some hard-core dead eye.

'It's a table, Miles, with four legs and a surface, which defines it as a fucking table and I am a Homicide detective, as is my partner here. As are the dead vics with throats cut, as are you – our person of interest. Miles, we know you leave your yacht at night on the Brisbane River, that you take your tinnie to Kangaroo Point, that you moor it at the Botanic Gardens and go off to get supplies or to get a pint or to fuck a nice young Malaysian bird on the thirty-third floor of that building across from the casino. There ain't much we don't know about you, Miles – except for what you might do in the Gardens deep at night. Like maybe killin' some folk. Because, Miles, we know you like a little bit of slashing.'

'What are you saying?' he asked as he casually leant back in his chair and crossed his arms.

'We got the records, Miles. You might recall I interviewed you a few years back. That was before you cut up the geezer in the Gold Coast pub, yeah?'

Miles froze.

'Yeah?' repeated Billy.

No response.

'Yeah,' said Billy with finality. 'Yeah, because you're a bit of a monster. And now here you are, in front of me and Detective Constable Ocean from the Homicide Squad because we think you might have somethin' to answer for with some dead gents who have been found with their throats cut in your patch. What were you doing last night?'

—

MILES WAS OUT walking last night, as he was the nights that Brian and James were killed. Occasionally dropping into a bar for a drink and a dance. But the night of the first murder, he was busy having a one-night stand with a hair stylist called Pamela from one of the salons on Eagle Street. They met at a pub in West End, a few kilometres away from his mooring on the river, where there was, as she told us yesterday afternoon, a loud and lazy New York punk band with the bassist leaning against the bar and staring into space as he twanged.

—

AND MILES COMES up to me and he said, Hey, who are you? And I said: I'm okay. And he said: What do you do? with a gentle and not unpleasant thrust of his body into mine as I felt his abs and his cock and I said, I work in the city as a hair stylist and what do you do? And he said, I live on the river, on a yacht and I do a bit of this and bit of that but I own the boat and what do you say, you wanna come back with me and have a look? With another thrust, gentle, not aggressive because if it was aggro I would have told him to get fucked but it was subtle and I'd been out all night and wouldn't mind some sex and he was hot and smelt okay and he wasn't drunk, he was standing tall, so I said: Yeah, let's do it and he said: Okay, take my hand and come with me, which I did, took his hand as I let him lead me out of the bar into the night, with a bit of rain and he talked to me about stuff I can't remember as we caught a cab around the corner, to the river and he helped me on to a little boat, a tinnie he called it, and put-putted across the river, which was pretty hairy, I can tell you, because of the rain, to his dodgy yacht and we went aboard and I swayed a bit with the swell but he caught me and led me down below and I took off his clothes and he took off my clothes and we made some precious love, all night.

Well, not all night because at some point – it might have been three or four – I woke up and I was naked and there was something sticky on me, on my breasts where his arms were folded, and I reached across to the light switch in the cabin as he was slumbering hard and strong, his arm gripped around me, and I turned on the lamp to get some light and I saw:

Blood. My breasts and my chest were covered in blood.

Dried, partially dried. His? Mine?

I jumped out of bed and shouted: Are you okay?

And he woke up and said: Huh?

He had blood on his hands.

'I have blood on me!'

'Oh yeah. Sorry about that. Let's go have a shower.' And he climbed out of bed and his body was crimson and wet. And blood dripped from him as he walked to the shower.

—

WHICH IS WHEN Pamela got him to tinnie her back to shore as quickly as possible.

—

'SO, MILES, TELL us about the blood.'

'There was no blood; what are you talking about? What blood? What are you talking about?'

'The blood, Miles, the blood on your body before you went and showered it off, the blood on the lady you were sleeping with at the time. On your boat. Where you live. November eighteenth. Thursday. Night-time. After you took her back to your boat and before she woke you up.'

'Pamela? Did she fucking dob me in? Fucking bitch. I'm going to ...'

'What? Miles? What are you going to do to her?' I asked.

I leaned in to him. After less than a year, I was still learning and I certainly wasn't yet an expert on questioning a person of interest, let alone a suspect. But there was something about Miles and his smugness that riled me. Billy could sense it, I knew, but he let me go. Got to drop the L-Plates some time. And, it was more than Miles. It was the case. Three victims in less than a week. It was the rain, the grey sky, the hammering relentlessness of blood and water, a river rising. It was Damon, it was mum, it was Nils and my stupid decision-making teen years that were coming back to me after I thought I had buried them and started anew. All of this morphed into Miles.

'Miles,' I said, 'hear me now and look into my eyes.'

Billy leaned back in his chair with a feline smile, closing his eyes, as if pretending to sleep.

Miles stared at my chest with an I-Am-Man-*Succumb* look and a flick of his tongue across his lower lip, as if I would swoon. 'Into my eyes, Miles. Not at my chest. Got it? Put your tongue back inside your mouth.'

He nodded lazily as if he had all the time in the world and there were a thousand girls out the front of the police station, all waiting to strip off and fuck him.

'You keep staring at my chest and I will rip *your* eyes out. Okay? Got it?'

'And she will,' said Billy from behind his closed eyes.

A ripple of anxiety flicked through Miles. He'd got it. Looked up at me. Meanwhile Billy reclined deep back into his chair with his legs stretched out.

'Tell me about the blood,' I asked.

'That Pamela, she's a fucking–'

'Stop,' I said and he did as Billy emitted a snore, soft and low.

'Where did the blood come from?'

'She had her period in the middle of the night and I roll over and I'm awash in blood and I threw her out of bed and dragged her into the shower and the sheets, well, they're wrecked, so I burn 'em; that's Pamela for you.'

'We understand you were sailing a few weeks ago.'

'The crime being?'

'We understand you sailed around North Stradbroke Island.'

'Again, the crime being?'

As we all well knew, there was no crime in sailing around an island, even if it had some resonance with our investigation. But fading resonance; there was no sign of a swamp daisy anywhere near Brian or Fabio. Maybe it had just been a random, unexplained diversion, forever unexplained.

We let him go. But not back to his boat. We had impounded it and, to add to our over-stretched woes, a forensic team was sweeping through it to see if there were any incriminating DNA matches to the victims.

—

WHEN WE RETURNED to our desks, there was a message for me. From Damon.

Thanks for last night. Great seeing you again. Number three, huh? Good luck catching your killer. He's out there, waiting for you xxx

Hey You

NILS.

I have found you, you who used to stab me, little bits, a millimetre here and there with your long-bladed knife, pretending it was foreplay, you who subjugated me, Nils, you who suggested I get a full-back tattoo and you who said if you can't afford to pay for it, fuck him. You said that to me, Nils. More than once because you needed me to affirm you. If I was to be worthy of your love and commitment, I had to mirror the pain.

And I did what you said.

But after you sculled a bottle of vermouth, you told me about a drunken rampage years ago in Alotau by some fishing boats, in the middle of the night, because it was fun. You don't remember that, do you, Nils? Telling me about the night in Alotau. Milne Bay. Be careful what you say, Nils. It might come back to you.

I have found you, you my lover, my killer, the end of my dreams, I have found you. Living in an apartment close to the beach, in Miami, on the Gold Coast. We are coming to get you Nils.

Are you my killer? You fit, Nils – Taranis, Ogmios, violence, slicing off a man's head, bragging about it, from years ago. Nothing to connect you to a swamp daisy but who knows, maybe you've visited the island? Who knows?

We will. Soon.

—

'GIRLIE, IT'S FOR YOU.'

My reverie was broken as Billy leant across the desk with the phone in his hand.

'This is Detective Constable Ocean, how can I can help you?'

'How was Damon?'

80

Mum. Talking to her leftover daughter.

'I'm at work. I'm working on a really challenging homicide,' I whispered, bending over, facing the floor so Billy couldn't witness my embarrassment.

'*That* I hardly need to be told. *That*, I read about every day. Damon told his mother you didn't like him.'

'Mum! I will call you tonight!'

'You never do. When was the last time you called me? Your brother Ronnie, he calls me every second day.'

'Because he works nine-to-five selling used cars that break down after two weeks.'

'Don't talk about your brother like that. He's worried about you too. Spending all this time with dead people rather than your family or finding a suitable man. You know, once you get to thirty, it's all over.'

'I'm going now. Okay?'

'You're always going, Gao Yi. Yes, okay. Go.'

And she hung up on me.

I handed the receiver back to Billy, who clearly had heard my side of the call. He didn't say anything, just put the receiver back on its cradle and returned to his Murder Book, adding in more arrows and question marks with his fountain pen. Spindly writing that only he could read. I once again reminded myself I'd made the right decision to stick with him as a partner.

—

I WAS BORN Wang Gao Yi.

Wang is my original Chinese family name and in China the surname always comes first. My dad's name was Richard Ocean. For a little while I became Yi Wang Ocean but, as the bullying cracked out of control at high school with the Asians attacking me because I was half Anglo and the Anglos, Greeks, Italians, Lebanese and every other non-Asian kid attacking me because I was The Chink, I formed a wall of anger and resentment that took me on a self-destructive road to mayhem and I changed my name. Lara Ocean.

That's me.

Nils

(I)

'HI NILS, THANKS FOR COMING IN. I'M DETECTIVE INSPECTOR William Waterson and this is Detective Constable Lara Ocean. Lara and I are working a case and we would like to chat to you. We're hoping you might be able to help illuminate a few things for us.'

'Hey Lara.'

'Hey Nils.'

'Long time ...'

'... no see.'

'How've you been doing?'

'Good. Detective Inspector Waterson is going to ask you some questions,' I said, deflecting to Billy.

I had told him some of my history with Nils – that we were lovers, years ago, when I was a kid, that he dumped me, broke my heart – but I didn't tell him the whole story. He didn't need it. I said, I probably shouldn't be in this interview, and he said: Nonsense. Nils gets out of line, I'll smash his fucking head in. Sorry ... 'scuse the French.

I said: Okay.

—

NILS WAS THE same but different. Still over two hundred centimetres tall with serious muscle. New hairstyle, though: a Mohican look, a narrow journey of spike running along the middle of his scalp, the rest shaved. He bristled like he needed to punch the desk every couple of minutes and he smiled non-stop as if to say: I'm a good guy.

I tried to look away, but he kept staring steadily at me. I didn't need to ask him if he was still with Rhonda, the girl he dumped me for. I had already checked, before we got him in, before we found him. Rhonda had left him six months after he left me. She came from Hamilton in New Zealand and she was a tall redhead with a razor-cut and she was thin and she had a beautiful body, better than mine. She had dimples and a soft smile. She played the harpsicord; imagine that.

Rhonda was dead. Smack. Overdose. No-one went to her funeral. No-one. I checked. I rang the crematorium and some guy remembered her: No, no-one, we just got the body. Some cops dumped it in the foyer and left before we had even asked, 'Who's this?' We put her in a cardboard box and incinerated her. Little thing, even though she was quite tall but, you know, in death, we all shrink. She had a pearl ring on her finger. She's out the back, under a yellow rose bush. Flowering now. Are you family? There was a man who we tried to call. Nils, I think that was his name. We discovered he was her partner but he never called us back. Never paid either. He owes us some money. Not a lot. The cardboard-box funerals are pretty cheap but you know, they still cost ... Hello? Are you still there?

—

'Why am I here?' asked Nils, his pale blue eyes not leaving mine.

'Well,' said Billy, 'I'm gonna be up-front and say that you are a person of interest for us in some recent incidents, and thanks for coming in because we want to ask you some questions; is that okay, Nils? A person of interest ain't no suspect. Alright on that, Nils?'

I pulled my gaze away and looked at Billy and he looked at me and gave me a nudge, knee to knee with a: *Keep it cool, girlie.*

'You're known to like knives, yeah?'

No response; he kept staring at me, those pale blue eyes, no flinching.

I stared back.

'Can you tell us where you were on the night of November eighteenth? Last Thursday.'

After what felt like hours but was, as Billy later told me, ten seconds, Billy leaned into Nils and said:

'Stop staring at her. The next moment I see you staring at my partner – and I know you have history, you two – the next moment I see you staring at her, I'm gonna cave your head in. Okay?'

Nils leaned back and kept staring at me with those pale blue eyes and I tried not to fall into them and he said:

'Come back to me.'

And for one crazy moment I wanted to, I wanted to fall into those pale blue eyes. But I could not possibly do that a third time. Not any more Nils.

And then I heard:

'Turn the fucking cameras off now! NOW!'

As Billy lurched out of his seat and grabbed Nils by the throat with an 'I will fucking kill you.' Nils said: 'I can't breathe,' and Billy said: 'Great, excellent' and 'Those cameras better be off because I am Billy Waterson and you know who I am.'

He leaned up into Nils's face, breath to breath and he said:

'I know who you are. You are a fucking viper. You are heroin. You are here to answer questions – Lara, get the *fuck* out of here.' And I ran. The last thing I heard as I closed the door to the interview room behind me was:

'I *will* fucking kill you if you ever, *ever* attempt to make contact with her. Got it?'

As he was being throttled, as I fled, I heard: 'Got it.'

———

I DON'T WANT you to think I was a victim. Because I wasn't.

I brought the knife into the relationship. I whispered into his mouth: Can I hurt you? and he said: Maybe, not really, what do you mean? And I said: Lie back and close your eyes, and I reached down to the floor and took my flick-knife and said: Tell me how this feels, as I drew the blade across his back, from his shoulder blade to his bum and then I pricked him and said, Fuck me now, and he did and as we both came together I stabbed him even more and there was blood, a lot of blood, and I licked it off him and he said: You are very weird, and I said: Be me.

I want to say I regret those times, that, now, as a Homicide cop, I am a different person and it's all behind me. But there are no regrets. That was me, that was then, I will carry it for the rest of my life, a flake of my life. And I sometimes wonder if, like a junkie, I could be triggered back into that dark sex and violence.

Becoming a cop saved me. Homicide kept me sane and alive. We live and breathe murder.

—

'So, WE'RE ALL comfortable?' asked Billy.

'Yes,' replied Nils, looking at the floor.

'The recording is back on – we had a little glitch back then, yes?'

'Yes.'

'Yes, and so I'm going to retrieve my partner, Detective Constable Lara Ocean. I'm going to get her to return to the interview. Yes?'

'Yes.'

—

'WE ARE GOING to resume the record of interview with Mister Nils Marnell. Where are you from, Nils?'

'I am currently living in Miami on the Gold Coast.'

'Good, Nils, great.'

Nils kept looking at the floor. Somewhat abashed. I had always imagined him as a Viking warrior. Unvanquished. As I sat and watched *him* being subjugated by an old cop with an English accent and the lover he once held in a captive thrall, I couldn't help but feel a little sad. It was me I was angry at. I was the one who fucked up. I fell into the darkness.

'And I was born in Denmark.'

'Great. Good, thanks for that, Nils,' Billy said as he slid a sheet of paper across the table. 'Can you have a look at that for us, Nils? If you wouldn't mind.'

'Do you recognise that? Nils?'

'Yes.'

'Illuminate us, old mate; what is it?'

'It's the Celtic symbol for Taranis, the god of thunder,' he said, keeping his eyes on Billy.

'You wanna take off your shirt for us? Can you do that for us, Nils?'

The merest eye-flick towards me and he stood, turned his back to us and removed his shirt.

Stretching from shoulder blade to shoulder blade and from the edge of his neck to the base of his hips was a massive tattoo of Taranis.

Nils, the god of thunder.

Fruit Loops

IN MY SHORT TIME AT HOMICIDE WE HADN'T ENCOUNTERED many big, high-profile cases. Of course, Brisbane being a capital city, there had been some which generated front-page news, which generated anxiety and pressure on the investigating crews. I had observed this from the desk I shared with Billy. Watch and learn. Kristo, our Officer-In-Charge, and even the Commissioner, leaning on them every day to get the media off their backs. *Just solve the fucking thing, all right!* was the consensus from up high.

It seemed to me, at times, that the identity of the actual murderer was less the priority to our esteemed Commissioner than the completion of justice. But I would never say that; just do your job and get on with it, Lara.

And high-profile cases were, as were virtually all homicides in Queensland, crimes driven by big emotion, committed by someone close, someone the detectives suspected or, often, knew, from day one. Then it became the hard slog of finding the evidence, the hairs, the fibres, the fingerprints, the DNA from sperm or saliva and matching them to ensure the case didn't fall apart in court. Motivation was and is important but only part of what is needed to get a conviction. A jury usually doesn't convict without credible motivation, a body, a link of physical evidence from accused to victim and a proven geographical placement between crime scene and killer. Usually, not always, all these boxes need a tick.

We had none of that. What we had was three bodies within a week, and one of our biggest gaping holes was motivation. Queensland may have had many unsolved crimes but in each, a motivation lingered like an alluring scent. It was pretty much always to do with a young and attractive woman and a thwarted and angry guy. Or a rainbow's bucket of money.

We were also missing a physical link between one of our suspects and the three victims. There wasn't even a social link between any of them. They lived in totally different spheres, which just went to confirm the randomness of the crime and the lack of motive.

And then there was the fact that Queensland had never experienced a serial killer. It had seen some extremely violent murderers, such as Tracey Wigginton, but they were an aberration. Serial killers were actually so rare that when I first heard the phrase back around the time I graduated from my criminology TAFE course, I thought it had something to do with murder at breakfast. I'm not kidding.

Fruit Loops were my guilty pleasure. Dad would often sneak me and my brother a bowl of them, when we lived in Cairns, before he died, before everything in my life went to shit. So now – but I would never tell Billy this, as he and I begin to realise we are investigating such a rarity in the world of murder – I keep thinking about the overly sugary, multi-coloured breakfast cereal.

I'm not alone. There's a cop I know, about my age, who works down in Melbourne. Tough and dangerous. Also works Homicide. He told me he had exactly the same reaction as I did.

Serial killers may have been around since the dawn of time and perhaps the most famous, Jack the Ripper, made his splash in the last century but, really, it wasn't until Hannibal Lecter graced the screen in 1991 that people, including cops, began to realise there was this whole new, beyond-creepy killer profile. The guy who won't stop. The guy who does not fit the mould of angry, jealous boyfriend or schemer or the carrier of vengeance. They exist, for sure, but they're as unusual as a UFO sighting.

And now *I* was working on a serial killer case.

I was scared.

Not of him, the killer. But of failure. The greater the profile of this case, and already we have media inquiries from all over the world, of detectives trying to solve the down-under exotic slasher who folds men's heads back, the greater the potential for failure.

If we didn't catch him, it wouldn't just be the Commissioner who would make an example of us, throwing us to the wind to cover his own arse; it would be the press and the public, all angry at our impotence and inability to keep the city safe from an evil predator. Seven months into my dream job and I could already see the exit door. There were a lot of us working the case but Billy and I were leading it. First in, first out.

Billy also saw the threat. The oldest and most experienced cop of us all. As he often told me, he had been slugging crooks when Kristo, our Officer-In-Charge, was in nappies. He had also been giving evidence in Homicide trials when the Commissioner was falling off his tricycle. Billy had no intention of going down, at the end of his career, with the mark of failure.

'You know what the likelihood is, don't you, girlie? Of catching him,' he said to me after Nils left the interview room, as we looked at one another, deflated. As much as either Miles or Nils could be our killer, and both men had the violence within them, we realised we were searching for a phantom. The normal rules of a murder investigation don't apply, Billy told me, which I had figured out anyway.

'He is meticulous, he has not left any prints, any firm sightings, any DNA. He has, maybe, left us a fucking flower and a Celtic symbol which is probably tattooed onto the backs of a few million young geezers with nought better to do with their time and money. He has also left us a grin, which he's cut into their faces – fuck knows why, maybe it's to laugh at us – and then ripped out one of their canine teeth. Probably one of them trophy things.'

And even if it is Nils or Miles, how do we connect all this? We are trying, using the usual routes, to identify whether they knew the victims, whether we have missed anything, whether there is a chance of us linking them to the moment of death, but we know it's most likely futile.

Because the serial killer does not choose his victims like other killers. This is new. This is driven by psychology.

We know our guy likes to kill middle-aged and well-to-do men, which possibly means he has a problem with his mother. Or father. Perhaps was sexually abused. But maybe not.

'We keep doing the Celt thing, we keep doing the sweep of North Stradbroke Island, we keep chipping away at Nils and Miles,' Billy said to me. 'And hope we, like our victims, get smashed by something random and unexpected because, girlie, to my way of thinking, these geezers don't get caught by investigation, they just get unlucky.'

Skater Girl

'HEY LARA, THERE'S A GIRL ON THE LINE AND SHE SAYS SHE might have information about your killer.'

Number twenty-eight thousand, two hundred and sixty-one. I'm being facetious but with our serial killer making news around the world, we were inundated with calls every minute or more. And, as Billy had said, this killer did not live in a vacuum, he did not visit us from another planet, he had a mother or a father or a wife or girlfriend or kids, and whoever that person was, they may be thinking he had been acting strangely or maybe they had seen a bloody knife or some bloody clothes. Within the deluge of crank calls there was, almost certainly, a sole lonely voice of someone who knew something.

Every lead had to be considered, regardless of knowing that a dead-end was almost always going to be the outcome.

Normally I tossed these calls to one of the lower ranks but there were only so many of those sorts of menial jobs you could toss to others before you became a prick. And I could never forget, I was twenty-six years old and seven months in.

I had been following up on a nagging instinct. One I had been trying to suppress. Was it possible that Damon had killed those three men? Surely, I told myself, he just had a creepy fascination with the case. Why not? It seemed as though the entire world had a creepy fascination with The Slayer, as he was now known, dubbed as such by the *Courier Mail* about two weeks ago.

We were almost three weeks in. Three weeks since James and then Brian and then Fabio, in a rapid spate, were killed. Three weeks of rain and storming, three weeks of fear, three weeks of a city increasingly feeling as though it was under siege.

I had been checking: Damon arrived in Brisbane two weeks before the first killing. He was living in Sunnybank, with his mother, in the old house next to my mum, waiting to hear back from the University of Queensland about a senior job as a lecturing professor. No criminal history. Which, to take a look at him, was not surprising. Nothing, from a scant check of the online newspaper *Vancouver Sun*, about killings like ours, when he was there, studying. I felt a bit guilty checking up on a friend.

'Hello?' I said, picking up the phone.

'Hi. Am I talking to a police person?' asked a scared-sounding young woman.

'Yes, yes, you are. My name is Lara. Can you tell me why you're calling?'

'We've all been talking about it, and we think she's the one.'

'Sorry. Hang on; back up. Can you explain to me what you're referring to?'

'The killings. The guys with their throats cut. She's a vampire.'

'Okay ... What's your name?'

Silence. Then: 'If you want me to give you my name I'm hanging up now.'

'Okay. No problem. Just tell me what you know.'

'She rides her skateboard through the Botanic Gardens at night and along the Kangaroo Point lookout. She worships Celtic gods and she's covered in tatts.'

Which was when I stopped staring at my computer, sat up and paid attention. We had deliberately kept the Celtic stuff out of the press in order to explore the underground world without sending out any alarms.

We'd been told about a girl, a midnight skater, a shadow who zoomed around Kangaroo Point and the Botanic Gardens. She'd been seen on the nights of the killings. A dark blur of teenage freedom out late when she should have been home asleep ready for another school day.

We'd tried to find more on her, like an identity, as she might have seen something but:

Teenage girl on a skateboard? There are hundreds of them.

Nothing turned up, and so we moved on. She wasn't a *lead*.

Because she was a she and she was a teenager. Whoever she was. Both Billy and I eliminated her before we even knew her identity. She didn't fit the profile. Teenage girl killer? Nonsense.

I put the call on speaker and gestured for Billy to listen. She sounded terrified.

'Okay, look, sweetie; hope you don't mind me calling you sweetie ...' I said in my best I-am-nice voice.

Billy nodded an affirmation to me as the girl replied, 'That's what mum calls me.'

'My name is Lara. Okay?'

'Hi Lara. Sorry, I don't want to waste your time or anything ...'

GET HER NUMBER AND HOME ADDRESS! NOW! Billy hurriedly scribbled onto a piece of paper and handed it to one of the analysts. Who ran back to his desk, passing the Christmas tree that one of the guys from another crew had brought in a week before. It was a real tree and the office smelt of pine needles. Cheap red baubles hung from its small branches.

'We are all a bit scared, though. I'm really nervous,' she said.

'That's okay, sweetie. No need to be nervous. You called her a vampire?'

'That's what we call her.'

'Why?'

'She sucks blood. She's evil.'

Which is when I nearly hung up on her, thinking I had been thrust into a teenage game or the fantasy of a kid who had been reading about Tracey Wigginton, the notorious Lesbian Vampire Killer from 1989. But Billy cautioned me in whispers across the desk: 'Stay on the call, let's listen to what she has to say.'

She kept talking to me.

'I mean: *hello*, she's not even eighteen and she's covered in tatts; she's a Goth; I think she has to be having sex with the tatt guy, and all of us, all of us, well, you know, they voted me to be the one to call you and I am *not* giving you my name, okay!'

'Okay. No problem.'

Because, after about fifteen seconds, Billy and I had it. Her name.

One of the analysts had clocked her number and ran the ID.

I know who you are, where you live, what school you go to, what your parents do. I am even about to find out your choice of subjects.

And now, most importantly, as Billy leaned in and peered over my shoulder, at the computer screen, as we looked at your end-of-year school class photo, I know who you are talking about.

Second from left, front row.

Skater girl.

PART II

JEN

Mary wore three links of chain
Every link was Jesus' name
Pharoah's army got drownded
Oh Mary don't you weep

One of these nights about twelve o'clock
This old world's going to reel and rock
Pharoah's army got drownded
Oh Mary don't you weep

Moonage Daydream

OUR GIRL'S NAME, THE GIRL WHO RANG US THINKING SHE HAD been anonymous, was Donna Mex. We drove to her parents' house in Ascot, up on the hill, not far from her school. Also close to where Lynne, Matt and Diane were suffering in their torment of grief. Donna's house had a big view of the river and the city.

The rain had stopped. Which is not to say there was blue in the sky. The last blue sky was in October. Which is when it all began. Light rain at first. Nobody really noticed or cared. Hard drizzle and then, after a few days, four or five weeks ago, like an ominous threat of war, suddenly breaking with cannon-fire, rolls of hard thunder and masses of rain. Rain for days. Rain for weeks. Always, through this, a pause. A break. A tease.

But the rain always started again. Sometimes violently, without warning, sometimes a light drizzle which built to a torrent. Rain had become the new normal. Its absence was unnerving. We had become so used to constant rain, hard, light, heavy, living under a grey roof with its always-shifting shades of blizzard black and white, with temperatures soaring into the high twenties then into the mid-thirties, that when it momentarily did stop, we would look up to the sky and wonder if now, maybe, finally, now, a crevice would open and the blue beyond, which we were yearning for as if we had been living underwater and needed air, look up into the sky and hope. But it never came. The blue. The last blue was October twenty.

Maybe it wouldn't come back. Maybe these were the end of days. Maybe the entire world would explode with the Y2K millennial bug.

We knocked. After a few moments the door was opened by Donna's mum, who had the look of a sparrow. Petite, wispy blonde hair and dressed in a white caftan. She was on edge. We were all on edge. Non-stop rain and a never-ending grey roof does that to you.

'Hello. My name is Detective Constable Lara Ocean, and this is Detective Inspector William Waterson and we would like to have a brief chat with Donna. There are no problems; she is not in any trouble, but she might be able to help us with some inquiries. Can we come in?'

—

BY NOW I had done a few face-to-face Homicide interviews with witnesses and possible killers and aggrieved lovers and parents of lost ones, and I had come to be sceptical about the meaning of body language. Sure, in some instances people look away and jiggle their leg and their hands might shake and their eyes might dart this way or that, which *may* indicate some guilt, an indication to Billy and me to hunker down and hammer them, but in my brief time in Homicide I have come to know that a reliance on a person's body movements as you ask them tough questions, determining guilt, is nonsense.

Donna jiggled, tapped her feet on the floor and drummed her hands on her knees like she was Ringo Starr. She had the body language of *The Texas Chainsaw Massacre,* but she was just scared, out of her comfort zone in what had always been, until now, a place of security, a place where mum and dad might yell at her every now and then but, essentially, a sanctuary. Home had been turned upside down by the arrival of two cops. Tears were welling in her eyes and when she stopped doing the hands-drum-roll, she shrouded herself in a cocoon of arms wrapped tightly across her chest and rocked slowly backwards and forwards. She had dark brown hair, cut into a bob, like a 1920s fashionista, parted in the middle with upturned swishes on either side of her cheeks. She had wide green eyes and stared at us in what seemed to be constant bewilderment, rarely blinking. Her mouth stayed open in a perfectly formed O which gave her the look of being in perpetual surprise.

Her mum, whose presence was necessary because Donna was underage, looked away, out through the large open windows into the garden and beyond to the magnificent view of the river and the city from their perch on the other side of the hill. There was a dog out there. A Labrador, who was chasing its tail, and she followed its progression as if watching the final game at Wimbledon.

Billy sat back and gave Donna a smile, not an indulgent smile or a threatening smile, just the sort of smile you would look at and feel comfortable with, like he was a dad, and I did the talking, leaning in with:

'Donna, you called us yesterday; it was me you spoke to.'

'I didn't. Why are you here?'

'You did. Hey. Look, we're the good ones. We come in peace, okay? There's no problem, you're not in any trouble, and if you want us to leave, we will.'

'Yeah, I want you to go.'

'Okay, no problem. Of course.'

We had rehearsed this. We were entering a new landscape. Of kids. Billy stood up, still smiling, as if to say: We are your friends, we respect your wishes.

I didn't stand. I leaned across to Donna and lied. 'My mum died when I was your age and I had to look after my little sister. I'm in my mid-twenties now and she's sixteen. You're sixteen, right?'

She nodded, eyes wide open and mouth in a perfect O.

'So I look after her, my sis. She's your age. I get it. Not only do I remember what it was like being sixteen, I'm living it every day. With her. So I get it. I get you just don't want to have to talk to anyone who carries a badge or is like, you know, the authority. I know you don't want to talk to me or the old guy – how about that after-shave, yeah?'

She smiled.

I had her. I was in.

'Why don't we, you and me huh, just have a walk in the back yard. It's stopped raining. For like eight minutes ...'

She smiled again.

'... and if I ask you a question and you don't want to answer it, you're going to say ... guess what?'

'What?'

'Fuck off, bitch.'

—

THE LABRADOR RAN around us, trying to engage us in a game known only to itself but every now and then would zoom off to chase a bird that had momentarily landed on the wet grass. We were walking slowly around one another, lazy and relaxed, circles, staring at the wall of trees on all sides of the garden, swishing away the occasional drip from an overhanging tree branch.

'Donna, that phone call; why do you think Jen might be of interest to us?'

'How do you know her name?' she asked, shocked.

Fuck, Lara. Your L-Plate status is showing. Lucky Billy didn't hear you mention Jen's name. Don't lead the person with your questions. You know that. You were taught that in the first week at the Academy; is it that hard to remember? Silly girl.

'But that's who you were calling about? Yeah? Jen White?' I deflected.

'She's weird.'

'How?'

'She does all this Goth-shit stuff with knives and tattoos.'

'What kind of stuff?'

'She brought a knife to school. Actually, she did that, like, heaps of times; she has this wide, long-bladed knife she keeps in her backpack next to her Kafka and tell me if you think *his* shit isn't weird ...'

'And what else? Why did you call us?' I asked, wondering who Kafka was; it rang a distant bell, but unlike Donna, I didn't go to a fancy school and I essentially left the world of education when I was fourteen.

'Lately she's been talking about sacrifice. Animals. People. She used to be normal, but now she skates in the middle of the night, through the city, along Kangaroo Point and she carries her flick-knife and laughs about how she might cut a guy and "bathe in his blood", she calls it, like a vampire, and then she turns up at school the next morning with a – "Hey, how are you? Guess what I did last night?" And we say: "What did you do last night?" And she says: "I bathed in blood." Like she's acting out Countess Báthory.'

—

BY NOW DONNA had become emboldened and was on an unstoppable roll, like a dam had broken. I began to recoil from what was sounding like a teenage snakedance: a roller-skating schoolgirl killer, near-decapitating men in the middle of the night in the heart of Brisbane, carving a Celtic symbol onto their chest, channelling Elizabeth Báthory, a seventeenth-century noblewoman who also happened to be the most notorious female serial killer of all time (for a twining moment in my mid-teens, I had thought she was cool).

I knew that if and when we ever found our killer, he (now *maybe* she) would be a mind-twister of a person the likes of whom I could barely contemplate.

But. A *teenage* female serial killer? It seemed highly unlikely.

But, as Billy always said to me, keep your mind open and let the evidence lead you. And so I did.

But perhaps I should have remembered my own childhood and how those bullying girls circled me to the point where stabbing myself or them seemed like a terrific way out to solve the end of anxieties, or so it seemed then.

Space Oddity

HERE IS WHAT I HATE: I HATE SCIENCE AND I HATE MATHS. I hate bugs and I hate stairs and I also hate elevators because I freak-out that an elevator will freeze and I will be stuck inside it for days and slowly die. I hate Kieren because he presses his body up against me with a 'Can you feel it?' and yes, I can but get it away from me. I hate Ms Peters because her body odour is fierce. I hate rain and I hate water, especially river or sea water because there are things in there, fishy, squirmy things that will eat you. I hate boys who wear aftershave and girls who put on too much lip gloss, and I love, this is what I love:

I love Proust, who wrote in bed, and Baudelaire and Colette and I love Emile Zola's *J'accuse!* and I love Jane Austen and Charles Dickens and Walt Whitman's *Leaves of Grass* and Damon Runyon and I love Enid Blyton's kids' books, especially *The Magic Faraway Tree* and I love *Autumn of the Patriarch* by Gabriel García Márquez and Patrick White's *The Tree of Man* and *Earthly Powers* by Anthony Burgess. I am going to study Literature at the University of Queensland and then go on to become a Professor of Literature and smoke a pipe and sit in an old green leather chair and be witty like Dorothy Parker at the Round Table in New York.

Oh! Let me tell you about Google. It was sometime last year when Annice rang me and said: 'Oh my God, you have to go onto the internet and find this thing called Google.'

'What? Google? It sounds like how to cook an egg.'

Now I love to go onto Google and watch the Spice Girls. (And did you know there's all this pornography on Google? I typed in 'Spice Girls' and up came all these images of, stuff, you know.)

I love playing *Myst* on the CD Rom my dad brought back from a trip to LA last year. I love skateboarding and I love getting tattoos even though I am under-age (there's a guy in the Valley who does them for me) and I love my Docs and I love my black-dyed hair and I especially love it when mum goes nutzoid at me after I dye it blacker and blacker. (She hasn't seen the tatts yet; I'm not stupid enough to get them where she can see them. Only someone who sees my naked body could know what and where they are and no-one is going to see my naked body until I am old and decrepit.) I love the breath and wind as I ride on my board in the middle of the night, after I have crept out of the house, dressed in black, hoodie and all, and skate through the Botanic Gardens and along the edgy peak at Kangaroo Point knowing that if I fall at the wrong moment, I will drop to my death twenty metres below. I imagine the release. I imagine what they would all think then. I love stabbing trees with my long-bladed knife. When mum saw the parcel (from the Asian supermarket in the Valley) all wrapped up in brown paper with string, she said, What's that? I told her it was a hair straightener and she believed me – she believes most of what I tell her; she ignores the rest and pops another pill. I love walking up to the girls at school who used to bully me, calling me fat and a dumb bitch and stupid, walking up to them now, years later in Year 12, no longer fat, certainly not stupid, maybe a bitch, and pushing the edge of my knife in through their uniform, into their stomach and saying: Remember me? You bully another kid at this school and I will slice off your nose. I love the way they freak out and tremble because we both know I am in total control. They have no idea of the things I know. The things I have done. The things I will do. Jingles and jangles, the good things and the bad.

That's what I love.

Oh! I love anchovies and olives, which is weird because nobody else seems to.

I hate my sister, but I love her too. She is gloomy but smarter than me, and I'm smart. She needs to get out more. Anthea is sixteen, going on seventeen. I am seventeen, going on eighteen. I am a Celt-Goth. She is a mega-Goth but hides it. She hasn't dyed her hair and she doesn't have any tatts.

I have dyed black hair and wear shredded black jeans and ripped T-shirts and I have tatts and I carry a flick-knife to get back at those little bitches who bullied me all the way through school because I was overweight and wasn't blonde or in their Group and because of my eyes, one green, one blue. It's called heterochromia, you stupid dumb-fucks and it's got nothing to do with having a split personality; get over it. I want to go to Paris. Davina is a bitch; she stole my tuna sandwich last week. Mister Tyson is hot and sometimes I dream about him having sex with me but I actually don't understand what sex is, *really*, aside from the porn I watch, which is not much because it makes me kind of squirmy but sometimes I go online at two in the morning and watch stuff; there's this guy called Peter North. I would never let him get anywhere near me but I told, I did, I told Emma, my best friend, the next day, to go look at the Peter North videos online – on Google – and she did, that night and the next day Emma came back to me in the corridor of the school and said: You are so naughty!

I didn't tell her I had found a couple of violent porn sites where men stabbed women, and women strung up men. Torture stuff. Shhh. I feel dirty after I watch a bondage scene where a woman dressed in black leather hurts a guy who's hanging from the ceiling and then ...

Then I found the snuff videos.

P-Plater

He kept staring at me.

On the floor above Homicide were thick woollen carpets and young women in short skirts and immaculate white blouses and high heels who whispered to one another with a sense of urgency from behind their desks in the wide-open space where, behind them, were large offices that housed the Deputy Commissioners and the Commissioner. It was the land of policy and media bites, statistics and ratings.

I had never been up there and never wanted to. It was not the land of crime or blood or sawn-off heads, of tears and anguish. It was the land of reassurance to the public and the government that all was well within the Police Service and, as long as they didn't cut our budget, all would continue to be just dandy because, minister, crime is going down (it wasn't) and violent crime is ... well, I'll tell you what it is: it is re-defined. Yes, minister, we have approximately ninety murders a year and when one takes into account the nature of most of these killings – passion or a lover's violent tiff – then we have stabilised the level of crime, so we are, indeed, doing an excellent job. So, minister, as crime is really going *down* – as you will see in the stats – what we would like to suggest is an increase in the budget to ensure this trend continues so that the government can put it out to the voters that we are, indeed, fighting crime on the streets.

Billy says I am too young to be cynical – just learn how to be a good copper and shut up, he says – but I get it from him; he never shuts up about all this stuff.

Three dead men, middle-aged, white and upper-middle class, heads sawn off and folded sideways onto their shoulders, mouths cut open into a horrid, frozen grimace – those dead men did not fit into that world view.

'What are you doing? Give me an update,' asked the Commissioner, a tall, angular man whose body, when he stood, alarmingly took on the shape of a question mark. He was in his forties and nobody in uniform liked or respected him because he came into this job from a PhD at Sydney (strike one) University (strike two) and had spent not a day, not a day, on the beat or in the presence of a crook (strikes three to eighteen). He had never felt the rattle of violence and threat beyond a B-minus for an essay. He had long eyelashes and, for a second, after he shook my hand without looking at me, I wondered if the rumours were true and that he used eyeliner (strikes nineteen to six hundred and counting).

His name was Johannes van de-something-unpronounceable. (Strikes six hundred and counting to seven hundred.) He was Dutch. No-one could remember his name. Or wanted to. He was known simply as The Dutchman. He kept staring at me, his eyes constantly falling back to me. I smiled, in that reassuring dumb-arse way that we do, but it made no difference. His office looked out to the Roma Street railway station. Outside, the sky was deep purple with shards of black, and rain bashed loudly against the windows.

Next to me stood Billy and Kristo Galantamos, our Officer-In-Charge, our immediate boss, who was jiggling like he was at a Suzi Quatro concert.

'We've all seen this movie before, right?' he said.

Huh?

'Boss screams at his underlings and says: Why haven't you done what you are meant to have done. Right?' He had an accent. Clipped. Afrikaans. Not my favourite but don't be racist, Lara.

Billy was meditating, eyes half-closed and smiling in an inoffensive way, and Kristo was nodding and I was trying to figure out if he actually did use eyeliner. Maybe it was natural.

'I've done the stats,' he said. 'And the stats tell me we have eighty-seven point five murders in Queensland every year. And have done for the past ten years. Sometimes there's a spike down and sometimes there's a spike up. Probably the weather. Like now, with this goddamned rain and threat of a flood. But ...'

But.

'... these figures are consistent and ...'

And.

'... almost every murder, and I am talking *murder* here, chaps ...'

Chaps!

'... gets resolved. Three-point-three percent do not – not a bad rate actually, but I didn't say that because we must strive for a one hundred-percent rate. Three-point-three percent – the unexplained, or the ones missing that vital piece of evidence to nail the perpetrator. And now we seem to have a goddamned serial killer. Super. Puts the state on the map in a beautiful way; sensational for tourism as we move into the next millennium: 'Sunshine one day, serial killer the next.' And all of the gentlemen, these poor chaps who got killed, upstanding members of the community. An accountant, a lawyer and an architect. These are *not* people who should be killed in the city of Brisbane. No?'

No.

Be obedient, Lara. Be quiet. Watch, listen, learn.

He leaned forward, flicking his gaze at all three of us, and I swear I heard Billy snore, ever so lightly.

'Please find the killer. I don't care who it is and I don't care how circumstantial it is; the DPP can figure that out and the onus will then be on them. I do not, the government does not, want a goddamned serial killer, a goddamned Hannibal Lecter walking the streets of Brisbane.'

Goddammit, I thought, me neither.

(Keep it cool, Lara. He is your boss and you are twenty-six, the only Asian and we can count the number of Queensland female detectives with the fingers of one hand. Don't be a smartarse. You are, actually, privileged to be in the office of the Commissioner.)

Leaning in once more, and he too was wafting aftershave but not Brut, he stared at Kristo and said:

'Kristo.'

'Yes Commissioner?'

'Get me an arrest and get me an arrest within the next six days. I don't care if it's a blind fucking monkey, just get an arrest. Six. Days. I would say seven because that's a nice round figure, but in seven days I am going up to Noosa with the family because my littlest is turning five and we are having a birthday party on the river, on one of those houseboats they have, and by the time I am on the Noosa River with little Chloe and the missus, I want to have put behind me the biggest stress of being Commissioner. Yes?'

'Yes Commissioner.'

'Good.'

As it seemed like the meeting was over, we started to leave. He was staring at me again.

'How old are you?' he asked.

'Twenty-six,' I replied thinking: Here we go, this will be the end of my time on the case. 'Going on twenty-seven,' I added, like a five-year-old who wants to be six.

'And you've been in Homicide for how long?'

'Seven months.' (Going on eight!)

I felt Billy move forward. I wanted to speak up before he, as I knew he would, defended me. I needed my own voice heard.

'I feel I am qualified, sir.'

'Why?' he asked and I inched forward as I felt Billy step back. I don't believe in ESP but I swear he got my message: I've got this.

'I am dedicated and focussed on this case, sir. I bring my study in criminology to our Squad, not to mention first-hand experience I would rather forget with evil bastards, and while I might look young, I am as ruthless and determined as any of the men on the floor below. I may not be an expert in Homicide, yet, but I am working with one. The most experienced detective in the building, in the state of Queensland, and it's the combination of his amazing experience and my fresh, young eyes that, I suggest, provides you and the department and the minister with the best team available. Our crew is growing, with many additional experienced detectives, and we, all of us, fully understand the urgency in finding this killer and we will not rest until we have taken him off the street and charged him.'

He held my gaze and the guys behind me said not a word. I could hear the roar of my heart. I was not used to speaking up for myself, not like this, not as a cop.

'Six days,' he said and then, to me: 'If this comes to trial, you dye your hair back to its original colour. You can get away with looking like a goddamn pop star at the moment, because you're Asian and a woman and we're lean on both, but not in the gaze of the Supreme Court. Yes?'

Yes, sir. Got it.

Satellite of Love

WHEN WE HAD A SERIOUS SUSPECT IN A CRIME, THE LAST thing we would do was go knocking on their door and say: Hello, you are a major suspect in a string of murders.

A little like how we had placed the outward circles around the crime scene itself, we gathered information until we had a 3D picture of the person, and of the what, why and how they might be the crook. Which was what we did with Jen White. Which was what we had done with Miles and Nils. Neither of whom had been forgotten. Billy and Kristo had assigned one of the crews to verify, double-verify and then triple-verify their movements up to, during and after the three killings.

Miles's boat had yielded no incriminating DNA. Same with Nils's apartment in Miami.

We had to move fast. Not that we really cared about the Dutchman's six-day countdown to his daughter's birthday party. We were, all of us on the floor, all of the crews, working on the serial-killer case, which we were now also calling The Slayer. Billy and I (all twenty-six years of girlie-me) were leading the investigation only because we were the first responders and Billy, whom everyone was scared of, said we were calling the shots and if any geezer had a problem with that, he'd chuck 'em out the window.

We had to move fast because it was only a matter of a short time before our killer struck again. And we weren't the only ones who knew it. The press and the public knew it too. Jack the Ripper's first six victims were killed within eight weeks. Our killer had exceeded that in the most terrifying of ways.

As I researched Jen, still sceptical that our killer could be a seventeen-year-old skater, I skimmed some Kafka, remembering soon after we left Donna that he was a gloomy Czech author and that some kids at my school in Cairns had a prize for anyone who could actually finish one of his books. There was a passage about wanting to die being the purpose of life. Eek.

Ring a bell, Lara?

I suppose all teenagers – well, most – are drawn to the lure of the dark. I certainly was with Nils, tatts and blades. But had the darkness led Jen White to butcher three men?

—

WOMEN DON'T OFTEN kill. About fifteen percent of homicides are committed by women, and almost all of them are a result of domestic violence or, as they called it when I studied criminology, Wife Torture, when a 'battered partner' can't take it anymore. Or infanticide, which is rare and usually relates to a place (like Queensland) where abortion is illegal and a mother giving birth imagines that she has no other solution to a birth she cannot cope with, for whatever reason. Or when the grip of postnatal depression proves too strong.

Unlike men – those who kill, anyway – who seem to think that murder is a sensational way to solve a problem despite the fact some rational thought or conversation might have actually done the trick.

It just didn't seem possible that a seventeen-year-old girl could be capable of repeat murders of such a ritualistic and grotesque nature. But Billy kept telling me that young women can kill, more than once, even though it's rare, and all the time I was thinking, I don't think so, not in this case, not with this level of brutality. But Tracey Wigginton was in her mid-twenties. And then Billy reminds me of Mary Bell.

She was pretty, an innocent face with a sweet little smile, black hair and a fringe. From the West End district of Newcastle upon Tyne, way up in England's north, on the east coast, where Billy reckons the locals have undecipherable accents. She was eleven when she strangled two little boys.

It was the day before Mary's birthday in 1968 when she strangled four-year-old Martin Brown in an empty dump of a

house in her working-class suburb in northern England. A couple
of days later she turned up at the Brown residence and asked to see
Martin. When his mum, who was in deep grief, explained that he
was dead, Mary said:

Oh yeah, I know that, I just want to see him in his coffin.

And his mum let her in. God only knows what this eleven-year-
old girl was thinking as she looked at the corpse she created.

About five weeks later, Mary and another girl, Norma Bell (no
relation) strangled three-year-old Brian Howe. Out came a razor-
blade, and no-one really knows who did what because Norma,
weeping in court non-stop and showing remorse and with a good
lawyer, got off and has not been heard from since. The blade was
used to mutilate Brian Howe, slashing his penis, cutting his hair
and carving an N – later modified to an M – in his stomach.

'Brian Howe had no mother, so he won't be missed,' is what
Mary later said, this cherubic eleven-year-old girl.

But it was revealed this little monster had a mother who was
an S&M prostitute working from home who would force Mary to
fuck her clients. From the age of four.

The moral compass on Mary Bell still swings in an endless
three-sixty because no-one quite knows, aside from the blunt fact
she killed two little boys, where the edges of culpability lie.

Maybe, as Billy believes, she was born evil. 'Ain't no lad in the
East End who didn't have a childhood of beatings and bashings,
ain't many lasses who didn't have the same along with fiddly-stick
uncles; every one in my street and the next and the one after that,
all of 'em, all of 'em had our share of that and none of us go out
and kill some kid geezer. Well, none of the others, that is.'

But still: Jen White? Seventeen-year-old Jen, from a wealthy
middle-class Brisbane family with dreams of studying literature?

But still, my little voice said: Lara Ocean? Teenage girl with a
knife, teenage girl with a gun tucked into the back of her jeans.
Angry and violent with something to prove. What makes you think
you couldn't have tipped over and slashed the throat of a random
guy, through your rage at the world?

—

'HERE'S THE THING, girlie,' Billy said to me after we had left the Commissioner's office and called Jen's school to arrange a meeting with her year advisor, 'take the space between improbable and impossible. Yeah, you in that space?'

Yes, Billy I am in that space.

'Our Jen, she fits inside that space. Yeah?'

Yes. But.

'It's not impossible?'

No. It's not. Is it, Lara?

All Things Must Pass

HANG ON; WHAT THE FUCK?

Cops at the front door? A squat guy with green eyes and danger, wearing a suit and shiny brown shoes with pointy toes, and this pretty woman, Asian with dyed blonde hair with a gun on her hip, smiling at me like we're about to all share a picnic lunch.

Why are they here? What have I done?

Well, okay, I did stab Mary-Anne a bit hard with my flick-knife, and I did threaten to slice off Donna's nose, and I did accidentally on purpose trip up Miss Preece in the corridor and she didn't believe it when I said, sorry, so, so, sorry.

'Hi Jen ... it's Jen, right?'

Yes.

'Hi. I'm Detective Constable Lara Ocean, and this is my colleague, his name is Billy Waterson, and we'd just like to ask you a few questions.'

—

AS WE HAD walked up to the front door we had passed through a pretty garden with rose bushes and frangipani trees and a pond that had been built in an eight-shape with trees of citrus, lemon and orange trees and pockets of jasmine and lavender and lemon myrtle and rosemary. The rain had stopped an hour ago. The sky was still full of dark clouds. Some days they would skidder quickly. Some days, like today, they would just hang. Not moving, creating the ominous.

As we were led inside by her mother, before she called out to Jen, after we had introduced ourselves, I scanned the house. Large rooms with floor to ceiling windows and thick white carpet and solid Balinese wooden furniture. It looked like a home. It looked cosy and the sort of place I dreamed of when I was a kid. There was a massive Aboriginal painting hanging on one of the walls. We knew that Jen's dad traded in art and crafts from places like Morocco, selling works to galleries around the world.

The Whites, like the others we'd seen on the hill, were well-off. By the staircase was a tall white Christmas tree with wrapped presents at its base. Christmas lights were flashing.

—

'MISSUS WHITE, WOULD you like to sit next to Jen as we ask her some questions?'

'What's this about?'

'Just some routine questions. If you could sit next to your daughter as we chat to her, that would be great.'

'Now, Jen, we're going to ask you some questions, okay?'

Okay.

'Did you go on the school excursion to North Stradbroke Island in mid-November?'

'Yes.'

'Was that a camping trip? Like, a wilderness thing?'

'Yes, we were there for a couple of days.'

Did I do anything wrong when I was there? I didn't; I hated it and stayed quiet and didn't talk to anyone for the whole three days. Why are they asking me about it? I am starting to get angry. I gotta stop that. I've been told to curb the anger when things start to go beyond my control. When I feel like I'm treading water or drifting in a life raft scanning for a horizon.

'Thanks Jen,' said the man.

'No-one remembers where they were on certain days or nights – I mean, who travels with a diary and cross-references that stuff, huh?' says the woman.

Huh?

'But Jen, can you tell us where you were on the night of Thursday, November eighteenth?'

—

No, I CANNOT.

What is going on here? The walls are creeping in on me and the ceiling is crushing down and I need to breathe ...

'There's nought to be alarmed about,' said the older cop, in a distinct English accent.

I don't believe him.

'What we'd like to do is take you down to the office for an interview,' she said.

My hands started to quiver. Deep breathing This is a mistake. All will work out. Be positive, Jen.

Anthea was hiding at the edge of the kitchen door so no-one could see her, but I could. She was staring at me with a: *There are cops in the house?* look. I tried to give her a reassuring smile – it's okay, it's just a weird fuck-up. There were tears rolling down her face because she knew that we were in an alternative universe that was bad, bad, bad. I dragged my gaze away from her after sending what I hoped was a look of reassurance; *Hey, it's going to be fine, it's going to be okay.*

She didn't buy it; she knew I was lying. Because she saw the fear in my face. As I felt the fear in my stomach.

And mum was, well, mum had taken a Xanax with her morning burst of vodka after she got out of bed, so although she was sitting next to me, she was really on Jupiter, and dad, none of us had seen dad for weeks because he was fucking that Serb girl from Sydney, pretending he was Peter North.

Lara Ocean, the female cop, had a tiny mole by the edge of her mouth, which reminded me of a story by Kurt Vonnegut Jr about the purity of beauty; but, as he wrote, there is no such thing because there is always a blemish. In other words, perfection is–

'So, if you could just come with us?' said Lara Ocean.

Okay.

'Missus White, you need to be with your daughter during this chat down in our office. Okay?'

Mum nodded. Maybe it's Saturn.

'Jen, before we go, would you mind getting us your sling blade?' said Lara Ocean.

'My what?' I asked.

—

'FLICK-KNIFE,' I SAID calmly. Jen stared at me, a little unnervingly, as if a coldness has fallen, and she said:

'I lost it.'

'Okay. No worries,' I said. When I glanced at Billy I could see that he didn't quite believe Jen about the knife, and nor did I. For the first time, the nonsense of a teenage killer started to dissipate.

The Place of Errors

'THANKS FOR COMING IN, JEN. IF YOU'LL JUST SIT THERE FOR us, that would be great.' I pulled out a chair.

I stared at the teenage girl who was a suspect in three brutal murders. She stared back. She had a round face with dimples and the most striking eyes, one blue, one green, like David Bowie.

'We'll get this happening in just a moment. Okay?'

'Okay.' She held the stare. Was that anger I could detect, below the surface of a sweet-looking seventeen-year-old?

'Just have a seat while I set up the camera and the tape deck and ... where did your mum go? Have we lost your mum? We need your mum; I thought she came up in the lift with us. I cannot talk to you without your mum.'

I shouted into the corridor outside the interview room, 'Billy!'

'What? I'm getting a glass of water.'

'Can you find Missus White? She's vanished.'

—

WE FOUND HER wandering through Missing Persons – how on earth did she get there? Don't ask; police headquarters is supposed to be secure – but here was our dilemma. Jen's mother had clearly taken some medication and was on another planet, and while, yes, she could respond and speak to us and give her approval for a record of interview with her daughter, we had to ask ourselves: would this come back to haunt us if, *if*, we ever took Jen to court? A defence lawyer might say the record of interview was invalid and nothing that my client said can be brought before the court.

Jen and her mum remained in the interview room while Kristo called the DPP.

'Jen, would you like a cup of tea?'

'No thanks.'

'Just remember, Jen, if there's a moment when you feel overtly –
you know the meaning of that word?'

She gave me dead-eye. Her year advisor had told us she was an
English Literature genius. Stupid me; I needed to focus.

'Okay, got it, sorry, I didn't mean to insult you.'

Jen leaned across the desk in the interview room and it was no
longer dead-eye and she said:

'The past is a foreign country.'

And I stared back at her with: *Is this relevant?*

'Look it up,' she said, 'because I can see it on your face; look it
up and check out the next phrase.'

I left.

I saw then, in Jen, what I thought I would see if I sat across a
table from Mary Bell. She gave me, Jen did, the shivers. This was
the second time I began to erase my initial disbelief in our serial
killer being a teenage girl. And replaced it with an open mind.
Don't reach a conclusion before you have all the facts, I reminded
myself.

—

THE DPP SAID, as long as the mother is in the room and can
respond to questions, you can proceed with the interview.

'Jen, if you could just announce your name into the microphone?'

'Jen.'

'Can you give us your whole name?'

'Jen. White.'

'Born?'

'You know.'

'We do but if could tell us, thanks, that would be great.'

'It was in the age of paradise.'

Even Jen's smacked-out mum sat up and stared at her daughter.

—

IT'S THOSE HANDS. That grip. The smile. Being guided out of the house. Being pushed. That hard grip; although she's tall she looks slight, the female cop, Lara Ocean. But she's not. She must do karate or some other Asian self-defence thing, because she has the grip of a lion.

The abject humiliation of being led out of our house, into the street full of nosy neighbours, hiding behind their curtains, her hands on me – that was when the tremors of fear started to ebb and were replaced by anger. I have not done anything wrong.

—

'YOU WERE BORN on May the eighth, nineteen eighty-two. Is that correct, Jen, May eight, nineteen eighty-two?'

'Yes.'

'Great, thanks. And Missus White, if you wouldn't mind confirming that you are in attendance at the interview here in the offices of Queensland Homicide with myself, Detective Constable Lara Ocean and Detective Inspector William Waterson?'

'Yes.'

'Great, thanks. Before we start I want to confirm that Jen, you are feeling comfortable and that we have offered you some tea or some water.'

Jen nodded.

'If you could – this is for the recording, Jen – if you could say yes or no, that would be great.'

'What was the question?'

'Are you being treated well and have we offered you tea or water?'

'Yes.'

'And you are not in any distress?'

'No.'

'And your mum is seated next to you, now, at this moment?'

'Yes.'

'Great. Thanks Jen. We'll get some sandwiches in here in a couple of hours' time so you can eat, but can I start with this.'

I pushed over the illustration of the twelve spokes within the circle – Taranis. 'Do you know what this is? Have you ever seen this image before?'

'Maybe,' she said.

'Jen, I know you're going to study English Lit after Year 12 and I know you are really smart. Jen, what is it? Yes, you know this image, or no, you don't?'

'Yes.'

I looked to Billy, who was doing his pretending-to-be-asleep thing, and back to Jen. Which was meant to be passive as if to lull the suspect/person of interest on the other side of the table into a place of relaxation. We both know the place of relaxation is a place of errors, where you can say the wrong thing because you are not totally, *totally* alert to the dangers that we, us cops, present to you. It is an obstacle course and we make the rules and if you deviate, we will take you to court and maybe to jail, for the rest of your life.

So, stay alert, little girl, because my partner here is like a cobra and will pounce on you within a millisecond if you waiver, if you falter, if you deviate. And those hands on you, my grip on your elbow, from which you flinched? Those hands will be on you for the rest of your life, so look into my eyes, and stay honest.

—

'TELL US ABOUT this image,' I continued, while next to her, Jen's mum tried to stay awake.

'It's the Celtic god of thunder,' said Jen.

'Whose name is …?' I asked.

'Taranis.'

'What does he mean to you?' I asked.

Billy was lying back, still passive, pretending to snore.

'He is all-powerful,' she said.

And I leaned in and said:

'But what does that actually mean to *you*? Do you invoke him? Does he come to you? Do you channel him? Is he within you? Do you, maybe, take out a silver-bladed knife at three or four in the morning and find a place on your arms or your legs or maybe even your back and draw blood for him? Because I read that sacrificial blood and Taranis are a thing, if you know what I mean.'

Still leaning back in his chair doing the non-threatening sleep thing, Billy, unseen by them on the other side of the table, gently nudged my leg with his patent-leather shoe. Reminding me again.

Too long a question, too leading a question. Too many questions in one. This girl was unnerving me. Focus, Lara. Even though the stakes were high and all the crews were watching me, everyone – including the Commissioner – was watching me, I had to stay alert and keep my mind clear.

Jen was staring, showing no emotion and holding my gaze, as if willing me to arrest her.

Staring at me, she said, a small voice in the room:

'Mum?'

'Yes darling?' asked the fog of Xanax.

'Do you think you should call dad?'

'Why would I want to call your dad?'

'He might be interested to know that his oldest daughter is being formally interviewed by two Homicide detectives and he might think that perhaps I need some representation.'

'What do you mean, representation?'

'A lawyer.'

'Oh. Yes. I hadn't thought about that.'

'You want a lawyer?' I asked Jen.

'I think it might be prudent, don't you?' said Jen as her mum rummaged through her bag and pulled out her new and very expensive mobile phone, called a Blackberry, which only came into the shops about a week ago.

—

SHE WAS SO excited when she got it. 'Look at me,' she had proudly said to Anthea and I. 'This is the future. If you girls are nice to your mother, then I might think about buying you one each for your birthdays.'

Mum likes to get the shiny new things and charge them to dad's American Express card. Last month she bought a Sony flat-screen LCD TV, first on the market and it cost her over fifteen thousand dollars. Lucky that his card is platinum.

—

'WHY DON'T WE step out for a moment, while you call your husband, Missus White. Interview with Jen White is being halted at,' said Lara Ocean, into the tape recorder, checking her watch, 'eleven eighteen a.m.' Click, off and out they go.

The Chink

'WHAT DO YOU THINK?' I ASKED BILLY AS WE WENT BACK TO our co-joined desks, our little island on the floor of the office, leaving mother and daughter alone in the interview room. The other crews who had been assigned to the case – working the North Stradbroke angle, the Goth and Celt scene angle, the possibility of a gay killer, the necessary but dead-end angle of a connecting point within their pasts that might have motivated the killer and any other angle – took a moment to look at us, knowing we'd brought Jen in. The same question in each mind:

Could it be her?

'Guilty as sin,' said Billy.

'Really? Why?' I asked, surprised by his rush to condemnation.

'She's cold, she's heartless, no emotion. Ruthless.'

'Maybe that's just fear. But even if it's not, would that make her a killer?'

'North Stradbroke trip, knives, god of thunder, skateboarder, testimony from the kids and teacher at her school; remember that?'

—

How COULD I forget. Girl after girl after girl, all saying the same: She's weird, she carries a flick-knife around school, and what's with the Celtic thing? And Bettany knows she's into Satan, like, worships him and stuff, rituals and stuff, and Olivia saw her in the Queen Street Mall one Sunday and she was, like, so stoned and ... and ... and, and –

Then there was her year advisor.

'Well, yes, it is true that Jen stands out,' she had said. 'Stands out, if you will, quite a lot from the other girls at the school. Her

124

parents are very nice and very wealthy; I think her dad has a Lexus and her mum drives the latest model Volvo and they are always here on sports days and evening events. You know, we have a mentor scheme where the little ones, just after arriving, are assigned a Year 12 girl as a sort of go-to person, to guide them, if you will, and Jen was assigned a girl, a nice little Asian girl and,' she'd said, looking directly at me, '*you'd* know – '

Said with a smile that I have stared into all my life, a smile I have fallen into, into a deep cave of: Who am I? A smile that is not patronising but so fucking is.

One of my first memories was that smile I've seen tens of thousands of times. It comes with: Asians are so good with numbers. Asians are obsequious. Asian ladies will make you a cup of tea and massage you. Asians are well, you know –

– *they're not like us.*

Billy had gently nudged my foot, under the table with a, *yet again*: stay groovy. I put on my happy face; yeah, we're not like you, we are subservient and thanks for reminding me of that.

'This little Asian girl was just great with maths and her family had recently moved from Singapore and this little girl, Frannie, well, her parents were rather horrified because Frannie, who would have only been eleven, started going home and swearing at the dinner table: f-this and f-that and we quickly discovered it was Jen, her mentor, who thought it highly amusing to teach Frannie to use the f-word at home. She is so intelligent. Jen. I teach her English, and her grasp of the novel is quite extraordinary. Aside from her obsession with Kafka – at least it's not Nietzsche – she is the most talented student I have taught; I mean, she can recite Chaucer! Who has even *heard* of Chaucer these days?'

Billy raised his hand. I followed.

She laughed. 'So, I suppose what I'm saying, detectives, is that she is terribly bright, quite dark, and –'

'Tell us about the knives,' I asked.

'Oh. Yes. The flick-knife?'

—

SHE TOLD US her name was Hortense and that she was from the
Seychelles. She had been teaching English at this very exclusive
all-girls school for decades. We were sitting in her office, which
was large and had massive windows with plantation shutters and
glass louvres with a view over the tennis courts, a lawn and, as this
school sat atop Ascot Hill, a sweeping panorama of the river below
and the city beyond. Her office must have been, when the school
was built out of hardwood back in the 1800s, part of a veranda
and, on the lawn below, girls would have played croquet and worn
long dresses.

There was a black and white photo, framed, on her wall, of
a Chinese man, in a Mao suit with girls all around him, staring
up at him as if he had come from another planet; it must have
been taken in the early 1950s. Soon after mum as a little girl and
my grandmother fled the mainland. In the photo, the girls were
all standing under a massive jacaranda tree, in full bloom; and I
could, looking out through the louvered windows, see the same
tree towering over the lawn, in full bloom again, its purple flowers
both in the tree and on the ground, a carpet of purple.

What was the Chinese man doing here? I wondered.

He was smiling, the Chinese man. Was he here with a delegation
of some kind?

Where is he now? I wondered. He must be long dead. I wondered
what his name was, if he had been married and had kids and if
he did, where they might be, now? I thought back to growing up
in Cairns, as a kid, walking to school with a plastic ice-cream
container on my head because the magpies would swoop down to
nut me, thinking I was a threat to their babies, kicking through the
floor of purple flowers, like the boys liked to kick through puddles.
Swish swish with cold noodles in my bag, which I would eat in
private, sometimes in the toilet because it was Asian food and I
couldn't be Asian because if I was Asian, I was The Chink.

Mum, just make me a sandwich! Please! Or money for a meat
pie! No more noodles!

—

'I suppose the first time we realised there was an issue with the flick-knife was about a year ago. One of the girls in Jen's class, Lucy, came to me and said she felt ... what's the right word? It's not as if Jen had actually *threatened* her, but the knife scared her, so I spoke to Jen and I confiscated it and I got her parents in and we all, including Jen, had a chat and she agreed not to bring it in again. Mum and dad were somewhat startled that she actually had a flick-knife, and that was pretty much that.'

'Sorry. You said the first time,' said Billy.

'Oh. Yes. Well. After that there were some other incidents.'

'Being?' asked Billy.

She started to fidget. 'Would you mind telling me what this is all about?'

—

'Oh, for fuck's sake; didn't you close the door?'

Turning around, I followed Billy's gaze to see Space-Cadet-Mum on our floor, walking from desk to desk, the brand-new Blackberry in her hand.

'I thought *you* did!' I barked back at him.

The other crews were looking bemused as, having now spotted us, she was quickly striding towards us, holding out her phone.

'Can you talk to my husband? He wants to ask you some questions.'

We both got up and began to shepherd her to the interview room.

'Sorry darlin', it doesn't work like that.'

'But he's in Dubai.'

'Good for him,' said Billy as we ushered her back into the interview room and shut the door behind us. Jen was sitting upright and hadn't moved.

'Have you made a decision regarding a lawyer?' I asked while she whispered into the Blackberry: 'They won't talk to you. I know, so rude. All right I will.' And she hung up.

'Yes, we have. My husband is calling someone now.'

Exit Strategy

IN MY FIRST WEEK AT HOMICIDE, I HEARD AN OLD JOKE ABOUT criminal defence lawyers. One of them is talking to her client behind bars and says: 'Okay, you stabbed him fifty-three times, then you ran over him twice; your DNA's on the victim and you did this in Times Square, so there are ten thousand eyewitnesses. Here's my plan to get you off.'

I laughed then, like every Homicide detective who hears it for the first time, but also like every Homicide detective I stopped laughing after my first murder suspect was charged and then, three months later, walked free from court. Not only does a cop feel a sense of anger that a guilty person has got off because the law is fucked, but a failure of conviction blows back on the cop's reputation. One too many failures, Billy told me, and the floor starts with the quiet rumblings about the colleague who's cutting corners, not being diligent enough, not caring, and soon you're not on a crew anymore. Then the rumblings stop being quiet, and the other crews not only refuse to work with you but agitate to get you off the floor for good, aware that their reps are also getting tarnished.

It's all well and good for the Dutchman to tell us we just have to charge someone to get the press off our back, and to leave the rest of it, the actual conviction, to the prosecutor. What happens, as Billy said to me, if we hand a brief to the DPP and then, hallelujah, another bloke gets killed in the same way a week later?

'I'll tell ya what happens, girlie. What happens is that everyone from the Dutchman down calls us idiots, throws us to the wolves, kicks us out of Homicide and blames us for the new death.'

—

128

JEN AND I glanced at one another as her lawyer entered the interview room and introduced himself by handing out his business card.

'Hello, my name is Bruno Albanese and I am representing Ms White. What, please, is the reason for her to be here?'

I looked up from the business card, which told me that Mister Albanese was a solicitor from a small suburban firm. Most likely he'd done the family wills and some contracting work for them. Jen's mum was a manager at a Honda dealership on Breakfast Creek and her dad was a wealthy art dealer. In my very narrow experience with wealthy people who travel the world, they fret about frequent flyer points more than anything and hate spending money, assuming that life is a triumph and they, therefore, shouldn't have to throw good money anywhere, certainly not at a lawyer because if you're not careful, they could bankrupt you, because the only person who cares about you is you.

Jen was staring at me.

—

I WAS STARING at Lara, who had just scanned the business card of my lawyer, dad's old school friend who, I'd overheard dad say, does a good 'mate's rate' because lawyers 'charge like wounded fucking herds of buffalo'. I don't think dad or mum or mister lawyer understand that I am actually in Homicide. Being interviewed in Homicide. Because I am a suspect in a murder. Or murders. We haven't even got to that bit yet. But what is abundantly clear is the word, the deed, the threat, the reality of Homicide. Dad, I would have thought that'd be justification enough for you to get, like, you know, a barrister, or someone with criminal expertise.

But no. Dad is in Serbia and mum is on Saturn.

It is up to me. To deal with this.

—

'IF WE COULD just return to this,' said Billy, indicating the image of Taranis, which was face-up on the table. 'Can you tell us what the god of thunder means to you?'

'I want to invoke the fifth amendment, as anything I say may incriminate me,' said Jen.

For the first time Billy sat up, eyes wide open, and stared at her with a *What the fuck*? And I looked at her and wondered if this is just kid-dumb or a tease.

'That is relevant solely to American law, Jen. There is no fifth amendment in Australia. You can choose to remain silent and not answer our questions, that is your right, but you cannot invoke the fifth because it does not sit within Australian law.'

—

FROM THE TIME they led me to the cop car out the front of the house with the street watching, Lara's claws digging into my flesh and Anthea looking horrified, to now, I had started to think this was all a big stupid fucking joke. I am not angry anymore. I am fucking over it. I wanted to go to the movies but instead I am sitting in an interview room with an old guy who smells of cheap lolly water and wears brown shoes that look like mirrors.

I am my own worst enemy. Who isn't? Well, I take the prize. Sitting in the interview room in Homicide, it started to feel like this was all simply ridiculous. At some point, soon I hope, the world of topsy turvey will return to its axis.

—

'LOOK,' SAID THE lawyer as he leaned forward in his chair, 'what's going on here? My client has come here of her own volition and is co-operating but you need to tell us exactly why she is here. I mean, for God's sake, we're in an interview room in *Homicide*. You think my client killed someone? Please, elucidate us.'

Before Billy or I could respond, Jen began to weep. Deeply. Alarmingly. And then she slid off her chair onto the floor and began to heave with pain and anguish. We called off the interview. After all, she was, legally, a kid.

They went home.

Was it an act? Was it real?

—

'WAS THAT DESIGNED to make us feel sorry for her? Throw us off the scent?'

Kristo had called us into his office after Jen, her mother and lawyer left. He, along with everyone else on the floor, had heard a teenage girl's distress from behind the door and then watched as she was led out of the interview room, sobbing, staring at us like we were Inquisitors from medieval Spain.

Or that's how it felt to me.

Was it just theatrics? Whatever it was, it told Billy and me that we needed to tread carefully with her.

'Give me an update. Tell me what you've got. Is she at all a realistic suspect? Because having a teenage girl weeping in my office makes me feel decidedly uneasy.'

'Guv, she is as good as the other two blokes. Which, truth be told, ain't no spring day of sun, as those two geezers are certainly violent and are into knives and have been seen in the proximity of the killings – Miles even lives smack-bang in the middle of where we found all three vics, on the river, in his yacht. Nils, he's a walking advert for death and mutilation. But the girl, she's a Goth, she's also into knives and the Celt thing, not as much as old mate Nils, but still, and she's recently been to Stradbroke Island for a school trip, and she rides a skateboard and we know there's been numerous sightings of a girl on a skateboard when the vics got done. So, you tell me, 'cause this ain't no slam dunk, this serial-killing thing.'

'The motive?' asked Kristo.

'We have to look at it a different way,' I said.

'Which is?' asked Kristo.

'The motive for the killer is different to anything we're used to; this motive comes from a deep psychological aberration. The killer wants to prove something or wants to show off with the arrangement of the bodies. It means something specific to him. He wants power over his victims and then, I guess, over his life because his life is empty. Or else none of that: he wants to kill just because he gets off on it, because it's a thrill.'

It's a serial killer. We don't know what the fuck we're doing because the traditional leads are worthless. He is, as Damon said, a ghost.

———

THIS IS WHAT Billy taught me in my first week. These were the essential requirements we needed to take a brief to the Director of Public Prosecutions, to consider whether a case was strong enough to proceed to court; in other words, to get a conviction. Before we arrest someone.

One: A confession. We all love a confession, because that nails it; I am guilty. Slam dunk, says the DPP. Done and dusted, case over even before I walk into the courtroom. Well, almost – as long as the confession is not rescinded and as long as the Homicide Squad can corroborate it with evidence.

Two: No confession, okay; is there hard physical evidence that connects the accused to the crime? Hair, fibres, semen, DNA. No? Okay; moving on.

Three: Eyewitnesses testimony? Dodgy, because most eyewitnesses are unreliable, but don't worry about that, because the jury will be transfixed by the little old lady who says, 'Yes, it was her that I saw.'

Four: None of the above? Guys, you're killing me. No DNA, no eyewitnesses, no evidence but all this circumstantial stuff about a freaking daisy from North Stradbroke Island, weird creepy shit with the victims' mouths and a god of freaking thunder? And she's underage? And she goes to maybe the most expensive school in the city and – hang on ...

———

'HANG ON,' SAID Billy as he stared at Kristo. 'Perhaps we could give the cage a bit of a shake.'

I had no idea what he was talking about. But it seemed as though Kristo did.

'She's pretty,' he said.

'Are you talking about what I think you're talking about?' I asked, now realising. They ignored me, the two men.

'Sometimes,' Billy said as he turned around to face me in his chair, 'you gotta let the tide run and see where it takes you.'

I was seven months into the job I had always dreamed of. I was sitting with the Officer-In-Charge and the most experienced Homicide cop in the state of Queensland.

I stayed quiet.

Jen Black

TOUGHEN UP.

In the interview room I didn't know whether to laugh or cry or stare at the cops or stare at the wall or put my arms around my chest or shoulders or lie on the floor and maybe try to sleep so that when I wake up it will have been a dream, all a dream, a bad dream but a dream. But it wasn't a dream, and I knew it wasn't a dream, and I kept on thinking: Why am I here? What have I done wrong? Homicide? That's dead people. That's murder. That's another universe. Surely, surely, surely, someone will come in and say: Oh, this is all a huge mistake, you have the wrong Jen, you wanted Jen Black, she's in the next room and she's the one who committed murder, not our Jen White, not her. But they didn't, they didn't come into the room and save me and the cops, Lara Ocean and the old guy, they are so driven; Jesus, when was the last time either of them laughed? Like, two decades ago?

—

I'M BACK HOME, on my bed, staring at my poster of Madonna on the ceiling, which Anthea and I struggled to put up – you try sticking a poster onto a ceiling. Her poster is of Satyricon, a black metal band from Norway. I'm trying to process what happened to me today and I'm thinking: What do they imagine I did?

Anthea walked in and sat at the end of my bed.

'What's happening? Has this got to do with those three guys who almost had their heads cut off?'

'What?' I asked. 'What are you *talking* about?'

'Don't you read the newspapers or watch the news?'

'No. What three guys?'

'One at Kangaroo Point Cliffs and two in the Gardens. Someone killed them by sawing into their necks and almost decapitating them.'

'Are you fucking kidding me?'

'Nup. Why would they think it's you?'

She reached out and held my foot, and I began to cry. Is this really happening to me?

—

I LOVE MY little sister, I hate her. She makes me laugh and she drives me mad. She is so selfish but so caring. We love different things and we hate different things. She loves heavy-metal music and sometimes sneaks out at night with her fake ID and comes back at three in the morning smelling of vodka and slips into my bed and says: Can you tell mum and dad that I'm really sick, when you get up in the morning? and I say, Yep, and she snores as she slumbers in my arms and I think: Where will we be, you and me, in ten or twenty or thirty years' time? Will we still be alive? Will we have kids? After mum and dad have gone and it's only you and me.

Deluge

(I)

I LIVE IN A SMALL TWO-BEDROOM HOUSE IN HENDRA, CLOSE TO the racetrack, in one of the many streets where, in 1999, it was still legal to have horse stables in your back yard and chickens in the front. It was a wide street with jacaranda trees along both sides of the grass footpath, which formed a canopy of branches, where most of the buildings were old wooden Queenslanders, small, compact, with a tiny veranda out the front and a patch of grass with a frangipani tree out the back. And then, peppered between them, were the larger wooden homes with the stables out back, which have been there since maybe the late 1800s. In the dark of pre-dawn as I lay in bed, my room facing the street, I listened to the click-clack of the horses being led by their owners, the trainers, down the centre of the street to the track at the end. They were my neighbours, old guys from another era with hopes and dreams of their horse winning big and them cashing in, who every weekend come back home, leading their horse down the middle of the street again, resigned but hopeful that next week will be the one. If I happened to be out on my balcony, I would wave, with a smile, and they would wave back to me.

That was my pre-dawn every day.

That morning, though, well before the click-clack of the horses, I woke, abruptly, in shock, to the burst of a thunderous crack that might have tilted the sky and the earth, its boom reverberating across the landscape of the sky until, many moments later, it shuddered beyond the horizon. Then the downpour, rain pummelling the roof and the street outside.

I had been dreaming.

I rarely remembered my dreams, still don't. My friend Didi once told me I should do a spiritual hypno-therapy course to recall them, write them down when I wake up and then meditate with white sage, but I didn't want to; I like my dreams to recede into the mist of grey as I jump out of bed.

I had gone to bed under the sound of light rain and now it was hard, relentless, like sheets whipping along the street. I got up, out of bed, stood at the front window. A phosphorus beam of yellow light, from a tall wooden pole, light arcing onto the gun-metal surface of the road, shimmered with the bluster of the wind and rain lashing down. I went down to the kitchen and made myself a jug of coffee and some noodles and sat on the couch, fired up my laptop and brought up Google, which Didi also told me about, breathlessly, earlier last year. Search:

Retirement in Fiji.

—

He didn't hit me.

Well, only once.

We were in the caravan, deep in the desert, not another human for hundreds of miles, and he rolled on top of me with bourbon-and-beer breath and said, Let's do it, and I said, No, I want to sleep, and so he started to do it and I said, No, and sat up and he whacked me, not in the face, but in the stomach and I felt a tide of air leave me, exhaling through me and I managed to sit up, my hands gripping the side of the tiny little caravan bed, and I said, Don't ever do that to me again, and he said, I will do what I want, and I said, I don't think so, and as he scrunched up his fist for another shot I two-finger poked him in both of his eyes and he yelped like a dog and roiled back onto the bed and I thrust my knee into his balls and leaned into his ear and said: You *ever* touch me, you *ever* come within a hundred-metre radius of me, you *ever* reach out to me, you *ever* even *think* about me, again, I will kill you. Got it?

He got it.

This was Guido. He sat, in my shitty history of no self-esteem, the spiral of hate, between Nils Part One and Nils Part Two.

I climbed over his insect-like body, coiled in pain, and put on my jeans and T-shirt and grabbed my hairdryer and my make-up and my few other clothes strewn across the floor of the caravan and I saw his gun, a .45, and I took that as well, knowing he would come after me, gun in hand and try to hurt me as I had allowed myself to be hurt by him because I thought I was shot, a dog, a half-caste with a place neither here nor there and as I stepped out of the caravan in the middle of a vast desert because that's how we (you) like it babe, we are traditionalists, scanning a three-sixty of nothing but for a dim and thin red dirt road etching its way across a dusty flat landscape with the awk awk of crows circling about me in the sketchy rise of pre-dawn, my boot hitting the dirt, scuffs of red dust scurrying around me as I walked, never looking back, don't look back, Lara. Do what it is you really want to do; be a cop, be someone, be a person, make a difference to the ones whose lives have been collapsed like yours almost was, by him, when he put the nozzle of the .45 into your mouth and his dick inside you and laughed and said: I am you; and you said nothing but quaked with a little fear and wondered when you would summon the courage to eviscerate him, cut him from head to toe.

—

BOOTS ACROSS THE desert. After the first day of walking, rains began to sweep across the arid land and the sky hung with gloom and sadness, crackles of grey and black, black and grey, blue, heavy onto the horizon, ripples of thunder, getting closer and closer, rolling across the ether towards me, pulsating me, twining around me, scaring me and then maybe dissipating but maybe not, and the threat of rain. Rain, deep in the desert. I see it now. I didn't then, back then when I was seventeen. After Guido, between Nils, the first and second time, before I shocked my mum by telling her I'd been accepted to train as a cop.

Eventually I made it home. Walking across the now-muddy landscape I reached an outback highway, empty and straight as a nail. But for the occasional dead tree, grey with branches sticking out like a mad woman's hair, the land all around me was so empty. I turned east and walked until a lonely chicken farmer picked me up in an old Bedford truck. He might have noticed the .45 sticking out the back of my jeans; if he did, he didn't mention it.

—

ONCE, A COUPLE of years later, Guido came for me with a Hey babe, I miss you, you miss me? And I said: Nup, go away and never come back.

And he didn't. The past is the past.

And some of it you can keep away. Where it belongs. In the past. And some of it –

—

EVERY NOW AND then, when I pulled the doona up around me in my house in Hendra and heard the click-clack of the horses, as I heard the pitter-patter of rain that might become a deluge with water rising up from the drains into the street, every now and then, I thought back to that hard walk across the desert, the outback of Queensland, out of the caravan, deep in the heart of the desert leaving behind a brutal man, a .45 wedged into the back of my jeans and on, on, on. Eventually to Brisbane. Long before I became a cop. But not so long before I went back to Nils. And everything that came with him. The tatts, the blood, the cutting, the collapse. Why did I keep going back to crisis?

Is that me, doomed to repeat this pattern of self-destruction?

Flotsam & Jetsam

BILLY WOULD SEND MONEY HOME TO HIS MUM. HIS Queensland Police pay cheque wasn't much, not back in the 1970s but he always managed to find a few quid, once he'd done the conversion from dollars, to send back to her. She lived in a council flat in the East End, a tiny little place that he also grew up in, after his dad had gasped his last. Billy grew up at the end of the war years, in the mid to late 1940s and by the time the 1960s came along, he had amassed so many criminal charges for robbery, he'd become well known on the streets of the East. So much so that by the time he reached the age of seventeen, with a long playlist of infamy, he saw two choices: life inside the slammer, and he'd already been in and out a few times, or a clean break.

With his mum's blessing, he caught a boat as a Ten Pound Pom, one of the many who took advantage of the siren-call from the ex-colony, in need of white-faced migrants. This was during the days of the White Australia Policy when Lara's Chinese family would have been turned away. As would have almost anyone not of European heritage.

Billy moved into a small wooden Queenslander in West End. On a large block, off the dingy main street, Boundary Road, so-named after the boundary between whites and blacks, Anglos and Aboriginals, from back in the last century, and still home to many Indigenous people from Queensland. In the 1980s he had saved enough (and his mum had passed on) so that he could buy it in cash. In the 1980s West End was still considered a bit of a dump. By 1999 it had become very trendy with outdoor cafes and bars pumping US indie rock, not that he ever listened, always still going to the same old pub on the main drag and having a beer with his

140

cop mates, walking down the memory lanes of crook-catching and regaling in the notorious local hookers, all gone now.

Billy was always wily. You had to be to survive the streets of the East End. He carried his wiliness with him as he arrived in Brisbane, knowing that he wanted to be a copper. Better to be on the right side of the law with this new life even though, as he slowly rose up through the ranks, well liked and respected, he knew that any copper worth his salt could get some on the side. Influence, money, girls.

Billy had always been gregarious, and his generosity at the bar made him quickly popular. He knew that to move up the ranks, skill and ability were important but being liked was much more critical.

So, when he came to Brisbane and became a copper, he also knew enough to reach out to people who might be able to help him, like flotsam and jetsam passing the shores of an island.

Police union bloke, good. Old coppers, good. The madams in the Valley who kept a record of all the cops and politicians and businessmen who went into the brothels for some good old fuck-fuck, good. And then, the newspaperman.

—

'Allo mate.'

'Billy, it's four in the morning for God's sake. What's going on? Have you got a front-page headline for me? Are you calling me about The Slayer?'

'I am, me old buddy. Got pen and paper?' asked Billy, sitting on his lounge, in the front room of his little West End home, wooden floor boards, walls covered in tourist paintings of the Greek Islands, mementos from his numerous holidays abroad.

'Hang on.' He heard rustling, then: 'Right, ready mate. Hang on. Let me get out of bed and get down to the study. I'll hang up and call you straight back – oh God, can you hear that rain? When will it stop old mate?'

Never. That's the point: it never stops, thought Billy as he waited. Here comes the flood, the deluge; I ain't not as much of a religious man as I should be and I think Noah, he ain't probably real but after weeks of this rainfall, streets and footpaths awash, I am starting to think of The Doom which me old grandpa talked about when I was four, before I got packed away on a train to live with a family who didn't want me, to escape them doodlebugs.

'Hi Bill. Sorry about that. My missus is a light sleeper and it *is* four in the morning so this better be good.'

'Got your pen and paper?'

'Actually, I'm working on a computer these days. Gotta keep up.'

'A person of interest ...'

'Hang on. I type on the keyboard a bit slow. One finger at a time. A person of interest ...'

'A young woman of seventeen years. Very beautiful, like Mata Hari ...'

'A young woman of seventeen years. Very beautiful, like ... can you spell that for me buddy? Who is Mata Hari again? Sounds like a cocktail.'

She-Devil

THIS SEVENTEEN-YEAR-OLD GIRL REVELS IN GOTH CULTURE. We cannot name her because she is underage, but this newspaper has verified her identity and spoken to many of her school friends, all of whom are terrified because she carries a knife into the school grounds at the exclusive St Mary's in Ascot. Parents, who pay a premium for the education of their daughters, told this reporter how scared they were that a killer, a teenage girl who would decapitate men's heads in the middle of the night in the Botanic Gardens and the Kangaroo Point Cliffs, is still allowed to go to class.

This reporter has it on good authority that police have all the evidence they need and will soon make an arrest.

St Mary's in Ascot could not be reached for comment despite numerous attempts.

—

THAT WAS THE story in the morning newspaper. Front page. I'd read it online before dawn. Delicately, the newspaper did not name her. Indelicately, they had a grainy, slightly fuzzy photo of her, blown-up from the Year Book class photo.

Billy.

How could you do this? She might be a person of interest, yes, but how could you allow the local tabloid to throw a hundred-thousand spotlights onto her, destroying whatever life she had before this morning?

After we left Kristo's office and when the floor was quiet and the others had gone for the day and it was only him and me left, as the darkness fell swiftly over the city and the rain began once more, I had brought it up.

'This is so dangerous, using the press to start a witch hunt for a kid.'

'What if she's guilty?'

'What if she's not?'

'We've got no other leads. Them boys, Nils and Miles, they're taking us nowhere.'

'Do you think I don't want a conviction now, too? Do you think I don't lose sleep because of the pressure to make an arrest? Do you think I don't hear the DPP and the Commissioner roll out the drums of war? But until we are sure. If we are wrong ... We can't make this go away, not at the expense of a frightened, confused seventeen-year-old girl.'

That girl could have been me.

'Do *not* bring the drums of war onto her. If we fail, we fail. We cannot allow an innocent person to go down.'

'She may not be innocent.'

'Until *proven* guilty.'

'That's what the court is for,' he replied, then walked away.

—

AND NOW HE'D gone and done it.

I wasn't stupid and I wasn't naïve. I understood that every police officer above the rank of Sergeant was a politician. It's not like I was shocked to the core and completely taken aback. I knew there was a culture in Queensland Police, corrupt, macho and arrogant. Even though it was yet to be a year, I had been in the toughest and most rugged Squad in the entire department. I knew how things worked. No-one had asked me to deliver a brown paper bag full of cash, no-one had asked me to turn a blind eye to some of the things that my colleagues got up to. Luckily I was in Homicide, where that stuff doesn't really come through the doors, not like in Fraud or CIB or the two giant pinnacles of temptation, Drugs and Vice.

I'd managed to stay afloat and just do my job.

During the first month, Billy had told me, with a sense of pride, how he got into the Force: 'I was in my late teens and had emigrated to Australia, pretending I was an upstanding lad with metal foundry work to me name and they didn't ask no questions, nought like, Billy, you ever killed anyone? Or Billy, you ever been in trouble with police back home in the East End? I travelled from Darwin, where I landed, to Brisbane and, knowing that I wanted to be a copper, I found where coppers ate their steak and tatters and canned spaghetti with pineapple – at the Breakfast Creek Hotel – and I sidled up to 'em, especially the lad in the union, and said: Me name is Billy and I just got Australian citizenship (which I hadn't but they never asked for proof) and can I buy you lads another round of beer, and by the way, I would like to become a fine, upstanding member of the Queensland constabulary. And I got accepted. Didn't have to pass no test; just paid for a lot of beers, and some bloke, name was Cyril who was high up in the union, Cyril says to me one day in the bar: You is in, mate.'

You is in, mate. Simple as that. The criteria was no criminal record, be a good bloke, a tough bloke, tell stories, drink a lot of beer and eat the T-bone with canned pineapple and spaghetti. This was during the late sixties, when the Queensland Police Force was unbelievably corrupt, and while those days had gone, they hadn't. Not entirely. You don't erase a culture. You adapt it.

That was me, having to adapt. That was me, being quiet.

That was me, feeling not so good. Feeling a little uneasy. That was me. Potentially fucking up the life of a seventeen-year-old girl.

Ashes to Ashes

DEAR MISS INNOCENT-OF-THE-MURDERS:

Hello. I am so sorry that you have been targeted by the police for the killings that I have done. When I did the killings in November, I didn't think that the police would come after an innocent person like yourself. I was very careful in making sure that I left nothing behind, nothing the police could track back to anyone, least of all me. Well, not careful enough because they have tracked whatever clues that were left behind, to you.

So sorry. I did not mean for this to happen. I had such a great time doing the killings, I just didn't think that an innocent person would get into trouble for them. I know you must be very scared about what might happen to you but if I could say that, generally speaking, an innocent person does not go to prison. Well, in Australia anyway. Not so much in America but lucky for you we live in Queensland and so I think you will be alright. The other thing is that it's obvious the police are desperate and have nothing to pin on you like evidence or else this story would not have been planted in the local newspaper. As far as I can tell, it is an example of how desperate they must be so I want to say to you that while you must be feeling very scared at the moment, don't be because I don't think anything bad will happen to you.

I was pretty careful at the places where I killed the men and no-one saw me, that's for sure. So I don't think the police have got anything. I don't know why they have come after you. I think it's really bad that they did, coming after an innocent girl. I think they should be ashamed of themselves. I think it's got something to do with that Asian cop. I think she is just trying to prove herself or something.

So, don't worry, okay?

I am not going to do any more killings now. I wanted to but it's not like any of the three dead men were part of a plan. They just happened and I felt really good about killing them.

I really wish I could show you how I did them, the killings, because I reckon you would be really impressed. Or maybe not. I think I might be a bit weird but nobody would know because I am really careful at hiding stuff like that.

I did want to do some more killings because it gets pretty addictive, especially if you don't get caught! But I don't think I can now. I think I have to rest up and stop. I hope that doesn't mean anything bad for you, like the police thinking the killings have stopped because you are a suspect in the public eye and that you would be scared they were watching you, which is how I would react if it was me in the newspaper this morning.

I am not going to send this letter to you for obvious reasons and I am hopeful that you would understand. And I just want to say, one last time that I am really sorry that you have gotten caught up in my fun. Really, if I knew that this was going to happen, I would not have done the killings in the first place. You probably don't believe me when I say that but it's true.

Yours Faithfully,

Me.

Sounds of Silence

BILLY WENT TO SLEEP, AFTER HIS CALL WITH THE newspaperman. The heat remained intense. Even before dawn. It was Billy's day off so he settled into slumber knowing he could sleep all morning. Outside it was wet. Dark. The black clouds kept the gloom in place. He liked to hear the sound of the rain on his tin roof. Everyone likes to hear the sound of rain on a tin roof. It's one of those kid things that make you feel that all is okay with the world, is what he thought.

And, as he slept, oblivious to the anger within his partner Lara, on the other side of the city, of the horror about to unfurl at Jen's house in Ascot, he remembered being a kid and the sounds of bombs.

Silent bombs. Doodlebugs.

Bombs that were dropped from a German plane way above the streets of England in what became known as The Blitz. The doodlebug was an effective incendiary not in that it caused catastrophe as buildings tumbled into rubble and debris and families died into smithereens in their sleep, but because it had a unique sound.

Or, in fact, two unique sounds: the first was a screeching high-pitched shrill as the bomb fell towards the earth, sounding its approach, awakening the people below, readying them for destruction wherever this one may fall and the next sound was of silence.

Ten or fifteen seconds before the bomb hit it was like it had gone away. And then: bam. With the silence came slow moments of terror. Which is why Billy liked to listen to the rain on the tin roof, why he liked to live in the raucous suburb of West End with its fights and screaming domestics up and down the main street, up into his street. Noise makes him content. Silence terrifies him.

After a few weeks of this shrill and then silent terror, his ma packed him off into the countryside. The government had responded to the Blitz by informing parents there was a scheme where they could send their kids, under the age of eleven, having registered them at the local council office and then taken them down to the local railway station whereupon they would be trained to Suffolk or wherever, in the country, where it was safe from the doodlebugs.

He waved goodbye to his ma and then after a bit of sleep and a rollicking on the train, he got to Nottingham (like the Sherriff) and they all trooped onto the platform and stood in single file and this geezer said, 'Follow me' and they did, being taken to a local town hall. Where they all sat on the floor in a circle and after some time local villagers, dressed in good clothes, came in and stared at them and walked around the kids and said, 'I'll take her' and 'I'll take him', and Billy was always the last, the very last to get chosen.

Don't Leave Me

ON THE OTHER SIDE OF BRISBANE, UP ON ASCOT HILL, WHERE Jen, Anthea and their mum lived in the house with big windows, soft Moroccan carpets and Indigenous artworks, in the still-dark of pre-dawn, Jen lay awake. She could hear the soft snoring of her sixteen-year-old sister through the wall and vowed to tease her, yet again, when they got up.

In the far distance Jen thought she could hear a helicopter.

Through the other wall, where her mum lay, she could hear the first stirrings. Megan had a routine.

Every morning Megan would wake up at four in the darkness and reach across to touch her husband Hugh, but for the past sixteen months it had been a cold and empty space and she would remind herself: oh, yes, that's right, he is in Sydney with that Serbian girl he pretends not to be with, and she (Megan) would hold herself, knees scrunched up into her chest and try not to get emotional and reach out to the pill box and slip a Xanax into her with a little tonic water, a bottle of which she always kept by her side, and slumber back to sleep, but of late, the Xanax wasn't really helping as it used to and a friend had told her about lithium and I might try some of that, she thought, as she then slowly climbed out of bed and padded across the floor of the bedroom, softly so as not to wake up the girls, into the corridor, turning on all the lights as she was afraid of the dark and gently, lest she tumble and fall, step down the stairs and into the kitchen where she would put on the kettle to make some Earl Grey tea (with just a splash of vodka) and, as it was rumbling, the kettle, to a boil, she would open the side door and artfully step out into the little laneway and down to the front of the house where there was a lawn with plants and shrubs, the names of which she could never recall, and lean down to pick up the morning newspaper which she loved to unfurl and read, with her tea and vodka in the slow approach of dawn, at the little table in the kitchen, not the dining room table where she and Hugh would host dinner parties, back when they were a couple, before he fell in love with the Serb girl and she did this, now, this morning. Sometimes she would have some toast as she did this, sometimes not. She would always go to the social pages to see who was getting married, that she would do first, go straight to the back without nary a look at the headlines on the front page but this day, this morning, before dawn and light and the sound of birds awakening, as she prepared to read the social pages with her vodka and toast to come, she noticed, on the front page, as she was actually turning it, she noticed an indistinct but clear-enough photo of her daughter.

And the headline, emblazoned across the front page:

IS THE SLAYER A SEVENTEEN-YEAR-OLD GIRL?

—

WHEREUPON THERE WAS a darkness falling across her vision, searing, this darkness, like black ink in water, into her skull, but she could still make out the kitchen and she could still feel her hands as she got out of the chair and steadied herself on the surface of the table as she walked to the cupboard and reached out for the vodka, as she unscrewed the lid again and swilled from the bottle; actually, not swilled. Sculled. Half of the bottle in one full stream of gulps.

As the cold flow of booze iced down her throat into a warm pool in her tummy, as she began, in her mind, to deal with this, as the darkness began to lift and her faculties of logic and thought returned, the phone went off. She reached to answer it, thinking: did I hear the phone ringing last night, like in the middle of the night? and thinking: who would be calling me at this hour, before dawn?

'Hello?'

'Is that Megan White?'

'Yes.'

'Oh hi. My name is Spencer Christianson from the *Courier Mail* and I'd like to ask you about the story in today's paper.'

She hung up on him. The phone rang almost straight away, again.

'Is that Missus White?'

'Yes.'

'Hello, this is Clarissa Rees from the BBC. I am calling you from London. Can I speak to you or your daughter, Jen, about the story in today's newspapers?'

She hung up.

The phone rang again. She pulled out the connection from its socket.

And that's about when a flood of brilliant white light illuminated the front lounge room, from outside, like there was an alien spaceship from *Close Encounters of the Third Kind* out the front and she ran to the front room to see four mobile TV broadcasting units, vans with lights and antennas and journalists with microphones being filmed and more vans driving up to join them and then pounding on the front door with a cacophony of 'Missus White!' 'Jen!' 'Open the door!' 'We have questions for you!' 'Jen, are you The Slayer?'

And then: the whup-whup-whup of a helicopter coming in closer to hover above the house and another beam of white light, this time from above and now her Blackberry is going off and –

And –

I lay in bed listening to all of this, now hugging Anthea.

'Don't leave me,' I said.

'I won't,' she said, and held me tighter.

'Close your eyes,' she said.

But I could not.

PART III

LIFE IS NOT LIFE

God gave Moses the rainbow sign
No more water, but fire next time
Pharaoh's army got drownded
Oh Mary don't you weep

Mary wore three links of chain
Every link was freedom's name
Pharaoh's army got drownded
Oh Mary don't you weep

Wacol

2015

IT'S FOUR IN THE MORNING. I'M WRITING TO YOU FROM THE Wacol Women's Prison in Brisbane, my home for the past fifteen years. In the previous century, and the one before that, women and men, found guilty of any crime which required incarceration, were sent to the notorious Boggo Road Gaol. A brutal penitentiary erected in the ashes of the convict days, stone and bashings, whips and subjugation.

My trial was fast-tracked through the system due to the Queensland Attorney-General responding to what he called 'community fears'. He passed special legislation to ensure I could be brought before a judge and jury in a 'timely manner'. They can do that, you know. A year ago, in 2014, the Victorian government brought in special and unique legislation to make sure that mass killer Julian Knight would stay behind bars for the rest of his life. Maybe they were inspired by the Jen White Queensland law.

Even though they fast-tracked it, the trial was delayed until after my eighteenth birthday so I would be up there in the box in the courtroom as an adult.

Thanks for that, guys. Thanks, Mister Attorney-General.

—

'IT'S REALLY QUITE nice,' said an officer of the court as he led me to the van that would transport me across the city, down south, to Wacol, where I would be stripped naked and showered with jets of hot and cold water and given the prison greens – all the while being told not to talk back, not to look at anyone, not to speak unless spoken to, not to have an opinion, not to smile, not to laugh, not to pretend you are innocent (Bitch, you fuckin' tell me you're innocent and I will fucking bash your brains in because I have been hearing that shit from bitches like you from the moment I walked in here). But I was told I could make a phone call, though only one, and I could talk to a counsellor. And then it was here's your ID card and your cell.

—

DAD HAD COME back from Sydney and left the Serb on her bed in Lane Cove, scrolling around with his credit cards, while mum appropriated the world of victim, but only for a little while – it didn't resonate with the luncheon set. Instead, it morphed into the psycho-speak of nature versus nurture. It wasn't her fault; I was born evil. Go read Robert Hare. Well, Hugh and I did *all* that we could and *more*, in providing her with the *best*, most loving environment a girl could *wish* for. I mean, look at the children in Somalia. Do those little girls grow up to be killers?

These were the dwindling conversations with the ever-decreasing set of mum's friends, in order for her to cling to a sense of meaning when not, in public, proclaiming my innocence and how outrageous it was that I, a mere teenage girl with a brilliant future, had been so badly treated by a raft of corrupt police.

DISPATCHES

(II)

THEY CAME IN waves.
Wave One.

Dad

By the time we were used to an encampment of press in the street and the anger of the neighbours, none of whom I liked anyway, we had got into a routine of siege. Do not exit the house, do not open the curtains, do not answer the phone ... do not, do not, do not.

For a week or two we just ate all the dried and canned food in the pantry. Then, when that was all gone, mum called up one of her friends and asked them to go to the supermarket for us, and the friend came over late one night with a box of groceries and refused mum's money. Then he left with a sideways look at The Slayer as I was reaching in to get some Doritos.

—

DAD CAME HOME.

To great fanfare, as if we were all meant to welcome him, as if he had been away climbing Mount Everest instead of fucking Serbia. Mum spent two hours grooming herself with make-up and crimson lipstick and straightened hair and a discreet squeeze of Chanel No 5 and a too-short dress and, three drinks later, a hello and a kiss while Anthea and I stood back and watched as he juiced his way back into our lives as if nothing had happened.

After the party died down and he had left the bedroom – where mum and him had fucked so loudly that Anthea and I had to go out the back and stare at the palm trees and talk about what sort of dogs we might get when we leave home – after the lunch that mum had worked on for two days when she heard he was returning (for me?) for her, in an 'all is forgiven' and 'I have left Serbia' flourish (you haven't, you liar; Anthea and I know she has you in her tight grip, her flowing dyed red hair and extra-sized boobs, her fake smile, her fake everything but for one thing: your money), after his favourite – steak-and-kidney pie with mashed potatoes and the swish-fuck of red wine and a let's-go-up-to-the-bedroom, huh? seductive smile – after all that, dad came down and dragged me out of palm-tree-staring reverie and said:

'Hey kiddo, you wanna come inside?'

No. But I did.

I left Anthea scrabbling around the edge of the pool, scooping out leaves, dodging the rain, and I followed him inside, into the lounge room with its fat white Balinese couches and icons. I sat, and he sat opposite me and said:

'So. This is pretty fucked, huh?'

I nodded. There are no words, dad.

He leaned forward and this is when – you know, there are big moments in life, and I have contemplated them through my years in Wacol, where you turn a corner, where you become *you*, a person, not the daughter or the girlfriend or the anything but just the *you*, and this was one of those moments, and I wonder how many of those moments are good, not bad – when he leaned forward and said:

'You can tell me. Okay. Just you and me …'

Don't, dad, please don't.

Please.

Please, dad –

– just don't.

'Did you do it?'

He asked.

———

WAVE TWO:

The Raid

Unlike what you see in the movies, the police who raided our house – about two hours after dad asked me if I had actually killed those three guys, whereupon I never spoke to him again, despite his entreaties – were polite. Hey, we're only doing our job and can we come in and just go through everything and Jen, can we have your phone and your laptop and if you wouldn't mind just going back downstairs in a minute and we promise we won't make a mess in your bedroom, and we are the good guys and do you have a key for that filing cabinet and look, nothing to be distressed about, Jen, but we are going to strip your bed and take the sheets – yeah, you know, just a routine thing we have to do – and Roscoe! where's the vacuum? Because Jen, nothing to be concerned about but we will be vacuuming the floor of your room, and can you take off your clothes for us? Thanks – Rhadika will be overseeing that; Rhadika! Can you come up and get Jen's clothes? We need them, okay; where are you? Rhadika? Sorry Jen, she's coming. Don't move. Don't do anything. Rad will help you take off the clothes. We'll get them back to you. We just need to send them off for a bit of testing.

Rad took off my clothes and bundled them, along with all my other clothes, into plastic zip bags without a word and left me in the bathroom. I sat there, on the side of the bathtub for an hour, maybe two, maybe three, as I listened to them ransack the house with the occasional distant shout of: 'Has anyone found the flick-knife yet?' And then finally I heard them leave, and there was a distant murmur from downstairs where I guess mum and dad had emerged and clinked some drink.

When I came downstairs in my sister's pyjamas and dressing gown, I noticed they were shaking. We were all shaking, although Anthea had vanished into a dark hole with her bedroom door firmly closed. Mum and dad were sitting on the couch staring at the floor and drinking vodka, and neither of them looked up at me, as I sat on the couch opposite and held my hands and also decided to stare at the floor, and after about twenty minutes I got up and said: 'Night,' even though it was only mid-afternoon and left them to their contemplation of how their oldest daughter had ruined, totally and completely, ruined their lives.

The cops didn't find the flick-knife because I actually *had* lost it, on the way home from school a few days before they turned up at the house that first time. Stabbing trees. And in the middle of an angry rant on the trunk of a ghost gum, one of my teachers drove by and I saw her out of the corner of my eye and fled, lest she see me with the knife because, you know, by then the knife had become a bit of an issue after I used it on the girls I hated and wanted to kill, as I sat in the office as the lady from the Seychelles talked to me about calm and surf and tranquillity.

—

I COULDN'T GO outside, which is what I normally did when
feeling depressed, because the front yard, beyond its low wooden
fence, was hostage to news crews and TV camera vans, like from
something you'd see in the movies – which made the neighbours
even more gracious towards us. And it had begun to rain again, so
the back yard was out unless I wanted to get drenched.

Mum and dad talked about the rain a lot. When they weren't
staring at the carpet and dousing themselves with vodka, that's
what mum and dad talked about. The rain. A coming flood. A spill
at the dam. A mass of water that would roar down the river until it
hit the city and maybe submerge houses like it did in the 1970s. We
lived on a hill with a view over the city and the river, so what did
they care? It's not like we were going to be submerged.

My not-friends were still going to school but we, all of us,
including Anthea, had just left the planet on a one-way ticket to
a dreadful passivity of waiting for something to happen. For the
police to make a move. And if they chose not to make a move,
would they tell us? No. If the Director of Public Prosecutions
(by this stage I knew this shit; I had spent the previous few days
reading how the justice system worked) decided not to prosecute,
then they – Detective Constable Lara and Detective Inspector
William Waterson – sure as hell won't be dropping over with cake
and balloons. They'll just move on to another homicide and keep
us in suspended animation.

But that would not happen. I might only have been seventeen
but, and I really don't want to sound vain and conceited, because I
am not, but with that rabid media and now with the TV cameras
on me, The Slayer, twenty-four-seven, there would be only one
ending; I was smart enough to know that the public, voracious
readers and watchers of my profile, could be sated in only one way.
Arrest. Trial. A guilty verdict. No other outcome was possible.

I bided my time, listening to the rain smash-smash onto the
windows of my bedroom, reading Franz Kafka's *The Trial*. Just
waiting for the next knock on the door.

The Next Knock-Knocking

BILLY AND I DIDN'T TALK MUCH AFTER THE NEWSPAPER headline. He knew I was angry and he'd taken on that man-thing where he became more strident and defensive, as if he had embraced the right and only action and I, a girl (girlie) didn't understand. It had me thinking: Maybe I *am* too soft.

It's all about the conviction, girlie.

—

MUM CALLED AGAIN. On the home phone, which I was starting to use less and less. Mum always had a special knack of calling at the wrong time. I was racing to work, knowing I was about to be drenched between the front door and the car when it rang.

I knew it was her.

I hesitated. I really did not want to talk to my mum. I reached for the door knob.

'Hi mum, I can't talk.'

'The killer is a *teenage girl*? She drinks the blood from the necks of her victims?' (No, mum, she doesn't. How many times have I told you to stop believing the tabloid newspaper? How many times did you tell me to ignore the tabloid newspapers?) 'Your brother is worried about you; I'm worried about you; Damon is worried about you. He wants to ask you out again, but you were so rude to him. I told Damon's mother you were just under a lot of pressure at work with the murders and that you would love to go out with him again, so I booked a table for two this Friday night at the casino.

Seven o'clock. Don't be late. It's very fancy and there's a two-for-one special on. Damon is looking forward to seeing you again. I had to tell his mother that you really did want to spend more time with him, and for her to tell him that it wasn't him but *you*. He's staying with her while he's waiting to hear from the university. You know where the casino is? It's not far from the police headquarters. I can send you the address and how to get there from your work. You can walk, you know.'

'Mum, I'm working a Homicide case.'

'If Damon is not the man for you, *c'est la vie*; we'll find someone else.'

Dark silence. Here it comes:

'You told Damon you were a lesbian.'

You are truly such an idiot, Lara. You and your too-fast, too-big mouth.

'I'm not. Does it matter?'

'Then why did you tell him? He's very keen on you, you know, and he's rich; he went out and bought a BMW last week, did you know that? Bright red. Why did you tell him that? Do you know how much that hurt me when Vera told me that you told Damon you were a lesbian? Lara, you have to stop with this murder business and settle down and get married. I know I'm old fashioned but you have to obey your mother. Understand?'

'I have to go.'

'Always you have to go. The booking is for seven at the casino. Friday. And be nice to him!'

'Mum, I have to–' And she cut me off with derision:

'Yes. We all have to.'

And hung up on me.

As I stepped out the door, I saw Billy on the street, sitting in our unmarked Camry as if he had been there for some time.

'I thought we might go down to Breakfast Creek,' he shouted, after winding down the passenger window. 'Have some eggs.'

'I'm not very hungry,' I shouted back, across the sweep of rain, still on the balcony of my house.

'Get in the car,' he shouted back. Not unkindly and certainly not in a threatening manner, more like he was just a tired father.

—

'POACHED OR FRIED? A bit of T-bone?' he asked me.

'No, maybe the muesli.'

The Breakfast Creek Hotel was an institution, an old and sprawling pub designed with some sort of French chateau look, built in the 1800s, overlooking a massive bend in the river. We could see expensive houses crowded along the alarmingly swollen banks, water lapping onto lawns and little pleasure boats tightly secured to private jetties. The river was surging – its flow moving down towards the ocean, behind us a few K's – with a frightening speed. I had never seen the river so full and moving so fast. Every now and then part of a tree would zoom past us, carried by the urgent swell. On a clear day you could see the city in the distance. Not today. Visibility was obscured by sheets of grey and silver rain.

Billy looked up to the hovering waitress with her plastered smile, but not as bad as the fake smiles you get at McDonald's, and I followed his gaze. She had a slightly nervous tic with her ball-point pen tapping the order pad and she lightly bounced from one foot to another. Her name was Daisy, said the name plate on her chest.

'Do you still do the tinned spaghetti with the T-bone? On the side? And with the pineapple?' asked Billy.

She looked at him as if he were reciting a Babylonian text. Christmas carols were playing over the sound system. *Hark the Herald Angels Sing.* It was December and with Y2K around the corner, with the city about to flood and a new millennium approaching, there was, despite the ho-ho of the music, an attempt to remind us that now was the time to remember Jesus. We were all on edge.

'It was the signature dish back in the old days,' Billy said.

'Ah. No. We don't have that, I'm sorry,' she replied, casting a quick glance around the restaurant as if looking for a manager, for help. 'But the poached eggs, avocado and salsa with bacon is really popular.'

'Twenty years ago,' said Billy.

Daisy looked alarmed. Food orders were meant to be simple. But not for geezers like Billy. She was staring at him, uncertain what to say. I was about to intervene and tell him to get on with it when:

'Twenty years ago, that old T-bone dish, that was all anyone ever ordered here. And you ain't never heard of it which just gives me pause, you know, to wonder where we will all be in another twenty years' time. That'll be another century, girlie. You'll be middle-aged and I'll no doubt be in the grave and young Daisy here might be the manager of this fine establishment. Poached eggs, tons of bacon and I don't mind a bit of avocado. Brilliant. Thanks love.'

Some people, no matter what their age, respond to eccentricity with grace and humour. Some people respond with fear. Billy was so far outside her world-view, and who could blame her; she might have been nineteen if that, she could only give us an uncertain smile, hoping it would suffice and then, order down on her pad, she did a predictably swift exit.

'Bacon kills you, you know that? Been scientifically proved,' he said to me.

'Yeah, I've read that.'

'Cancer.'

'Yeah.'

'And over-cooked meat. Like, charcoal meat.'

'Yeah. I read that too,' I said.

'Me dad, he nearly died of cancer. Combination of the fags and the mine. Coal.'

'Sorry to hear that, Billy.'

We both knew how it would go when we stopped tiptoeing around the growling beast under the table. He would be angrily defensive about the leak to the press. I would be angrily disappointed. He was the teacher and I was the student. We both knew the dynamic was about to turn because the student, the rookie, needed to be impressed by the teacher, the expert. And when the dynamic turns, as it inevitably must when the student gains confidence and emerges as her own person, all that would be left is sadness and regret. We both knew it. We were stalling.

'He was a cunt – 'scuse the French. But he was. Beat me every night. Got the scars to prove it. On my back. Not for any reason.

Just for being alive. Beat my sister, Georgie, when she was four, maybe five. She came home from school and da, he's tanked from being in the pub all day and thinks: Oh, yeah, smashing, let's get out the leather belt. Well, he started and little Georgie started screaming and me ma, God rest her soul, she was upstairs and out of it and on the laudanum, which I threw away after I killed me da. I did. I did. As I heard Georgie scream I thought: Kill the cunt – 'scuse the French. So, I did. I went down and got the carving knife we used last Sunday on the roast, baked rabbit, because you didn't get chicken or lamb or beef back in them days, and I stabbed him. And I buried him in the back yard. Oy, what's this?'

'Complimentary avocado salsa and grain bread, sir,' said Daisy with a smile and a flourish.

Billy looked at it as if it were radioactive and then pushed it across the table to me. 'For you,' he said.

Did my partner just confess to murder?

As if reading my mind, he said: 'Stabbed him. No-one missed him, none of us reported him missing. Only Shooter Kransky, who came over one day, a week after, and said, Your dad owes me money, and I said, Me da's gone to Ceylon. First thing I could think of. Later I find out that Ceylon stopped being called Ceylon in nineteen forty-eight and changed its name to Sri Lanka. But Shooter, he had some brain issues, so he just walked away and that was the last of it. Ain't done no killin' since I got to Brisbane.' And with a smile: 'Straight and narrow, love.' And then he said: 'You're angry.' He was talking about the newspaper story.

'I am.'

'You wanna make a thing out of it?'

'I don't know.'

'Don't.'

'Why?' I asked.

'Because if you do, no-one will trust you. No-one in Homicide that is.'

'She'll get Life.'

'Life ain't life. Life is maybe fifteen years. Still be able to have a kid when she gets out. Long as she plays by the rules in the nick.'

'She's seventeen.'

'Eighteen when she gets to court. What, you reckon she's innocent?'

'I didn't say that.'

'What'cha saying then?'

'That it was you who told me, again and again: Let the evidence lead you. Don't let assumptions or desires lead you.'

'Yeah. Well, we'll see about that then, eh girlie.'

The Qantas Bag

JANUARY 1, 2000.

Wave three:

It's four in the morning and I'm standing in my bedroom, looking out through the windows into the front yard below, listening to the rain. It's dark; dawn will soon come. Off in the distance, coming up towards me, around the spiral streets that lead to the top of the big hill, are the lights again. Red and blue. Just the lights. Red and blue swirls like mini-spaceships. The road to the top of the hill is a corkscrew, and I stare out the window watching as they go around, these lights, in ever-escalating circles. No sirens. Just an eerie silence.

They are coming to get me.

Again.

But this time they are coming to take me away.

And I am not coming back.

Not for a long, long time.

And when I do, come back, way off into the future, when I do return, I wonder if this house, my home, will still be here. If mum and dad will be here. If Anthea will be here. I don't think so. I think that when I return to another world in the faraway future, they will all be different people.

Maybe they won't recognise me and maybe I won't even recognise myself.

Happy new year. Happy new millennium. Normally I would be able to see the fireworks display from my room but tonight they were cancelled because of the storms. I turned on my computer at a minute past midnight. Guess what? It turned on. I went to Google. It came up on the screen. No Y2K. We're all saved.

Christmas Day was great fun too. Talk about a tableau of the doomed, shuffling deck-chairs on the *Mary Celeste*, me, my sister and mum. Under the ghostly white tree that Anthea chose from a mail-order catalogue.

I've had a little bag packed for about a week. Since Christmas Eve, actually. Sitting by my bed. A pair of PJs and two T-shirts and my jeans and trackie pants and some socks and my hand cream and toothpaste and toothbrush (but not the battery one from the bathroom, just a cheap one) and skin cream because sometimes the skin on my face goes dry and some chewing gum and tampons and undies and two sports bras and two pairs of black tights and my runners. And, wedged into one side, a book, *The Trial*, which kind of sums up my life now, and on the other side, The Bible, not that I am religious, I'm not, but I figure that when I go to prison it will be for over a decade and it's a big book, you know, it will take me years to read it and one of my teachers told me it had some of the best stories of murder and deceit and betrayal and lust, so it sounds pretty good; I know they probably hand you a Bible when you pass through the gates of prison but I want my own.

It's mine, not theirs.

So, I picked up the bag – a small purple Qantas travel bag that dad gave me a few years ago, after he'd come back from Hong Kong – and walked down the hallway, down the stairs, to the front door. I opened it and stepped outside, under the stoop so I didn't get wet, and waited for the swirling red and blue lights – coming for me in silence – which would transmogrify into real things, police cars with police officers with an arrest warrant and handcuffs and, because I am an underage girl, even though I am The Slayer, with a fawning, gentle approach.

If you could just come with us, Jen, that would be great.

———

'CAN I HAVE a look inside your bag, Jen?' asked the policewoman, not Lara, as she unzipped it anyway, before I agreed, and she ruffled around inside it to ensure there were no knives or hand grenades or C4 explosives or Smith & Wesson pistols, one of which she had holstered to her hip.

Three cars had pulled up. I watched the cops climb out and stare at me.

They were nice. They have always been nice.

Mum and dad were sleeping through all of this. I heard them go to bed about two hours ago, after yet another hard night of drinking on the dark side of the moon. I had been quiet as I left my room to wait for my impending incarceration on the doorstep of the house, watching the shards of rain blustering across the front garden.

'Thanks Jen,' said the policewoman as she handed back my bag. 'Do you understand what is happening here?' We were standing out of the rain, but she was dripping wet.

'Yes. You are arresting me for three murders I did not commit, and you will now process me into the system and then, at about eight o'clock this morning, you will bring me before a magistrate as that is the first port of call for this legal abomination, before we get to the trial at the Supreme Court.'

We both had to speak a lot louder than normal, because of the rain.

The policewoman stared at me and said: 'Maybe we should go inside and tell your mum and dad what's going on. We don't actually need to have them accompany you at this point of arrest, but perhaps they should be alerted to this development.'

'No. Let them sleep,' I said.

After a moment, she shrugged, as if she didn't care, and said: 'Okay then,' and took my arm gently and ran me towards one of the three vehicles. I climbed into the back seat, drenched, and separated from the front seat by wire mesh and metal bars. She closed the door on me, and the driver, a guy, started up the engine as she jumped into the front passenger seat.

As we began to drive off I saw Anthea in her pyjamas, standing at the front door. I think she was crying but it was hard to say with the downfall of rain.

As I watched the house, my home, disappear from view, I thought I would never see it again. I tried not to cry because I had told myself that it was time now to be steadfast. That all things must pass.

Deluge

(II)

'WHOA, WHOA, WHOA! WHAT *THE FUCK* IS THAT?!' SCREAMED the female cop from the front seat. 'Back up!' she yelled at the driver, who had stopped the car and was just staring ahead, down the road in the pre-dawn dark in the middle of an otherwise-empty Brisbane city.

'Is that ...?' he asked.

'It's a fucking wave!' she shouted. 'Back up! The river's burst its banks.'

And it had: like a lava flow, this dark, hard-to-see swell of water maybe two or three metres high rushing along the street, towards us, sweeping away parked cars in its wake.

The driver thrust the car into reverse and screamed back up the street, then reversed up Edward Street and climbed a hill. He stopped, put the car into park, and we watched as the dirty black water swept down through the street below us.

A yellow Volkswagen, upside down, passed by in the onrush. Were there people inside it? I wondered. Are they, he, she, the owner, dead, lost in the wash of flood or are they at home in bed, in gentle warm slumber?

TWO HOURS EARLIER

Standing on the ramparts of Wivenhoe Dam, staring at the massive body of water that snarled and flowed in circles and swells, gently smacking the concrete edge of the dam, the massive body of water which stretched back kilometres off into the distance, in the rain, the thunderous monsoon-like rain, in their thick raincoats and galoshes and waterproof hats, Ray and Liam stared at the impending crisis. The water level was less than one centimetre below the dam's edge. When the wind angrily caroused its way across the surface of the water, splashes rolled over the edge, waves. And behind them, on the other side, far down below, the Brisbane River, the serpent that runs eighty kilometres through the city and finally to the mouth, the ocean.

The noise of the tempest all around them.

'If we do nothing,' shouted Ray, 'the dam will spill and the river will flood.'

'Yep,' shouted Liam. 'But if we open the sluice gates to release some of the water into the river below, it will flood.'

'The water's going to breach the walls of the dam in about ...'

'I'd say in about two minutes!'

'Fuck. With this volume, we have to mitigate flood flow; otherwise our options'll be even worse. We should control it,' said Liam, resigned.

'Okay, yep, let's open the sluice gates and release some of it!'

'Fuck!' Liam shouted yet again.

—

AND THEY DID.

Flood water moves quickly. Flood water can move at up to four hundred and thirty-four kilometres an hour. Within moments, the outlying farmlands near Wivenhoe were deluged, in some places up to twenty metres underwater, and then the gush arrived in Brisbane city, running through the suburbs and the city in a rapid ten-metre swell. Before long people were drowning, cars were upturned, streets were underwater, houses were submerged and the city centre itself, mostly low-lying, was completely flooded but for the few hilly areas like Ascot. Boats and yachts were torn from their river moorings and floated unmanned towards the mouth of the ocean, passing suburbs in the inundated flatlands.

—

I COULDN'T HELP it. I started to giggle from the back seat of the police car, staring down the street to the rising pool of water on the cross street. I'd been good up until now, resigned to my fate but the realisation that the river had finally, after months of build-up pressure, burst its banks and that the city was going under, well, my controlled demeanour went under the surface and everything just seemed fucking ridiculous.

Roma Street Police HQ was about two hundred metres away from the river. Its foyer and ground floor would be under oily black flood water with maybe a few tree branches and some small dinghies; the force of the flow would have ripped through the main doors and windows.

'Now what do we do?' shouted the policewoman to her partner, who had no ready answer, just a dumb shrug. 'And you,' she said, turning around to face me. 'Can you shut up with the giggling? It's not helping!'

'I'm not here to help you,' I said as the giggling intensified. I stared at the black wave of river water in the city street and could not stop laughing at the absurdity of it all.

I was Alice in a dark and fucked-up wonderland, the night of Noah, the night of the dawn of the new next thousand years, the night of a massive joke which was a massive fear called Y2K. The last night of my freedom, the first day of my chains. Don't mourn, Jen. Don't weep, Jen. It's all going to be okay, Jen, because there is nothing, nothing at all, that you can do to change the outcome Jen.

The policewoman glared at me. She was nothing like Lara. She was hard and her face seemed to dwell in sharp angles. She had short hair and looked, to me at least, as if she'd been beaten through childhood and was deciding to take out a bit of revenge on anything that came her way, that she could get away with.

'Let me tell you something, Jen,' she said angrily, 'and I'll tell it to you for free: you think you're cleverer than us but you're a smartarse. You belong to us now. Cops and the court. And if you keep up with the attitude, you'll find yourself in a world of great and memorable pain.' She turned back to the driver.

'Fucking bitch. We'll take her to the lock-up in the Valley. Radio through and tell the Homicide detectives to meet us there,' she said.

He reversed up to the crest of the hill, turned right and sped up Ann Street. It was still dark. It was still raining. There were no cars on the roads and no people.

I didn't listen to her warning. That, as it turned out, was a big mistake.

Dispatches

(III)

'YOU'LL BE ELIGIBLE FOR PAROLE IN FIFTEEN YEARS' TIME, okay. Life is not life,' said Ian, my Queen's Counsel, as I was led away by the bailiffs in the Supreme Court. As the floor was giving way to an impossible void of black and white, shifting worlds of startling nothing. As I tried to see if mum and dad were in the audience, but couldn't see them. As Anthea was crying hysterically. As I was calculating: 18 + 15 = 33. As I was thinking, I'll be thirty-three years old before I am eligible for parole, but the judge just gave me Life, which is, in my case, a twenty-year term: 18 + 20 = 38.

Originally, I was banking on a decade. 18 + 10 = 28. But then, while in remand, I got to hear about Tracey Wigginton, the Brisbane Lesbian Vampire Killer. She was convicted nine years ago, for thirteen. Everyone in remand, from the guards to the girls, looked at me weirdly: how come The Slayer has not heard of The Lesbian Vampire Killer? We thought you guys were related or something.

I thought I could hear people shouting that the judge had been too lenient, that he'd fallen for the *She's still a teenager* and *She's never been in trouble before* lines put forward by Ian. I thought I heard people calling for me to be tortured and hanged.

—

AFTER I WAS taken away that dark morning of January 1, 2000, formally arrested and sent before the magistrate in an emergency special session, mum and dad woke to discover I'd gone and Anthea told them I'd been driven off by the police. Dad hired a QC, which is the best you can get. Mum had been on dad to do it since he'd come home but Anthea told me she heard him say he didn't want to spend the money, thousands of dollars a day, and anyway, he said, Anthea told me, he thought it would all blow over, it (me a suspect) being patently ridiculous.

Ian was on a pathway to becoming a judge on the High Court, so Anthea said, which is the top court in the country. He was very tall, old, wore a white three-piece suit like Tom Wolfe and spoke softly and he said, at the beginning of their first meeting: 'My fee is ten thousand dollars a day. It's a lot of money, so I need to be very up-front with you about this here and now. Expect to pay no less than half a million dollars for my team and I to fight for Jen's acquittal.'

'I'll need to take out a loan against the house,' replied dad, which is what Anthea told me. This was after I had asked her why they had moved into a small house in Bald Hills, north of the city.

'They lost the house. They lost everything,' she told me.

—

I WAS LED downstairs to a holding cell, a small concrete room with a narrow concrete bench on the back wall and an old-fashioned door with bars, like you see in the movies, and told to sit and wait. Which I did. I stared at the yellow-painted concrete wall that surrounded me. Why is it yellow? Who chose that colour? Where are they now? And there was, on the other side of the cell, a tiny hole and within this hole was a tiny insect trying to extricate itself and welcome itself into the cell of hell.

Life is not life.

—

AFTER A WHILE, the prison van arrived, backing into the underground car park area, which is connected to the yellow-painted cells, and I was escorted into the back of the van, also just like in the movies, and the back door was closed and locked and I sat on another bench as the roller-doors rose to let the van out into the city.

Did I tell you about the press inside the courtroom and outside the courtroom? Also, how people erupted in cheers when the guilty verdict came down, how their glee smothered the emotion of my sister, how the victims' wives burst into tears and later one told the press how relieved they were that justice had been done but wasn't it a shame that Queensland abolished the death penalty in 1922. She took my James away from me and our children; I hope the bitch stays behind bars until she's too old to have children; I hope she dies behind bars. I hope she rots in prison and dies a horrible, long painful death.

I saw her say that on TV, in jail, and I knew she would carry those feelings towards me – wanting me to die painfully – for at least another forty or fifty years because Lynne was only in her mid-thirties. By the time her hate for me – and the hate of the other widows – dies, when they all die, I will be in my mid-fifties, maybe my sixties. And after they all die, if I am still alive, their hate will be carried on, towards me, by their children. Hate will stalk me for the rest of my life. For the rest of my life, there will be people who'll want me to die in great pain and they will think about inflicting great pain upon me every day.

—

As THE VAN left the confines of the court and swept up onto the street I could see and hear dozens of press people running alongside it, shouting at me and trying to snap a photo through the barred, grimy windows. Pop-pop-pop of the flashes as they held their cameras high above their heads, hoping to get me in frame.

—

BRISBANE CITY TO Wacol is about a thirty-minute drive.

Be thankful, Jen, that you're not going to Boggo Road, which kept prisoners in the most awful, primitive, violent conditions, where men would be beaten and women raped and the place justly earned its reputation as one of the most Dickensian of all prisons in the country. I did a presentation on it for a Year 10 History class.

In comparison, my cell in Wacol is almost three-star; the decor is pale Greek-island blue with cream walls and a polished wooden desk and shelves. A highly polished metal toilet with no seat is bolted to the floor in the far corner. Above the toilet, on the wall, is a mirror. Made from metal, not glass. To its side is a window, framed with the same pale blue and also not made of glass.

I have blue towels and a doona on my narrow single bed, which is up against the wall opposite the desk. Under the desk is a circular metal stool, also in the pale blue, bolted to the floor and it swings out so I can sit on it and write my dispatches. To me, to you, to whomever. Not mum and dad, that's for sure. I'm writing to you now at four in the morning, before the doors will be opened and the routine will be adhered to. I am renting a flat-screen TV, from the prison, and I go to the library. I am not allowed internet.

Wacol is not a prison. It is a correctional centre. I, and my fellow-prisoner comrades, are here to be corrected.

The point of prison was, originally, quite simple: to punish the perpetrator for their crime, to make them as uncomfortable as possible by depriving them of freedom and sunlight, making them eat gruel and perform hard labour. Thus, rapes and beatings were part of the deal. Hence a place like Boggo Road. And then the point of prison became two-fold but with each fold being in a paradoxical battle with the other. Since sending prisoners on a convict ship to a dumping-ground land mass, Australia, there have been many so-called scientific ideas on how best to deal with prisoners, such as in Port Arthur, down in Tasmania, in the 1800s, where some inmates were made to wear cloth-masks over their heads so they couldn't see another person and be in solitary twenty-three-seven; to the 1970s, when something new crept in: rehabilitation. While once you might have been on a chain gang like in that Paul Newman movie *Cool Hand Luke*, now you are starting to participate in cognitive-therapy sessions so that when you are released we did more than just fuck you with the best punishment we could summon. You are – and we did this to correct you – trained to become a better person, an adjusted human being, able to contribute to society. But in order to get there, and indeed to be paroled, you need to face something else.

Atonement.

Without atonement, there can be no parole. But, the thing is: I am innocent. So, how can I atone for crimes I did not commit? I can't.

And I won't.

Dispatches

(IV)

THE VANISHING

MUM AND DAD VANISHED. ANTHEA TOLD ME THEY'D MOVED to a small house in the almost-rural suburb of Bald Hills on the outskirts of the city, but I never saw them. They never visited. Anthea used to tell me they intended to. That rolled on for a few years then shuffled off-stage.

It's okay.

Actually, it's not, but I understand, I do. They were never the doting type. Mum worked full-time as a manager at a Honda dealership around the corner, down the hill, and dad was always flying around the world buying and selling art. Anthea and I got to appreciate that our birthdays were a stopover in their otherwise self-focussed world. It's not like they were nasty or horrid or hit us or didn't care for us. Dad once sent Anthea and me on a weekend trip to Sea World on the Gold Coast. A town car picked us up, dropped us off and there was a nice manager waiting for us in the foyer of the hotel with our tickets, all-inclusive for the week and any problems, to give her a call or just come down to the front desk. She told us we weren't unique; other kids were sent alone because their parents were just so busy but loved them and wanted the best for them. Often kids from the UAE, she said. Last month they had a couple of wealthy kids from Malaysia. Nice kids, too. Parents flew them in on a private jet.

My parents were there but they weren't. They always told us to call them if there was an issue and they would always apologise for being so busy but they loved us and after a while, you know what happens? You not only get blasé about it, but you build in so many mechanisms to cope, to be independent, you grow up really fast and you tend to not doorstop them for a problem, not wanting to bother them. Knowing you can deal with it yourself.

And in the wake of trauma, I get it. I do. It's easier to ignore it.

—

I HAD A sort-of friend. Albano. He went to Churchie, the all-boys school. We met at one of those inter-school dances where teachers try not to look bored, and kids look awkward, chew gum and hover hands over pimples. We became sort-of friends and we started to meet in the mall on weekends and go to the movies. This was when I was fifteen. Just before the Goths and the Celts came to visit. Anyway, his mum died. She had a weak heart and it finally took her. Albano had known and he would occasionally mention it, but it was no big deal. Until she died and then, of course, it was a huge deal. He texted me. *Mum just passed away.* Texting had been around for a year or so and it was great because you didn't have to speak to people. I didn't text back. The next day he texted me again. *Funeral is on Saturday.* I didn't text back. A week later, another text. *Hey. Just wanted to see if you were okay. Miss you.* I didn't text him back. I couldn't. It was trauma and all I could do was turn my back on it and pretend it didn't exist.

For a moment, I thought I might have glimpsed Albano in the courtroom, in the crowd of people watching me. But I can't be sure.

I have brought great shame on them. Mum. Dad. And, you know, kids shouldn't bring shame on their parents. Kids are meant to bring pride to their parents. They were high-fliers and had money and a nice house and now their lives have been re-defined in the most hideous way, by me. They had The Slayer living under their roof. With people asking: Did they know? And people answering: They must have, it's inconceivable they didn't. That's what people would have said. I didn't hear it. Nor did Anthea but you could hear it, bouncing from house to house across the city.

How could they have not known? And, if they *didn't* know, then what dreadful parents they must have been.

There's no way out for them.

I know they love me.

Actually, I don't.

They don't. Not anymore. I killed that for them. How can you love a triple killer? Because if you do, you are doomed to an endless embrace of despair.

—

ANTHEA VISITS. SHE'S married now. She and Robbie (who has also never visited) bought a house in Ascot, not far from where we grew up, up on the hill looking out over the city and river. They have two little kids. She shows me photos. The girls, the munchkins. Jen is a little terror, she didn't crawl; well, she did but only for about two months before she started to walk, and Anthea and Robbie are worried that she won't develop her fine motor skills. They have done a lot of research on what to do about that because, you know, when she becomes a teenager it could have a psychological impact on her and so Robbie is now doing a kid football thing with her. Maxi is adorable and will break the boys' hearts when she grows up.

Robbie works in finance and he was lucky to escape the GFC. I was vaguely aware of the Global Financial Crisis and sub-primes but I hate the news and, anyway, that sort of stuff means shit in prison. Same with climate change. Who cares? Let the world burn. You're in fucking prison. I told her I was very happy Robbie still had a job.

Anthea and I, we never talk about why I am in jail. She knows I am innocent. Unlike mum and dad, who also know I am innocent but do nothing except stay inert and silent in the wake of the trauma, Anthea is supportive – she keeps me on life support.

I never really paid much attention to her. She was my little sister, so it was her duty to be out of my way, to not talk to me. I used to push her over a lot and she would go running to mum, or dad if he was home, and whinge and I'd get yelled at and blah blah blah. She'd creep into my room and steal things, and I'd use my make-up to paint her up as a scary clown with a big red nose and an extra big smile so it looked like her mouth went up to both sides of her face, up to her cheekbones. She would cry as I did this and I'd hit her like all big sisters hit their little sisters.

But, when she grew up a bit, she became nice to me, and she was so supportive when I was in the court. The only one, really. I have learned to rely on her. In my lonely little cell, she is all that I have.

—

BY THE WAY, how's mum and dad?

I ask this every time she visits, and every time it's met with a fake mention of them being okay, and after a moment I change the subject back to her house and the renos and the kids and what Robbie's fave meal is. (Pad Thai.) It's easy to lapse into silence during these visits because, you know, I am a convicted killer and she is indulging me. I love it when she visits, but when we reach the water's edge where mundane chatter turns to uncomfortable silence (Don't leave, just stay a little longer) I say things like:

'Did you know that Pad Thai was created as the Thai national dish after the King of Thailand declared a need for unity and identity, after the Second World War?'

'You were always the smart one,' she'll say, but not in a nasty way. The older sister thing never entirely goes away, I guess.

Backtrack, Jen.

'How are the butterflies?'

'Yeah, good. Thanks. I better go.'

'Okay. Thanks for visiting.'

'No worries.'

'Love to Robbie and the kids.'

'I will.'

'Say hi to mum and dad.'

'Bye.'

'Bye.'

'Love you, big sis.'

'Love you too.'

—

DOES SHE TELL her kids that their aunt is in prison for the gruesome murders of three men? Do her kids even know that I exist? Do they look into their mum's photo albums from when she was a kid and ask: 'Who's that?' And if they do, what would she say? Oh, that's your aunty Jen. Why haven't we met her?

Well, she's The Slayer.

Sister Death

'I TRIED TO CALL YOU.'

'Oh sorry, I must have had the phone off.'

'You were at the prison again, weren't you.'

Robbie and Anthea and the two girls have a big house on the Ascot hill, an old Queenslander with wide wrap-around verandas, four bedrooms downstairs and a massive, renovated lounge, dining and kitchen area with polished wooden floorboards and some very modern hip art and, on one of the walls, a breathtaking display of mounted butterflies. More than a thousand of them, the most extraordinary array of shimmering colours. A hundred wooden framed cabinets, each with specimens from South America, Africa, Madagascar, Papua New Guinea, India, Australia – from across the globe – carefully pinned to a white acetate backing and encased behind glass. Shimmering, translucent, colourful beauties, once flying, now frozen.

The kitchen is gleaming white and modern, and in the evening they usually drink Cloudy Bay Sav Blanc at thirty dollars a bottle but on a special occasion they might reach into the cellar for a Soave or a Chenin Blanc or, on very special occasions, a Margaux White Burgundy. They have floor-to-ceiling windows that offer a view of the back yard, a sweeping lawn and lush sub-tropical garden, dominated by a hundred-year-old mango tree. Pink wisteria drips from the wooden side fences. They met at a mutual friend's party around the corner and have been married for eight years. Anthea was shy about socialising but one of her loyal old school friends told her to get out more and stop living through the shadow of her older sister. Robbie's Porsche is parked down below in the 'car accommodation' as the real estate agent put it, and her BMW, big enough to take the kids to school, next to it. Robbie is negotiating a job with HSBC, which will stratosphere him even further into the rarefied world of global finance. He has three iPhones.

'Were you? Tell me.'

'Yes. I did. She *is* my sister.'

'Don't get all defensive on me. She is also a serial killer.'

'She's innocent.'

'Hey, you wanna have this conversation again, sure; I've got to get up at three in the morning to talk to Lagos, but if you think it's more important to have a conversation about your sister, then fine; I'm with you.'

'Mum!' from down below.

'You want to hurt my career prospects,' he said, 'then go ahead; you want to be loyal to The Slayer, go ahead.'

'Don't call her that!'

Anthea stepped forward and leaned in, pinning him with a hard glare. He took a step back. Sometimes Robbie got a little scared around his wife; she had a cold intensity. Sometimes he felt as though she might do to him what she'd done to the thousands of butterflies they had in the house. 'I told you, when we were dating, I was the sister of a convicted killer. I told you that if it was a problem, walk away. I told you I would remain loyal to her because she was innocent. I told you I would not advertise it but I told you she was part of my life. And you said?'

'Mum!' Getting closer. The girls now coming up the stairs.

'I said, okay. All right! I said, okay.'

'Mum!'

'And remember what else I said? I could have told you about my sister while we were naked in bed, after sex, when you were in the flush of love, but I chose to tell you over lunch in a formal situation. Because remember what else I said? I said that, in the years to come, you being cool with my sister might wear off and you might start to change your mind, and remember what you said?'

'Yes. Fuck! All right. I said I would be good to my word forever.'

'Mum!'

Parents are good at a rapid and complete abandonment of tension and distress when it comes to the kids – if they want –

so Robbie and Anthea (because they did want) turned to the munchkins and said:

'Hey girls, what's up?'

'Mum! We found this.'

One of her photo albums.

'Who's this? She's in, like, every photo with you when you were growing up.'

—

BEING THE YOUNGEST of two sisters was, for Anthea, about being second. Second best, second last, second in line. But, as she now well knows, given she's a mum herself, it also meant you got away with a lot more, because the anxious-parent smothering has been expended on the first born. This she remembered when her own little Jen came along, vowing to keep a balance in her care and not to put the second born in second place.

For a little while, up until she was twelve, Anthea resented the distant and dismissive older sister who enjoyed tormenting her, but when puberty kicked in, Jen changed and became what the rule book says an older sister should be: a caring person. After Anthea turned twelve the sisters became close and, instead of defining one another as the enemy, they united into a single force against their parents. That was when dad's absences from home, for work, became less something to brag about (my dad is in Paris at an art auction) and more something to be ashamed of (my dad doesn't even know what year I'm in). The glitz of his overseas trips and glamorous gifts faded and morphed into feelings of abandonment, not at all helped by Jen's discovery of a tranche of nude photos of a woman – the girls named her Miss Serbia – and the realisation that his absences had more to do with an alternative life in Sydney, instead of life back home. Life with them.

And mum? At around the time the sisters were recalibrating their attitude towards their father, they began to redefine their mother. Instead of her being hilariously absentminded, she now became a space-cadet addicted to pain killers and culpable for not doing enough to keep dad within the confines of home.

As the years progressed, as the invisible countdown to Jen's arrest and imprisonment crept towards them like a wraith, shepherding them both to that fateful time in 1999, when life and all it meant collapsed into darkness, between the ages of fourteen to sixteen for Anthea and fifteen to seventeen for Jen, their mum and dad increasingly acted out the roles the girls had defined for them. Everything they did was yet another confirmation in the minds of the sisters that mum and dad were spiralling away from them. All the while, of course, with smiles and love, sent from these other planets, gifts and trips, to keep up the façade in the minds of the girls.

Jen's arrest and imprisonment tore Anthea asunder. And, in the wake of their parents' inability to deal with the momentum of inevitability but for the occasional flash of coherence – such as when they paid the legal team its massive weekly fee – Anthea became closer to her sister than ever. In a funny way, she thought, their roles had reversed. Jen was now like the second born, surviving at the behest of her sister because survival at the behest of herself was increasingly difficult.

—

'GUILTY' WAS THE word that brought down the hammer. Jen had told her to expect it. Jen had told her that there was no other possible outcome, not even after the scary tattooed Mohican had taken the stand and given his evidence. One thing about her older sister, thought Anthea: she is deeply capable of dispassion.

While Jen had been abandoned by everyone – Who would want to be associated with a gruesome killer? – Anthea kept a band of loyal friends; her close friends at school, a couple of boys from the brother school, with whom she'd hung out at the school dances, then in the mall and at the cinema. They were sympathetic. Some were curious. Some stayed quiet in their support. Some boasted. Many of her online friends in her Yahoo chatroom offered their support, but, to her horror, she developed a following, known as 'Sister Death'. Which freaked her out and made her shut it down.

The school had told Jen and Anthea to take a leave of absence. Jen was in Year 12, was just about to start her exams with plans of a gap year in 2000 backpacking around Europe before studying Literature at uni. Anthea was in Year 11 and had a dream that made everyone scoff with bafflement: she wanted to be a lepidopterist.

'Where the hell did that come from?' asked Jen when she was nine and Anthea was seven. Anthea shrugged. 'I like butterflies.' She didn't know. Where *does* that stuff come from? It's not as if it's inherited. One December day when she was six, she asked Santa for a butterfly net. She got it; it was a peculiar shape, wrapped under the tree. All that day, after mum and dad had woken and they'd unwrapped their presents and breakfasted on hot chocolate and French Toast with maple syrup, Anthea ran about the garden in search of – vainly – a butterfly to catch.

Now she has thousands of butterflies, dead and mounted in wooden cabinets, behind glass, in the lounge room. Butterflies from field trips to PNG and South America and elsewhere. Now she is a lecturer with a PhD, at the University of Queensland, in her specialised field, in the Zoology department. UQ is the institution that her older sister always dreamed of attending, before going on to the Sorbonne and then NYU, to become a literary guru.

—

AFTER THE CONVICTION, and after her parents lost everything and moved away, Anthea dragged herself back to school, a new school, finished Year 12 and went straight to UQ. She graduated six years later with a Degree, a Masters' and then the PhD. During the Uni years she waitressed and made money writing essays for other students. Through all of this – her reinvention – she changed her name to Anthea Black. It was the first thing she thought of and she wasn't in the mood for greater invention.

No-one knows, but for Robbie, that she was once 'Sister Death'. She managed to erase that online profile. Because she was underage, there were no photos of her in 1999. And the press wasn't overly interested in the little-sister angle; far more intriguing to them was how responsible the mum and dad were, for the killings done by their daughter.

Robbie was okay, as okay as a man can be when his potential girlfriend 'fesses up after a few dates. Once that news had worn off and he'd said he was shocked but otherwise okay, she said it was important to her that she remained loyal and supportive to her sister behind bars. And again, he said, that too was okay, he understood loyalty but just don't involve him and if and when she ever gets out, keep her away from him.

At the time of that conversation between them, a couple of years before they got married, Jen was a decade away from being eligible for parole.

Monstrosity of Nature

IT GAVE ME A STRANGE, INVASIVE SENSATION WHEN I SAW JEN in the courtroom and watched her going down for the crimes I committed.

I didn't mean for this to happen. She was like a bunny, caught in the lonely glare of a massive spotlight, knowing she was going to be found guilty as so-called friend after friend took the stand and said things like:

'She bragged about bathing in blood and chopping off men's heads.' That was Clemmie, who was seventeen years old and whose boyfriend was keen on Jen and so Clemmie's testimony was riven by jealousy and revenge but not aggressively challenged by the QC and not at all by the judge.

The people of Brisbane needed to know that The Slayer had been found and would go down – to allay those horrid fears, especially when so much of the city was still underwater and fifteen people had died in the floods on New Years' Eve, everyone waking up on the first day of 2000 to find deluge and ruin.

After Clemmie, the small Irish prosecutor who reminded me of an attack dog, brought forward another three school 'friends' who all gave roughly the same evidence: Jen was a dark and dangerous Gothic Celt who carried a flick-knife to school. In a moment of extreme drama in the court, flashed onto TV screens across the globe, one of the girls stood in the witness box and pulled up the edge of her school shirt while pushing down her school skirt, to reveal a scar she said was the result of Jen stabbing her.

That was Donna. She told the court she was the person who rang the police. Which led us all to the here and now. Donna's teenage flesh and victimhood in the courtroom. Gasps. Not even

OJ and the glove could rival this as a glimpse of Donna's naked hip was seared into the minds of men and women, good citizens all. Moments like these are the moments that condemn the accused; not evidence, or lack of it.

Then there was Mary-Anne, who told the enraptured court that she had overheard Jen laugh about cutting the throat of a man and pulling back his head, sideways, through sinew and muscle as she sat astride him and watched him die.

None of this should have been allowed, because none of this could be corroborated, but the judge ruled it all admissible.

And then all that ridiculous and totally circumstantial 'evidence' about a flower from North Stradbroke Island called a swamp daisy and how Jen might have picked some while on a school excursion and left it on the scene of the first killing, and the details of how she was into the Goth and Celt scene and she knew who Taranis was, the god of thunder; her and a few hundred million others.

But, as the Irish-accented prosecutor said: 'It's not our business to know *why* a set of heinous crimes were committed, but it is our business to ask by *whom* – and the evidence will lead to one person and one person only: Jennifer White, the accused. A monstrosity of nature.'

But the bad part, the worst part, the part that meant Jen was going down, without question, was the knife.

Bad, bad, bad.

She was never going to break free from the knife.

Which was obviously planted by one or both of the cops because my knife, the killing slicer, was back at home, in my army corps duffel bag.

—

PART OF ME felt sorry for her and part of me felt relieved that it was not me who was going to be found guilty. Another part of me, the unemotional part confirmed what I had already thought:

Time to stop now. No more killings possible. You've had your run. Four dead and sliced. The first one, and the other three.

I have to confess, I was having trouble with this. My head was telling me one thing: stop! and my heart was telling me the opposite: do it again, it's so much fun!

What am I going –

Oh, here's Lara to give evidence! Wow, she's dyed her hair back to her original black ... as she walks to the stand.

Doli Incapax

As one of the two lead investigators, I gave evidence for more than two days, studiously not looking at Jen. And trying not to look at Nils, who had somehow snuck in before I took the stand. He wasn't meant to be inside the courtroom as he was a witness for the defence. Their alternative killer as a way to deflect focus on Jen and cast doubt on the case against her. What was he doing here? Trying to creep me out? I would have him removed after I'd given my evidence.

Billy had already gone through the sequence of events, from the moment he and I arrived at the first crime scene to the day we charged Jennifer White with three counts of murder. My testimony echoed his. From the point of view of the prosecutor, a nutty little Irish guy from the DPP office, to whom I took an instant dislike, all smugness and condescension, it was important to hear reiteration, but also very important for him, aware and sensitive to some media reports of Lindy Chamberlain revisited, to have a young woman supporting his case.

We arrested and charged Jen when she was seventeen. A minor. She was to turn eighteen in a few months' time – great birthday party that would have been – whereupon she graduated into the real world, where her name and likeness was legally reported, where all the restrictions that were provided to a person underage were lifted and they could be – even though she already had been, thanks to Billy and the tabloid leakage – exposed to the public.

The law is clear on this and it comes down to *doli incapax*, which is Latin for 'incapable of evil' because you are too young to understand the ramifications of what you have done. Mary Bell was eleven when she was brought before the UK courts for two murders; the background of her dysfunctional home life was irrelevant to the prosecutor, who did not care about the why but only the *Did she do it?* Did Mary understand *what* she was doing? When she killed those two little boys, did she have an awareness of 'evil' (if such a thing exists)? Did Jen White understand, even though she was much older than Mary Bell but still, in the eyes of the law, a child at the time, did she understand that the killing of three men by sawing into their heads to the almost-point of decapitation was an evil act completely alien and repugnant to society?

In a case like this, even in the backwaters of Queensland, 2000, a tribe of psychologists was brought in to examine the accused. Sixty years earlier she would have been hanged from a tree branch in the Botanic Gardens, branded a witch. I'm not exaggerating; it's Queensland.

'Please tell us your name.'

'Detective Constable Lara Ocean.'

'You are with the Homicide Squad?'

'Yes.'

'You attended a crime scene at Kangaroo Point Park on the night of November the eighteenth last year, nineteen ninety-nine?'

'Yes.'

'Please tell us what you saw.'

Alotau

IT'S A LITTLE-KNOWN FACT, BECAUSE IT'S HARDLY EVER observed, that the prosecutor of any case that comes before an Australian (or Commonwealth) court has a primary obligation and duty not to get a conviction, but to get the truth. It's that simple. Even if the truth happens to imperil their chances at winning, it is what they must strive for. Because court cases have become battlegrounds of legal egos driven by a media gaze and big bucks on the defence side, the truth always takes a backseat to combat. Winning. At any cost.

The defence, of course, has no such obligation, which is why Jen's QC, a tall, elderly, distinguished-looking man, forced Nils onto the stand and why, when Billy and I briefed the DPP on the case against her, outlining all the avenues we had pursued including the other major suspects, he chose to ignore them.

Miles and Nils were good for the defence. They each had a violent history, were scary looking and carried a male arrogance that tends to freak out ordinary jurors who've come from safe-town.

Miles, and especially Nils, who looked terrifying with his body covered in tatts and his mohawk, were also brilliant diversions in one of the basic rules of defence: create reasonable doubt by throwing out some very solid alternatives as to the killer's identity.

Billy had given his testimony. I had given my testimony. I had ensured that Nils was removed from the court and would not be allowed back in until his time as a witness.

Miles had given his testimony which was the same as the dead-end information that Billy and I sourced from him in our record of interview. Aside from being a slimeball, it and he didn't have the same electric effect on the jury as did Nils.

—

HE STRODE TO the stand. Long strides and a footfall that bit into the floor. He was wearing a hired black suit but even that couldn't mask the tattoos which covered his neck, hands and fingers. He was the illustrated man, presented as your Freddy Krueger nightmare come alive. I watched Jen recoil and her eyes pop wide as she followed his walk through the court.

I also saw that Nils was nervous. His hands were shaking and his gaze was darting around like that of a meerkat. He looked at the judge and quickly looked away. He looked at the jury and quickly looked away. He looked at Jen and quickly looked away. He looked at the prosecutor, as if for help, and quickly looked away. He looked at me. And held his gaze. As if I, sitting close to the back of the court, was a safe harbour, as if the days and times of subjugation would anchor him into, now, a place of strength and control.

I smirked and shook my head, as if to say: Loser.

He looked away.

—

IT WAS IMPOSSIBLE to know if the prosecutor believed that Jen was guilty. His job, dismissive of any irritants like the truth, was simply to nail her – and he did so, going at her like a rabid brute. He knew all about Nils, and he knew that Nils would be a problem. The jury would freak out when they saw him and instantly think that a six-foot-something guy with abs and tatts, and with a history of knifing, would be far more capable of the killings than an eighteen-year-old girl.

But Nils was all circumstantial, and Jen's case was being driven by hard evidence, which had turned up at the last minute, allowing us to finally charge her with the three brutal murders.

Still, with Nils on the stand, the prosecution took a hammering.

—

'THERE YOU GO again,' said the QC, who spoke in a soft voice, mostly reassuring, sometimes with gentle exasperation. 'Yet another lie to the court.' He turned to the judge, turned to the jury. 'Your Honour, good people of the jury, in all my time as a representative of the court – and that has been a long time, believe me – I have never come across someone who has such blatant disregard for the truth.'

The judge let it go. The judge seemed to be happy to let pretty much everything go. He was the Ito of Brisbane but without the live broadcast. And, unlike the star-struck Judge Lance Ito, who eagerly presided over the OJ Simpson case in Los Angeles, keeping signed photos of movie actors in his courtroom desk, Jen's judge, although preening in the glare of an international press focus and tabloid fascination, was constrained by the narrow confines of Brisbane, not LA and no movie stars. Still, word had it that he'd passed on the important message to the press photographers that the right side of his face was preferred to the acne-scarred left.

The QC, Ian McDonald, turned back to Nils and smiled, as if seared by regret.

'You seem not to be able to help yourself, so let me elucidate for you. In nineteen ninety, you were in Papua New Guinea, is that correct.'

'Yes, sir.'

'Hooray, an honest answer. How long were you in Papua New Guinea?'

'About a year.'

'Can you recall when you arrived and when you departed Papua New Guinea?'

'I got there soon after Christmas and I left sometime in November.'

'And which parts of Papua New Guinea did you visit?'

'Port Moresby.'

'And?'

Nils flicked his gaze to me. Only I knew of this. Well, maybe he'd told some other girls in his inebriated bragging but only I could have revealed this to the legal teams. I had, of course I had; I was bound by my duty to tell the DPP all that I knew about Nils.

He then had chosen not to reveal it to the defence. Which, technically, is illegal. But you know, it's combat.

Ian and his team had done their homework, and nothing the Irishman could do, alarmed and eager to object on any grounds, would stop it.

'I'm sorry?' asked Nils.

'You arrived in Port Moresby on December the twenty-eighth. Is that correct?'

'If you say so.'

'I do say so.' As photocopy evidence from Air Niugini was tendered. 'You remained in Port Moresby, staying at the Mountain View Lodge for three nights. Yes?'

Nils started to jiggle his knee. He stared down at the floor.

'And then you flew, on the first of January, to where?'

Nils looked up and stared at him. A couple of moments passed before Ian repeated himself:

'To where?'

'Alotau.'

'Alotau,' repeated the QC. 'And you stayed in Alotau until November that year, when you flew back to Port Moresby and then on to Cairns. Correct?'

'Yes.'

'Do you recall the evening of August the fifteenth?'

'No.'

'Oh. Really? You don't recall that evening? The fifteenth of August?'

'No. I might have been drunk.'

'You *were* drunk. If I may read from the police record, from the evening of August the fifteenth, nineteen ninety.'

He had the original police file, an ancient-looking, wide, green leather-bound book. PNG police didn't have computers, not outside of Port Moresby, and all crimes and misdemeanours were laboriously written, in fountain pen, on every lined page. I was reminded of Billy's Murder Book. The judge had a photocopy of the relevant extract. As did the prosecutor.

'Three a.m.,' started the QC, reading. 'Constable Oscar Youngman and Sergeant Misto Laurie attended Sanderson Bay.

Deceased man on the ground. By the water's edge. Deceased man is local taxi driver, John Floyd. His head has been brutalised. Also at the scene of the crime and arrested by Constable Oscar Youngman and Sergeant Misto Laurie was an Australian man, Nils Marnell ...'

The QC paused, looked up at Nils.

'That is you, yes? Nils Marnell?'

Nils nodded.

'Yes or no, please.'

'Yes.'

He continued reading: '... who was holding the death weapon, a long-bladed knife, which was covered in blood. Mister Marnell was drunk and told the arresting policemen that he had no idea how Mister Floyd had come to be killed. Ambulance arrived at four a.m. and John Floyd was taken to hospital. Mister Marnell was taken to the police station and has been charged with murder.'

'I got off!' said Nils. 'I was innocent!'

But it didn't matter, not to the jury.

Nod Once

THE JURY LOOKED SUITABLY OUTRAGED BY NILS. JEN'S QC
had done his job. Doubt established.

Nils knew it. He wasn't on trial but he knew that he had
successfully managed to put himself into the cross-hairs of the gun
and, if by chance Jen was acquitted, Homicide would be all over
him to placate the public cry for the killer's blood.

I stepped out of the courtroom, passing Jen who was in her
lonely box of hell. Out on the city streets the sky was blue and had
been for some months, since the night the river burst its banks and
black water ran through the streets, upending cars and flooding
houses and shops. By the time of Jen's trial, the city was still
mopping up. A mildewed damp permeated like the smell of wet
carpets, hanging over Brisbane. People had died. Dogs had been
swept away, downriver, into the sea. Houses had been crushed like
balsa-wood toys. Newspapers reported that the flood would cost
hundreds of millions of dollars. People who had built along the
river were desperate and homeless. The insurance companies were
arguing the pedantic divide between 'flood' and 'rain', the latter
being something that no-one had cover for. The government was
outraged and vowed to force the insurance companies to grow a
heart, which was as unlikely as imagining that Brisbane wouldn't
be flooded again. There was also a bit of a debate going on as
to the wisdom – or lack thereof – of opening the flood gates at
Wivenhoe Dam and releasing two thousand cubic metres of water,
every second, into the river, causing the flood. I didn't think that
issue would be resolved for years.

I went home, ordered a pizza with anchovies and olives from a
joint in Hendra, opened a bottle of Chardonnay. I ate, I drank and
I fell into bed.

Whereupon, in my slumber, I dreamed.

Of that day by the beach, when my dad cooked the chops on the barbie and my dickhead brother ran around me in circles as I tried to build a sandcastle, sticking bits of tea-tree and broken shells into the ramparts so the enemy could not scale it, as mum lay on her back, in the shallows of the warm water, by its edge, little waves gently undulating beneath her, lifting her body up then down before they settled onto the sand, her arms outspread so that she resembled a starfish, or so it seemed to me, with her fingers softly tapping into the water like she was a pianist.

I am a light sleeper. Well, I am now. I wasn't, not when I was a kid, not until Nils, when I began to realise that angry strife in the way of an unwanted and forced fuck or a singular howl from the man in the bed next to me, followed by gin and vermouth, smack and smacking the caravan wall, that all of these things and more could erupt at a moment's notice. When I began to realise that sleep was a landscape of potential outbursts.

So, I heard the first footstep, as the intruder entered my house, very softly, through the back door.

I froze.

It's easy to remember all the research about shutting down and freezing up when an assault occurs, it's very much something else to break away and do something.

But I did, I did do something. I got out of bed. And I stood there, next to the bed, hoping that what I had just heard was a possum on the roof, all the while knowing that I was deluding myself, thinking: Should I stay here and wait because maybe he might just steal my handbag and then leave, or should I open the bedroom door and confront him? (And why, Lara, are you still such a scaredy-cat that you sleep with the bedroom door closed?)

Another footstep, getting closer.

My police-issued Glock was in a secure locker at headquarters. Check it out at the beginning of shift, check it in before you leave, at the end of shift. I really like the hard, compact metal feel of my Glock pressed against the side of my hip. I haven't used it yet and hope that I won't, but I very much wanted to have it then.

—

MY BEDROOM DOOR opens inwards.

As I reached out to the handle, it swung open, hard and fast.

The force of it knocked my arm away and smashed into my forehead, blinding me in the dark and I lost my balance and stumbled backwards, falling to the floor.

He ran at me.

He was in the dark. There was no moon. All I could see was his shape. He was a tall man and was wearing black: black jeans, black T-shirt, black hoodie and black runners.

As I reached up to whack him with my closed fist, ignoring the pounding in my head and trying to blink away the blood streaming from my forehead into my eyes, he reached down and put a massive claw-like hand around my throat. The grip tightened.

He leaned in to me as his face was touching mine. I could smell him. Like I had smelt him night after night as he wrapped his oily body around mine, the smell of perspiration and blood and semen on his unwashed body and Juicy Fruit chewing gum tinged with cigarettes and vermouth and beer on his breath.

'Get off me,' I struggled to say as Nils lifted my head up off the floor with the grip of his hand and moved in closer to me and said:

'If you *ever* make a move against me, or if any cop makes a move against me, I will come back and hang you from the fucking rafters, chop off your feet, your hands, your nose, your tits and then shove my knife inside your cunt and cut you up to your fucking chin. Nod once for, Yes I understand, Nils.'

I nodded once. My eyes were bulging and I was about to pee through a greater terror than I could have ever imagined.

'And you know I will, don't you? Nod once for, Yes I understand, Nils.'

I nodded once.

'And if you happen to dob on me, like you dobbed on me to that English cop partner of yours about my past, if you happen to tell him or anyone of this little visit from your good old ex, then I *will* come back.'

He reached around to the back of his jeans and pulled out a long-bladed knife.

'Remember this?'

He put the tip of the knife close to my eyeball. 'Stay very still, Lara, because this razor-sharp flick-knife is about three millimetres away from you and some very nasty pain and a forever I-Can't-See.'

I was frozen.

'I'm going to leave now, and I will never hear from you again. You will leave no further footprint on my existence.'

And with that he released his grip from around my throat and climbed off me. He swiftly left the bedroom. I heard the back door close after him. As I struggled for air, as I reached out to the wooden bedframe for support as I stood, blinking the tears and blood from my eyes.

The Knife

I CALLED IN SICK. I TOLD THE BOSS I'D NEED A FEW DAYS, back on Monday, and he said that was fine, the jury had retired to deliberate and the odds were looking great. Jen was going to be found guilty, of that he was certain. 'Take a week. Celebrate. You deserve it. We got the bitch,' he said before he signed off.

I hadn't slept. After Nils left, I had a long shower and put on a clean set of pyjamas, but not before I took a carving knife from the top drawer in the kitchen and went through the house checking that all the doors and windows were locked (realising that I had left the back door open because it's Brisbane and everyone leaves a door open because houses don't get broken into; it's safe in the suburbs) and that he wasn't lurking out the front or in my back yard.

I held the carving knife as I stood in the shower. I held the carving knife as I put my pyjamas into the washing machine. I held the carving knife as I sat on the couch in the lounge room waiting for the dawn to arrive. Dawn came. I didn't move.

I thought about different ways of killing him and getting away with it. I am, after all, a cop who specialises in murder. If anyone could get away with it, I reasoned, it would be me. I knew where he lived and I could easily surprise and disarm him, kill him, pile him into the back of my car and drive out west, a day's drive, and dump his body down an abandoned mineshaft in the middle of the desert and no-one would ever know.

It's not that hard to kill and dispose of a person, but the problem is there would have been traces. There always are. CCTV perhaps, a motive, a couple of petrol receipts from the trip to the desert and back again, although I could have paid with cash. But then I had a very strong motive, what with our shared past and me having dobbed him in to Homicide. And how would I have explained the mileage increase on the car? And maybe there was some DNA in the boot, maybe some blood and gore drizzled through the plastic sheeting I wrapped him in, and did anyone witness a tall, lithe woman carry a very large thing wrapped in black plastic or maybe wrapped in a rug?

And then, while I rolled with the fantasy of killing Nils – it seemed to be doing me good, resetting my equilibrium – I began to think about me.

Is there a killer in me?

No. I don't think so, even though I've just been assaulted and terrified by the angry rant of violence of an old boyfriend who, incidentally, just popped his profile up to Suspect Number One in a triple-murder investigation, even though a teenage girl is about to be found guilty, because she is a teenage girl and pretty (and yes, yes, there is the knife, that damned knife) but let the fantasy slide, Lara.

I did.

I let go of the carving knife, got changed and drove around the corner, to Racecourse Road and sat on the footpath at one of the outdoor cafes. I ordered a glass of Chardonnay, which I sculled, another, which I drank at a more sedate pace and a chicken caesar salad and enjoyed the sunshine. It was hot.

Here's to me, with a week off from work. By the time I did return to work, Kristo had drawn a red line through the names of James, Brian and Fabio on our whiteboard, signifying that all three murders had been resolved with a conviction.

—

BILLY HAD RUNG and asked if I was okay, and I said I was. We hadn't spoken much since he contacted me the night before Jen was arrested and charged, to tell me about the knife.

It just seemed too good to be true but, you know, it happens. And I was seven months in, compared to his twenty-one years in Homicide. He's the legend, I'm the rookie. I had three murders to my career before this case. He had hundreds.

He wasn't very good on the stand, Billy. He was nervous like Nils but, actually worse: very nervous. Even though giving testimony in a court is a fundamental part of the job for a Homicide Investigator, some detectives can't shake the stage fright. Kristo had suggested that Billy and a couple of the others who had the same problem take an acting class to get over their anxiety, but you can imagine how that went down.

Even though Billy and I were essentially giving the same evidence, it was up to me. I had to not only reiterate the police case against Jen, I had to make the jury listen and pay attention because, as the prosecutor told me, they hadn't heard a word that Billy had said.

———

THE CASE AGAINST Jen rested on a lot of circumstantial evidence: the swamp daisy, the flick-knife she took to school, the late-night skateboarding through the edges of the city, the Celtic world which led to the Taranis carving on the chests of the three victims and the sacrificial nature of the face and head mutilations, the upwards slicing of the mouth and the removal of a tooth. But there was the knife. Really, it was all about the knife.

'Tell us about the knife that Detective Inspector Waterson found,' asked the Irish prosecutor.

Billy wasn't in the courtroom. I tried not to look at Jen. The discovery of the knife was fortuitous, but that happens. Places which might have been overlooked the first time around, not searched properly, can yield valuable evidence. It happens. It happens a lot, Billy told me; he'd seen it many times during his career; lucky, last-minute stuff. The knife turned us around, from a case reliant solely on circumstance to a slam dunk.

'A knife was discovered.'

'Where? Please?'

'In her school locker.'

'Which you had already searched?'

'Yes.'

'And so, Detective Constable Ocean, let me pre-empt my colleague from the defence: How was it that, having already searched the school locker belonging to the accused, you did not find the knife earlier?'

'It was hidden.'

'Hidden where?'

At the back of the courtroom, the door opened and a person entered to sit and watch the proceedings. Damon. He smiled and winked at me. Since mum's command that he and I go to dinner at the casino – the two for one special deal – which I put off, citing work and could we do it after the case was behind me, to which he said: Yes and good luck, Lars, since then, I had totally forgotten about him. He had fallen right off the suspect list, not that he was ever on it. He just had that morbid, childish curiosity about the salacious killings, that's all, is what I had told myself.

'Down the bottom, at the very back, hidden behind some gym gear,' I answered.

'And what did you do with the knife, after you found it?'

'We took it to be analysed.'

'For?'

'Fingerprints, DNA.'

'Were there any fingerprints on this knife? And, if it might please the court, I will enter the knife into evidence now.' He held up the plastic bag.

'Noted,' said the judge.

As they went through the process of admitting the knife into official evidence, I turned back to Damon. He was staring intently at me. So was Jen. But I didn't catch her gaze; that I kept away from.

'Were there any fingerprints on the knife?' I was asked again.

'Yes.'

'Whose?'

'The accused.'

'What else did you learn from the knife, from the forensic analysis?'

'There was DNA.'

'DNA from? DNA from the accused?'

'Yes.'

'Anything else?'

'Yes.'

'What?'

'There was blood – leading to another DNA source.'

'And the blood, the DNA, this second contamination, if I may, whose was that?'

'The victim, our first victim.'

Reckoning

WAS SHE GUILTY?

The jury said so.

They deliberated for three hours, about the same time a Darwin jury took to convict Lindy Chamberlain for murdering her daughter, back in 1982. In that jury room, there were no deliberations. They had all agreed, well before the trial was over, possibly even before it had begun, that she was going down. Presumably the same thing happened with Jen's jury. Despite the horrifying imprint that Nils had indelibly put upon each of them, it was the pretty teenage girl who was going to be found guilty. Because there was also, of course, the knife with its blood match and, try though he did, her QC could not get the jury to express scepticism over the last-minute discovery of the evidence. The only actual evidence that tied her to the crimes.

Lindy Chamberlain was found guilty through some blood tests – which were later revealed to be not blood but rust inhibitor and milkshake. The analyst had stated the tests were conclusive, at the behest of the investigating police, who were under extreme pressure from the government, who were under extreme pressure from the press, who were under extreme pressure from the hungry public to get the bitch behind bars.

Like Jen, Lindy Chamberlain had no motive to kill. The prosecutor made one up and there was a lot of drivel about her baby being killed as a sacrifice in the wilderness, a bit like the blood sacrifice Jen made to her god of thunder, Taranis.

And also, like Jen, Lindy Chamberlain was young and pretty. Subjugation rarely happens to a woman who is not and it certainly doesn't happen to a woman who fails the meek-and-bashful test.

—

I DON'T REALLY talk about my criminology course and what I learned; cops don't like it when another cop quotes facts and stats. Cops like blood and semen stains, body hairs and fibres, fingerprints, broken alibis and insurance payouts and, for the past ten years, the holy grail, DNA.

For me to talk about the 'she-devil' complex or the 'third wave' and their impact on how male police and lawyers and judges behave when considering the possibility of a female killer would only invite derision, then anger and then push-back.

I can speculate, as I did when I studied this, about the notion of an attractive woman, who is seen by men as a nurturing, loving, earth-mother, falling under the black grip of suspicious violent behaviour. The creation and then subjugation of a she-devil reaches back to the witch-hunts in Salem and even further back to Cleopatra, the wealthiest and best-known woman on the planet whom the Romans derided as a whore.

But I won't speculate, not to Billy, not to my colleagues, because I'd be dancing solo on a desert plain. I could quote them facts, about the huge spike in focus, from police and law courts, on the potential of women's criminality whenever a wave of feminism grew. Like in the United Kingdom after women successfully lobbied to vote in 1918. Like in the United States after women were forced back into the kitchen following their 1940s wartime service, all because the men came home. Like in the 1970s after the publication of *The Female Eunuch*, when American cops were quoted saying that if bitches want equality, they will fucking give it to them; they were talking about jail times. Like now, in 2000, a few years after third-wave feminism appeared, after a black woman named Anita Hill was harassed by a group of older white men when she appeared in the US Senate to testify about sexual assault. But I won't quote them these facts, all of which I kept on recalling, as I drank too much Chardonnay during that week, while the city around me burst out in celebration that Jen White had been sentenced to life imprisonment.

Because what's the point of dancing solo on a desert plain? Better to take control of my own life and chart my own trajectory.

Leaving those who would reach up to pull me down, the men I have known and the men I will come to know, marooned in their own narrow, singular orbits.

—

THE LAST TIME I saw Billy was over lunch at the Breakfast Creek Hotel, his go-to restaurant. He ordered a T-Bone but didn't bother asking for the tinned spaghetti or the pineapple slices. He had suggested we get together to celebrate the conviction of Queensland's first ever serial killer because we would go down in the annals.

It was a week after Nils attacked me. The bruising had gone down and my murder fantasies had gone away. I locked my doors and windows assiduously and I'd taken possession, illegally, of a Beretta pistol, hand-delivered to me by a local biker at the behest of my friend from Melbourne, a cop who had also recently joined Homicide, in Vic Pol. I kept the pistol in a shoebox under my bed.

I had now clocked in twelve months with the Brisbane squad. The four months from arrest to conviction must have been a record in Commonwealth law, but that's how the state government wanted to play it. Be tough with crime and get a speedy result from the jury, appease the people, call an election.

'I heard you put in for a transfer? Out of Homicide?' Billy asked as he took a long swill of beer. I was drinking peppermint tea. We were sitting outside, on the veranda, across from the creek which ran off the river. We were sitting in the sun and the river was moving slowly, back to its normal level, as if the tempest of 1999 was a chimera, as if it hadn't really happened. I imagined the river as a beast, a blood river, which held not only secrets of those lives it had taken but which lurked as a silent and smiling reminder, running through the heart of the city, which at any time could turn on us and become a raging monster once more.

'Yeah. I thought I'd get some training in the other squads,' I replied.

'Fraud?'

'Yeah. I hear the crooks are charming.'

'Was murder too much for you? It gets to some people. No shame in that,' he said.

'No. I just want to get experience with all sorts of crime. And, you know, I want to climb the ranks. Become an Inspector one day. So, have to do the boards, move around, one step back, two steps forward.'

All of which was true. Over the course of the year and with an increasingly narrow focus on one series of crimes I had begun to feel the need to broaden my understanding of how Queensland Police worked. If I stayed in Homicide, I would be defined by murder, maybe eventually turn out like Billy. Cynical, ruthless, jaded. He and I had been lauded for the capture of a vicious serial killer. We had made the world news. He had grinned at the cameras; I had shunned them. That too was part of my reasoning for leaving Homicide after just one year: I was craving the normalcy of crime that did not involve such high stakes. There isn't very much in police work that is nice; you're dealing with people who rob a 7/11, abuse their child or partner, defraud a pensioner's life savings, murder. But that was the world I had chosen, a byzantine world of human frailties. I was happy here in this world and I knew, after a year of killings, after more years in the other squads, that I would never leave.

'Good move,' Billy said and drained the last of his beer. 'Do you think I planted that knife?' he asked without warning.

'Did you?' I replied.

'Of course not. We had enough to get a conviction without it.'

'I'm not sure that we did, Billy.'

'We used to fit people up in the old days, back in the seventies and eighties. Not anymore. Too hard.'

'How come? How is it too hard?'

I didn't mean to be combative, although there was an angry Lara, the one with the dyed-platinum hair, ripping away at my conscience. *Did we get it right?* Or, more to the point, did *I*?

'What do you mean by asking me that?' he said, his eyes narrowing. 'You think I did do it, yeah? Is that what you think? Me, Billy Waterson, plant the fucking knife to get a conviction? I didn't do it. I didn't need to. We had enough to get a conviction anyway.'

'Billy, calm down for fuck's sake. That's not what I said.'

He ordered another beer and stared at me. 'But that's what you think, isn't it?'

I didn't answer. I had no answer. He found a knife, late in the investigation. It happens. Would Jen have been convicted on circumstantial evidence alone? The flower, the trip to North Stradbroke, the love of the Celtic world, the testimony of the school friends of her threats and stabbings, the skateboarding, no alibis and an anger that made her want to hurt men, as the prosecutor alleged without a shred of proof. Would she have been found guilty if she was an eighteen-year-old guy who fitted into all those categories?

Who knows? Who can say? Not me. But as my mum had noted, the killings stopped after she was arrested.

'I should go,' I said and got up from the table. Our food hadn't arrived, but he didn't seem to care.

As I walked away, cloaked in confusion and sadness, I heard him say:

'You're stupid, you're naïve, you'll get nowhere.'

The Year of Our Lord 2000 and, Be Praised, a New Millennium Has Arrived

I celebrated Jen's conviction with a kill.

I knew it was wrong, to go off and do one more, after all that my head and my heart had gone through, the great debate. But I did it.

I succumbed.

I left home. I had on my backpack and in it, my blade.

—

He and I had talked and I advised Him that this one had to be different. A sacrifice, yes, like the last three but not like the first, which was different and many years ago.

This one would not be a fear but an aoife. A woman. Important, I told Him, that we choose a different type of victim, and unlike the last three, that this new one would never be found.

So, with that understood, I set out, with my blade inside my backpack, to claim her.

It was April in the year of our Lord 2000. Jen had been dragged before the courts just before the end of the last century and convicted shortly thereafter. Her trial didn't last very long. Justice was swift on poor Jen.

Since the rather shocking moment when I read the newspaper and discovered the cops were going to make her the killer, I had managed to deal with the feelings of guilt. It's a terrible thing that has happened to her but I have to be selfish and think of me.

I remember the morning of January 1 in the year of our Lord 2000 when I woke up and was terrified that all of the information on my laptop was going to explode into the ether of Y2K when I turned it on but, like everyone else on the planet, I had been tricked and deceived into thinking that a terrible event was going to occur. Just like all those Christians who often think that Jesus H, their Saviour, will return to earth on a certain date, time, day and place to embrace them and take them back up into the sky. Stupid people. And sometimes I think that people would find *me* and my musings with Him to be silly.

I am not mad. I am not insane. I talk to Him and he talks to me and I follow His guidance. It's no different than if you spoke to God in a church, and nearly everyone I know does that. They are not mad, nor am I. I just talk to another.

To people on the streets, in real life, on the surface, I conduct myself as a regular, normal person. No-one is truly aware of what is really happening in my mind. As I walk along a footpath or through a park, casting my gaze upon people with a smile because everyone likes a person who smiles – it tells them that they are nice – I appear unthreatening. Safe.

Which is why she smiled at me. Because I smiled at her. The aoife was young, barely in her twenties. She was, sad to say, homeless. No fault of hers, I'm sure. She had likely run away from home, perhaps due to some form of domestic abuse. She looked as though she'd been on the streets for a while, which was the point of me smiling at her.

My target. My next kill. He agreed. A person who has been on the streets for a while is a person no-one really cares about. A homeless person like her is anonymous and has already chosen to absent themselves from normal life. So, when I kill and dispose of her, she won't be missed.

New type of victim. Young. Aoife.

New type of kill. No head fold.

New type of hunting ground. I have left my familiar territory of Kangaroo Point and the Botanic Gardens to venture where

Miss Homeless is living. Still the Brisbane River but far away from before.

Miss Homeless aoife has chosen to live in one of the last remaining abandoned wharves along the river, in Hamilton, not far from the mouth of the river and the ocean beyond. Most of the wharves have been torn down and apartments are being built but a few remain, giant husks of brooding buildings, warehouses that front onto wooden piers, all of which are condemned because the massive logs that make up the piers are cracked and rotting, pieces falling into the water below. The flood didn't help. The river rose and covered the piers, the waters rolling through the old warehouses and out the other side, onto Kingsford Smith Drive, the four-lane highway that leads to the airport.

The warehouse she was camping in was huge; a vast empty dark space littered with rusty machinery, massive hooks dangling from the ceiling and old conveyer belts, long ago abandoned. The wooden doors were incredibly thick and tall, intended to be bolted, locked with huge metal chains and padlocks, but after the flood one had come apart and presumably this was how she found her way in. This was how I found my way in. I have always cruised along the old wooden piers, ever since I was kid, at night. Last week, on a midnight haunt, I noticed the open crack and stepped in to find myself in this deep gloom; in the distance, on the other side of the warehouse, was a little lean-to and this person sound asleep.

I crept up to her and peered down and said to Him: We have found the next victim. Let's come back, You and me, next week, and cut her up.

—

HERE I AM.

Two in the morning. She was sound asleep as I stood over her. Knife in my hand. I could hear the swell of the river beneath me. No moon tonight.

I knelt down and sat on her. She woke up straight off and stared at me but not really at me because the tip of my knife was at the tip of her nose. My knife is very, very sharp. Razor-blade sharp. I said:

'Open your mouth.'

And she did. She was really scared. I could see it. I could feel it. I could smell it. I liked it. Her fear gave me a thrill. I could feel the rush, as it was beginning to come, the endorphins. I fought against it, though, because I needed to remain in control. Maybe later. Maybe after We have dispatched her.

'Pretend you're going to kiss me,' I said and she duly obeyed and slowly pouted her lips.

I cut them off.

She screamed, but I was prepared. I stuffed a tea-towel into her very bloody mouth. She tried to writhe, trying to buck me off her, but I was prepared. I held the dagger up high and plunged it down. Then I sat back and opened up her top, a dirty flannel shirt, and dragged the tip of my knife down her chest, from just below her neck to just below her belly. Not deep but deep enough for a warm flow of blood to spill out, onto the concrete floor. She was panting, breathing hard, in-out, in-out. She had the confused look on her face they all get. *Why me?* is what they are thinking. She was in great pain and unable to move, pinned as she was to the ground. I pulled out her canine tooth with a pair of pliers. To be added to the trophy board. Wrapped it in tissue and placed it in my pocket.

I had noticed a large piece of metal, part of some old machine, possibly an engine. It was just sitting on the ground, covered in dust, a relic from the days when the factory was active. I thought I could use it. The finale. Before I disposed of the body. I crossed the floor and picked it up. It was very heavy. I carried it back to her, lifted it up high and dropped it.

The old warehouse was full of valuable things. I wrapped her bloody body in some old chains, rolling her into them and then dragged her by her feet across the dusty floor towards the big old roller doors, through the open crack. Out onto the wooden pier and towards the edge, the river. She was heavy and the chains got caught in the splintered edges of the old wooden beams along the pier, but I got her to the edge, and I was about to roll her in when I heard:

'Hey!'

I spun around. It was a kid. Must have been out doing what I used to do. Hanging around the old wharves. He was frozen. Hard to tell if he was young. He was about thirty metres away. He wasn't moving. I rolled Miss Homeless into the river below. The chains were so heavy, she sank beneath the surface without a sound. I turned back to look at the kid and he was still there, still frozen.

I ran.

The other way, of course. I knew the old wharf area well; up ahead was a metal fence to keep people like me out but someone, years ago, had bent part of it back, and I managed to squeeze through it and ran into the park next door. Where I hid, behind a massive strangler fig tree, its roots spread wide and deep into the ground. Just before dawn, convinced the cops had not been called, I emerged and went home.

If the kid thought he saw a killer dispose of a body, he didn't tell the police, or if he did, they didn't pay much attention because after about two months, I started to breathe easy, confident I'd got away with it.

But.

I said to Him: I think that was a warning. I think We need to retire. That was too close. We nearly got caught and when it comes to killing people, she was as perfect as you could get. Homeless, abandoned, hidden.

And He said:

Yes.

And then, before We left this alone, this part of Our lives, I reminded Him that, in the future, in the far and distant future, Jen White would, one day, be paroled. And then We might strike again. Back, then, to a new spate of head folds.

And He said:

Yes.

And Jen?

She is now about to get parole, nineteen years later.

PART IV

KARIN

God told Moses what to do
To lead the Hebrew children through
Pharaoh's army got drownded
Oh Mary don't you weep

Moses stood on the red sea shore
Smotin' the water with a two by four
Pharaoh's army got drownded
Oh Mary don't you weep

Sunburnt Country

'NEXT UP IS JENNIFER WHITE,' I SAID.

'You will have read the file and no doubt remember the case with all its tabloid glory, quite some years ago. We'll bring her in, via the video link, in a minute. She's been in Wacol for fifteen years now, for the three murders and this, as you will have also read, is her first parole hearing.'

—

THE PAROLE BOARD meets once a month to make its collective determination as to whether a prisoner is eligible to be released. Each prisoner's file is emailed to us a week before we gather, in a rather dull boardroom on the fourth floor of the William Street government administrative office block, a depressingly ugly brown stucco building with 1970s fashionable concrete blocks protruding beneath each of its narrow grimy windows – Queensland's testament to Stalinist Brutalism, some twenty years after it was in vogue in only the USSR.

The carpet hasn't changed since the 1970s, and even though smoking in offices has been banned for decades, we can still sniff the generations of ciggie-puffing bureaucrats. Each prisoner's file is massive, with case details ranging from the crime-breakdown, the sentencing details, records of all psych reports, the criminal's history within the correctional facility, information regarding support systems for when and if they are released back into the community and, sometimes, victim impact statements on why they should not be released back into the community.

And signs of atonement.

Contrary to Hollywood expectations, good behaviour is not taken into account. Only its absence. 'A prisoner is *expected* to behave well,' I instruct all members on their first outing in the boardroom.

As president I take the top chair, sitting at the end of a long wooden table. Around me are my twenty-two fellow board members. Morning sun blasts through the small narrow windows, creating shafts of pale yellow across the room.

Outside it's thirty-two degrees and it hasn't rained for eight months. Cattle are being shot dead, farmers are committing suicide, drought relief is being debated in parliament across the road and the sounds of a crowd protesting against forest clearing can be heard as they march along the street below.

I'm young to be in this position – late thirties – but I was also one of the youngest QCs in the state. My husband, Warren, is also a QC. We have two teenage daughters who attend Clyde, an all-girls' school and a house not far from where Jen White and her family lived back in 1999.

Brisbane is a small town, and Warren and I have a high profile. We often attend art-gallery openings and book launches; we try to maintain an active involvement within the girls' school. When I was offered the job of parole board president by the Attorney-General, a dumpy cowboy called Ray, everyone told me they weren't surprised. But I was.

I'm proud of my career, and I won't deny I have toyed with the hope of an appointment to the bench. Maybe even the High Court. We are tremendously busy but try not to work on weekends; that's scheduled as family time with the girls, usually starting with pancakes on Saturday morning. Yum cha on Sundays and a family movie on Sunday night, lights out, all huddled on the couch eating nachos and popcorn. (I make the nachos, Warren does the popcorn; he gets an easy break because it's just a microwave thing.)

Our girls are our greatest joy. Beth is twelve and Di is thirteen. They both have an issue with buck teeth and wear braces. Beth loves Lorde and Lady Gaga. Di swoons to Frank Ocean. Whenever they go out, they resolutely keep their mouths closed and do not smile or speak because they are totally freaked by the tooth thing.

—

'I NOTE THAT her parents have never visited but her sister has kept up regular contact. What's the deal with an outside support system?' asked Nellie, a mid-forties professor in science and technology at Griffith University.

'There's a report from her social worker; where is it?' We all shuffled through the thick files on Jennifer White.

'Here. Westaway House, in Southport, has agreed to put her up while she finds a job and her own place.'

'Did anyone get a phone call from Ray last night?' asked Clive, a mid-twenties nurse who was named Young Australian of the Year for his work in youth suicide awareness. Clive was the youngest by far and while he exhibited self-assurance, he was a little needy and easily intimidated.

'Ray who?' asked Nellie.

'Ray the Attorney-General. Ray, our boss.'

'I did, yes,' I said carefully. 'He's not exactly our boss, Clive.'

'He sure sounded like it last night.'

'Did anyone else get a call from the Attorney-General last night?' I asked the rest of the table.

Fifteen heads nodded. A majority of the vote. So bloody inappropriate, though I couldn't say that out loud. 'Right, well then,' I said instead. 'We all know that the Attorney-General has expressed concern regarding Jen White's parole because of community concerns.'

'First,' said Nellie, 'Ray is a cowboy who wears a Stetson to parliament when he's not mustering cattle on his property; he only got the job of Attorney-General because the Premier needed to curry favour with the redneck vote. Second, Ray cannot tell us what to do or what not to do. Someone should give him a lecture on the separation of powers. And finally, this young lady who has been incarcerated on the flimsiest evidence –'

'There was a knife,' interjected Clive.

'With the first victim's DNA,' added Susan, who was in her late fifties and a private-sector advisor to the government on building a greater rapport with China for the benefit of local Queensland businesses.

'Yes, and we all know there remain unanswered questions about that trial, especially in relation to the knife. And do we think one of the investigating homicide officers at the time was pushed out of the Service by his ex-partner when she became Commissioner?' asked Nellie.

Since Jen had been incarcerated, there had been a growing online movement to protest her conviction, citing rampant sexism and dodgy evidence. She hadn't exactly reached the profile of Lindy Chamberlain, who was found innocent and freed after giving birth while in prison, but Jen's case was growing in notoriety.

'It's not our job to rehash innocence or guilt but to look at the situation of the prisoner. Jen has a social worker on the outside, tied up to a secure and registered place of accommodation within the ambit of the Salvation Army and she has a family member who has agreed to vouch for her, financially and emotionally,' I said.

'Ray said the public would frigging freak out if she was released back into the community,' said Clive.

'And have you read the submissions from the families of the victims? The widows of the three men, and their children? Grim. They'll come after us,' added Susan.

'Granted, it is an emotional case,' I agreed, 'but we can only work to the criteria we are given.'

'Which takes us to the issue of rehabilitation,' said Nellie.

Yes, well indeed, I thought as I prepared to set up the video link with The Slayer. Not a lot in the case file on atonement, let alone an acknowledgment of the crimes, despite multiple sessions with prison psychologists. But Jen does seem to have ticked all the other boxes.

Except the one she can't tick. Community outrage, herded by a Stetson-wearing cattle farmer who probably didn't even know how a parole board operated until one of his advisors warned him of this upcoming decision.

—

'Hi, hello, Jennifer? Are you there? It's Karin Jones here, the president of the parole board.'

'Hello Ms Jones. Hello, members of the parole board. It's Jen here; you can call me Jen or Jennifer.' As the image of a thirty-three-year-old woman with short brown hair and the most striking eyes crackled into focus.

My Nights with Enrico

IN THAT OTHER REALITY, THE ONE FROM WHICH I ABSCONDED when I fell down into The Doom, The Fall, when the grip of homicide encircled me and carried me to the bottom of the ocean, head first, plunging me into the sand with a *Get this bitch* –

In that other reality I studied literature at the University of Queensland and wrote my Masters on Jane Austen (I had realised that Kafka was a teenage aberration of gloom and Goth, like Sartre and Joy Division) and then did my PhD on the works of the Chilean writer Roberto Bolaño, in the context of magical realism and how poetry can infuse the definition of the novel, with allusions to Gabriel García Márquez and Leonard Cohen and his impossible-to-read but wonderful-to-read *Beautiful Losers*.

Like the characters from Bolaño's masterpiece *2666*, the only book to make me cry, I was a literary academic who travelled the world to give lectures and occasionally sleep with men (or women) after a night of raucous argument and singing and dancing in Barcelona and drinking Rioja or absinthe like Baudelaire and Rimbaud and Modigliani, Proust, Oscar Wilde, Lord Byron and Erik Satie whose piano music I listen to in my cell, much to the bemused chagrin of my fellow inmates. The Girls. And we danced and we danced and told stories and woke up under the dawn of a Paris sky and dreamed about *la joie de vivre merveilleuse*.

That is the other life. The other reality. The one to which I cling as I lie in my cell trying not to listen to Anne wail in the cell next to mine.

Anne's meth-addled boyfriend, who goes by the name of Dragnet and is a biker, blew off the head of their eight-year-old daughter when he mistook her for a fifteen-foot cop like Godzilla, or at least that's what he told his biker mates who just came in to tell her the bad news that little Blissy is dead and now in heaven.

I close my eyes.

In my other life I never married but I had many lovers and we would dance and laugh, and Enrico, he was the Brazilian on the beach in Senegal, he said to me: Don't you want children? And I said to him: Yes, maybe, I don't know but it's impossible because I am on this remote island called Wacol, Enrico, but my sister has kids and she shows me the photos of them as they slowly grow up.

—

THERE WERE A lot of *I nevers*.

Never went to the Year 12 dance, never graduated, never studied at uni, never went out on a date, never had sex with a boy, never cooked spaghetti carbonara like my mum used to, never drank a glass of wine (only a hit of mum's vodka one night whereupon I promptly threw up), never smoked a cigarette, never drove a car, never went overseas, never ate risotto, never even kissed a boy, never went shopping with my own credit card, never held my sister's babies (who are no longer babies), never got to forgive dad for asking if I was a killer, never got to turn sausages on a barbecue, never got to wake up and think: Fuck it, I'm going to sleep in and not get up, never got to go down to the Valley and watch the ravers and dance all night long to eccies. And, funny:

Since the conviction I haven't felt anxious until now. Now, before I talk to the parole board.

Because, you know, it's the routine. They wake you up, you do this by a certain time and go to bed at a certain time until, after a few years, you get used to not making a decision because there are none to make. Oh, okay, there's chicken or beef and should I embrace or ignore Rosie, who wants to be my lover and maybe I will, because there is this thing called *loneliness* and there is this other thing called *the press of flesh* where I hunker up to her in bed and we just hold each other tight; no clothes, no nothing, just us and maybe we look into each other's eyes and maybe she touches me and maybe I touch her and maybe she exhales a soft whisper as she orgasms and maybe I do too, that whisper into me as I inhale it and take in her breath and as I orgasm, she inhales my breath, like we capture one another in a moment of unexpected intimacy.

We don't talk about why we are inside.

Everyone knows who I am but no-one has ever brought up the crimes.

And I don't to them.

And I love Rosie but I would never tell her that but I think she might feel it, as she sucks in my breath, as I exhale into her open mouth.

Rosie is hoping to also get parole.

She says: Come and live with me, after I get out, because you know what?

What?

I have a farm that has trees, tropical fruit trees, like mango and rambutan and papaya, mangosteens and star fruit and it's up in the north, deep in the north, past Cairns – lover, my lover, my sister, my lover as I stroke my fingers through your hair and peck your dimples and stroke you in that place where I can, feel your hot breath flow into my mouth, lover, I had this little farm before I did what I did. I've never told you what I did, have I? Why I'm in here. Do you want me to tell you now as I flutter a kiss upon your eyebrows, do you want to know?

No.

Ha-ha – I'll tell you anyway. I cut him into six pieces and cooked them up in a pot. Pot roast with spuds and carrots and quite a bit of garlic because he had sweat issues; slow cook, eight hours, and then I invited his mum and dad over for Sunday lunch, to feast on the beast they had spawned. Touch me ... as she exhaled into my open mouth as I –

Do you still love me, lover? Did I go too far?

As she caressed me.

No, you didn't go too far. You never will.

—

'HELLO. IT'S GREAT to be with you, and I hope I'm not too nervous as you ask me questions.'

'Okay. Look, there's no formal structure to this, so let's just start, shall we?' said Karin.

'Okay. Thanks.'

'Jen, tell us about the murders and how, sixteen years later, you feel about them, about what you did.'

'I didn't do them.'

'Jen, it's very important for us to understand how you have processed the murders and how you feel about them, in terms of moving forward,' said Karin as the others around the table nodded in agreement.

'I didn't do them.'

Karin drew breath and stared hard. 'Jen, you were found guilty of three murders, and our job, or part of our job, is to assess your consideration of those crimes. For us to release you back into the community we all need a very clear understanding of where you are, sixteen years later, on the crimes.'

'Yes. I understand. I am not stupid. I'm innocent. I did not commit any of those crimes.'

Following a silence of about ten seconds, during which the parole board members stared at the screen then at the table then at Karin, she said:

'Thanks for talking with us today, Jen.'

And a zap and her image was gone.

—

I COULDN'T HELP it. I was angry. I have a problem with anger. Still, after all these years being in jail. Next time, Jen, next time, be nice.

Heat

'HELLO JEN. IT'S KARIN JONES HERE AGAIN AND I HAVE THE parole board with me. It's been over a year since we last talked with you, and your lawyer has made another request for us to consider your parole. You have now been in prison for seventeen years. Can you see us?'

'Yes.'

'Great. Well, we can see you. We have all the documentation – Westaway House will still put you up, until you're able to pay for your own accommodation, and your social worker has again made a recommendation on your behalf and your sister has confirmed, as she did last time, that she will vouch for you financially and emotionally. The prison has come back to us and confirmed that you've not been in any trouble there. One thing to be clear on, for all of us, is: parole is not a *right*. The judge in your trial sentenced you to Life but, you know, Life is not life and, in your case, after nearly seventeen years, it is appropriate that we, once again, consider your situation in relation to the other stakeholders and make a determination as to whether it is timely that you be released back into the community. Sorry, that was a bit of spiel; do you understand what I just said?'

—

BY NOW, AT the age of thirty-five, Jen is beginning to show her age – just a trace – with a couple of grey slivers in her hair. Aside from that, she remains trim and vibrant with those intense eyes staring unrelentingly and that angry righteousness that will destroy her chances of getting anywhere.

—

IT HASN'T RAINED in more than a year-and-a-half. The entire state of Queensland is suffering its longest dry spell in history. The heat is intense. Baking waves of arid dust roll across the outback. The air-conditioning in the William Street building has crashed and emergency fans have been purchased, the last ones in Brisbane, everything sold out, before the next shipment arrives from down south, plugged into the beige-coloured wall and are shooting hot air across the long table.

No-one wants to be there. Everyone wants to be home or on the little man-made beach on the other side of the river, in South Bank. At least there are plastic bottles of cold water. At least the fridge in the boardroom is still operating, which is saying something because the aircon overload is so intense, the city has been hit with rolling blackouts. People are demanding a new election as the government can't even guarantee a basic service like electricity.

—

'YES. THANKS. YES, I understand,' said Jen.

'When we last spoke we tripped up on the issue of culpability. Because you were adamant of your innocence ...'

'Look, I just have to say, I did not do it. I am innocent.'

Zap. Image closed. And it wasn't an electrical malfunction.

Cowboy Ray

RECEIVING A PHONE CALL FROM THE NEW ATTORNEY-General at eight in the morning on a Sunday as I was making the girls' breakfast was completely unexpected. The new coalition government had just swept into office the night before. They hadn't yet been sworn in by the Governor. Votes were still being counted but the *Sunday Mail* headlined a swing against the old and an in with the new.

'Is that you, Karin?'

'Yes. Who is this?'

'It's Ray. I'm the new Attorney-General but don't tell no-one or else I'll have to kill you; state secret until Thursday. Come into the dining room at parliament – I'm gonna open it up just for you and me, tomorrow. Lunch. Twelve. Yeah?'

Yeah. Sure. Ray. Without the surname. But it's Queensland. The Premier is Betty. The Treasurer is Shane.

After an election, the mechanics of government are still, silent, dead. It takes about two weeks before everything revs back to life with a return to normality, especially when the opposition party has trounced the existing power, when aides and advisors are scrambling and a man who was, a week ago, mustering two hundred thousand head of cows is now one of the most powerful people in the state.

And in charge of the entire legal system.

—

THE PARLIAMENT DINING room, at the top end of the city, is a very large, high-ceilinged, Victorian space in which ladies in aprons whisper as they serve you, and the cutlery is silver and heavy and ancient and you are asked if you might like the lamb with boiled potatoes and mint sauce or perhaps the beef with mash and horseradish. There is a salad to start: lettuce, orange and processed cheese. Salt. No pepper. Which is what Warren told me to expect as we rolled around in bed on Monday morning before we roused the girls out of their eternal teenage slumber.

Warren said that if the new government was Labor I would get pineapple slices (from a can of Golden Circle) on top of the lettuce, but because the new government is conservative, pineapple is banned.

Sweet equals fruit equals radical. If you're lucky, you might get a slice of orange with some processed cheese, he told me. Orange slices are safe, not radical.

'Babe, you're going to hate it, and why is Cowboy Ray asking you out to lunch before he gets – and the government gets – sworn in?'

'I don't know, but I have to go.'

'Whatever you do …' leaning over to kiss my lips and down into my neck and down and girls, don't wake up, not just yet.

'… do *not* come home in a Stetson hat,' he said afterwards.

—

WARREN AND I met at the finishing line of a memorial Gelignite Jack car rally in Birdsville. To commemorate the famous 1954 Redex Trial race through the outback, we had to drive vintage cars – but not too vintage or else we'd all break down. I drove a 1970s five-litre LH Torana SL/R 5000 sedan. Bright yellow.

I won.

Warren came second in a Ford Fairlane V8. Bright red.

We hadn't really noticed one another as the drivers gathered at Longreach two days earlier. We drove six hundred and fifty kilometres to Mt Isa, stopped, stayed the night, got up at dawn after too much partying and drove another seven hundred kilometres to Birdsville. Then we partied again, big time, for two nights and three days and by the time it was all over I had found a genuine partner. We were both from Brisbane and we were both lawyers and we were both aiming to become QCs. I'd grown up in the bush in Longreach and he'd grown up in Ascot. I'd been sent to an exclusive all-girls school and he'd been sent to an exclusive all-boys school.

We had many mutual friends and he was the first man I'd met who didn't have a problem with being bettered by a woman.

The car race was across outback desert. Massive swirls of red dust would almost sweep you off the dirt tracks. Back in 1954, the legendary Gelignite Jack sorted out any objects in his path, like boulders, by throwing a stick of gelignite out the window of his car, blowing them up and clearing the way.

Warren and I thought the law should be like that: don't let anything get in the way of getting the result.

I'd been into car racing since I was twelve. On the roads outside Longreach no-one cared how old you were when you drove, as long as you could see over the dashboard. I rolled my first Holden ute at the age of fourteen and narrowly escaped death at the age of seventeen when I skidded off an embankment and landed in a dry creek bed.

I've mellowed now. We've both mellowed. We are upstanding citizens of Brisbane and we enforce the law. The judiciary looks up to us. We take our daughters sky-diving on their birthdays, and the Torana is parked in the back garage. It's still registered. On our wedding anniversary we back it out, down the driveway and then go to Brisbane airport. Which is under federal jurisdiction. Which means the state police do not patrol the roads. There are a few near-empty roads down near the mangroves by the mouth of the river, where you can hear the ocean. And we gun it. Him first. Then me. Crack the ton and then make love in the back seat, like we did that first night in Birdsville. And then we drive back home.

—

I ARRIVED EARLY.

In keeping with the wild and independent we-do-it-our-way ethos of Queensland, the very first parliament was in a convict barracks building. Now, as I walked up to the entrance gate, I looked across the impressive 1860s sandstone building on the other side of the Botanic Gardens built in a blend of French and English imperial muscle with rows of archways and colonnades. Like every other Brisbane schoolkid, I had done the obligatory tour, trudging along the wooden-walled corridors and peering into old rooms with thick scarlet curtains, bored out of my brain, staring at the Assembly, thinking how small it was and how relieved I was when I finally climbed back onto the bus.

'Hello, my name is Karin Jones. I'm a bit before time. I have a ...'

'Oh yes, we are expecting you. If you go up those stairs and turn left and then right you will be in the dining room. The minister will be with you shortly.'

—

'YO! KARIN! HERE she is!' he said as he walked with long gaits into the otherwise empty dining room. Two frightened-looking women hovered close to the kitchen holding menus printed up every morning with the date in the top right-hand corner. Printed up today, especially for Ray and me.

'Beef or chicken?' asked Cowboy Ray.

'I think I'll just have the salad,' I replied.

'The salad is terrible,' he said, 'but I might convince them to bring out the pineapple. You want a beer? Wine?'

'No, thanks. I'll stick to the water.'

'You know who I am?'

'Yes, sir.'

'Then you know ... oh, here she is! Honey! Over here. I'm going to have the chicken but you know what? I have a big hankering for a chicken parma, lots of cheese, you get me, and my colleague here, she's going to have a salad and you have the pineapple, yeah? She wants the pineapple and bring her some garlic bread because we all know that eating only salad will kill us and bring us a bottle of your best red wine and my colleague here is going to drink some water so the best water in the house. Got that?'

Yes, sir.

'On air you go,' he said, to which I thought: *What?* but decided not to push it. (Many years later I heard it again and asked: What does that mean? And I was told it was a 1950s BBC phrase used on set, just before the cameras were turned on; we are on air. So, go.)

'I've got this parole-board thing and I want you to run it. Yes?'

'Sir, minister, I'm not sure I'm qualified for that – it is a tremendous honour but I am sure there are others who would be far more suitable than I am.'

'Bullshit. I need a smart, innovative person because ...' As he leaned across the table, inviting me to do the same, which I did. I could smell his breath of red wine. 'Because I know nothing about this stuff, nothing; all I know is that if they do the crime, then put 'em away for the rest of eternity, but my advisors, all young folk, like you, they tell me to not be like Fred Flintstone, it's a new century and stay with the times. So, what of it?'

Let me talk to my husband.

Who says yes.

Let me talk to my kids.

Who say yes.

Thanks Ray. The answer is:

'Yes. It's an honour, it really is but will you allow me my independence?'

———

AND NOW HERE I am, years later, in the slow grip of pressure where he and I are going to do battle over a person neither of us has met.

Jennifer White.

Eighteen Years In

'HELLO JEN, IT'S KARIN HERE AGAIN, ALONG WITH THE REST of the parole board. How are you?'

'Okay, thanks.'

'Today is your third time with the parole board. Your support system is still in place and your sister remains committed to you upon an early release, should that occur, and the prison social worker and your pastor support your application to return to the community. We also note that you have continued the sessions with your psychologist and you've created a literary class for the other prisoners and you're studying *Moby Dick*, which is certainly not the easiest of books to read, let alone study, all of which we think is great. But we need to come back and look at this nagging issue of culpability. If we may.'

'I am innocent. I did not kill any of those men.'

'The jury found you guilty, Jen, and it's critical that you – indeed, this is a crucial first step – that you acknowledge your crimes.'

'I did not kill those men.'

Zap. Black. Bye Jen. Not the right answer.

—

AT THE AGE of thirty-six in 2018, I'm now the longest-serving inmate. Not a record of achievement I would have imagined. Girls come to me for advice. Girls come to me in tears and they come to me for drugs and knives and I tell them I don't do that shit. I'm like the Old Mother Hubbard of the prison. The Old Girl. Old Jen. Go ask Jen, she's seen it all; there's nothing that Mother Jen ain't seen. She's seen the suicides, so if you're feeling black with thoughts of harm, go see Old Jen and she'll straighten you out. She's seen murders where bitches slash other bitches, mostly across the face so their men won't wanna fuck 'em anymore, but Jen's seen more than that; she's seen girls stab and twist and head-kick another girl to the eternal mother up above. So, if you're feeling as though you wanna kill another inmate, go see Old Jen and she'll talk you down, reminding you that what you really want, above all else, is to get out of the prison, walk your way past those razor-sharp wire walls that encircle you. She's seen girls who shrivel up and can't move as if all energy has sapped from their very life-force, so if you feel like you can't move or think or lift a foot or a hand, crawl to Old Jen and she'll advise on how to combat the death of life when you're not actually dead. Even some of the guards go see Old Jen for a bit of advice on what to do with their wayward husband or irascible kids because even though Old Jen don't have neither, not in her life because she went down a teenager and us girls made a bet that she's never been fucked, not by a bloke but we'll never win or lose that bet because Old Jen tells us she ain't never going to tell us if she has or not.

The floors are polished linoleum. Light grey framed by dark grey edges. The buildings connect through outdoor cloisters. Around us, in every direction, is green lawn. But now it is brown and dead because of the drought and the water restrictions that kicked in a couple of years ago. The flowers died too. Beyond the scissor razor walls of metal are walls of forest. We're under the flight path.

I do the art classes and I lead The Girls in the literature classes where we talk about books, and Daphne does the massage and meditation classes, and Rosie and me, Rosie and me …

Rosie. Danger-green eyes, deep as the ocean and a buzz-cut slicing into both sides of her head, tearing through her soft blonde hair; and muscles from being the tough girl and a smile, gentle and loving, from the side of her mouth, lest anyone see a semblance of vulnerability. With a 'Come hither, Jen,' moment that always consumes me.

Who would have thought I would enter into a relationship with a girl called Rosie who is older than me with kids and a dead, murdered (pot roasted) husband, and whose body has a softness

I not only caress but crave; she is going to get out before me; her parole comes up on June 24 and she will get out, she will, she has been in here so long and she is scared about getting out and as she twines her body around mine as we touch, I say: Wait for me and she says: I will, come and live on my farm with the tropical fruit. And she will wait for me; I believe her.

—

THERE WAS A dust storm. We were kept inside. The sky turned red then it turned brown then it turned burnt umber and the walls of the buildings shook and we, all of us, stared out through the windows. No-one said anything. We were all lost in our own thoughts. The sky was deep burnt umber for a long time and the cloud of dust swept in and enveloped the entire prison. It had been hot that morning but now we were encased in an even greater heat. Is this hell? I wondered. Is this what hell looks like? Hell comes from the sky? I always thought it was beneath me, far below the surface of the ground. None of us could see out through the windows. Just a wall of thick dust. Later, we were told that the dust storm was made up of top soil from out west. Top soil and desert red outback sand. Merging together as a great thunder of wind swept down from the sky, unearthing the land, ripping out layers of ground and then blowing across the city, then out into the sea.

I think Rosie is drowning me; you know when you are in love, captivated and lost within the sea, the undulating, massive crash of waves, some as big as eighteen metres, as you are submerged by love and the threat of loss.

It's time for her to leave.

She is being released today.

—

'I'LL COME BACK and visit you next week,' she says.

We both know it's shaky. Freedom rewires all promises made inside. But I hug her and she hugs me and I say: 'Can't wait.'

'Stop being innocent.'

'But I am.'

'No-one cares. Play the game.'

'But I am.'

'No-one is innocent,' she says. 'Be guilty, find remorse and then you'll be out.'

She's been telling me that for ages. Everyone has been telling me that for ages. No-one wants to listen to a person who says they're innocent because that's what everyone says, all of the guilty people inside.

Be guilty. Then and only then will you be free.

And with another kiss, she turns. I watch her leave. Down a corridor, escorted by two prison guards, and just before she vanishes around the corner, there is a pause and she stops and she turns back to me and I feel the warmth from her smile all the way from the other end of the corridor. And then she is gone. My Rosie. She is gone.

Wait for me.

No-One Is Innocent

PAROLE WAS A GIVEN. PAROLE WAS MY RIGHT. PAROLE WAS almost the first thing my QC mentioned when the judge gave me Life. 'You'll be eligible in about fifteen years' time,' he said, which I didn't really hear because I was so overwhelmed with what had happened to me but, as I was being driven, in the back of the van, to Wacol, my new home, parole became the beacon of light that was all and everything I clung to. The actual sentence of Life Imprisonment had been fully replaced by parole.

Which, as I was now finally starting to realise, was not actually a given or a right and no amount of being a good girl and not bashing up guards or injecting smack or killing other inmates was going to substitute the acknowledgement of my guilt and, ergo, my atonement. Because, as I now realised after eighteen years of stubborn anger, the girl cast as The Innocent, unless I changed and did a one-eighty, would be stuck inside this sterile hell for a lot longer.

Myra Hindley went down for Life, at the age of twenty-four, in 1966 after the jury took two hours to find her, along with Ian Brady, guilty of the horrid Moors Murders, the killing of kids. She was told she'd be eligible for parole after twenty-five years, which would have been 1991. But government after government changed the laws, and she died in prison in 2002. Sometimes Life behind bars actually is Life.

—

I HAD HEARD the burst:

To be paroled, I had to be guilty. I had to be the killer. Thanks Rosie, I am going on a fast track to embracing my guilt.

241

—

I STARTED WITH the widows. Of the three men I was supposed to have killed –

Stop, stop: of the three men I *did* kill.

There is a thing called victimology, which I read about in the prison library, which is run by a (like me) thrice-killer, of her husband, his lover and their baby. Sheree. Kind of like a 1970s earth mother with rolls of tummy and she put her arms around me on the day I went in and said, 'I need to do some work in here, is that okay?' And she said, 'Sorry to hear that Rosie has left you; I am always around for you,' and I smiled, falsely, and said, 'Thanks Sheree, can I sit over there, at that table?' Her breath always smells of licorice.

Victimology is a criminalistic study of the victims, their characteristics – female, blonde hair, Asian, dark skin, light skin, red skirts, pony tails, works in a bank or a kitchen – which might then, stepping into the mind of the killer, start to provide a profile of who he is.

Or, more to the point, who I am.

—

I'VE OFTEN WONDERED who he is. The real killer. I'm going to extinguish him now, the man who put me here, erase him out of my mind, make him invisible, no longer an entity with a heartbeat but, before I do, one last consideration of the man, the killer, who shut down my past eighteen years.

Where are you now?

What are you doing? Do you live in a house with kids and a wife? Maybe you have a dog. What do you think about alone in your bed? You haven't killed for the past eighteen years, since I was convicted, so I wonder how you've managed to keep those secret, longing desires from turning into actions. It must be hard for you. Not to kill. I read about the way you folded back the heads of your victims, resting their almost-decapitated heads onto their left shoulders, the way you cut into either side of their mouth creating a bizarre grin and the way you carved Taranis onto their chests, the way you pulled out one of their teeth – how did you manage to squash what must have been a massive rush of satisfaction for you?

I can't imagine it. It makes me want to vomit. But now I must. And will. In your footsteps. Where are you now? Are you still alive? Are you that man covered in tattoos? Nils Marnell. Who terrified me with just his appearance. Who chopped at a man's head in Papua New Guinea. Are you that man? Whoever you are, maybe you died soon after I was convicted. Maybe you went to prison for something else. Maybe you found God and turned your wicked life around, into the arms of angels.

I am scared of you. You fill my nightmares.

But now you no longer exist, because I am about to become you.

—

THE PAROLE BOARD is going to want to know why I did it and how I did it.

I want to kill middle-aged white men. They are wealthy but not extremely so. The first one lives in the Ascot/Clayfield part of town, which is where I lived, upper middle class, and he and his wife are settled and well off. They, all of my victims, work in the city. They wear suits and ties. They like to go out at night. They walk through the Gardens or along the Kangaroo Point clifftops. Is there a connection? Something that links three men walking alone at night, alongside the Brisbane River. In the rain, too. This was just before the river burst its banks, when the city had been deluged with rain for over two months. Just like we are now afflicted by drought, year after year.

Why do I want to kill them? Why have I targeted these men? Why not younger men? Why not women? Am I gay? Was I abused as a child? Am I the victim of domestic abuse? Was I a young woman who wanted to take it out on married men? But women rarely kill; all the killers in Wacol did it because the cheating, lying, evil, brutal husbands got what they deserved after too many years of meting out bashings, when finally, murder became the way out for these women, even knowing that prison would follow. The amount of times I have heard, 'At least the cunt is dead.' Followed by, 'I saved myself,' or 'I saved my kids.'

Even my gorgeous Rosie – who cut and diced then cooked her husband with carrots and spuds – did what she did because he would beat her and place a hot iron on the soles of her feet while she slept and vowed to chop off her fingers.

Maybe it's just the thrill. I've read and studied that too. No childhood issues. No anger issues. Just the thrill of a kill. The rush of a hit, like a jab of smack. Was it that? A hundred and fifty years ago, prosecutors would often cite menstruation as a common motive for a woman to kill. My prosecutor alleged I had anger issues towards men. Is the motive as prosaic as 'It was fun'?

I don't think you are a woman. I'm sure you are a man, but whatever led you to kill as you did, it is of no relevance to me. Because I am the killer. I did it. Not you.

Anger towards men is as good as anything. Why not, as I embrace my guilt and seek atonement, agree with what the prosecutor has already said.

But I must also explain Taranis. In my mind, somehow, as I cut your throat and fold back your neck, cut the edges of your mouth and pay homage to the god of thunder, I must feel as though I am communing with a violent Celtic culture. Do I *really* believe I am making a sacrifice to a make-believe god who existed in the minds of people two thousand years ago? That is either really twisted or really childish. Or am I just appropriating it to be cool? To stand out from the other killers? To leave my mark on history? To be remembered? Have I written a diary? Maybe I have. I think I have. I think I wrote down how it felt to kill each of those men. Did I snip a lock of their hair? No. It's the teeth. Why not ears? Didn't the prosecutor mention my love of Ogmios to the jury? The ears of his followers tied to a golden chain, linked onto his tongue? The teeth have to be a trophy. Yes? Teeth last. Ears would go mouldy. Have I formed those teeth into a hidden chain? Is it hidden in a box in an attic? Like Robert Hansen, the Canadian serial killer who took the lives of at least seventeen women; he had locks of their hair in a box in an attic. The police ignored him for ages because his victims were prostitutes, so it was their fault they got killed. (He got 461 years. That's Life on steroids.)

What is it about my victims that sheds a light on me?

What is it about me that sheds a light on them?

Did I know them? Did I cross paths with them? Or maybe I knew their kids? Did any of their kids go to my school? Was I a seventeen-year-old schoolgirl having sex with them? Would I meet up with them in a bar in the Valley with a fake ID card and then lure them away so I could kill them?

What did I say to these men? Did I say anything or did I rush at them with my knife? And we'll get to the knife, the method of killing, in a minute because that too is going to tell me something about who you are, Jen.

Stay with *them*. Be patient. Build up the stories and profile of who they were, try to find a common link and then create your motivation. The why.

Then create the how.

James

JAMES. VICTIM NUMBER ONE. THIRTY-SEVEN, MARRIED TO Lynne with two kids, Matt and Diane. It says here that Lynne read out a victim impact statement to the court and screamed at me for taking away her husband. It says here that Matt and Diane were in the court and had to be led out because they were weeping.

I cannot remember any of this.

James was an architect, working out of a modern city tower with Thai and Japanese restaurants on the ground floor and an expensive cocktail bar on the rooftop. He worked long hours; he had his own key and therefore after-hours access to the office space. He would often get to work at seven a.m. and leave at six p.m. Sometimes later. Like, eight or nine. James liked then to go to the Valley, and there is a hint that he was bi, a suggestion he had a lover down there at a bar called CRASHED, but on the night I killed him he'd been to see his friend Nick, who lived around the corner from Kangaroo Point, and then took a slow walk to the highway to hail a cab. Nick was too drunk to drive his friend home, and James said he needed some fresh air.

James was short and trim. He went to the gym. He was good looking. Thick brown hair and a nice, warm smile. The sort of guy you might linger a glance upon. And I think he knew it too. I think he was a little vain but he was a good and caring father. He and Lynne were childhood sweethearts which was nice and they'd holiday on Lord Howe Island every year.

Perhaps James and I were lovers and I discovered this other lover down in the Valley, which infuriated me; I could handle him being married because he kept telling me he was going to leave her: Just wait until you turn eighteen, Jen, then we can run away together.

But maybe I discovered he had a secret gay life with this guy in the bar called CRASHED.

James lived a couple of streets away from my house. His daughter did not go to the same school as me. But maybe, on those days I played truant and hung in the city mall, maybe instead of doing that I went around to his house and we had sex. Maybe I wrote about him in a lover's diary, which I have since burnt.

He was a soccer player, and he encouraged his kids to play the game and pretty much every Saturday the family would drive to the local field and watch the game and, according to the victim impact statement from his wife and indeed from testimony regarding his character, from friends and colleagues, he would never engage in aggro like the other soccer mums and dads.

He was just the sweetest guy.

Yeah, he was and I killed him.

I think he was my lover and I got jealous and killed him because of that. But what about the other guys? That's a lot of middle-aged lovers, Jen. Let's just put that scenario on hold and move on.

Brian

BECAUSE THEN I KILLED BRIAN. HE WAS ALSO THE SWEETEST guy. He had a silly mop of hair and would sing Chuck Berry's *My Ding-a-Ling* at parties. Also married, to Jacinta. With three kids and two dogs, and they all lived in Paddington on the other side of town. Not as upmarket as Ascot but a wealthy inner-city suburb. Jacinta read out a victim statement too. I'm reading it now. I skipped over Lynne's because it made me sad, but I have to read them because I have to show great empathy for these wives, widows, whose lives I tore apart.

I made an application to the court to have these transcripts sent to me. I didn't have to wait very long; Anthea paid for them.

Anthea and I don't talk about the murders. We don't talk about the trial. We don't talk about who might have done it, who the real killer might be and where he is now. We talk about everything but the killings. It's better that way.

Brian was a solicitor for a city law firm. He had a thing for old Renaults, which he restored in his garage. I killed him in the Botanic Gardens, on the other side of the river from where I killed James. Then I killed Fabio, less than a week later, also in the Botanic Gardens. Look at those dates: I killed three men so quickly, one after the other. Fabio had had a late dinner, on his own in a restaurant across the road from the Gardens and decided to take a walk afterwards.

I could have had sex with James. At a pinch. Even though he was old enough to be my father. But Brian? Eek. No. He was pretty ugly. Yeah, he was the sweetest guy but he had a big nose and fat lips and he looked as though he'd sweat a lot.

The Third Man

THIS IS WHERE THE LOVER ANGLE GETS REALLY DIFFICULT. No-one is going to believe that I had sex with three random middle-aged men. The prosecution suggested I had a rage against older men and left the issue of motivation there, not really bothering to linger on why, moving on to the evidence, circumstantial and otherwise.

Otherwise meaning the knife.

The knife has haunted me every day and night for the past eighteen years. Who planted it and how, and how, also, did they get my fingerprints and place them on the blade, along with James's blood? But those worries are gone now because it was my knife and I did hide it in my locker at school and I forgot to wipe it clean or throw it away because I was overwhelmed with the rush of my first kill. And, to explain the knife and the other two kills, well, that's easy. I went and bought another knife. Bigger. Longer. Sharper.

I could get away with being James's lover; that would work. But also with a guy from Paddington? And another guy called Fabio? They must have been a spontaneous attack of blood lust. I must have been waiting for them, on those two separate nights, in the Gardens, having got the thrill of it after James. And because I had gotten away with killing Brian in the Gardens, it had become a secure environment for me to kill Fabio.

But if James's murder was driven by raging jealousy, why didn't I stop there, once I had scored my revenge, the revenge of a teenage lover-girl thwarted by her middle-aged man who'd been playing up with another lover down in the Valley?

How did you find out about the other lover? You followed him, yeah, because you were suspicious. Yeah, that works ...

... actually, maybe it doesn't.

Maybe the lover thing is just too much; they are going to ask me where we met and how it happened and how many times and they might also want to know what his house looked like and what he said about his wife; you know, on reflection, it's going to be too tangled to spin that web of lies. Just be a female Jack the Ripper. Easier that way. Keep it simple, Jen. Blood-lust. No other motivation: you just wanted to saw into the heads of three random guys.

Which takes me to the gory bit. I'm not exactly squeamish but this is disgusting and, again, I blocked it all during the trial. I had no clear memory of what the police said about how the victims were killed, not until I began to immerse myself in the killer, reading the trial transcripts, to become him. I have a vague memory of the courtroom being full and people gasping in horror and the widows, who sat together holding hands and staring at me every minute of every day, weeping, and I think there might been an adjournment when the judge said we should take a break.

But here it is in black and white.

The victim was initially struck from behind with a strong blow to the back of the neck. This blow was most likely from a machete or similar type of blade, its width less than a millimetre. In each of the three murders, the blade cut deep into the back of the neck, causing the victim to fall. In each of the three murders, a second blow was sustained to the side of the neck and around to the throat, where the accused then proceeded to slice into the neck. In each of the three murders, this led to near but not complete decapitation. Then I cut into the edge of their mouths and created a grotesque-looking smile, and then I pulled out one of their teeth, a maxillary canine, third from the middle, the one that looks like a long fang.

None of the guys I killed was tall. Each of them was my height or a bit shorter. And I caught them by surprise, from behind, so there was no lingering issue with the fact that a seventeen-year-old girl had the physical wherewithal to do it. I guess I must have sat on them while I finished them off. And contrary to what you might imagine, sawing off a person's head – or almost – is not especially hard. Just apply pressure and don't stop. In other words, it was pretty quick, each of these killings, which helps explain why I wasn't seen by any witnesses. But there was eyewitness testimony from two different people who said they had seen a person on a skateboard, wearing a hoodie; it might well have been a girl.

It was a girl.

It was me. Me, the killer.

Where did I get the knife, or was it a machete? How on earth does a person get a machete? Maybe it was a kitchen chopping knife like those wide-bladed ones that Chinese chefs use to chop a chicken or a duck. I could have got one of them easily. I went down to the Valley, into Chinatown to one of the Asian supermarkets and got it there and packed it away in my school bag next to my actual knife, my flick-knife, which I had gotten from an Asian market in the Valley, the one that I kept secret from mum but used to stab trees and some of the girls at school, little stabs, not big I-am-going-to-kill-you stabs.

Well, this speaks to a significant level of premeditation, Jen, so ... why. Tell us *why* you committed these murders.

I've been wondering that myself as I now grapple with my guilt and desperate need to atone and seek forgiveness through my process of rehabilitation and thanks for asking that question because it's like, you know, what I've been going through with the therapy sessions where I get the chance to consider and reflect upon my past behaviours in order to erase automatic responses and enter into a really strong, you know, process of behaviour modification but, yes, I think it was me watching all the porn and then going down into a rabbit hole of violent S&M and bondage and finally, like a junkie, staring at snuff movies. As I look back and reflect, I think that unleashed an anger towards men. You know, seeing them subjugate women in that way, made me want to subjugate them.

How does that sound? Will that do?

Additionally, as a teenage girl in search of an identity because of self-esteem issues, which is, sadly, so common with teenage girls, I fell into the grip of the Goth and Celtic world and this had a twisted, violent influence on me and so, as I killed the three men, I imagined myself invoking this god of thunder. Also, Ogmios, which is why I desecrated the bodies by cutting the mouths and removing the teeth and carving Taranis's spoke. Being in prison has really allowed me to escape these thoughts and, as my psychologist attests, I have not had these thoughts for many, many years now. I am a completely different person.

How does that sound? Will that do?

I feel so ashamed and embarrassed by this and so remorseful for the hurt I have caused the families of my three victims. And I also have to confess to the parole board, and this has been hard for me to acknowledge, that yes, as the prosecution said, I felt this rage against men. I think it also relates to my father, in that he was largely absent as I grew up. I loved my father and still do but he was never around as much as I would have liked and I think, as I strive to really understand this, that I built up a growing anger towards men like him. You know, successful, middle-aged married men. This is also why I stupidly invoked the cult and god of Ogmios with the cutting of the sides of their mouths. To humiliate them. Same with the removal of the canine tooth. To humiliate and then debase them.

How does that sound? Will that do?

I have been working really hard to deal with these issues, and strange as it may be for you to hear this, being inside prison for all these years to this point where I am in my late-thirties, I feel I have really come to terms with this and I certainly have no such anger issues regarding men or my father anymore. I have also been working on addiction therapy and I am totally comfortable with, you know, one of the parole provisos, if indeed I am granted parole, not to drink or smoke, and not to go online. Ever again. I am more than happy to give my parole officer my IP address should I actually get a computer so he or she can ensure that this promise is adhered to.

How does that sound? Will that do?

Nineteen Years In

2019

'EVERYONE HAS THE PAPERWORK? ALL CAME THROUGH ON the emails last week? And we've all read the file?'

Nods of assent.

'Great. So here we are, yet again; this will be our fourth consideration of parole for Jennifer White, and I know a couple of you have recently joined us, but Jennifer has been, as we all know, incarcerated at Wacol for nineteen years. She was eligible for parole four years ago but we have floundered on the very serious issue, or perhaps I should say issues, of her guilt awareness, remorse and empathy for the victims; Jennifer's past refusal to even acknowledge she was the killer of the three men has been a block for us to consider releasing her back into the community. Especially considering the current climate and a very heightened public awareness of this issue given some of the terrible murders that have occurred in Melbourne by recently released offenders and the controversy in London about the so-called Black Cab rapist whose victims caused such an outcry that the government was forced to act. All of which means *our* public and government gaze is upon us.'

'Did anyone get a phone call from Ray last night?' asked Susan.

A shuffling of silence as it became clear that I was not the only one to receive a phone call from Cowboy Ray last night.

'Look, let me say this, and I have been president of this board for some years now: Ray, or any other permutation of Ray, in other words, a government minister, has no sway over our independence. Which is what I told him, again, last night. We will, as we must in order to preserve our corporate and individual integrity, make a decision without fear or favour. Are we in accord with that?'

Twenty-three nods of agreement.

'Good. So, look, because this has been a very long and protracted process for Jennifer and for us, I have asked that she speak to us in person today. She's being held in a room downstairs and was transported by the prison officials earlier this morning. I know it's old-school, but, as we have all read in the reports, it seems that this woman has made a rather significant turnaround in not only accepting her guilt but in asking for forgiveness. It's also noted that she has found God. Now, the number of killers and rapists who suddenly find God in prison, when confronted with incarceration, is monumental. I am as cynical about this as you will be. As always, we go into this interview now with the best intentions and the understanding that a prisoner does need, at some point, to be returned to the community for his or her future and with a healthy dose of scepticism.'

And then the phone, a speaker phone in the middle of the long and wide table, rang.

Very few people had the number (and all cell phones had been turned off as we all filed into the boardroom). I pressed 'Accept'.

'It's Ray here. Your boss. I know you are about to consider the parole of Jennifer White and so I am going to give you a message from not only the Office of the Attorney-General and the Office of the Premier, with whom I have just been speaking, but also the Office of the Public and it is this: Keep her inside; do not parole her. Am I clear?'

I didn't hesitate:

'Minister, we appreciate your concern in this matter. The parole board is independent of government. We will, as we always do, take into account public concerns and government concerns. Thank you so much.'

And hung up on him.

Turning to an assistant, one of three in the room, I said: 'Bring up the prisoner.'

—

THEY WOKE ME early. It was still dark. 'Time to go,' they said. I had hardly slept. I had been thinking about Rosie and wondering where she was. In the few years since her release, there had been contact. A postcard sent from the Seychelles. Two words:

MIssing YOU

and

xxxxxxxxxx

I'd had a shower the night before and the prison guard said I could wear real clothes, not my prison uniform, and they handed them to me at reception while it was still dark. Two guards stared at me and then at their phones as I changed into the suit Anthea had bought for me from Country Road: pale blue with a crisp white cotton shirt. When I was growing up, I hated clothes from Country Road. Mum used to wear Country Road. It was a symbol of being old, middle-aged, boring. I like them now.

I climbed into the back of the van and looked out through the metal grill, as it rumbled from Wacol up into the city as the dawn played out some sketchy blue.

My first dawn in ninteen years. In my cell, my window is angled towards the sunset. Which is great. I love the sunset. The orange. The descent. But the dawn is the ascent, and that was how I felt.

—

THE DOOR TO the holding cell opened and a guard, Mia, stepped in and said, 'Time.' I followed her up old and worn concrete stairs and then down a corridor and into a large boardroom with a lot of people sitting around a table and I smiled and nodded out of deference and Mia sat me down and handcuffed me to my chair and then stood behind me.

'Thank you for agreeing to see me,' I said.

—

NOT FOR A second have I thought this woman was a killer.

The absolute lack of motivation for Jen – I mean, *why* did she do it? – the absurd circumstantial evidence about teen interest in Celtic Gods and a North Stradbroke flower at the first crime scene but not the others, the all-too-convenient discovery of the knife. If we were in America and she had OJ's lawyers, she would have walked out of that courtroom on the first day.

I would have gotten her off, had I been her QC. Even with the knife and the matching DNA.

Even with a public and government baying for her to be found guilty. I would have put Nils Marnell in jail.

But she was, in the eyes of the court, guilty, and thus I have to treat her as such.

And here she is. Now getting close to forty, hair mostly grey, quite buffed and looking a little like Linda Hamilton in the *Terminator* movies with muscle and those mesmerising blue-and-green-eyes, staring, for the first time, with a sense of *humility*.

The stridency, that stare-me-down in anger, that's gone.

—

THERE WERE TWENTY-FOUR faces staring at me but I stared back at the one that mattered. Karin Jones.

A face, finally, to the voice. She looked nice. She looked like you'd want her to be your mum. She was about my age, a bit older. She had blonde hair, tied back and was wearing a casual light brown suit which looked like it had also come from Country Road. There was an understated diamond ring on her wedding finger and she wore a thin gold chain around her neck. She was calm and still. She looked confident and smiled at me. There wasn't a trace of judgement about her.

'Good morning, Jennifer. We understand, from your social worker, that you have prepared a statement for us.'

'I have. Yes, if I may read it and then answer your questions? Would that be acceptable to the board?'

'Yes. It would.'

I took in a deep breath and looked down at the piece of type-written paper in my shaking hands.

'Dear Members of the Parole Board, firstly I would like to apologise for you having to listen to my blanket and stubborn refusals to engage in any sense of discourse over the past four years.

Over the past *two* years I have come to an awareness of my guilt and culpability for my crimes. This was triggered by the discovery that my father was, and still is, dying of cancer.'

I wasn't expecting sympathy. After all, we all have someone, somewhere, dying of cancer. Or if we don't now, we will.

I watched them all search through their thick file on me to find the letter from the doctor confirming that yes, indeed, my father was in the later stages of terminal cancer.

'My dad's impending death made me realise that I had to take ownership of my situation and confront the evils of what I have done and then, once I had done that, to seek repentance and find true guidance into the future so that I can become a better person. I am now ready to answer all your questions.'

'Thanks Jennifer. We have read the report by your social worker, who has been committed to you for many years, and she has reiterated that were you released, there is a home for you to stay in and she would provide monthly reports to your parole officer. We note the letter from your pastor also, but I'm sure that many of us would like to talk to you about the actual crimes and why you perpetrated them, what led you to murder these three men and how. This is not to hash over the evidence but an opportunity for us to understand your state of mind and, to be frank, for us to be completely comfortable that there is no chance of recidivism.'

I smiled.

No chance of that, I thought.

Drums of Thunder

THE POLITICS OF GRANTING PAROLE ARE COMPLEX. NOT IN every case, but certainly in high profile ones like that of Jennifer White. It is neither the role nor an obligation of the parole board to inform the public – or, indeed, the families of the victims – of an impending release. Vigilantism is never far from the veneer of a cultivated society, so on my watch, when a murderer is to be paroled back into the community, it is managed as quietly and unobtrusively as possible. They have served their sentence and now it is time for them to make a new life. Condemnation stops as they walk out through the prison gates and back into the community.

Aside from Cowboy Ray and his agenda to keep The Slayer behind bars for the rest of her natural life, I had to be mindful of the three women who lost their husbands twenty years ago.

They have not been quiet.

We don't advertise it when a person comes up for parole; there is no public register of potential parolees, but the whispers are loud enough for interested parties to hear. The last couple of times that Jen was brought before the board, the whispers reached the widows and they made some loud and inflammatory statements. They are driven by emotion and revenge, I understand, but I am driven by justice. Emotion can have no place in my world of consideration.

I did not make contact with them.

Nor did I inform the minister of our decision.

My husband would say I am not the best politician in the world, and he might have a point. I could hear the drums of thunder, of course I could. They were getting closer.

Unfurling

ANTHEA WAS WAITING FOR ME, OUT THE FRONT, IN THE CAR
park, standing beside her brand-new white BMW, covered in a thick
sheen of dust because washing your car, even with a garden hose,
has been banned for the past three years. She is thirty-seven with
two kids, and I am thirty-eight with an emptiness in my history.

The guards slid open the gate and said good luck and I nodded
and carried my purple Qantas bag with my twenty-year-old
pyjamas and my Bible and my Kafka and I stood there, on the other
side of the wire and as she came to me with a smile, I crumpled and
fell to the baking concrete and wept, the first time I had shown
emotion in twenty years. Emotions don't exist in prison. Emotions
will get you sliced.

I wept. I was free. There was an endless sky. There was wind
and maybe, because there were dark clouds to the west, maybe it
would rain later today, for the first time in five years, making it
the worst since the drought that lasted, down south, from 1996 to
2010. And maybe, if it did, I would feel the rain on my face and I
could stand in the rain for as long as I wanted and I could have a
hot shower afterwards for as long as I wanted.

She knelt and gently pulled me up and held me and wiped my
tears with a tissue, with a smile and said:

'It's okay. I'm here.'

'I'm sorry. I don't mean to cry. I *promised* myself I would *not*
do this.'

'It's water on your cheeks. What do you want to do? I mean, we
have to get you to the parole officer to check in and we have to get
you to Westaway House before this time tomorrow, but ... what do
you want to do? Now?'

I was shuddering.

Nineteen years had come to this: a baking hot concrete slab out the front of scissor wire and the clap-clap sound of guards' boots as they walked back down to the building behind us.

I was vibrating, I was shimmering, free.

'I want –'

What *do* I want? I hadn't actually thought about this. The girl who went into prison is not the girl who stands before you now. I don't know what I want. I *would* have wanted a Whopper from Hungry Jack's in the mall, in the city where I used to hang in my danger-girl world, or I might have wanted a chocolate donut or maybe some lemon chicken from the Chinese down the road or a Meatlovers pizza covered with mozzarella, or maybe I would have wanted a trip to the beach or to Noosa where mum and dad took us when we were little.

'I would like to see your kids,' I said. 'I would like to hold them and say hello. Do they know about me?'

———

THEY DO NOW, after my husband and I had that fight after the kids bounced up the staircase with the photo album –

I'm *sorry*, okay? I am *sorry*. I thought I'd hidden it, but she is my fucking *sister*, okay –

And they asked me who was the girl in the photos, so many photos, as he strode off in that passive–aggressive way he has perfected and got a glass of wine from the fridge and put his hands on the breakfast bar and glared at me as he scoffed the wine, as I sat the kids down and said: Look, your mum has a sister.

Why haven't we met her!? We have an aunty! Yay! Where is she? Can she come over now? Will she bring us presents?

There was a pause. Robbie enforced it. I looked at him as he swilled the wine and turned his back on me with a *You do what you need to do ...*

'My sister's name is Jen ...'

'That's my name!'

'... and she is my older sister and she's been away for the past twenty years.'

'Where?! Has she been to Hollywood? She looks so pretty and she's got eyes like David Bowie. She must be a movie star. I bet she's been out with Vin Diesel.'

'He's gay.'

'He is not! Where did you hear that?'

'I read it.'

'Yeah, like John Travolta and Tom Cruise and Justin Bieber.'

'He is so not gay!'

'Girls! Stop. Your aunty will be visiting us soon and you can ask her about living in Hollywood, okay?'

'Yay!'

'Yeah. Dad?'

'Whatever,' said dad.

Later, as we always did, we made up and I pulled back on the erasure of the man I had sworn to love and I do, but sometimes I hate him.

—

'YOU SPENT THE past nineteen years in Hollywood,' said Anthea as we drove away from Wacol with my gaze firmly not on the rear-vision mirror. 'You went there at the age of eighteen and sought fame and fortune but didn't quite make it but it was a great time and now you're back.'

'How's Robbie?'

'He's good.'

'Are you okay with me staying tonight?'

'Yes, of course.'

'Because I can go straight to Westaway House.'

'No. It's fine.'

It wasn't. But I stayed silent. I didn't know how to argue with her. If someone lied to you in prison, you just hit them with a claw hammer or whatever was at hand. I'd lost the skill of traversing the waves, the undulations, the hidden meanings of a conversation. I was adrift, it suddenly occurred to me as we drove towards the city. The incarceration surrounded me with walls of black and white; I knew she was lying to me, I knew she did not want me to come back to her home and I knew, I knew, I knew but I was tired and I wanted to see her kids. I don't know any more how to embrace the conversation of the oblique battleground, if I ever did.

Anthea told me she had just come back from a field trip to Sri Lanka where she had observed a Banded Peacock Butterfly, which was, she told me, extremely rare. I had never really responded to her quaint obsession with butterflies which has become a very successful career for her. Sometimes, when she came to visit me in prison, she would bring a newly published journal on butterflies and I'd look at the pictures of the beautiful colours on their wings and wonder if she still caught them, let them die then pinned them onto a large board with a little historical bio under each of them, listing their Latin name. Or if, in the world of respect for all things animal, she just watched them as they flew about their natural habitat.

—

EVERYTHING HAD CHANGED and nothing had changed. As Anthea drove me into Brisbane city and then to Ascot, I saw new highways and buildings. What was once a huge paddock with horses, close to the airport, was now a modern block of offices, like something out of Silicon Valley with overpasses and six-lane highways, and there still was the Toombul shopping centre where I would hang out before I got Goth-cool, and as we drove through the streets of Ascot and Clayfield, but not past our old house, all the memories came rolling back. The McCubbin house, the Ord's house, the park where I would lie on the grass and stare up at the Norfolk pines, Miss Emily's house. I just sat there, in the passenger seat – we didn't say much as Anthea drove – and clasped my hands in my lap and fretted about meeting Robbie and got excited about meeting the girls. As we passed the old school I slammed shut my eyes for a moment and counted to fifteen and when I opened them again we were pulling into a driveway hidden behind a tall, thick hedge of golden cane palm trees lining the footpath. We made our way past a dry, wilted garden and a massive mango tree to one side and on the other the oldest-ever frangipani tree. Along the fences, bright red bougainvillea scattered flowers on the ground. They had survived the drought but the lawn was brown and dry. The house was a large Queenslander, all wood, with wide verandas, raised up off the ground on thick wooden poles, painted white.

'Here we are,' said Anthea.

'Wow. It's gorgeous.'

'Thanks,' she said a little awkwardly.

Our old home was two streets away. I knew she lived on the hill, I just hadn't realised it was so close to the past. 'Robbie's parents are just down the other end of the road, so he wanted a place nearby,' she said.

'And close to the girls' school. So, that's convenient,' I said.

I grabbed my Qantas bag and followed Anthea up the wooden steps onto the front balcony and then into the house. We stepped into a spacious open-plan area with a huge kitchen and dining space opening onto a lounge room with floor-to-ceiling windows that slid open to a back yard with a pool and another mango tree, its branches hanging low. But more than the view, I was taken aback by the wall of butterflies, all mounted in wooden cabinets and covering an entire wall.

'Wow.'

She laughed. 'Robbie says I shouldn't bring work home. I'll show you your room. It's downstairs.'

I followed her to another large area below, with four bedrooms and a games room for the girls with an on-the-wall flat-screen TV and couches and beanbags.

'Here,' she said as she opened the door to a room with a queen-size bed and turquoise-painted walls with a sliding door that led out to a Japanese-inspired garden. There was an ensuite, which was huge. Everything was huge. White carpet, soft pastels, silent.

I tried not to cry.

'Thanks Anthea,' I said.

'Hey sis, here's my suggestion: go have a shower or a bath and then maybe a sleep and there are some jammies hanging in the cupboard and when you're done and dusted, just come on up; Robbie will be home around five and the girls will be home about three-thirty. They're so looking forward to meeting you, the Hollywood diva, they'll be thrilled to know you're here. They'll absolutely want to cook you dinner.'

I cried.

She held me.

'It's okay. I love you.'

'Thanks. I love you too.'

She closed the door; softly. I ran a bath, I poured L'Occitane bath salts into the water and I immersed myself under the surface and closed my eyes and thought: When was the last time you did this? Like, driving with Anthea from Wacol, to here: When was the last time you were in the front seat of a car?

Nineteen years ago.

Thank God for my sister.

—

As I LAY in the bath, I let the killer slide out of me. He had inhabited me as if I had a demon inside, as if I were possessed. I had welcomed him in; I had to. He walked with me and dreamed with me. He whispered to me. He made me proud of the killings. He gave me a sense of purpose but all the while, as I was consumed by his dark evil, we knew it would be only for a certain period of time. Like all great lovers, my dance with the devil would come to an end and in the bath as I wallowed in the smell of French lavender, I purged him.

I climbed out of the bath and stood naked, letting the water run off me. I was innocent again. I was me again. He had served his purpose. He had allowed me to embrace those vile deaths, he had made a killer out of me, he allowed me to dream at night, of cutting men, he allowed me to become angry and vengeful, even though I was confused because it was always his anger and vengeance, not mine; I had to decipher him. But now he's gone.

Just a puddle of warm water on the floor. Soon to turn cold, soon to dry away and be no more.

I was Jen White again. Nineteen years later and I had returned to me.

I didn't even think about him. The actual killer. I had left him on the floor, a puddle of water.

I didn't even think, not then, that he might be somewhere, unfurling, like a monster awakening from a long and precious dark sleep.

—

'HELLO JENNIFER.'

He was home early. He was standing behind the kitchen bench with a glass of wine as I came upstairs. He was wearing a sleek dark suit with a red tie, unloosened around his neck, and his hair was slicked back with a lot of gel. He had squirrel eyes and a longish nose. Mum would have thought he was handsome, and I guess he was. He reminded me of a young Alain Delon, the French actor I fell in love with when I was thirteen after watching one of dad's VHS tapes, *Le Samouraï*, about a hit man who lived underground with a caged bird. But Alain Delon was charismatic and sexy. My sister's husband was not.

'Hi. Robbie?'

'That's me,' he replied. I hadn't noticed them before but the lounge area had many photos, not just on the fridge, but framed and on the walls, of Robbie and Anthea and the girls and my parents. They were holding the girls and laughing for the camera. Grandparents do that, making up for the lack of love and attention to their children, atoning with adoration to the next generation. Kids have no idea, just thinking that granny and grandpa do all the stuff that mum and dad won't.

Robbie wouldn't look me in the eye. He looked at my neck, my mouth, the top of my head. Never my eyes.

'Anthea has just gone out to pick up the girls.'

And then: 'It might rain.'

'We need rain,' I replied, like a moron.

'We do,' he replied, also like a moron.

I nodded and smiled and there was an awkward silence for about five seconds, until I said:

'Gorgeous house.'

'Yeah. We're happy with it.'

'So, you work in the city?'

'Yep.'

Another five seconds.

'You grew up around here, Anthea said,' I said.

'Yes.'

I think this was called being passive–aggressive. I've read about it, seen some people on TV who are like this. This was my first real-life experience with it, and I wasn't sure how to navigate it. In prison we just said what we meant and used fists or crowbars when language got too hard.

'Uh-huh. Okay. I just got out of prison. This morning.'

No answer but a lengthy gulp of his wine. He has not offered me any, although I could not take it anyway because drinking alcohol would break my parole.

'Yeah, I was there for nineteen years. It's kind of weird, you know, coming out after nineteen years and everything has changed. I'm so happy for my sister, for getting married, having this beautiful house, two adorable girls. I'll be leaving in the morning; it was very, very kind of you to let me stay here tonight – I'm a little disorientated, as you can imagine – a bit like walking on land for the first time in twenty years after being at sea, so yeah, I really appreciate it and by the time you get up in the morning I'll be gone.'

He nods. 'Good,' he says.

Good.

He says.

And we just stood there, him behind the kitchen bench with his wine and me at the top of the stairs in the pyjamas Anthea had left in the cupboard for me. To assuage any further awkwardness, he brought out his phone and began to play with it and I wandered over to the massive display of mounted butterflies and marvelled at the Costa Rica exhibit.

—

I HEARD THE sound of a car pulling up outside and doors slamming and the hammer-hammer of feet in school shoes as the two girls raced up the wooden steps and smashed open the front door and ran down the corridor into the lounge room with excitement and then stopped, staring at me, goggle-eyed, ignoring dad as mum breathlessly hurried up behind them, carrying school bags, which she dropped to the floor and went to Robbie and kissed his cheek (he didn't look her in the eye either despite the imploring look I saw in her eyes). The girls have not moved but kept staring at me and me back to them. Searching ourselves.

Freeze frame, broken by:

'Girls, this is your Aunty Jen.'

To which they shouted, 'Yay!' in unison and ran towards me like two rackets of energy and almost knocked me over as they encircled me and hugged me and kissed me and said:

'Tell us everything!'

Thank God for the girls.

Liar

I AM THIRTY-EIGHT YEARS OLD AND THIS WAS THE FIRST TIME I'd had a kid sit on my lap. It felt good. One perched on each knee and arms clinging to my neck, hanging on. I felt like a Mother Octopus.

'I was scared,' I said to Maxi and little Jen, who stared up at me in rapture while mum and dad did some silent angry things behind the breakfast bar. 'I arrived in Los Angeles wanting to be a movie star but with nowhere to go and no-one to see.'

'But you were pretty?' asked Maxi, who is eight.

'Yeah. Maybe. Everyone in Hollywood is pretty or ruggedly handsome, and I caught the bus and I went to Santa Monica Boulevard and found an apartment and began to see if I could get a screen test; but that's enough about me for the minute ... tell me about you.'

'Yay!'

'Maxi, you're the oldest, you go first, and little Jen, take my hand, darling, and hold it tight as we listen to what she has to say. Okay?'

'Yep, okay Aunty Jen,' as she gripped my hand and looked up, once more, into my eyes. Little Jen is six.

'I'm going to be like mum and open a zoo,' said Maxi. 'But not like an old-school zoo. Totally no bars or cages. Yuk. A wild park where animals of the savannah can roam freely. I know there are parks like this in Victoria and Kenya and San Diego but mine will be the best. I have already started a crowdfunding site to buy the land and then the animals,' she said with the essence of a green venture capitalist.

'There's an animal park in China where the lady got eaten by a lion,' said little Jen.

'No cars in my park,' said Maxi. 'I'm building a monorail.'

'Like in *Jurassic World*!' exclaimed little Jen.

'You are such a moron,' replied Maxi.

'I am not!'

'Jen. Tell me about you,' I said, trying to defuse them.

'I'm going to Hollywood like you,' she said with a puff of her chest. Maxi was about to ruin that dream, I could see, so I swiftly gave her a warning smile and she resisted the temptation.

Kids.

'Tell us more about *you*, Aunty Jen,' said Maxi.

'Well, it was very scary arriving in a new city and, you know, how many others want to be a movie star? But I persisted.'

'And?' asked little Jen.

'Did you meet Vin Diesel?' asks Maxi.

'I did.'

'You *did*?!'

'Yeah, we went out together one night; I had bumped into him one night. I had bumped, like really bumped into him,' as I bumped my fist gently into their legs – they hadn't moved, all legs and feet and kid-insect-itchy and I loved them, I wanted to take them home with me as they looked up into my eyes with focussed adoration and I'm sorry kids, I'm lying but it's a good story: 'We were at the Chateau Marmont – you heard of the Chateau?'

Shaking heads, a frown and sadness: 'No, sorry, Aunty Jen, never heard of the Chateau,' until, a beat later, little Jen says with excitement:

'Is that the place in Versailles?'

I laughed and hugged her and told her how clever she was to know about that; but, no, that was the Sun King's palace, Louis the fourteenth, who was the precursor to the French Revolution where –

'They chopped off Marie Antoinette's head!' shouted Maxi.

'With the ...' Pause here, little Jen concentrating hard. 'Gill-thing.'

'Guillotine,' I say. 'Clever girl!'

'What did they do with her head?' she asked, brows furrowed.

'I don't know, darling.'

'I reckon they fed it to dogs,' said Maxi.

I hugged them tighter. Off into the far distance of my vision, I could see Robbie drinking more and shaking his head and Anthea reaching out to him, both of them behind the breakfast bar, an almost-silent tableau of marital anger played out on the edge of the stage. I'll be gone early in the morning, okay. Please, just chill and let me, if you may, let me hold your girls and rollick with them.

'You crazy critters!' I said with an even tighter hug.

'We are *not* critters!' And they mock-punched me. 'Critters are alligators.'

'There are no alligators in Australia, you dummy,' said Maxi.

'There are.'

'There are not. You are *so* stupid!'

'I am not,' said little Jen.

Tears welled in her eyes. I had been there. Quite recently, when emotion swelled everything else. Like: That morning. Like: That evening. Like: Now. When the emotional assault was just a bit too much to bear.

That was little Jen. She was the one who said there were alligators in Australia and she was wrong but, you know, who gives a fuck and now that Maxi had begun an assault on her to verify the truth, I had to step in (off in the corner of my eye I could see that Anthea was getting furious with Robbie but stay focussed, Jen, stay and hang with the kids). 'Well, you know what, it doesn't matter if there *are* alligators or crocodiles or any sort of critter because there *might be*. Okay?'

Okay, Aunty Jen.

'The Chateau Marmont was, is, a very exclusive and expensive hotel and still exists, in Hollywood, and that's where very, very famous people go, like Marilyn Monroe or Clarke Gable or (*get with the twenty-first century, Jen!*) Justin Bieber or Kanye or Frank Ocean or Rhianna. It's known to be the most famous, and I was there one night. It's on Sunset; do you know about Sunset?'

They shake their heads solemnly. No. Sorry, Aunty Jen.

Don't even ask about Clarke Gable.

'Sunset is the biggest and most fantastic street in Hollywood, and I was there in the bar at the Chateau and this man comes up to me –'

'Kanye!'

'Jay Z!'

'And guess what?'

'What?!'

'Brad Pitt came in ...'

'*No!*'

'Yes.'

'I was sitting by the bar and he looked at me and I looked at him and –'

'*No!*'

'Yes. Ha ha,' And ...

(... and I miss Rosie; where is she?)

Anthea came across and joined us. 'Hello, big sister, telling tall tales about movie stars with your nieces – who seem to like you; maybe more than grumpy mum?' as she perched on the edge of a couch.

'Brad Pitt came across to me and said, Hey you wanna go out for dinner? I know this great Afghan place around the corner and my friend George might join us and I'd like to hear your life story.'

'Brad. Pitt. Ohmygod.'

I started to feel guilty; they are my nieces, after all. 'I'm making this up,' I said. 'I never got to meet Brad Pitt but I wish I did; he is so cool and a great actor. I just spent most of my time there going for auditions and working as a waitress.'

Their faces fell; maybe I should have stuck with the fantasy.

And then, to interrupt us all, the sounds of angry walking across the wooden floorboards and a door slamming. Robbie had gone. Stormed off. I hugged them a little tighter and noticed that their reaction suggested this might be a regular occurrence. Anthea gave us a forced smile as if nothing had happened.

'Hey! Let's cook up some fried chicken and chips. Yeah?'

—

AFTER THE GIRLS went to bed I did too, but I didn't sleep. I didn't want to pry into Anthea's life and I knew, anyway, that it was all about me. Who needs a convicted murderer as a sister-in-law?

I heard his car come into the driveway at about two and a dishevelled fumbling of keys by the front door and soon after, I heard their bedroom door open then close and some angry whispers and then silence.

At dawn I left. Walked down the hill and caught a bus to Southport on the Gold Coast, down the M1, where I eventually found the parole office and sat on a concrete block out the front of the building, staring at the closed Korean restaurants and watched the traffic roll by in both directions, waiting for it to open.

The Price is Right

I MADE GNOCCHI. THE GIRLS LIKE GNOCCHI. I ALWAYS MAKE
it from scratch, with potato, adding some parmesan. Just as we
were sitting down to eat, the phone rang, the land line and my
instant reaction was correct:

Ray.

'Hello? Karin speaking.'

'You didn't do what I asked.'

'Minister, I'm just about to sit down to eat dinner with my
family; can I call you back later tonight or in the morning?'

'Certainly, but before you go, let me tell you this: You released,
against my direct orders, a criminal back into the community.
A criminal who will most likely re-offend, and if you think
the parole board is above the rule of law, you are wrong. This
prisoner, this woman, needs to go back into prison now. And, as
your minister, I am instructing you to get her back into prison.
Tonight.'

'Minister, I cannot do that. She is out on parole and the only
legal way for her to be returned is if she breaches the terms of
parole. I cannot put her back into prison for no reason.'

'I want you to do it.'

'Minister, I cannot. We work and live by the rule of law and I
can only be beholden to that.'

'I need your loyalty.'

'Minister, I am loyal to the Office of the Attorney-General and
to the rule of law in Queensland.'

'But not to me? *Me*.'

'Minister, I must abide by the separation of powers. I am loyal
to the Office of the Attorney-General, the laws of Queensland, not
to a person.'

'I don't give a fuck about any of that. Get the bitch back behind bars within twenty-four hours or I will sack you, replace you and get a parole board that does what I say. On air you go.'

Girlie

'HEY, WASN'T THIS ONE OF YOUR EARLY CASES?' ASKED MY assistant, Simon, a young semi-bearded guy in his mid-twenties. Millennial. When I started, when the Force was still the Force rather than the Service, facial hair was not allowed. (But dyed-blonde hair was.)

He was showing me an internal memo that listed the people who had recently been released from prison. We get an update on this, no-one else, not the press, not the victims' families. Which can (and does) cause anger and distress. But the job of the parole board is narrow – and that's to protect the prisoner and ensure that they are afforded a smooth return into society.

Jen White had been released. Not before time. Nineteen years was a long stretch for Life. Life is not life; it's usually fifteen to seventeen years, especially when the prisoner was as young as her. Nineteen years is when memories and outrage have faded, as long as the prisoner can demonstrate remorse and won't be considered a danger to the community. Jen was a teenager when she went in. Now she is middle-aged. Society has had its justice.

Still, I wondered why she was released four years after she would have been eligible.

—

I BECAME POLICE Commissioner six years ago. The Dutchman sat in the chair for another nine years after Billy and I 'solved' the Slayer case. He was replaced by a rank-and-file guy named Jackson who fitted a standard profile: male, full white, a cop since seventeen, in his mid-fifties, safe, beloved by the conservative government. Jackson was fair, pleasant and did nothing. He died of a massive heart attack arriving for work one morning. There's a plaque for him downstairs, next to the main entrance.

Then me. By then I had climbed the ranks and worked in every department, even fisheries and livestock, and in each of those departments I learned a lot and I earned respect, up and down the line. Every department I worked in gave me a new understanding of crime within the fabric of our society and the people who dedicated their lives to it. I sound like I'm making a speech but I came to believe it. I had arrived at the top floor and was a deputy commissioner.

I had the ministerial tap, I did the interviews but, after all that, I was voted in by the rank and file. Me, a part-Asian woman. There have been female commissioners in the past but not in Queensland. And not many; you can count them on the fingers of one hand. And there has never been anyone who wasn't white with European genealogy. Most Asian cops are in the specialised Asian Crime Gang Squads, fighting the Triads or Yakuza or the Thai bikers. Up until recently the three other Asian cops were assigned to the Asian police liaison team, in Sunnybank, not far from where I grew up, without a weapon or powers of arrest.

Our government, with its second term narrowly won, is like so many all over the world now: schizophrenic. Half of its ministers are hard-core right-wing cowboys like our Attorney-General, and the other half are leftist greenies, all of whom have formed an alliance to hang on to power.

The Police Minister is progressive, and when she approached me to take on the job, she asked if I could lead the Service more deeply into this new century and, at the same time, try to drive out some of the old (and not so old) dinosaurs who liked to think that policing was about bashing suspects and trouncing around with teenage girls at the annual Schoolies week, showing off their guns from a balcony on the thirtieth floor of a Surfers' Paradise unit with three semi-naked underage girls hot on vodka and valium (the VV). That was the culture I agreed to manage.

There would have been some jockeying for the position between the other deputy commissioners and maybe even some of the assistant commissioners but remuneration was an issue, even though the wage is unspeakably massive for anyone, let alone a tattooed girl who grew up on the south side; over four hundred thousand dollars. Some of the top guys were leaving, off to other states that paid more. I didn't haggle. There comes a point where you wonder how much money you need. I'm still living in Hendra. Same house. I'll die there. I bought a new car, a black BMW, but I still look for the specials at Woolworths and never get a bottle of wine that costs more than ten dollars.

I went around to the deputy and assistant commissioners and told them I'd been asked to throw my hat into the ring and said I wasn't in the mood for a political fight; that sort of crap is best left to the politicians, and they all supported me. Expect for a couple of old guys who tried to white-ant me but the minister clobbered them with smiles and transfers to the far north.

It's a full-on job. I have more than eleven thousand police officers working for me, in a capital city of almost two and a half million in a state of almost five million people, in a vast area of almost two million square kilometres, from dirt-red outback specks of remote communities to the wild tropical jungles of the far north, crocodile-infested swamps and waterways, no roads and tens of thousands of square kilometres of dense unmapped rainforest, from the Torres Strait Islands, just south of Papua New Guinea to the glitter of Noosa with its thousand-dollar-a-night accommodation to the Florida-inspired glitz of the Gold Coast. I try to travel across all the regions and I try to be on top of all the crimes that confront us now, from cryptocurrency hacking of billions of dollars to a kid running a red light. From sex slavery to overfishing. From cattle duffing (yes, it still exists) to premeditated murder, from terrorist threats to hate crimes. I have a Facebook account, set on private, with a fake name and sixteen friends, all of them cousins from Hong Kong and Cairns. Damon is not one of them. (I haven't spoken to him since the frightful night in the Mexican cantina serving Indian food. It closed after six months. It's a Uyghur restaurant now.) In my role as Commissioner, I oversee official social media accounts on Facebook, Twitter, Instagram, YouTube and Pinterest as well our website and numerous blogs. Our FB page has almost a million likes.

I pressed 'like' under the guise of my FB pseudonym. The day after the minister had asked me to run all this.

—

THE CHINK THING was irrelevant. Surprisingly. We are good at finances, remember (which is a complete fallacy but who am I to disabuse their belief?) so the union welcomed me because there were some serious issues with overtime and penalty rates and some mad-crazy stuff inherited from Victoria where, the longer you work, like in Homicide, the less you get paid by the hour. The union reps, who are hard-core, old-fashioned guys from the eighties, signed off on me within seconds, as soon as I said I would fix this craziness and ensure all the staff are treated and remunerated fairly. Not to mention arguing for a pay rise, long overdue. Not to mention arguing for more cops on the street, despite the inevitable new focus of fighting crime with drones, facial recognition and sitting behind a computer. Governments were leaning towards online in the reporting of crime and pulling right back from personal interaction. It's all about money, but I told the minister that I would not be that type of commissioner. I said to her: 'I don't know if you have ever been burgled, but as the most common crime it's quite devastating for home owners to be so violated, and generally they want police to attend their premises, to talk to them and to reassure them something will be done about it.' In the future they will go to their computer, if it hasn't been stolen, tick a few boxes, write a quick summary and hopefully wait for an arrest. Not cool.

I, and I knew the troops felt the same, appreciate old-school human interaction.

My decades-long experience as a cop on the beat, in Homicide, Rape, Fraud, starting off as a scared constable behind the counter then on the footpath, to now, had, I hoped, earned their respect. Not like The Dutchman who was big with the online approach. I was in for the long haul and they knew it; they knew I had their backs.

I had long ago stopped dyeing my hair blonde. I think it was the night before I testified at Jen's trial. I am no longer, and have not been for years, a rebel.

Mum died a few years ago, still at me, right through her last days of cancer, to get married and have babies. I'm not a person who carries regret but I was sad she passed thinking she was a failure in not having delivered me into marriage. Her duty. Up to her last breath, I kept on apologising that I'd not done the right thing for her, steadfastly refusing to get married, let alone have a boyfriend, failing to be the filial daughter, the good daughter.

Almost right up to her last breath, she was still at me about Damon.

'You lost him, you silly girl; now he's a millionaire living in the Silk Valley.'

'Silicon Valley, mum.'

'You're in your forties now, you can *still* find a man, you are still pretty, even though you are getting to be middle-aged and then, when you hit fifty, it's all over, young lady. Then you'll be an old lady.'

I wept at her funeral and I have a photo of her on my desk, next to another one, a sun-drenched shot, framed, of me and my brother and dad at the barbecue with the chops and mum, dripping wet, laughing, as she ran out of the water, the shallows where she had drifted like a starfish. A passer-by took it. An old man with a fishing rod. Took the photo, gave the camera back to dad and walked away. I wonder if he's still alive and, if so, what happened to him.

—

THE SKIRT WAS the issue.

In conservative Queensland with a Service that, not so long ago, championed men like Billy, my skirt was a problem. The guys could deal with an Asian, but taking orders from a girlie, that was, even in the second decade of the twenty-first century, asking a lot. The last bastion of subjugation; would they allow themselves to be told what to do by a girl in a skirt?

I addressed it directly. With the help of the union, we had a meeting in Roma Street and I stood up in front of about three hundred cops and said:

'I have been asked by the government to be Commissioner and I want this job because I know I will be a good commissioner to you all and to all the officers who are not here today but who report to you.'

I was wearing a formal black suit. Below-the-knees skirt and black shirt and jacket. A man would not have to spend twenty minutes the night before deciding what to wear to address the rank and file. A man would put on a suit and tie. A woman stands in front of the mirror and worries. Too brash? Too girlie? Too confronting? At the knees? Below the knees? Certainly not above the knees. Below the knees equals matron. On the knees ... just a smidge below. High heels? Flats? Make-up? I like a bit of rouge but no rouge, not today. No perfume. I was up at five a.m. Clack-clack outside the house. Got to work at eight. And there we were, hello all, at nine-thirty in the morning ...

I strode to the podium. I was strong, forthright but not too strong or forthright because then I would be a bitch.

'You know who I am and I know all of you. I have been on the beat for over twenty-five years and you know I am tough and fair and honest. What you want to know is this: Will she get pregnant? Will she get emotional and cry? Will she go mad when it's that time of the month? If I have left anything out, let me know now.'

Stunned looks from three hundred men. *Did she just mention her period?*

It's a cliché but you could hear a pin drop. Not one of the guys was prepared to register what I had said, so they sat there, frozen. You know, that thing that's not to be spoken about. But I spoke about it, then, in front of three hundred men.

'In my campaign to earn your support, because there is no effing way I will take this job unless I have your support, I want you to consider my past history here in the Service and know that I will work to your best interests. And no, let's just prick [giggles] that balloon. I will not get pregnant. My lover is the Queensland Police Service and he can't impregnate me [laughter] and no, I will not get emotional and cry because I did that a long time ago, during some dreadful years that I would rather forget about which gave me an inner strength that led me here, to Roma Street, to the pride of the uniform in which we all stand in today, with that wall of steel we all need to survive and move forward. None of us will forget the past, right? Where we came from and what moulded us into who we are now, right? How that relates to us on the job and, especially how that relates to our partner and kids when we get home. As your Commissioner, I will ensure that you and those who work for you have the space and the respect to have a – don't you guys laugh at me – holistic world.'

No-one laughed.

'And the that-time-of-the-month thing?'

I paused. I had rehearsed this.

'Just don't come anywhere near me.'

I was in. I was embraced. Three hundred guys laughing and standing and applauding.

—

I GOT MANY congratulatory emails and a few cards through the mail.

Mum, how about this? Is this good enough? First female part-Asian Police Commissioner in Australia. Are you proud of me now? Will this substitute for being a left-over woman? Will this do? Mum?

One of the cards was from Billy.

Hello Girlie.

It's Billy Waterson here and I hear you win the prize and become Commissioner! Well done to you. I always knew you would go far and while I may not have been your best teacher in the world, I hope that some of the time we spent together helped you get to this great position. The boys all tell me you are a very, very good and wise person now and I don't doubt it.

Silly old me when I last saw you, saying you'll get nowhere and you know nothing and you being naïve. Oops. Sorry for that. One last word of advice, Commissioner. Don't ever retire. Jackson had it right. Die on the job.

Bye for now but if you ever feel like a beer and a T-Bone you know where to find your old mate Billy W.

x

—

BILLY AND JACKSON, my predecessor, were old friends. Billy was, through patronage from the top office, allowed to stay on the job way after he should have retired. He was old when I worked with him in Homicide. He was ancient when he was finally eased out. Well into his mid-seventies. I did it quietly and gently and authorised the payment for a celebration party at the Hilton Hotel, in honour of his long service. I heard back that he said nice words about me in his speech and even went so far as to mention my outstanding work as a young rookie Homicide cop with dyed-blonde hair and Doc Marten boots, on a case that probably none of them in the room would remember.

Was Jen guilty? The jury found her so. The killings stopped after we arrested her. Did Billy plant the knife? Sometimes crucial evidence turns up at the last minute. It happens. Would she have been found guilty if not for the knife? Who can say? That's an alternative world, the world that spins in the opposite direction. Not the real world.

Loyalty

'Thanks everyone, for being on this emergency call at such short notice. As I'm sure you're all aware, our minister, the Attorney-General, has expressed very strong reservations about the decision we took in paroling Jennifer White yesterday, and last night he instructed me – and us – to return Ms White to prison. Which, of course, we cannot do unless she breaks any of the circumstances of her parole. I have, as of this morning, been advised that she spent the evening with her sister and family and is currently attending a meeting with her parole officer in Southport on the Gold Coast. She will be going to Westaway House as agreed and then, I am told, will be looking for employment. Clearly there are no reasons for her to be returned to prison. I have made this clear to the minister again this morning, but he remains adamant that she must not remain in the community. I am holding this call to advise you of the situation and, quite frankly, to let you know that we might be sacked from the parole board in an illegal, in my opinion, and totally inappropriate measure.'

No-one spoke.

'Does anyone want to say anything?' I ask.

No-one said anything.

—

'Tell me she's back in prison.'

'Minister, as I told you last night, I cannot, nor can the police, put her back in prison unless she breaks the terms of parole.'

'You have until the end of the day.'

New World Order

'I WAS EXPECTING YOU YESTERDAY.'

'Yes. My apologies. My sister picked me up and I stayed with her in Brisbane. Because the terms of the agreement state that I have twenty-four hours to register with you in person and it's now about twenty hours since I was released, I thought that would be okay. Sorry, I didn't mean to cause any problems.'

He might have been thirty years old. Probably late twenties. He had pimples, and shuffled papers on his desk. This boy is my ruler for the next part of my life. He will ordain my future.

His name was Gary.

The parole and probation office had the sterile, functional atmosphere of government spaces that dehumanises a person the moment they step through their doors. Prison chic. Bland wall colours, bland lino on the floor, bland plastic seats. At least the police stations were old, brick, Victorian, crumbling, harbouring the crush of miseries for over a hundred years. They had personality. Not this place, located on the ground floor of a glass-and-concrete building jammed between a Korean restaurant and a second-hand bookstore boasting over one hundred thousand books. The main highway, which spanned the coastline, was a block away.

The street windows were frosted white. The small waiting room was designed for minimum comfort. An angry-looking woman sat behind a solid plexiglass wall. You tell her who you are and she tells you to wait on one of the plastic chairs until finally the door to the side opens and your name is called and you go into a small, lifeless room with no windows and are told what you cannot do.

No drinking, no smoking, no crime of any sort, not even jaywalking. Report in to the office once a week and we will also

284

do spot checks on you. Advise us when you secure a job and a new place to live; we must have your address and employment details at all times. If you begin a relationship with another person, you are legally obliged to reveal to them that you were convicted of three murders and spent twenty years in a correctional facility. If you fail to make this admission you will be in breach of your parole and, furthermore, we will check, we will visit this person at his, or her, place of work and ask if you have informed them of your past.

'Anything you don't understand?' asked Gary.

'No. Thanks. I understand everything.'

'Good. Day one: let's do a urine sample and make sure you're clean.'

The Crucible

NEWS, 'FAKE' OR OTHERWISE, REFLECTING A SET OF FACTS OR 'alternative facts' is no longer the domain, as it was in 1999, of print. At three minutes past five that afternoon, just in time for the free-to-air TV news broadcasts, which were still watched by over two million Australians every night, a series of tweets burst into the ether, from the Twitter account of the *Courier Mail*.

—

SLAYER KILLER RELEASED BACK
INTO COMMUNITY
Families of the three victims of notorious Slayer killer, Jennifer White, were shocked to learn today that the woman convicted of the 1999 crimes has been allowed to go free.
'Nobody told us,' said Lynne Gibney, the wife of the first victim, James Gibney. 'You would think the parole board would have advised us or maybe even asked us what our feelings were. It's a total disgrace.'
A spokesman for the Attorney-General declined to comment.

And, for those who didn't have Twitter or get their news online or log onto Facebook, the print version of the newspaper would lead with the story on page one, next morning.

—

'HELLO, IS THAT Karin Jones?'
'Yes,' I replied as I drove home, up the Ascot hill, navigating the narrow, winding roads, listening to the ABC news, which

286

had kicked off the evening bulletin with a weather alert that another dust storm might be heading in the direction of Brisbane, accompanied by the dire prediction from the Bureau that this drought, which had ravaged the state, decimating the lives and well-being of thousands of farmers, had no end in sight.

'Oh hi. I'm calling from the office of the Attorney-General. He has asked me to advise you that your position as president of the parole board has just been terminated, as have the roles of the other twenty-three appointees. This will be going out in a press release within the next five minutes. Thanks. Bye.'

—

'HELLO PREMIER, YOU wanted to see me?'

The Premier of Queensland scraped into power the second time around with the merest of votes and spent weeks cobbling together a coalition from her party with a right-wing group that was anti-abortion and anti-immigration and anti-welfare, and a left wing Green party which advocated the total opposite.

'Yes. Hello Ray. Oh, don't bother sitting down; this will only take a second. You will rescind the dismissal of the parole board and you will do it now, before the press release goes out. Go. Do it now. Thanks Ray. Good to see you.'

'But –'

'The controversy of a convicted killer being released on parole I can handle, as can the government. The outrage that would follow a return to a tyrant's redneck justice, I cannot. Nor can the government. Go. Now.'

—

BUT IT WAS out, the story. They both knew it could blow in either way. As he hurried down the corridor back to his office, to shout at his staff not to press 'Send', Ray comforted himself that it wouldn't be hard to stoke the flames of the mob. The burning torches of Salem were not so far away, and he would inflame them. That's what the people wanted. Her blood.

Giving it to them could do nothing but boost his popularity. Like every politician, even the stupid ones, he dreamed of being leader.

——

RAY CAME FROM an industrial farm in the north west of Queensland, one of those farms which had grown since the 1950s into a space of over a million acres and hundreds of thousands of cattle and, as a little boy, he would step onto the veranda of the homestead which his family had owned since 1835, and he would survey the three-sixty of land, flat and arid in all directions and think: this is, one day, going to be all mine and Cowboy Ray, when he was a teenager, driving in his white Holden ute, to woolshed parties with birds and blokes from around the area, from around a radius of at least three hundred K's, would scull tinnie after tinnie of XXXX and then grab a bird and drag her outside. If her boyfriend would try to stop him, Ray would punch him in the guts. He would drag her outside across the dirt and into the bushes well away from the woolshed, under the sky of bright stars because they were in the middle of nowhere with not a town, let alone a city, anywhere near by, and he would throw her onto the ground, deep into the heart of the darkness where no-one could see them and fuck her then ejaculate onto her face, which was his signature act, while her boyfriend was anxiously running through the bush calling out for her, knowing of Ray's reputation, knowing that she was being raped by him, also knowing that Ray was the most powerful man in the area and actually, more than that, the boss to pretty much all of them so if you spoke out against him, you would lose your livelihood so let's just drive home honey and not really talk about this, okay? Until one day a girl called Lil whacked *him* in the face as he tried to fuck her, when he was vulnerable, pulling out his dick and bashed his head onto the ground as she straddled him and said: you ever do that again, Ray, to me, to any girl, I swear I will fucking kill you.

And he never did. (That again.) Lil grew up to be a human rights advocate with the EU and Ray grew up to be the most redneck politician in Queensland.

It's Not Like We Meant It

BETTANY WENT INTO FINANCE, WORKING FOR HER DAD. Together they raise money for start-up apps. Clemmie studied architecture but only lasted two semesters. Bronnie went straight to Spain and drank and partied for a couple of years before coming home. Chloe was engaged before she finished Year 12, and Mary-Anne had an issue with smack but is now clean. Donna is the only one of them, twenty years later, who isn't married, living in Ascot, in a big house and driving a four-wheel drive and taking the kids to St Mary's where they all went and where their mums all went.

They meet every second Tuesday at a cafe with the best French cakes, in the hip Racecourse Road just down from the – you guessed it – racecourse where, in their late teens, they would go, dressed in expensive clothes and hats as if they were debs at the real Ascot.

With the Brisbane River at one end and the Doomben racetrack at the other, Racecourse Road is less than a kilometre in length and one of the most exclusive streets in Queensland. Double Bay in Sydney and Toorak Village in Melbourne come to mind. Knightsbridge and Fifth Avenue also come to mind. On both sides of the road, wedged into the footpaths, are ancient Poinciana trees towering into a canopy over parts of the street. Nearby is Ascot Hill where they all grew up and now live, where Jen and Anthea grew up, where Anthea and Robbie live, where Karin and Warren also live.

A rarefied world. Soft and rarely threatening. There were divorces, there were tantrums, there were lying boyfriends and cheating husbands but there always are, everywhere. Still, the women, some nineteen years after they left their girls' school, some nineteen years after they sat like startled rabbits in the witness box at the Brisbane Supreme Court and gave outlandish evidence, have managed to keep it together and exude a calm and a sense of control and confidence.

Normally when they gather on every second Tuesday they chat about the hubbies, the kids, the next holiday abroad and the local restaurant scene, especially if a new one has recently opened up to good reviews.

Not today.

'She's out,' said Clemmie.

They had all seen the front page of the newspaper; even in 2019, they still got the hard copy delivered every morning.

'Do you think she'll come after us?' asked Mary-Anne.

'I don't even remember what I said,' said Bronnie.

'Wasn't it you who said she drank blood?' asked Donna.

'I did *not* say that!'

'Someone did.'

'We might have lied a bit or, you know, maybe *embellished* a few details.'

'She stabbed me with her knife,' said Donna, who had dramatically lifted up her shirt and pushed down her skirt to reveal the stab wound, in the courtroom. The OJ moment. 'I have no regrets,' she added aggressively.

'Me neither,' said Bronnie. 'I think we should forget about it. And Mary-Anne? There's no way Jen's going to come after us. I mean, it wasn't us who sent her to prison for twenty years. It was her.'

The other women nodded and then reached for the menus and Clemmie decided that a bottle of Champagne might be in order, not to celebrate but to calm the rattles within.

'I mean, it's not like we meant her to go to prison. We were just telling it like it was,' she said.

'No-one can blame us,' added Mary-Anne.

'No, we did what we had to,' agreed Donna.

'I just feel sorry for her mum and dad,' said Clemmie. 'Imagine if your kid turned out to be a serial killer.'

'Or a mass shooter, like those kids in America. How often have you read about a mum coming home to find cops out the front of the house, telling her that their son has just shot dead half the classroom.'

'Jen and Anthea's mum was really nice. Whatever happened to her?' asked Donna.

If You Ever Come By Here

Hey Rosie, it's me. Guess what? I got out, I got parole, I did what you said and they let me go free. So, now I'm living on the Gold Coast, in Southport, which is pretty gronky but it's *so* nice to see the sky and be able to go for a walk along the water whenever I want to.

I got your postcard. The Seychelles? Are you kidding me? Wow. I had a teacher from there. Did I tell you that?

Anyway, so, you know, I know it's tough for us being out of there, and I know circumstances are different and you might have a guy or a girl who may adore you, but …

See me.

Yes?

Please.

I miss you.

Let me know. I've put my sister's address at the bottom of this missive. (You remember when you said to me: What the fuck is a missive? And I told you and then we lay in one another all afternoon?) I'm living in a halfway house, so a little bit on the move, but my little sister will pass on any letters or postcards.

Hope you are well. Love you. Sending this to your ma and pa's address. xx Jen xxxx

—

Dear Miss White,

Thank you for your letter to our daughter Rose, which we received last week. Rose often mentioned you and she was genuinely fond of you and we are sorry to inform you that she died eleven months ago. After leaving the prison she had some challenging times and even though she sent you that postcard from the Seychelles, she did not go there. She found the postcard in a second-hand shop. She drifted a little bit and fell in with some bad crowds and ended up in Humpty Doo, just outside of Darwin. She had plans to open a laundromat but this did not occur. She committed suicide. Normally we would not share these intimate details with another person because we are still grieving very much for the little girl we brought into this world, but we are because when we arrived at her unit in Humpty Doo, there was another postcard, this one from Malta, addressed to you but without a stamp and saying how much she missed you and loved you and wanted to see you once you had left the correctional facility and returned to normal life as she had. She also wrote that normal life was tragic and hard and she hoped you would have a better time in it than she was.

Yours sincerely,

Mr and Mrs Rogers (Parents)

PS Good luck.

—

A WEEK LATER I got another postcard from Rosie. From Goa. *Hey babe, I love u.* And a week after that I got another postcard, this one from Antananarivo – *Hey babe, come to Madagascar and join me on a trek. I love u xxx*

Both postmarked the same day of the card from the Seychelles. Her handwriting was faint, hard to read and I guess the post office took a bit of time to determine Anthea's Brisbane address. No return to sender. So, you know, they did their job, the post office, they got the cards to me eventually.

And then they stopped arriving.

—

THE BROADWATER IS an estuary of shallow water on the Gold Coast, spanning from the village of Main Beach with its glitzy restaurants and oyster bars and elderly haw-haw men in white suits and Camparis, up past the bustle of gronky Southport and then on, past the staid Labrador, and in its northern reaches you can look across to Stradbroke Island. I used to come here as a kid, with Anthea, sometimes on our own, sometimes with mum and dad.

The ocean, wild and choppy, feeds into it, a deep flow of water churning through an open channel and every dusk you can watch the fishing boats chugging out, returning at dawn. Over there, on that side of the Broadwater is a narrow spit of land with the Palazzo Versace Hotel and Sea World and a Sheraton with Bentleys parked out the front, and, further up, on this side of the Broadwater, is a wild area of stunted trees in sandy hills, and just past them is the Pacific Ocean, where waves smash onto the beach. Back on the other side, across the estuary and along the Gold Coast Highway, is a beautifully crafted park where kids play and mums and dads have picnics and healthy people do tai chi at dawn and poetry readings in the evening. Pelicans swoop and the occasional houseboat sits on the water.

I walked along the water's edge. The grass, which should have been green, was curled up and dead. There were clouds in the sky but it wasn't going to rain. People had begun to ignore the promise of rain clouds, knowing they would drift away, leaving the ground hot and dry, like it was yesterday, like it would be tomorrow.

She was gone, really gone – dead. It's easy to say and write, but harder is that feeling when you wake in the morning and reach across to her and she is in cinders and will never come back to you and all you have are memories, cinders of a past life when you held one another and laughed and argued and felt the swell of flesh and for all of that: you too are dead.

With her death, you also died. But.

You know: *c'est la vie*. Which, I guess, is the only way I can get through this.

Sometimes I wonder if I will meet her, on the other side.

I am free, out of jail, nineteen years later. No matter how alluring are the tentacles of grief, as if tempting me to sink into the black where abrogation of life is without stress and anguish, no matter how easy it would be for me to just end it all now, I have a new life to commence and I've been waiting for nineteen years, for me to return. And here I am. No Rosie. Just me.

Outed

ANTHEA HAD PREPARED ME FOR MY ENTRANCE INTO 2019. Orientation, she called it. Like arriving in a new country. A lot of it I already knew, having watched TV and read journals and books. Everything from AI, China's quantum computing, facial recognition, 3D printing, #MeToo, Donald Trump, Alexandria Ocasio-Cortez, the likelihood of WW3, last year's Man Booker Prize winner and, because it was my crazy sister, which butterflies would be extinct by 2030. I had been tutored well. Or so I thought. I knew what to expect. Or so I thought. Little things, like the bath, like walking along the street, deciding on the spur of a moment to take a midnight stroll – they were the most profound. Little things were the things I didn't forget.

What I wasn't prepared for was being thrust into the public arena again, through the tabloid press, again.

I had devoted so much time to the killer's profile, the victims and how they died, and on the wonderful fragments of freedom I would taste, that it didn't occur to me the press would come after The Slayer again. Call me naïve.

And, like the night I stood with my Qantas bag, watching the police drive up the hill towards me, knowing that the end of that journey would be a conviction and prison because nothing else would placate the anxious public, I knew now that the end-point to the front-page news about my release would not be a lifetime of scrutiny, it would, after pressure on the government, be a new law enacted to put me behind bars again, once and for all. This time, Life would mean life.

There was also something else, something that had bothered me as I prepared to be paroled. I kept this to myself, my own private fear.

That the real killer would take advantage of my release and kill again.

I am no longer him. I am now his perfect alibi.

And now that the newspaper has outed me, he too will have thought through to the end-game, knowing that his window of opportunity is narrow.

But I have an advantage. For now. To make his kill, he needs to know where I am. No good striking out in the Botanic Gardens again, repeating The Slayer's – Jen White's – signature of the head-fold, torn mouth, tooth removal and the Taranis etching unless he can be sure I cannot account for my whereabouts. It will be a crisis if it's discovered that I was seen by the occupants of Westaway House at the time of his killing.

So, he needs to be close. He needs to observe me, follow me and determine my routine, not that I have much of one at the moment. But he could lure me out into a place where there are no CCTV cameras. Be vigilant, Jen. In the meantime, I have the upper hand. The newspaper has outed me as being released and free to walk the streets of Queensland but they don't know I'm living on the Gold Coast.

Not yet.

He can't do anything until he knows where I live.

He will be looking for me. He'll find me. The media will find me first and he'll follow.

It's only a matter of time.

Fairy Dust

I HAD TO GET A JOB. IT WAS EXPECTED, BY GARY MY PAROLE officer, that I would find employment so, at the age of thirty-seven I did what all first-time job-seekers do: I went to McDonald's.

I went to the one closest to Westaway House, in Southport, across the road from the Coast Guard and the Broadwater and off in the far distance, on the other side of the expanse of calm water, the channel to the sea, churning and deep green.

The manager might have been twenty, in what was becoming a depressing series of men a decade or two younger than me in roles requiring me to listen with respect and jump to their cues. He took me upstairs to a break room where the chairs were yellow and red and a TV repeat-screened an animation on how to be the best employee at McDonald's.

'Tell me about you,' he said.

'I've been in Los Angeles for the past twenty years, trying to make it as an actor and I just returned home last week.' Did I just break my parole by lying?

'Great. And so, were you looking at a long-term future with McDonald's?'

'Um. I hadn't really thought about that. I was just looking for a job. But, yeah, of course.'

'Short-term future, then.'

'Not quite sure.'

He tapped into his iPad.

'I like your eyes.'

Okay. Thanks. Do I have a job?

'Here's the thing ...'

Here's the thing:

'In a few years' time, there won't be any jobs here. Not for humans. It will be all AI robots who look like humans. Not yet. Not for a few years but that's the future, so if you want a future with McDonald's, you need to take that into consideration. That said, Jen, we do have jobs, now, part-time, and if you're interested, even though you are a lot older than the usual McDonald's employee, we can make this happen. Because you're still very pretty.'

Still.

Very pretty.

I'm not sure if it was the ageist or the sexist comment that threw me. The last time I was sitting across from a young guy, I was seventeen and we were flirting, talking about going to the movies. I wasn't equipped for this. This had not been part of Anthea's 2019 orientation. I felt as though I had suddenly been transported from that seventeen-year-old girl to this middle-aged woman in a millisecond and that those intervening years were catching up to me in slow-motion waves. I felt disorientated and, for the first time, I felt my age. For the first time, sitting on a yellow plastic chair being interviewed by a boy for a stupid job at McDonald's, I felt those twenty years and, as much as December 1999 had just bunched up against March 2019 with nary a gap between, those twenty years also felt like twenty thousand.

I resisted the urge to punch him, which would have been a breach of my parole. Instead I smiled, got out of the yellow chair and left.

—

I WENT TO Bunnings and said to the employment officer, a guy in his sixties with old-fashioned tatts down his arms: 'I worked for Bunnings for a week when I was seventeen and I was wondering if there might be any job vacancies.'

'Okay,' he replied uncertainly, as he looked at me. There was a pause, which I broke:

'I've been in prison for the past nineteen years and I just got out and I desperately want to start a new life and I will work hard and I will do anything – serve coffee, sweep the floors, stock the shelves – and I will always be on time and never be sick. I know the robots are coming and in a few years' time there won't be people like me even asking for a job because those jobs won't exist anymore, so if you could consider me, that would be great.'

'Do you want to tell me why you went to prison?'

We were standing in the timber section, planks of wood in all sizes on either side of us, a faint smell of pine and resin. 'No,' I replied.

'Nineteen years; I can guess. All right. Give me the name of your parole officer and I'll call him and say you've just been hired. Start tomorrow.'

'I'll start now if you want.'

And I did. He showed me where to clock on and off and gave me a uniform, which I put on excitedly and proceeded to work a shift that made me feel more independent than any time in my life. I was earning a wage. I could pay my bills. I could go shopping without having to ask Anthea for yet another loan.

—

INSTEAD OF CATCHING a bus, I walked the five-kilometre journey back to Westaway House. It was close to the Broadwater, back a street from the Gold Coast Highway; three modern two-storey buildings and one old, tumble-down wooden Queenslander, all joined together and hidden behind a tall brick fence with a sign out the front advertising weekly and monthly rates. The sort of place you'd expect to see a sign excitedly promoting colour TV. Inside were dark, narrow corridors and tiny rooms, smaller than my prison cell. Single bed and a wooden table. There were common rooms in each of the three buildings and open courtyards, concrete with a thousand tufts of grass and weeds and too-thin men and women stretched out in the heat in the door-stops or by the fence praying for a cool breeze. I'd only been there a day but I'd already counted four visits by the police. Nearly all of my neighbours were, like me, ex-cons and nearly all, unlike me, had a meth problem. Nobody slept. I don't think any of the rooms had been cleaned since the 1970s.

But I was free to come and go.

It was going to be a good hour's walk from Bunnings to Westaway, along the highway. Under a Caspian sky I walked past the neon of the Harbourtown shopping centre, smelling the sizzle of Big Macs and Whoppers, Indian food and tacos, hearing the bang-bang of death metal and rap as cars zoomed past me, headlights on, with the occasional *Hey sister!* I was Dorothy, off to meet the Wizard. Imagining myself lifted up into the sky, like she was. Off into the south-west were shots of lightning, towards the ocean, with the occasional sprinkle of rain but the heat was fierce and the drought had yet to break. There was a fairy dust of sunbeam before the twilight came and then it was finally dark, the highway lit with cars going in both directions, this way and that, as the overhead street lights, dull yellow at first and then blizzard white, zapped on.

I felt someone. I turned around to see. There it was. A blue Mazda, driving slowly behind me.

I was being followed.

The Ex-Con

I ASSUMED THE RENTAL COMPANY HAD RUN OUT OF WHITE vehicles, because a white Mazda would have been hard to spot due to its ubiquity. The blue car went past me on the highway then about three minutes later, it passed me again and then I saw it parked up ahead at a juncture in the road so, I guessed, as to determine which way I would go.

I went into a Sushi Train across the road from a Centrelink office next to an abandoned car lot where two lanky girls who looked South Sudanese were playing makeshift hockey and sat and grabbed the cheapest plate. Through the windows, I could see the blue Mazda, about thirty metres from me, engine on, windows dark.

This was faster than I'd expected. Maybe it's me and 2019. Anthea told me that everything goes in rapid speed now. Think dial-up to wireless and apply that to everything you do and everything in life, is what she said. Not that I quite knew what she was talking about. I had last used the internet when I seventeen, the night of December 31, 1999, the night of Y2K.

The thing about Mister Blue Mazda, who is undoubtedly the media, is that he doesn't know it's definitely me and if he takes a photo and says this is The Slayer twenty years on but it's not, he and the newspaper will go down into defamation hell. He probably knows I am staying at Westaway House and he will follow me there and do some more research to ensure he is correct before he zooms back to his computer and sends through the confirmation.

I couldn't call Anthea. She was over an hour's drive away and she had her own life. I didn't have any friends, any support. I couldn't leave the Sushi Train and walk around in circles for the rest of the night with a journo trailing me. I took out my phone, which Anthea had given me after I came out and dialled.

'Bruce, hi, it's Jen, you know, from today, at the store.'

'Where are you?'

'I'm at a Sushi Train across the road from the Centrelink on the highway, just down, like a couple of Ks from the store.'

'Don't move. I'll be there in five.'

—

ON MY WAY out of Bunnings, after my short shift finished, the old guy with tatts who had hired me came up to me and I thought *Here we go* but no, he gave me a slip of paper with a phone number scribbled onto it and he said:

'Comin' out is tough. I know who you are. I did the research. I'm okay with all that because it seems to me you were fitted up big time and badly. I did fifteen and I ain't telling you neither. Here's my number if you ever need to reach out, like AA, you know, we gotta protect ourselves.'

—

'THAT'S THE BLUE Mazda?' asked Bruce as we pulled out of the side road.

'Yes. It's been following me since I left the store.'

'It's the press.'

'Yeah, I think so.'

'I'll lose them,' he said as he drove out of the car park like we were in a Hollywood movie and zoomed up the highway, back towards Harbourtown as the blue Mazda came out behind us and tried to catch up. Moments later, in the dark of headlights and a red light up ahead, he spun the car in an alarming one-eighty and drove over the concrete median strip and high-tailed down the opposite laneway, taking a quick left into the street next to the abandoned car park then a right, then a left, then a right, then another right. Then he stopped and stared into the rear-vision mirror. I was gripping the edge of my seat.

'I used to be the getaway guy. Best of times, until I got done. Let's go home, back to my place.'

—

I DIDN'T SLEEP. I heard the surf.

Bruce lived above an empty garage, at the end of a courtyard looking across to the back of a Thai massage parlour, The Healthy Dragon, which fronted the hectic four-lane Gold Coast Highway. From his balcony I could glimpse the Broadwater. The Thai girls ate noodles in the courtyard below, smoking and drinking Coke as he and I ate pizza from Vinnie's Italian around the corner. I felt like I was on stage, in a Tennessee Williams play.

We didn't talk. We just ate. I was so tired, and eventually he said: You take the bed, I'll take the couch, and I said: No, you take the bed and I'll take the couch, and we argued about it for a while until finally I won and lay on the couch with a doona on top of me, listening to his snoring and thinking about the person who helped destroy my life. The person I would be meeting in the morning.

The Slow Circling of Ravens

As I left the courtyard one of the Thai girls was hanging out washing; it was six a.m. and already over thirty degrees. Total blue sky. Great for tourists but a symbol of continuing dread for locals, especially the few farmers left on the land.

I saw her as I approached the vegan breakfast place on the highway, with a view across the water. She was there, waiting, her long black hair pulled back and wearing sunglasses, I suppose because she was one of the most recognisable women in the state. While I'd carried the days of my age into my face, she had not. She must have been in her mid-forties but she didn't look any different from the last time I saw her, when she avoided my gaze during the trial.

I sat down on the other side of the black marble table. A small vase of rosemary sprigs between us.

'Hi.'

'Hi. I'm Lara.'

'Yeah. I know. I don't think I could forget you. Thanks for meeting. I didn't expect to see you,' I said.

'Why did it take you so long to make parole?'

'I had an issue with my guilt, and thus I had an issue with atonement, and thus I got knocked back and it took me a rather long time to find out that I was in fact guilty. Once that happened I found atonement like one might find God. Why did you agree to meet with me?'

'Let's get a couple of things out of the way first and before we do that, can you stand up for me and also put your bag on the table.'

I knew this was coming. 'Sure,' I said. After all she is the Police Commissioner.

I stood. She hugged me like we were great friends in the collusion of a secret, like we were sisters who hadn't seen one another for decades, like there was nothing antagonistic between us, nothing that might be a problem, an issue, like we were on stage together, dancing a slow dance and she put her arms around me and whispered, 'This will only take a second,' and she patted me down as if we were now lovers, her face so close to mine, I could feel her breath – inhale, exhale – of cinnamon and she said, 'You know why I'm doing this, right?' and I said, 'Yep,' and then, when she was confident there was no phone on me with a recording device, she stepped back and said, 'Thanks Jen,' and then she rummaged through my bag and found my phone and said, 'Can you turn that off for me and would you mind removing the battery as well? Thanks Jen.'

Twenty years ago she had also invaded my personal space by escorting me out of our house, her hand tightly gripping my arm, but I guess it would be impolite to mention that now. Back then, back when she got up close and personal, her breath smelt of vodka.

Our waiter's name was Herod. 'Hello, beautiful people, what can I get for you this morning?'

I got black coffee, short, she got black coffee, long.

'We have the most super Thai omelette on spelt bread, ladies ... the best breakfast on the Gold Coast.' He spoke with a German accent, or maybe it was French. He was good looking. He made me wonder if I would ever have another partner and, for the merest of moments I had a flash of Rosie's smile.

'Why did you call me?' she asked.

'Why did you pick up?' I asked.

'You first,' she said.

'Okay,' I said. 'You sure you don't want the Thai omelette on spelt? It's my shout. I just got a job. My first real job ever,' I said.

She smiled. 'You must be excited.'

'The little things,' I replied.

'So,' she said.

'So,' I said and took a deep breath. 'He's going to do it again. Now that the press have revealed that I'm on parole. He's got a perfect opportunity to kill again and he will. That's what they do. Kill and keep killing. The only thing that's more important to them than killing is survival and while my jail-time forced him to stop, so you wouldn't go looking for him, re-opening the case, my release allows him the opportunity to do it again. That's why I called you. Because wherever he is, whoever he is, he is planning to do it again. I will take the fall. It's a perfect crime. He'll get away with it.'

There was a long moment. She didn't move but then took off her dark glasses and said:

'What makes you think that?'

'I'm innocent. You know that, right?'

'I can't make any comment on what the court decided; that's not up to me.'

'Not in your purview.'

She smiled, looked away for a moment, then back at me. 'At first, when I heard the name, I thought Kafka might have been your boyfriend.'

I laughed.

'I cannot, and the police cannot, respond or act upon crimes that *may* happen.'

'What are you reading?' I asked.

'Huh?' she asked, thrown askance.

'What book is by your bed?'

'*The Crippled Tree*,' she replied.

'Han Suyin.'

Surprised, she nodded. And then, because I knew the book and the story of Han Suyin, she became embarrassed.

'It's not because ...'

—

I LEFT THE rest of the sentence hanging. None of her business, but she just saw through me.

This all came about after mum died. When I felt an obligation to understand, come to terms with, to rationalise, my mixed-race heritage and, in particular, my Chinese sensibility.

—

'No,' I QUICKLY said, 'it's not because Han Suyin was half-Chinese and half-Western – it was her mum, yeah, she was Flemish? – and that she wrote about the agony of being neither here nor there, in one place or the other or ... I'm sorry, I'm so sorry. I can be such a smartarse and pretentious and please forgive me. I love Han Suyin, especially *A Many-Splendoured Thing*; I have read all of her works and are you sure you don't want the Thai omelette on spelt?'

—

I HAD TURNED my back on Chink-World, which is what I called it in times of self-hate or maybe it was self-pity. After mum died I felt guilty, that I really had been a bad daughter. That she deserved more. The left-over marriage thing was really just the pointy end to her protective need towards me. She was only being what a mum should be, striving for what she thought was best for her daughter. And I stomped on it.

So, in an effort to atone by actually reading about her values, what shaped and formed her, I picked up a book by another part Asian woman.

—

WE ORDERED THE Thai omelette on spelt and Herod was very happy and I said, in an effort to deflect the awkwardness between us: 'So, Herod, if you don't mind me asking, where is that accent from? France?'

'Oh no, I am from the Seychelles in the Indian Ocean.'

We both did a double-take as we each had a weird but flimsy connection to that speck of an island. Which I discovered much later.

—

'WHAT MAKES YOU so convinced there will be more killings like the ones you were convicted of?' she asked in a diplomatic skating-around of my guilt or innocence.

'The same reason that made you drive down from Brisbane to see me. Because he can, before they put me back in prison.'

'You're not going back to prison.'

'I am. Unless we catch him first.'

Widows

'SHOW 'EM IN,' SAID COWBOY RAY.

They had walked through the main entrance, a little nervous, despite the angry righteousness of their cause. Parliament House in Brisbane, like all such establishments of power and law, was quiet. That's the first thing Lynne and Jacinta and Becky noticed as they walked down the thick-carpeted corridors to the office of the Attorney-General, being led by his advisor, a slightly nervous guy in his late twenties wearing an ill-fitting light grey suit. 'Follow me,' he had said and they did, almost tippy-toeing along the corridors, every now and then catching a glimpse into an office where people sat staring at screens or talking in hushed whispers. This is government? they thought, as the advisor led them around a corner and said, 'Wait just one sec,' and vanished into an office. They could hear muffled voices and he then re-appeared and said, 'the minister will see you now,' holding open the door to Cowboy Ray.

He stood up from his desk and greeted them. He had a massive beer gut and a shock of red hair and wore cowboy boots, white moleskin pants and a blue-and-white striped shirt. Lynne, who grew up in Ararat, in the Victorian Western District, who went to parties at wool sheds, where all the boys would turn up in their white Holden utes, dressed exactly like this, as if it were a bloke uniform, almost recoiled but she, and the others, had things to discuss and get done.

'Lynne, Jacinta, Becky, I hope you don't mind me calling you by your first names, have a seat. Do you want some tea or coffee or water?'

No thanks, we're all good, they said as they sat on the couch.

He left the desk and dragged a chair to sit in front of them with a sudden look of despair. 'I got your letter and I want to thank you for expressing your grave concern about the recent release of Jennifer White and your anger at the decision made by my parole board. I share your concern and your anger and it embarrasses me that the parole board made such a terrible decision. Against my instructions, I might add.'

'She should be back in jail. She should never have been released,' Jacinta said a little more loudly than any of them expected.

'I agree,' he replied.

'That's not good enough,' said Becky.

'I agree,' he replied.

Whereupon there was a moment of uncertainty; these women, these widows had come to the meeting expecting a fight and no gain.

He leant forward and said, 'What say we hold a press conference where you three ladies can express your feelings? What do you think about that?'

And all three said: 'Yes.'

'On air you go, then!' he said and turned to his advisor, who had been sitting in the back of the office, discreetly, listening to his boss while swiping on Tinder. 'Jimbo! Make it happen and make it happen within the next hour.'

Jimbo ran off and Cowboy Ray smiled at the three ladies and said: 'The Premier is overseas at the moment, in Guangzhou leading a local business delegation to explore investment into Queensland, so we won't need to inform her.'

The Gunfighter
or A Serial Killer's
Mid-Life Crisis

I'VE SEEN THEM.

I know who they are. The widows. It's not like I have been stalking them with a morbid curiosity about how they are coping or a morbid pleasure in seeing their grief and the grief of their children – grown up now with kids of their own, the grand-bubbies of my fears – no, nothing like that, just a bump or two in the supermarket whenever I happen to be in the same area that they live in, and happen to be in the Coles or the Woolies or the bottle shop, getting a bottle of vino or maybe a little vermouth or some voddy. In the aisle of the supermarket I occasionally see them with their trolley full of grief and sadness. I never let them see me.

Never, ever.

Ever, never.

Stay hidden, stay in the shadows, like I did in 1999 and on that last aoife kill in the year of our Lord 2000 on the dawning of the new millennium.

Hello.

Did you forget me?

Were you waiting for me to return? Do you miss my head-folds? What do you think might have happened to me? Since we last spent some time together, that time I took Miss Homeless and rolled her up in big industrial chains, and dragged her body to the edge of the river and threw her in.

That was nineteen years ago and remember how we signed off? Back then?

Of course you do.

We agreed to meet up again. Now. Well, the now being defined by when Jen was to be released on bail. Free in the world again. Free for me to kill again, to pin yet another massive and climactic kill – the end of a career, a killer's swan-song – on her.

Jen.

Free on parole and she kills again. This kill even more audacious than the last three, the trio of summer, ninety-nine.

That's how we signed off. With me vowing to return to the blade, to Him, Taranis and Ogmios, those twin gods who I adored and followed and spoke to, every day, back in the days when blood and pain were my beautiful friends.

I've told you about my dad before. Remember? How he would take me to the Ekka and how I would get an endorphin rush on the rides. How I could relate that rush to the heart of my soul to the killing of the fears, that special trio in November ninety-nine. Punctuated by two aoifes. The first one, years earlier and the last one, Miss Homeless.

My dad also used to take me to the movies, when he bothered to notice me. We can't really call him the best dad in the history of the world, but he never hurt me.

Well, only once.

One night dad took me to a movie in a movie theatre in Brisbane which is long gone now because it used to screen old black and white movies and on this night we went to see an old movie called *The Gunfighter*, starring Gregory Peck, who played a very famous and very dangerous cowboy gunman called Johnny Ringo and he made his fame at the O.K. Corral. The movie had him as an older man and his fame preceded him. Everywhere he went there would be a young buck, eager to do a quick draw on him. But you see, and this was the point of the movie, he wanted to retire. He was over it. He'd done his killings in his youth and now he just wanted to settle down.

He gets killed in the end. Sorry: spoiler alert.

That's me. The Gunfighter.

I'm sort-of over it. I still have the blades, sharp and shiny, but they are hidden and I haven't actually touched them, stroked them, let them pierce me, for a long time.

It's twenty years on and I am twenty years different. Ogmios and Taranis are for babies. Did I really believe in that? I've still got the trophies but I hardly ever look at them. They are from another life. Another me. A very immature me.

You know – we do some fucked-up stuff when we are young. That's what it's all about, being young: fucking up. Or, that's what it should be about.

I have different priorities now. It's not like my bones are aching or that I am old and fat and short of breath; I look after myself. I could jump a fear like I did twenty years ago, no problems at all.

It's just: could I be bothered?

I was a little worried about this – about an ebbing of desire – about ten years ago. Stuff happened and I started to wonder when the fuck will she get out and how long does a person have to wait to do something which was super-exciting in 2000 but maybe not so much anymore.

And the widows.

At first I just laughed at them and wondered if I could break into their houses and chop them up, pubis to neck and chop up their kids, into quarters, like they did in ancient England and Viking-Land. Scatter their limbs to the dogs of Blood River.

Then they started to haunt me with their canyons of gloom. I caused that. Maybe it wasn't so cool after all. I keep guilt at bay. I'm strong in that regard. I won't succumb for, to do so, will invite an encirclement of monsters that I don't think I could corral.

So I had moved on and let the past float back into the past, like tendrils of mist.

—

BUT.

—

I DID ENJOY it. Didn't I? I'm feeling like the drinker who hasn't tasted alcohol in twenty years. Self-enforced abstinence.

When you go to AA, you're told that even though you may have stopped drinking – he or she or it, being alcohol – is always there, a shadow to your every day and he or she or it, being alcohol, is just behind you, doing push-ups. Waiting for you to turn around and embrace yourself again.

Have I ended up like one of those married couples who sit over dinner in a restaurant not talking to one another? Have I let twenty years of waiting turn me into a boring husk? Has the waiting emasculated me? It makes sense, doesn't it? That after twenty years of waiting, you discover you're no longer as interested as you thought you'd be. You're like an old guy on the golf course or sitting on the deck of a cruise ship.

I guess the question is, then, should I leave my blades where they are?

Or should I not?

Should I revisit the buzz and thrill of the blood-spurt and the ride to the victim's last breath, sitting astride them, their face grinning up at me, their eyes fluttering to death as I grind myself into them as if we are entwined like lovers, me giving them the embrace of death? Or should I let it go, as a fond and warm memory of the person I once was?

Guangzhou

ALTHOUGH SHE HAD A SLENDER MAJORITY IN GOVERNMENT, the Premier decided it was important to take local business leaders on an official trip to China, even though one of her advisors warned her that, while away, as these things often occur, there might be a coup against her led by one of the maniac rednecks with whom she had formed her fragile coalition. The Premier heard the warning but, you know, what was she going to do? Stay there, in Brisbane, to ward off any threat, instead of doing her job by enticing Chinese investment?

She went and took thirty-five leaders of business and they arrived in Guangzhou where, during their first official state meeting, a breakfast, one of her advisors came up to her with a phone and direct live-line link via WeChat to a feed and said:

'You better look at this.'

—

'GOOD MORNING, MY name is Ray Conway and I am the Attorney-General of our great state of Queensland and I would like to introduce you all to three very strong ladies, strong because their husbands were taken, in the most horrific of killings, twenty years ago by a young woman, Jennifer White, also known as The Slayer. Not only did Jennifer White saw off the heads of her victims, she sucked their blood like Dracula. This beast of a killer has just been released back into the community and it is my wish that she be returned to prison immediately. I expressed this wish to the parole board but they ignored me because, it seems, they would rather have a dangerous killer on the streets than listen to the Attorney-General. I have expressed this wish to our great Premier, who is currently out of the country, in China, but she has not yielded to my concerns. Jennifer White is a grave danger to men, and women, and kids, in our state. Once a killer, always a killer. She needs to be returned to prison immediately.'

He stepped back, took a breath, surveyed the media and tried not to smile.

'Okay, that's enough from me. Now I'm going to hand over to three of the bravest women I have ever met: Lynne, Jacinta and Becky. They will explain why they also believe that this convicted murderer needs to be incarcerated for the rest of her natural life.'

Whereupon the Premier felt a deep sinking feeling. Ray had, in the most grotesque way, appealed to the mob, all of whom would rise up in anger and ignorance, and condemn her. If she did not act in response to appease this angry, ignorant mob whose drumming whispers were now, right now, becoming the banshee cries of retribution, she would be overthrown by the end of the week. And in politics, one's ethics don't mean shit when it comes to survival.

Silence in Salem

WARREN SAID TO ME: IT'LL BE FINE.

I said back to him: No, I don't think it will be. I'll be sacked by nightfall.

And I was.

Sacked by lunchtime.

—

WARREN HAS A long-standing appointment tonight. It's important for him, catching up with his footy mates at the clubhouse. He's on the board of the team and they just played their way into their first grand final in almost two decades. I said, 'It's okay, you go. I'll be fine. It's not like it was a shock. Go. If you don't it'll look as if we're cowering. So, just go, and make sure you get an Uber home.'

The girls are asleep; they don't know that mum's going through a stressful time. I cooked them macaroni cheese and we sat on the couch and watched a funny movie, which we've all watched before, *Les Fugitifs*, a French movie, an antidote to sadness.

Now it's midnight. Warren texted me to say he'd be home soon.

—

IT DIDN'T COME as a surprise. The entire parole board was sacked. All twenty-four of us. Talk about a night of the long knives. We all knew the past. We all knew the precedent. I had told them, just so they understood the context of our decision to release Jennifer White.

In 1986 a woman named Wendy Lange was found guilty after the court was told she'd paid two men to murder her husband. She became known as The Black Widow because a few days before they killed him she bought a black dress on special at a local clothes store; indeed, she got an extra ten percent discount because she told the shop owner that her husband had just died from cancer.

She was eventually released on parole but the then Attorney-General started to generate pressure through the *Courier Mail*. Our state newspaper, one of Rupert Murdoch's most profitable, is not known to refrain from sensationalism, and it went crazy with The Black Widow, a lot like they were now doing with The Slayer. That Wendy Lange was an attractive young woman only made the story more urgent for a frenzied mob. Tony McGrady told the president of the then parole board to put Lange back in prison. The president replied that he couldn't. But she's come out and started to work as a prostitute! shouted back the Attorney-General. Yes, replied the president, she has, but that is completely within the confines of the law, because prostitution is not illegal in Queensland.

They argued back and forth until the Attorney-General sacked them all, two by two, until there was only one left, who then resigned.

Lange didn't go back to prison. She hadn't broken the law, and O'Grady wasn't able to enact a new law – one of the new and increasingly popular special-purpose laws drafted for the benefit of a single criminal only – that would allow him to put her back behind bars.

In 1996 a new parole board released back into the community a man named Ray Garland, who had gone down for sex crimes. In April the next year, he broke into a house in Mackay, way up north of Brisbane, and kept fourteen people hostage; he raped three of them, two women and a sixteen-year-old boy. During the siege, he fired more than forty shots at police and is now in prison for the rest of his life, never to be released.

That's the special-purpose law: ensuring that a person will die in prison.

That's what our current Attorney-General, Ray Conway, will try to achieve with Jen.

She will go back inside. She will never be released. She will die behind bars.

And he will move as fast as he can. And, now, there is nothing I can do about it but stand by and watch. I hate being a passive observer. Nellie, from the parole board, suggested that we send a letter to the *Courier Mail*, that maybe all the others would sign it too. I told her I didn't think that would have much sway. She sighed and hung up.

I felt unclean. Could I really remain silent? Acquiescent? Was that the sum of these past years? Bending to the will of a fuckwit who'll probably be voted out next election and die in the dust surrounded by cows. Is this the rally-car girl who raced the desert in honour of Gelignite Jack, a man who used sticks of explosive to solve a problem?

I don't think so.

Billy

I THOUGHT I HEARD RAIN ON THE TIN ROOF LAST NIGHT BUT when I woke to the comforting sounds of the horses being led down my street and looked out the back window as I made my first coffee for the day, I realised it must have been a dream. It hasn't rained more than the occasional shower for more than six years. It's all everyone talks about, if only for a passing moment. One day the drought will break, just as the river broke its banks twenty years ago.

The daily newspaper had another front-page story, this time justifying the removal of the entire parole board 'for the sake of justice'. They had yet to confirm where Jen was living but I noticed a reference to her Southport parole office. If the killer wanted to track her moves, he now had a place to start.

My phone buzzed. Checking the ID, I saw it was my old partner.

'Girlie,' he said.

'You're up early,' I replied, staring out at the darkness.

'Did you get a phone call from the office of the fuckwit who calls himself our Attorney-General last night?'

'I did, yes. You did too, obviously.'

'Asking you to put out a media release supporting his decision to sack the parole board? To say The Slayer needs to be behind bars for the rest of her life?'

'I told him to fuck off,' I said.

'You're the Commissioner; you're not allowed to speak like that, especially to a minister of the Crown. Good gracious me, girlie.'

I laughed. 'I told him that, in my capacity as the Commissioner, it would be inappropriate to make any comment, unless asked to by *my* minister. What did you say to him?'

'I told him to fuck off. But I like an embellishment and he can't do no harm to me, not to Billy Waterson. So, I says to him, loud and clear: Fuck off. Cunt.'

I laughed again. For a moment the rookie girl, a little uncertain of her step with her first big case, in the shadow of the mentor, returned to me.

—

As I LEFT home, a vibrant red began to creep up towards a dirty sky filled with grey clouds.

Lately I've been listening to edgy hard rock – Violent Soho, The Amity Affliction, Catfish and the Bottlemen, a distant cry from the old days of U2 – but this morning I plugged in the ABC news. The Justice Emergency was, of course, the news of the day.

There is a growing excitement with governments and some police commissioners – mostly the ones like the Dutchman: cops with a PhD and little if any footpath-walking – to embrace not just the prevention of crime but the anticipation of crime. Communities and individuals are encouraged to report suspicious activity. Terrorism, drug deals, domestic violence ...

The anticipation of crime is all about utilising new technologies to get ahead of the 'crime harvests' driven by 3D printing, drones, hacking, the placing of spyware in your washing machine or toaster, a chip no bigger than the tip of a needle embedded into the motherboard of your phone, allowing it and the crooks to download all your passwords, bank account and credit card details. To fight this, governments are working with universities and people like me to chart every person in the state – every person to whom, as Commissioner of Police, I have a responsibility, to ensure their safety and well-being – and to then essentially download everything they do, say and think and correlate this data in order to predict whether they might commit a crime. If they might hack a computer, bash their spouse, abuse a child or kill someone. And once the computer has made the prediction, we'll send around the cops and incarcerate the citizen until the state is assured that they are no longer a threat.

If this sounds like a Tom Cruise *Minority Report* approach, it is. The future is here. Most of us just haven't seen it yet but, as much as the past walks alongside us, so too do the years to come.

The push to return Jen White to prison is because the monster might kill again.

—

WHEN I GOT to work, Simon was waiting for me in the foyer with a black coffee, as he always does, around dawn, every morning. He had a hand-delivered envelope, dropped at reception yesterday afternoon. My name was written in pen.

'It's safe to open,' he said. 'I had it checked for anything nefarious. It's just paper and ink.'

I opened it on the ride up to the top floor. It was from Damon. Twenty years after I last heard from him.

Hi Lars, be great to see you again. Hope you are well. I know you are insanely busy with the new job and congratulations on that too!

With a phone number, a Facebook link, a Twitter link, an Instagram link, a UQ email address and a personal email address.

Twenty years of nothing and now, as the press is going mad over The Slayer, up he pops.

I asked Simon to cancel whatever I had going on at lunchtime.

What If?

'ALLO GIRLIE,' HE SAID AS I SAT DOWN AT THE OUTDOOR table in a courtyard with Moroccan-blue umbrellas. 'Wanna beer?'

'No thanks,' I said with a smile. He still wore a suit, dark blue today, with a white shirt and purple tie. His shoes gleamed. Patent leather with pointy toes, as always.

It was, actually, good to see him after so many years. 'How's retirement? Still living in West End?' I asked, noting how incredibly fit he looked at the age of eighty-one.

'Retirement's brilliant,' he said, as if surprised. 'Met a bird online. She's from Mauritius. Ever heard of Mauritius?'

'I have. It's close to the Seychelles,' I replied.

'That bird at the school. I remember her. Had an old black and white photograph of a Chinaman in her office. Standing out the front of that big tree.'

'You noticed that?' I asked.

'I notice everything, girlie. Ain't nothing that Billy Waterson does not notice. The trained eyes of a gangster turned copper.'

He was sitting, as he always did, as all Homicide cops do, with his back to a wall. Instinct. So a crook can't come at you from behind.

'What's it like being Commissioner?' he asked as he caught the glance of a passing waitress and pointed his finger at the now-empty beer glass, indicating a refill. 'You want one of them green teas or just some soda water?'

I turned to the waitress. 'Soda water. Thanks.' She scuttled off. 'It's great,' I replied. 'Who would've thought,' I added.

'Me,' he said, with a look of satisfaction. 'Could tell that a Wolverhampton mile away.'

'You could? No, you're just being nice.'

'Too old to be nice. It's true. Fuck me. The first time I saw you, after Kristo says, you is being paired with the girl and me saying, which girl? There's a girl in Homicide? And him pointing and me looking at the Asian ...'

'Part Asian,' I corrected him with a laugh.

'That, and the fucking dyed hair and your fucking Docs and your fucking attitude; straight off, I knew you'd touch the flag, if you wanted to.'

'Thanks Billy,' I said genuinely.

'You's here about The Slayer, aren't ya?' he said, small talk finished.

I sat back. This was going to be delicate.

He was waiting, as if daring me to bring up the knife.

'I don't want to talk about the knife,' I said.

He didn't say anything.

'She was convicted, fair and square,' I said. 'She's done her time and we've both repudiated the Attorney-General's call to put her back inside.'

'He needs to read his fucking law books.'

'But,' I said carefully, 'what if, just to put out a hypothetical, what if, just for the sake of argument, what if her release triggered a copycat or, again, just to be hypothetical, one of the other suspects we looked at, at the time, chose to take advantage of Jen's release to kill someone?'

'Miles is dead,' he said flatly. 'Died a few years back when he fell off his boat on the river, shit-faced with a ton of grog in him. Body washed up by the Stamford Hotel, in the middle of a Japanese wedding. No loss to the world there.'

'Uh-huh,' I said, leaving a silence for him to fill.

'Them other two. Nils, and what was the name of that geezer you said was creepy but we didn't pay much attention to?'

'Damon.'

'Him. The Scientist. Them, I dunno. They might be still out there.'

I told him about Damon's letter. Breaking the silence after twenty years, after Jen's release.

'I hate coincidences. No such thing as a coincidence in a murder investigation.' He leaned forward and stared at me. 'Why don't

I do a bit of moonlighting? Check 'em out, them two lads. See what they're up to? What do you think about that for an idea, Ms Commissioner? On the quiet, of course. Not wanting anyone to know that the two original investigators had gone back to look at the case. Yeah?'

'Yeah,' I said.

And not once did we have to talk about the knife.

The Fix Is In

IT WAS A CHOICE BETWEEN THE BEATLES AND A CONFESSION.

Billy had just made his way into Homicide. He was twenty-seven years old when he began his life as a rookie, nine years off the boat, a Ten Pound Pom, then the youngest-ever cop to be admitted into the hallowed squad. It was 1964, the year of The Beatles' Australian tour and Brisbane was their last stop.

Billy and his mentor, an ancient and dangerous bloke by the name of Rooster Henning, who was born in 1898 and joined the Force after losing a foot at the battle of Passchendaele in Belgium in 1917, who walked with a bad limp and an ivory cane that he would often swing hard onto Billy's neck whenever he was displeased, worked out of the old Queensland Egg Board building in Makerston Street, in the city, overlooking the river. The Egg Board building had been taken over by the Force two years earlier, as their new home.

They were hunting down a killer.

Two weeks earlier, a young woman by the name of Violet Lazar had been murdered with a hammer, which had been left at the scene of the crime in Boundary Road, in West End, not far from where Billy was renting a small wooden house with a green lawn out the front and another lawn out the back, a far and distant cry from the concrete wasteland of the home in London where his ma still lived, surviving mostly on the quid he'd send over to her from Brisbane once every two weeks. Violet, all lipstick and rouge, was a lady of the night but Rooster drummed into Billy that it didn't matter if she was a three-legged albino from Rhodesia, she was a person whose life had been ripped away, one of God's children and the divinity had been altered by her abrupt ending. Thus, they had a God-given duty to find the

gent who had sent her to heaven a little too early, even if it was
His will.

They had tracked down a man by the name of Giuseppe who
lived in a boarding house not far from where Violet would often be
seen on street corners in nylon stockings and short skirts. Alone.
At night. Made for murder. Take it from me, young William, said
Rooster, all God's children need to be cared for and it's up to fellas
like us to do it.

Thus, they had Giuseppe, who did a little bit of this and a little
bit of that and not a lot of anything, in a sweat-room, being a
concrete cell out in the courtyard of the old Egg Board building,
tied and handcuffed to a chair, semi-conscious from the bashings.
Rooster first, Billy next. *Whack. Whack.* After a little while,
Rooster – who was sixty-six and well past the official retirement
age, not that anyone would mention that to him because they were
all scared of him, all the suits and all the pollies up in parliament,
especially the Premier because Rooster was blackmailing him for
adultery – after a little while, Rooster began to tire and had to sit
on the floor.

Giuseppe was, as it turned out many years later, innocent of
Violet's death; however, at the time, in the concrete cell, Billy and
his mentor Rooster were convinced otherwise and, without an
admission of guilt, they had decided to bash him into making a
confession. The problem: Giuseppe was remaining steadfast in his
innocence and was refusing to acquiesce. The other problem: Billy
had, against great odds, managed to purchase two tickets to see
The Beatles at Festival Hall, also in the city, and he was going to
meet up with Edith, his wife of one year, out the front, in exactly
eighteen minutes from his last punch to the side of Giuseppe's head.

If the little turd did not confess now, or within the next ten
minutes, Billy would miss rendezvousing with Edith, who'd told
him, 'If you are late, if you are even one minute late, William
Waterson, I will go inside without you.'

And she had both tickets.

And she would.

Edith Waterson: Soon to be slain by a drunken driver while
walking along Ann Street in the city, on her way to church, one

Sunday morning, the drunk having stolen the car and zig-zagging his merry way through the otherwise-empty streets of Brisbane city, only to come to rest in blood and carnage, his and Edith's.

Billy wept for a year.

And Billy still, to this day, now, in 2019, goes to that place in Ann Street, every morning, way before dawn, on that anniversary of catastrophe and lays a bed of roses, yellow, her favourite.

Where is she now, Billy? he asks himself.

To which he replies: She is in heaven and I, too, I too will soon be there. Wait for me, Edith. I still have things to do down here. Crooks to catch.

I love you, he whispers to the bunch of flowers in the anonymous cradle of remembrance where there was once a haberdashery and where now there is a supermarket.

Edith Waterson, born in gun-country, Ipswich, was hard and tough and Billy knew she'd just walk into the foyer of Festival Hall without concern – *you spend too much time at work, working with the dead, William Waterson* – and watch the concert on her own.

Edith Waterson: *Remember me*, she had whispered into his ear, a lost breath, a haze, a float of mist, black, grey, white, *remember me*, she had exhaled her breath of love onto his mouth, Billy inhaling her love, her last breath as his tears fell onto her face, as he enveloped her into his arms before Rooster had called him and said: 'Mate, don't cry. You've got family and it's called the Force.'

But he did.

Billy, he did. He cried. He cried from that day in late 1965 to now, in 2019, and he will cry until the end of days without another knowing of it.

Billy was too scared to tell Rooster he'd gotten two tickets to see the famous Beatles because, like all people of a certain (old) age, Rooster thought the pop group was dangerous. They had long hair. Well, they didn't, not really, not like they would, later, in the Abbey Road days, but any hair that wasn't short back and sides was a threat to Western civilization. Frank Sinatra and Bing Crosby, even Elvis, had short hair. Proper short hair. Long hair on men (ignoring history) was, according to Rooster, a sign of being a pinko, a Commie, a beatnik. Billy was (rightly) scared that Rooster would clobber his ivory cane onto him with disapproval.

Billy loved The Beatles. He loved *Love Me Do* and *I Wanna Hold Your Hand* and *A Hard Day's Night* and these songs gave him a swirl of pride, them being from Liverpool with accents and him being from the East End with an accent.

Eighteen minutes. Giuseppe was broken, bruised, beaten. But silent.

Edith was waiting.

Seventeen minutes.

'Boss,' said Billy.

'William?' asked Rooster from his place on the floor, sweat dripping off him.

'I don't think this geezer is going to tell us what we want to hear.'

'He's guilty.'

'Yeah, boss, I know, but I think we have to let him go and find some evidence. I don't think we'll get a confession.'

Giuseppe couldn't speak and could barely hear what they were saying. He was recalling a time when he was a kid in Cagliari, riding bikes up and down hills with his eyes closed. A dare to the world.

'You wanna let him go? This wop pile of shit?'

'He's not going to confess, boss, and we've been holding him for three days now. And we haven't even arrested him,' said Billy.

Rooster clambered up off the floor and, for a moment, Billy was sure he'd get a caning.

Sixteen minutes.

'Fit him up,' said the older cop. 'Bring in the fix.'

'The what?' asked Billy, confused.

'Don't you know nothing, young William? Forge a confession. Then go to his house and plant a hammer with some blood on it.'

And he did. The next day. Billy did both, forged a confession and planted evidence that would send Giuseppe to Boggo Road for fifteen years. By the time he got out, another bloke had confessed to the crime of killing Violet but, by then, Rooster was dead and Billy didn't care as fixing up crooks had become second nature, along with the other young cops in Homicide who, like him, had to be told by a weary mentor how things got done.

The Beatles were unforgettable. Mind-blowing. He arrived out the front of the concert hall just in time, a minute to spare with Giuseppe still tied and cuffed to the chair in the concrete cell, unconscious and slotted into the system of bad policing.

That night, much later that night, he and Edith danced in the streets, alone, doing the twist, pretending to be Ringo Starr and Chubby Checker, all rolled into one. That night they swooned and made love under the stars and told each other they would remain entwined forevermore.

So, by the time Billy got to Jen White some thirty-five years later, he was well experienced in the art of bringing in a fix.

But only if he thought the crook was guilty and if the mundane issue of evidence was proving to be a major problem. If evidence or lack thereof was stalling the process of letting a guilty person walk without being charged, Billy's simple maxim was: make it up.

By 1999 things had changed and the old days of bringing in the fix was frowned upon. Largely. Not entirely. Scrutiny was the issue. In the old days, when Billy was working under Rooster, cops were revered. Like bank managers and real estate agents. In the old days people had respect. Then, blow me down, the ABC broadcast an hour of horror one Monday night in 1987, called *The Moonlight State*, on Four Corners, which lifted the lid on what every cop in Queensland already knew: the state was deeply immersed in rotten corruption. Cops scrambled, politicians scrambled, the government was tossed out, old cops like Rooster (who was dead at this time) were tossed out or, worse, put in jail.

The fix was in but, this time, it was in on the entire police force.

Billy survived. Didn't have to dob in anyone, kept himself under the radar and vowed to be super-careful in the future when it came to a little bit of brown paper bag bribery or turning a blind eye to a mate who had committed a crime and, of course, to fitting up a crook with some dodgy evidence.

So, with all of that, Billy knew he could not tell Lara of his plan. She was idealistic and good-o, cheers for that but, at the end of the day, it comes down to putting the crook in the slammer. In any which way. As long as you think the crook is guilty. Don't let a lack of evidence get in the way of a good conviction.

It was simple.

He wandered down to the Valley, to one of the Asian supermarkets and got himself a long-bladed knife, wondering how they'd gotten a free pass in selling stuff that was ordinarily illegal to own. Knives of all sizes in one dingy part of the store.

Then he went to the evidence room at the cop shop and lifted Jen's fingerprints and carefully laced them onto the handle of the knife, then he took some of James's dried blood from the shirt he wore the night he was killed and rubbed that onto the blade of the knife, then he carried it in a plastic bag up to the girls' school in Ascot, went to the already-searched locker that belonged to her and stuffed it down the back. Later, he called one of the lads in one of the other crews and asked that he do another search of Jen's things at the school and waited for the applause.

Kristo summoned him into his office.

'Did you plant that knife, Billy?'

'Boss, would I do that?'

'Yes. Did you?'

'No. Not at all. Not never, boss. Scout's honour.'

Kristo didn't believe him. The Dutchman didn't believe him. None of the other detectives in the squad believed him.

But for Lara. Young Lara, twenty-six years old, the youngest detective ever in Homicide, his protégé. The idealist.

Lara was not naïve and she knew of her partner's reputation. Unlike Jen, Lara read the newspapers and knew all about the controversies within the force, now a service. But she wanted to believe Billy.

Because Billy was her guide and mentor.

So, she did not ask him if he'd planted the knife. She took her scepticism, drew a red circle around it and placed it in an ice box in the freezer, never to be thought of again.

And there it has remained. For almost twenty years.

Any semblance of guilt for having been part of a ruse to put Jen in jail, for twenty years, in abeyance. After all it wasn't her, it was him. After all, these sorts of things happen. Evidence can suddenly turn up at the last moment, even evidence in a place that you've searched before. After all, the killings stopped once Jen had been arrested.

After all –

———

'BUT WHAT OF the consequences?' Billy had asked Rooster while he forged a confession on behalf of a broken Giuseppe.

'No such thing as a consequence, William Waterson,' replied Rooster. 'Not when we are doing the Lord's work in putting evil behind bars.'

Billy didn't buy that but said nothing.

Because he knew there were consequences. There are always consequences.

They are called guilt.

They are called the reckoning.

They are called atonement.

They are called '*Who are you?*'

They may be wraiths and they may be actual places or events but they are real.

If truth be told, Billy would have rather fitted up Nils. The Viking with his attitude and history with Lara was a far better candidate.

Nils was good for a fix. Billy had rarely seen such a good candidate. However, there was a problem of him (Billy) shouting at the video geezer who was supervising the interview with Nils, when he (Billy) had lost his temper and ordered the cameras to be switched off while he grabbed Nils by the throat and threatened to kill him because he (Nils) kept staring at Lara.

And, unlike Jen, Nils had some alibi issues. Some dodgy low-life motherfuckers kept banging on about how good mate, old colleague Nils was at a Miami bowls club on the night of the first murder, despite Billy not being able to verify this. Billy really wanted to put Nils away. He hungered after the Viking. He hated Nils because Nils had hurt Lara and Billy loved Lara like the daughter he and Edith never had. He wanted to hurt Nils to the end of days to show Lara how much he cared for her.

Knowing, of course, that she would be furious about such protectiveness.

So, to expedite the case, he brought on the fix. To Jen.

But what of the consequences? he asked himself.

There will be none, he told himself.

He knew he was lying to himself – the worst sin of all, lying to one's self.

—

THUS, BOTH BILLY and Lara, in 2019, in an unspoken pledge, agreed to see if there might have been another killer, not Jen, not Jen who lived almost twenty years behind bars, every day of those twenty years they had to justify, to themselves, without ever mentioning her name but knowing atonement, if it could ever come, would lift a terrible burden and allow them to rise into the sky.

Billy had, as it happened, never stopped thinking about Jen and what he did to her. And to Lara, casting upon her, Lara, the guilt of sending an innocent kid down the river.

The Medium Is
the Message

I HATE BEING HATED.

I got used to it in prison, knowing that a hungry population beyond the walls despised me for the Slayings, knowing that my name and profile was on all those Famous Serial Killer websites and occasionally on television in a sweaty, panting doco-drama in which I was played in dramatic reconstructions by a blonde with an over-generous cleavage and contact lenses that exaggerated my one-blue-eye-one-green-eye, glinting like a devil's glare as I plunged my knife of death into the unsuspecting victims and then leaned down, out of shot as if about to suck their blood. I knew all this, but prison insulated me. Mostly. The walls of incarceration kept me safe from prying lenses.

Even though I was on Planet Wacol, I was not completely isolated from what was happening in the outside world. I was aware there existed a twenty-four-hour news cycle. I was aware of changes in technology. Anthea's orientation had also helped.

But neither of us had thought about the terrifying swiftness with which a story can go viral, a word I used, twenty years ago, to describe something medical. And how a simple Tweet can change your life in the space of a second.

—

AS THE BUS from Westaway House rumbled along the highway, I looked out for the occasional glimpse of water at the end of the side streets. It was my third day at work. There were no clouds in the sky. I'd heard the news that, since Lara Ocean and I had talked, the parole board had been sacked, that the widows of 'my' victims were on a revenge rampage and that the Attorney-General was itching to get me back behind bars. I was getting anxious and feeling powerless. And I knew that the killer would be too. We both had a closing window of time.

As the bus rattled up the Gold Coast Highway, I got a text from Bruce. Another thing that Anthea had forgotten to tell me about the new world is that hardly anyone makes a call anymore. Landlines barely exist and message machines must have gone out with VHS.

Where r u it read. I still couldn't bring myself to join the new revolution in the English language.

A few minutes away from work. I replied, complete with the full stop.

Get off b4 last stop he replied.

2 late, I replied, enjoying my first foray into text-speak.

—

AS THE BUS pulled up and I climbed off, I saw why he had texted me the warning. The Bunnings car park, at five to six in the morning, just before opening time, was brimming with people who didn't look as though they were out to buy a drill.

'There she is!'

Maybe thirty people were hovering near the front doors as a couple of staff members looked on nervously. I paused in my walk towards them, which only made them all stare at me more intensely. They all began to film me with their phones. A couple of them started running towards me.

I ran, quickly, away from them. I thought I saw Bruce, standing by the entrance. I'm not sure if it was him. It was hard to tell as I was fleeing. But I never saw him again.

I ran up the verge and dodged traffic across the four-lane highway and scurried into the massive car park that surrounded the Harbour Town shopping precinct, a low-level open mall. Only a twenty-four-hour fruit and veg market was open. I found one of the public toilets and locked myself in for an hour. By that time, my escape from the crowds of justice had gone viral. The first real sighting of The Slayer in twenty years. One of the clips had over twenty-six thousand hits on YouTube.

I didn't cry. I was numb. I hate being hated.

Bruce texted: *r u ok*

I didn't text back. That part of my life had just closed.

Anthea called the minute she saw the footage, posted online by the mainstream media. It had just gone seven o'clock. She told me to wait, she would be there in just over an hour.

I tried to call Gary to leave a message saying that I was changing address, to move in with my sister. But I had run out of credit on my phone. I'd do it when I was in Anthea's car.

The Stranger

RAIN CLOUDS HAD APPEARED FROM NOWHERE. OVER THE years as the state went from a deluge to a parched land of aridity, I had seen, from behind the prison wire, rain clouds form and even thunder, sometimes, but never any rain. Like a gigantic tease, a slow burn of dry torture.

'Do you think it might rain?' I asked Anthea, as we sped up the highway, back towards Brisbane in the early afternoon. Anthea had texted me throughout the morning as I sat huddled on the toilet seat, in my cubicle, waiting. Texting me to say she had been held up. No matter.

'Maybe,' she replied. She seemed distracted, and who could blame her. Big sister Slayer is coming to stay.

Drops of rain hit the windscreen. I counted them. Eight.

And then no more. She didn't even bother to turn on the windscreen wipers.

'Robbie's away. Did I tell you that before?'

'Yeah. You did. In Singapore. For a week, then on to Shanghai for a few days and then to Lucerne. Why is he going to Lucerne?'

She shrugged. 'Dunno.' Kept driving. Looked at the clock on the dash. 'We'll have to stop by the school and pick up the girls on the way home.'

'Great!'

—

NOT SO GREAT.

There are three schools on Ascot hill, all of them exclusive and two of them for girls only. Little Jen and Maxi were at Clyde, a different school to the one that Anthea and I went to. Because the streets were narrow and winding, with gracious old homes snug next to one another with thickets of palm trees along the side fences providing privacy and a carpet of purple jacaranda flowers on the footpaths and streets, pick-up and drop-off became a bit of a hectic maze for frazzled kids and parents. Expensive cars jostled for space, most of them lining up in an orderly procession of pick-ups, managed by smiling, efficient teachers. Little Jen and Maxi were waiting for us inside the art school, both holding cardboard Easter sculptures. Anthea found a park and we walked up the hill towards the front gates. The school was old sandstone, built in the 1860s. Gargoyles leered down from the arched rooftops. I was wearing sunglasses and a peaked cap that Anthea had on the back seat. I was travelling incognito. I was The Slayer, hiding out on the hill. I could have stayed in the car but I was scared.

Scared of being left alone. Scared of life. Rattled.

'Oh, by the way,' Anthea said suddenly, as if remembering something, 'mum and dad are coming for dinner. I hope you don't mind. I couldn't cancel at the last minute.'

'Sure. Of course. Totally,' I replied, utterly terrified at having to see them again, for the first time in twenty years.

As if to read my thoughts, she said: 'They'll be cool. Don't worry. It'll be fine. They know you're staying with us.'

As we passed through the gates, ornate, huge, like something from an Edgar Allan Poe story, I heard a, 'Oh, hello,' as if the greeting had slipped out with nary a thought.

I turned to see Karin Jones, the former president of the parole board. With her were two teenage girls. They were staring at me, boggle-eyed. They knew who I was.

'Oh. Hi,' I said, embarrassed.

'You're ...' She left the sentence hanging, the *What are you doing here?* unsaid.

'Hi Karin,' said Anthea. 'This is my sister, Jen. She's staying with us.'

'Oh. Hi Anthea. Okay. Well. Good to see you both. It's looking like it might rain later. Here's hoping. Bye.' And with that she and her daughters scurried off. An odd encounter. But, even odder when, after I'd taken a couple of steps, I paused and turned around to see Karin down the footpath a bit, staring at me.

I was feeling more and more like Alice in the land of topsy-turvy where people walked on their hands and all that seemed to be, was not. Deep breathing, Jen, like Rosie taught you in meditation class.

As we approached the art school, prominent with cut-out animals pasted to the windows, I asked, 'How do you know her? Ms Jones.'

Anthea shrugged. 'The school. We often get rostered on to help out on the sports days. They just live around the corner. I knew she was in charge of the parole board and she knew I was your sister, but we never talked about it. At all. She's very careful about that sort of thing. Shame about the sacking, though.'

We stepped inside the art school, and straight off I knew that my nieces had either seen the viral clip or had been told about it; or indeed had, in the past couple of days, discovered that Aunty Jen not only lied about Hollywood, she lied about being an evil killer. I was a stranger to them.

'Aunty Jen is coming to stay with us for a while,' said Anthea.

They stared at me without speaking. It wasn't just anger and uncertainty in their eyes.

It was fear.

Break and Enter

I HAD SAID TO THE POLICE MINISTER, WHEN SHE OFFERED ME the job, 'If we could keep the social functions to a minimum, that would be great.' And she said, 'Yes, of course, the government understands that employees at your level need their own time at home, even if they aren't married.'

Never believe a politician.

I was at my third for the week, a local upgrade to the Safe School Program being announced by the minister to an array of educators and 'leading citizens' (myself included; will this do, mum?) in the State Library, part of the modern complex of buildings housing the museum, conference centre and performing arts theatres. I had my phone on vibrate, just in case there was an emergency, and right on cue I felt the buzz. I checked the caller ID and quietly got up from my seat. I hastily exited the big room to an adjoining balcony where a couple of women were sneaking an illegal cigarette, blowing the smoke into the afternoon. The river was below us, a brooding mass of water moving rapidly past. The postcard-view façade of the city, its tall glass buildings lit up, with streets of neon lights snapping on. Dusk was approaching; the blazing orange of the sunset reflected off the buildings and the water.

'Hi Billy,' I said.

'This ain't the first time I've said it but I dunno what you ever saw in this geezer.'

'Where are you? Who are you talking about?'

'Old mate Nils. What a creep. I've just broken into his unit. He lives above a motorbike repair shop in Southport on the Gold Coast. There's a bonza nineteen sixties Norton down there.'

I ignored the break-and-enter bit. Billy loved to break into houses. He told me long ago, with great relish, that he did his first at the age of seven when he nicked a TV for his mum, carried it along a dark and narrow laneway, dodging cops, and then tuned it to the BBC while she slept upstairs in their council flat.

'Don't worry. He's not going to catch me. Him and his sixteen-year-old girlfriend are eating at the Chinese around the corner.' I could hear him as he moved around the apartment.

'He likes a knife, doesn't he? And I'm not talking about steak knives. I'm gonna send you a couple of photos.'

And within seconds, they arrived.

Carefully laid out on a side table: an array of long knives and swords. I counted eight Samurai swords and what looked like Viking swords. Then a new photo came through of another table, in another room, on which were laid out Celtic-inspired knives, short blades, long blades and, again, swords. Another photo, of a wall: framed paintings of Celtic gods. There was Taranis. There was Ogmios with his smiling mouth and pierced tongue with its chain of human ears. Another photo. This time, of Nils. In his early fifties, he looked fiercer than ever. His entire face and head had been tattooed. He looked like a lizard man.

'He's going out with a sixteen-year-old?' I asked, horrified but not entirely surprised.

'At least he's consistent.'

'God help her.' The age of consent in Queensland was sixteen. It was disgusting but it was legal.

'What do you wanna do? There's about forty grand worth of A-grade banned weaponry in this apartment, but there's the issue of illegal entry to said apartment.'

The smokers tossed their butts into the river, which annoyed me, and in a moment of Nils-related anger I felt an urge to bust them for smoking in a confined public space and for littering. But I let it go. They went inside, smiling at me as they passed.

'Is there anything to suggest he might be planning an attack?' I asked.

'Like a wall board with targets, dates, times and locations? Like in the movies? No, girlie, if there is, it's in his head.'

As I heard Billy move around the unit, commenting on its grim imagery and weapons, I couldn't help but wonder if he was, twenty years after the fact, in The Slayer's den.

'You know what to do,' I said and signed off.

Happy Families

THE GIRLS WERE SEATED NEXT TO ONE ANOTHER AT THE dining table, the wall of mounted butterflies behind them. Anthea and I were on the other side. It was a formal tableau. It was a formal talk. Their eyes were on me. I said nothing.

'Twenty years ago, when I was sixteen and your aunty was seventeen, when we lived in that old house around the corner with grandpa and grandma, something very bad happened. I never told you about it because your dad and I didn't want to upset you and we didn't think it was going to be necessary. Well, now it is. Your Aunty Jen was wrongly blamed for killing three men. There were a lot of bad people who wanted to put Aunty Jen in jail, and they did. It was very, very unfair. Aunty Jen hasn't been in Hollywood for the past twenty years. She was in prison and she just got out. She did not commit those crimes that those bad men said she did. She went to jail an innocent person. You remember that story your dad and I were talking about; that man in America, Valentino Dixon, who spent twenty-seven years in prison and he was innocent?'

They nodded. They didn't speak. They weren't looking at their mum. They were staring at me.

'Same thing. It happens, and it happens a lot. I told Aunty Jen to pretend she had been in Hollywood because I didn't want you to know about this terrible thing that happened to her. But now she's out and we're going to look after her.'

They nodded. They didn't speak. They were staring at me.

'People are saying bad things about her. And these bad people will keep saying bad things until they get bored and start to say bad things about someone else. We've talked about the nasty stuff on social media, haven't we?'

343

They nodded.

'And this is another example of when social media gets out of control and people get hurt. If any of your classmates say anything that upsets you or use social media to message you something that upsets you, something about Aunty Jen, ignore them, block them, don't answer and tell me or your dad or Miss Hepburn at school. Okay?'

'Okay mum,' they both said.

There was a silence. None of us were prepared for this and none of us knew how to act. I smiled at them and said:

'Thanks girls.'

They smiled back. Hesitantly.

—

DAD STARED AT me with glassy eyes. He had gotten dramatically thinner. He had a lot of grey hair and he swayed on his feet. He was carrying an open bottle of vodka. The cancer had hollowed out his cheeks and eye sockets. I tried not to cry as they walked inside. The girls clearly loved their grandparents and ran around them with buckets of enthusiasm.

'Hi dad. Hi mum,' I said. Anthea was in the kitchen, behind the breakfast bar. Dad was led by the girls to one of the couches, where he sat looking more uncertain than I had ever seen him.

'Hi mum,' I said again.

She gave me a tight smile; it didn't quite work, a little wobbly on the edges. She pulled a bottle of gin from her bag.

'I'm drinking gin. Would you like some gin?' she asked too loudly, staring at me as if we'd never met. She then called across the room:

'Anthea, I think Jen would like some gin!'

'I can't drink, mum. That's against my parole.'

'I went to Country Road yesterday and bought myself a pair of jodhpurs. Pink. What do you think about that?' she said to me.

—

IT DIDN'T GET any better. Anthea cooked roast duck, which mum, gin-addled, said was over-cooked, while dad sat and stared, as if Death was on the staircase leading up from below, while the girls were allowed to play with their iPads at the table. 'We'll make an exception tonight, just this once,' is what Anthea had said, knowing that we were all on the *Titanic* of family dinners.

Neither mum nor dad asked about me. They didn't talk to me. Oh, sorry, mum told me she had also bought herself a pale blue linen dress on sale. What did I think about that?

I wasn't upset. I had been resigned to the vacancy of my parents for a long time. I didn't blame them; they weren't to blame. I blamed myself. I bankrupted them, I ruined them, I forced them into all this. Not by asking, just by being.

Oh yes, but it was circumstance, wasn't it? Wrong time, wrong place, wrong girl, world gone wrong. I wasn't the killer. It was him, whoever he was, who had ruined their lives, my life, Anthea's life, the lives of James, Brian and Fabio and their wives and their kids and mothers and fathers and grandfathers and grandmothers and their best friends and all those who wept for the loss of the three men who were slain by him, whoever he is, wherever he is. It wasn't me. It was circumstance. Wrong world. Fate smashing into my little orbit, obliterating me and all around me, little galaxies of doom and regret.

But, at the end of the day, when all is said and done, after the buzz-saw clack of the last sunlight, it was me.

I slid him out of me in the bath. But it's his shadow that walks alongside me with the sun of day.

History, the Killer

I was now back home, on the couch with a hot chocolate and a tub of Maggie Beer's burnt fig and caramel ice cream, watching *The Tudors*, the TV show about Henry VIII, my current go-to chill before bed. Catherine Howard was about to sleep with another man, charting her course straight to the chopping block. I was shouting at the screen – 'Don't you know his history? He is a serial killer! He kills his wives, you stupid girl!' – when the phone rang.

'Jeez, girlie, you really can fuckin' pick 'em.'

'Hi Billy,' I replied. 'What are you talking about?'

'Damon Connelly. Your other creepy geezer-mate.'

'Have you broken into another house?' I asked.

'Haven't had so much fun since the night I clobbered Ratty McWilliam back in the East End days. Yes, I have. I told you I would check on these blokes and here I am, inside this place. Ain't nothing here. Nothing. Well, there is. There's a bed on the floor, one of them Japanese beds ...'

'Futon.'

'Yeah. That. So far. It's a big house for one geezer. Nothing on the walls. No furniture in the lounge room. Nothing in the dining room. That futon thing in the bedroom. Oh, hello! There's a blood orange in the kitchen, on the bench. One. And a very fucking sharp, expensive-looking, unusual knife sitting next to it. The blade on the knife is odd. Looks Celtic? I'll send you a photo. The fridge is empty. So is the freezer. Is this bloke an alien? Don't worry, Ms Commissioner, I'm here alone. Old mate Damon is in Sydney for a conference on string.'

'That would be string theory.'

'Just making sure you're awake and concentrating. Who would live in an empty house? Do you reckon it's because his head is stuffed full of maths and quantum mechanics?'

'Maybe,' I said.

'I'm walking down the corridor to the other rooms. How come we never brought this bloke in to question?'

'There was no reason to. At the time he was just someone who wanted to know about the killings. It was probably entirely innocent, a way to break the ice with me. I only mentioned him to you this morning because of the letter he sent. It was like his presence around me was only to do with the killer. Can't drag a guy into the office for that. We would have needed a lot more – like, evidence, a motive, anything – but there was nothing.'

I heard him open a door and step into another room; clearly Damon's house had wooden floorboards.

'Oy. Fucking beard,' Billy said.

'Sorry? What? A beard?'

'It's cockney, love. Beard. Means "weird". And it's what I am staring at in his end room.'

Two Shadows

I HAD ACTUALLY REACHED A DECISION. LAST NIGHT AS I LAY in bed. I thought to myself that it was just all too hard. My heart's not in it. The world is full of CCTV, not like twenty years ago. There are satellites in the sky recording the every move of people below. There's infra-red imaging, people on the streets are so much more alert to a suspicious-looking person in a hoodie carrying a back-pack, walking down a street, walking through a park. Fear won. Everybody is scared, be it from a serial killer or a terrorist, people are constantly on edge.

Not a good time to be killing randoms on the street of any big city. Not like the old days.

I carry a special pride in being Brisbane's first serial killer even though nobody knows my name. And they never will.

But, at the same time, as I look back to those days and think about the killings and the fun I had, I have to admit a certain degree of embarrassment. Not of the actual blood, the slicing of their necks and the looks in their eyes as I rode them to their death, straddling them as I sawed, not that. That was awesome. Those feelings I will always treasure. More, the Goth and Celtic stuff. The carving of Taranis into their chests. It seemed like a brilliant flourish at the time. Now it seems like a juvenile detail. I wish I hadn't done that. Same with the cutting of their mouths giving them that evil grin. I really loved doing that, at the time. But now, same thing. I fear that, in the annals of serial killing, history will not be so kind to me. History will say I was a mixed-up muddled killer, leaving too many clues. I should have just taken the teeth and folded their heads onto their shoulders and left it at that.

So, while I was indulging in some self-criticism, I came to the conclusion that my work was best left alone.

And there is always the danger of getting caught.

I grabbed a lucky break back in ninety-nine and while I'd been planning to kill again upon Jen's release, storing up for a grand-slam, it might be best to let it all slide. I have a lot to lose now.

Back then, in ninety-nine, I had fuck-all and even less to lose.

Different now.

Then, guess what?

Ray, the fat-fuck Attorney-General, sacked the entire parole board because they wouldn't break the law and illegally put Jen back into prison. So, now with them all out of a job, guess what? He is going to make sure she is on a fast train to Wacol.

The news just did my head in – totally galvanized me, spun me around in a U-turn. Realising that if I didn't kill again very soon, like I was planning to, all those years ago – the swan-song – I would never, ever, ever-never get the chance again.

All doubts erased. All concern for Jen gone. All worries about getting caught, gone. I can do it. I am smarter than all of them. Fuck the CCTV, the satellites, the fear in the minds of suspicious passers-by, fuck it all. I will rise again and I will not be thwarted.

If people knew who I really was, they would gasp with shock. I don't like to brag but all this is just between you and me so allow me: what success I have achieved in being two people, the surface normal and the inner dark, the killer and the ordinary, twins walking like two shadows on either side of me. One shadow, cut off your head, the other shadow, can-I-help-you-across-the-road?

I have to move fast.

Jen will be back behind bars within days.

The Rainbow Sign

ANTHEA MADE CHOCOLATE MOUSSE, ONE OF THE GIRLS' favourites, but after the disaster of the dried-out duck, mum announced that she and dad had to go. It was late. They needed to get ahead of the traffic, even though all the traffic had long delivered its drivers back to their homes in the peak-hour rush. Anthea fretted, as did I, about mum driving on gin but she insisted she was fine and still under the limit and dad seemed not to care. Nor did she, for that matter, as they wobbled out of the house without saying any further goodbyes.

The girls went to bed. They kissed me on the cheek before they went downstairs to their rooms. That made up for the empty cold of the evening.

Anthea said that mum and dad just needed a bit of time, now that I was out, but that they would come around and accept me. She told me that dad was looking better and she hoped that mum really was under the limit.

She was going to stay up to complete some marking on assessments that were due and needed to be posted onto the uni portal by midnight, so I hugged her and went downstairs.

I slept in the same room I slept in three nights ago. It felt like three years ago. My life was on fast forward at the same time it felt like it was in slow motion. I didn't sleep. Up on the hill, it was quiet. The streets were narrow and lined with trees and everyone went to bed at a reasonable hour. The total opposite to Westaway House down on the Gold Coast where the smack- and meth-heads groaned and popped all night.

The dawn came at about five. I got up at four-thirty and quietly went upstairs, careful not to wake anyone. I poured myself a glass of water and padded across the floor to the wall of windows that looked and opened out to the back garden. I could hear the sounds of birds. I loved to listen to the sound of birds in the dawn, when I was a little girl. When I had some dreams that didn't involve prison.

I wish I knew their names, the names of the birds. Which made me think about my sister and her obsession which then turned into a successful career with butterflies. Where did that come from? Was that an inherited thing? Hardly; mum and dad were as flummoxed as I was when it developed into a full-blown fascination, like with me and books. Where does that sort of stuff come from? Are we not made up of so many infinite possibilities, an accumulation of events and attitudes and angers and loves and hates, or is it simply pre-ordained?

I poured myself another glass of water and ambled across to the wall of butterflies. There had to be more than a hundred cabinets, all framed in polished rosewood with a glass front, like a series of paintings hung close together in one of those eighteenth-century European palaces. In each were twelve butterflies, all mounted in perfect symmetry. Three across, four down. The bigger ones at the top, the smaller ones below. All with their wings spread. It was extraordinary. Maxi had said that her mum knew the name, the Latin name and the English name, for every one of them. And its history and, for many of them, its scarcity.

I'd never seen so many colours.

There was a rolling crackle of thunder far away and, now that the dawn had arrived, the sky was overcast. A moment later, rain began to sprinkle.

At the very bottom of the display wall, at floor level, were cabinets holding Aboriginal artefacts. I hadn't paid much attention to them before, dazzled by the butterflies, but now I took a closer look.

The artefacts reminded me of dad and his jaunts around the world selling Aboriginal art into galleries in Paris and London and New York. Look at him now, I thought, sadly, as I knelt on the floor to examine the collection.

I assumed Anthea had permission to mount and show them. There can be dark spirits associated with Aboriginal artefacts and, as a matter of respect if nothing else, you needed to get approval for putting Aboriginal art on display; I remember dad telling me that, telling me that there were some pieces even he could not look at.

One of the cabinets held strings of necklaces. Mostly what looked like shells, although maybe they had come from Papua New Guinea. Under them was a necklace made of long teeth, like shark's teeth but there was a little printout beneath it saying they were kangaroo teeth. They were strung with a red ochre string.

And then my gaze turned down, to the last necklace. Which was also made out of teeth. There were only five teeth on this necklace and I recognised them immediately because they were a part of my research when I became The Slayer.

They were maxillary canine teeth, the same teeth removed from 'my' victims twenty years ago.

PART V

ANTHEA

The very moment I thought I was lost
The dungeon shook and the chains fell off
Pharaoh's army got drownded
Oh Mary don't you weep

I may be right and I may be wrong
I know you're gonna miss me when I am gone
Pharaoh's army got drownded
Oh Mary don't you weep

Trapped

I HEARD JEN GET OUT OF BED, ON THE OTHER SIDE OF THE wall. I heard her climb the stairs, trying not to wake any of us. The girls would sleep through an atom bomb, especially on a school day. I heard her softly pad across the floor above.

I heard a roll of thunder and then light rain.

I had been dreaming about the Blood River. Again. I try not to. Actually, I had been quite successful in stopping that dream from invading me at night, pretty much since Maxi came along. Someone had said to me – was it Phoebe? – anyway it was someone and they'd said to me that when you give birth there are many things that change. Profoundly. But, she said, the biggest change was that you were no longer the most important part of your life. Suddenly there was somebody else who was the centre of gravity of your existence. Your child.

Of course, not all mothers or fathers have this massive axis tilt in their perspective of identity, but I did.

And so, with the birth of Maxi, my first-born, the dreams and memories of Blood River began to cease.

Now they're back. Not surprising, I guess.

—

THE CABINET WAS locked. They were all locked. I couldn't smash the glass and grab the string of teeth. Anthea would know.

Maybe it wasn't what it seemed. It couldn't be. My sister? Could *not* have killed three people. Could *not* have allowed me to go to prison for twenty years.

It was absurd. I was living on another planet. It had to be a simple mistake. Teeth from an Aboriginal tribe, something that dad must have come across years ago, which he handed down to Anthea when they sold the home and moved to Bald Hills.

That was it. That was the only explanation.

And, another thing: there were five teeth. The Slayer only killed three people. So, there had to be another explanation. It couldn't be what it seemed.

Unless there were two other victims that nobody knew about.

———

'MORNING!' CALLED ANTHEA as she emerged from the top of the stairs with Maxi, who was walking like a zombie, still half-asleep. In her cat-patterned pyjamas, she walked across the room and hugged me as if I were a vertical cushion she could go back to sleep on. 'I don't want to go to school,' she mumbled into the fabric of my pyjamas.

'How did you sleep?' Anthea asked me.

I stared at her. *Is there another person inside you? Can there possibly be a monster lurking within? The one everyone thought was in me?* 'Great. Thanks,' I replied. 'There's been some rain.'

Maxi still had her arms around me.

'Yes, the weather bureau said the drought might finally be broken this week. Lord knows we need it. Poor bloody farmers. Max! Time to wake up, sweetie; you want Vegemite or cheese sandwiches for lunch?' she asked as she pulled out food from the fridge. The girls' school backpacks were open and laid out on the breakfast bar.

'No carrots,' mumbled Maxi.

'Okay, but you know the rule. You've got to have some vegetables.'

'I'll get some chips. Can you give me money for the tuck shop?'

'Chips are not vegetables. I'm giving you some celery.' Little Jen, also still in her pyjamas, her's patterned with roosters, staggered into the room and, also like a zombie, walked across to the lounge and dropped into it. 'Do I have to go to school today?' she asked and then went back to sleep.

'Sis?' asked Anthea. 'The girls will be walking home after school this afternoon. All right, girls? Mummy won't be able to pick you up.'

They mumbled assent.

'I'm so far behind with my assessments and I have to cover for one of my lecturers at a tutorial,' she said to me.

I was having trouble keeping it together; my brain was going bang-bang in a series of up-and-down spirals, like the one and only time I rode a rollercoaster, at the Ekka when I was a kid and dad rode with us. It's not that repeat killers can't be parents. They are, after all, sons and less so, daughters. Usually the object of abuse, but not always. BTK – Bind Torture Kill – one of the most horrible serial killers ever, had an ordinary childhood and then came to fantasies of bondage and torture as a teenager. He has a daughter who, even after the shock and horror of discovering her father was BTK, forgave him and has written about that forgiveness. It can happen. People are strange. Anything can happen. I get that.

What I was having trouble with, what was surrounding me like a wall of impenetrable incredulity and disbelief, that bang-banging in my fucking head, was that the killer could be my sister. I couldn't get past that; it had to be wrong. It couldn't be her. It just couldn't.

'Sorry, what?' I asked.

'Are you okay?' asked Anthea.

'Yeah. Sorry. I was just distracted. Sorry, what did you say?'

'There's some spag bol in the freezer; perhaps you could microwave that for them, if they're hungry? I should be home by six, though.'

'Okay. Sure. No problem.'

She reached into her pocket. She was already dressed and ready for the day. 'Here's a spare set of keys if you want to go out.' There was a moment where she looked at me. I could feel the five teeth behind me, in the cabinet, as if they were biting into my lungs.

'But probably best not. Just in case the press track you down. Lucky we have a big driveway and a hedge out the front. No-one can see in. You're safe and anonymous here.'

No. I think, sweet sister, I am fucking trapped here.

Songs of Love and Hate

THEY'RE BACK.

The choppers hovering above the house and the camera vans out the front and the hounds of press with a relentless bang-bang on the front door, all day and all night with a, 'Mrs White! Megan! Are you there?! We just need to ask you some questions!'

Hugh, he sleeps. He's pretty much been asleep for the last twenty years, since she was found guilty and our life fell apart, friends fell apart, family fell apart, the house in which we lived fell apart, the world that we had, fell apart. The centre certainly did not hold. It opened up to become an abyss, but we clung to its edge and, with the kindness of some, we managed to return to life. His cancer is aggressive. It won't be long.

He feels so guilty. He thinks it's his fault.

Of course we know she is innocent, the victim of a tragic and very terrible misunderstanding but –

– as the years wore on and as our lives crumbled, her guilt just seemed to become more entrenched. It was almost as if our defence of her gave way, crumbled and all that was left was an evil little girl who I had mothered and he had fathered.

He thinks it's because he would tell Jen about the Blood River. His horrid story. He thinks that's why she became a killer of unimaginable cruelty. I told him, for years I told him that she was innocent, that she was not a killer, that the police had set her up, that the court had got it wrong, like they did with Lindy Chamberlain, but the entreaties fell away, like ramparts of dust surrounding a fortified town.

—

WE'RE IN BALD Hills, a suburb way north of Brisbane, on its edge actually, before you get onto the freeway which will take you to the Sunshine Coast. We have a house next to what used to be an old Golden Fleece petrol station, which was the last fuel before Caloundra, our house over-looking farming flats and bordered by the South Pine River. The Bonnie View Tavern is where we go to eat when we think we should leave the barriers of home in this new life.

We live in a tiny one-bedroom house made out of fibro, which is really asbestos, but we don't talk about that. There are weeds in the garden and next door is a Syrian family who sometimes give us home-made lollies. They cannot speak a word of English. They have two daughters and I look, sometimes, at their daughters and think: I hope it works out for you, for all of you.

Numb, you have to be numb, so I did Xanax with lithium and he did the voddy and then he did weed and now he's doing meth. 'I can control it,' he says to me every morning when I slumber awake at like ten or eleven, thinking: What happened last night?

We spent eight hundred and sixty-three thousand, two hundred and fifty-eight dollars on her legal fees. Of course, that bankrupted us. As we knew it would.

But you do that.

You do that for your child. Even though you know you are about to enter the end of the world as we know it.

We did not go to the court very often. We were there when we heard 'guilty' and when Anthea, love of my life, little Anthea now with her two gorgeous daughters, when she fell to the floor and wept and a medic had to be called in and they carried her out on a stretcher past this very tall, tattooed and rather horrid looking man with a Mohican haircut and he scared me and I followed Anthea. To the hospital. I think Hugh was with me. I can't remember.

—

I HATE HER.

I tried not to. After all, she is my first-born. I try to remember holding her and feeding her and the first crawl and the first walk and the first word which was 'chocolate' (where did that come from?) and that first day at school when she had proudly dressed herself in her new uniform and marched off with her backpack and when she started to become a young lady whom my mother would be so proud of, with her stupendous knowledge of literature, having read *Don Quixote* at the age of eleven but then the darkness slowly falling, the Goth stuff and I knew that when she became a teen it would be challenging, doors slamming and angry looks and rebellion (I mean, who am I to complain? I ran off with a guy called Buster and fucked him from here to eternity when I was thirteen) and the darkness and how do you reach out to your kid, a hand of love extended, like in that famous painting by Michelangelo in the Sistine Chapel with the almost-clasp of hands, how can you do that? Love, anger? Is there a rule book?

I tried to be strong.

But the hate just grew like a cancer. And like a cancer, despite all that you do to try and halt it, it just keeps on growing.

At least I have Anthea. At least one of them turned out well.

Although Hugh's sense of guilt is silly, I did make Anthea promise me that she would never tell her children the story of the Blood River and she told me she wouldn't.

Do It

I HAVE A DRIVER AT MY DISPOSAL, IF I WANT TO RIDE IN THE back seat of a car while working. My staff tell me I should take advantage of it more often but I love driving and I love driving fast (as fast as the law will allow) and listening to very loud music. It helps me relax and makes me concentrate on whatever is bothering me. Whatever needs resolution, if I can find it.

Like, this morning, Nils and his illegal stash of very dangerous weapons.

Billy had made two anonymous calls: one to Southport police to alert them to the arsenal of blades, and another to the parents of a missing sixteen-year-old runaway to disclose their daughter's current address with a recommendation they advise the local police instead of trying to rescue her themselves.

Damon wasn't bothering me so much as perplexing me as I cranked up the volume of the go-to music of the month, The Amity Affliction.

In his back room, the 'beard' room, was an X-ray. Of a man. Hung from the ceiling, about three metres high and two metres across. Placed upon a pale red background, it reminded Billy of a bad day at an avant-garde art gallery, where 'them pooftas put on bullshit and make tons of money'. Lucky Billy was out of the Service. These days he'd go down in a heartbeat for some of his language.

He'd sent me a photo of the X-ray. After he'd sent me a photo of the blood orange and the sharp-bladed knife. I don't know what unnerved me more: the X-ray of a man on the wall or the knife on the kitchen table.

The X-ray room didn't have the look of a room where art was displayed. Instead, it had the look of a room in a disturbed person's home.

And the knife wasn't an ordinary knife. It was striking, with a polished wooden handle and a strange metal surface to the blade. Like it had been burnished in an ancient cauldron. It took me straight back to the Celtic days and all that talk of sacrifices. Damon's knife also looked incredibly sharp. I did a little research and discovered it was a Nesmuk Jahrhundertmesser knife, made in Solingen, Germany and costing over nine thousand dollars. Made of Damascus steel and based on a design from three and a half thousand years ago. Which, Billy and I agreed, is a lot of knife to cut up a blood orange.

Nils looked like a killer. He looked as though he could cut open a man's neck and fold back his head. He was covered literally from head to toe in terrifying tattoos and had his own martial-arts security troupe of tattooed thugs. Damon, on the other hand, was a professor of advanced mathematics at the University of Queensland. He did not look the part. He did not act the part. And I couldn't bust him for the crime of owning an expensive knife and having creepy art in an otherwise-empty house.

What do I do with these two? There was no basis to bring them in for questioning; and anyway, I was supposed to fly up to Rockhampton this afternoon for a meeting with the district commander and then dinner with the Mayor, the council and community leaders.

Billy had suggested that I allow him to reach out to a couple of retired ex-cops and get them to surveil Nils and Damon, being happy to jump at any chance to get back into the scent of the game, under the radar. Just in case.

I'd said, before I went to bed, after Catherine Howard's head had come off, that I'd think about it.

I rang him from the car phone.

'Girlie.'

'Do it,' I said.

'Copy that,' he replied.

Sold Down the River

I HAD THE HOUSE TO MYSELF. I SAT OUTSIDE, IN THE GARDEN, on the grass, which was dry despite the earlier spot of rain. It was like a walled garden, each side covered by thick bushes and trees. I couldn't see any of the neighbours and they couldn't see me. I lay back and stared up at the sky. Dark clouds moved so slowly I had to measure them against the wall of trees to determine if they were moving at all.

I mean, sure, back then she could be steely-eyed and maybe a little too intense.

I mean, sure, she used to ride a skateboard and creep out at night, like I did, at different times and going places I didn't know about.

I mean, yeah, she was into the Goth world with that really heavy Norwegian black death-metal band.

I mean, she knew all about the Celtic world because I had that book about the gods, including Taranis and Ogmios.

Sure, she burned black candles and had a book on Aleister Crowley, the so-called 'wickedest man in the world', devil-worshipper and all-round wanker who invoked demons for blood sacrifice.

She would have had the physicality to knock over the three victims, from behind, forcing them to stumble, lose their balance and fall to the ground.

I mean, yeah, she was on the Year 11 and Year 12 school trip to North Stradbroke Island and could have picked some swamp daisy flowers. She liked flowers, but she liked butterflies more.

And she was the only one who stayed loyal to me. When the verdict came down, she fell hysterically to the floor of the court and had to be taken out by paramedics, which could have been brought on by seeing her sister go down for Life. Or it might have been the shock of realising that I had actually been convicted for her crimes. It could have all been out of guilt.

But there's nothing in the consideration of my little sister that says, *I'm going to kill three men, randomly. I'm going to slice open their neck and fold their head back onto their shoulder, then cut their mouth into a grotesque grin, rip out one of their teeth and carve the symbol of Taranis into their chest.*

I mean, a person like that wants something. I know; I became that person. I wanted the thrill because the adrenalin rush was impossible to deny and impossible not to embrace. I wanted people to be in awe of me as they would be of thunder and Taranis. I wanted them to fear me and I wanted that fear to spread across the city, like a spill of ink, black and indelible. I wanted to feel the warm rush of their blood, bathe in it. I wanted to be immortal.

Did she?

Have I misread the person closest to me?

—

I WENT BACK inside and sat on the wooden floor and stared at the string of teeth. I could have called dad and asked him if they were from his collection, but that wasn't a possibility, not after last night and the past twenty years. I could have waited until Anthea got home and asked her, but that wasn't a possibility. I took a photo of them. I could have sent it to Lara, but I wasn't going to drop my sister into a well of suspicion like I had been dropped twenty years earlier; I knew there was no turning back once the shadow of doubt crossed over you, especially if you were innocent. As she must be. Because there had to be a very simple, obvious, explanation; I just had to find it.

I went downstairs and into her bedroom. It was theirs, but it was hers. The scent of lavender and the soft pastel floral cushions and doona cover were hers. The thick white carpet and impeccable order were hers. Same in the bathroom, all gleaming white with expensive toiletries. It was like an advert for L'Occitane. Sprigs of dried lavender. Reproduction Matisse on the walls. A Balinese garden outside, through French doors, with a fountain and bougainvillea in earthenware pots. Her wardrobe was full of clothes, and none

of the boxes hid anything that might reveal the world of a serial
killer. Only expensive shoes. Her chest of drawers full of clothes
and jewellery. There were three strings of pearls and two antique
diamond-and-ruby rings. Earrings were in a special box.

It was a large downstairs area. Four bedrooms, two on either
side of the hallway, which led to a large family room with couches
and bean bags.

There was a bar fridge containing a lot of white wine. DVDs
and games and remotes were scattered on the floor. This was the
messy room.

I walked back upstairs. Off to the side of the large open lounge
and dining room with the kitchen and breakfast bar was her study
and Robbie's office. Both were small and intimate. His looked like
what you'd expect from a boring guy who worked in finance. Hers
had the appearance of a university professor's: a desk full of student
papers and a wall of books and journals. Her degree, her Masters
and her PhD were all framed on the wall. On her desk was a vase
of dead yellow tulips, their stems had flopped over and the petals
scattered across the pages of an open book from something called
the Annapurna Natural History Museum about the six hundred and
sixty species of butterflies in Nepal, alongside a laptop. I tried to
log in but couldn't guess the password. I went through all the desk
drawers, carefully checked the titles of all her books. I looked for the
killer's toolkit, a backpack of blades, knives and a pair of pliers.

Not there.

This is what it is, Jen, I said to myself. This is an office in the
house of a geeky zoology professor who specialises in lepidoptery.
Who has, by chance, some teeth in a wall mounting, next to feathers
and butterflies; is that so odd? It's just a coincidence. Go make some
bacon and eggs, brew up some real coffee, the breakfast you've
been dreaming of for years, with that sourdough bread she told
you about, and then sit on the couch and binge-watch Netflix, if
you can understand how the remote works. Spend the whole day in
your pyjamas and don't have a shower. Do whatever you want to do
whenever you want to do it, without anyone telling you otherwise.

As I began to walk out of the office, a curtain of darkness lifting
off me, I paused. Something had caught my eye.

Dad had given me the purple Qantas bag, with a zip along its side, small enough for a twenty-year trip to jail. He had given Anthea a blue Ansett bag, which I liked a lot more than mine. Her flight bag had a picture of a red and white jet flying upwards on its side and I thought it was better than the little white jet picture on my bag. I used to try and steal it from her. This was when we were really little, like when I was ten and she was nine. When we fought all the time.

And there it was, after all these years, sitting on top of her bookshelves, perched at the back.

After almost thirty years, there it sat.

I reached up to get it. I don't know why. I couldn't reach it. I grabbed her desk chair, moved it to the shelves, stood on it and reached up to the bag. I don't know why. Still standing on the chair, I unzipped the bag.

There were three knives or, I should say blades, inside. Rolled up in oilskin and then in very thin leather. There was a cleaver, like the ones Chinese chefs use to chop up ducks. There was a very long bladed stiletto and a small machete. They were all gleaming clean and very, very sharp. I traced one of my fingers along the edge of the cleaver, no more than a centimetre and it drew blood.

They were razor sharp.

I stared at them.

What happens now? I asked myself.

I have no fucking idea, I answered. Your sister is not only a monster, but she betrayed you. Life-and-Death betrayed you. The sister you loved who must, actually, hate you.

What happens now, Jen?

Because you told Lara that the killer was going to strike again because he – but he's not a he anymore – can; her last chance to kill again.

Hey, little sis, are you planning to kill again? To set me up? To set me up for the big fall, whereby old sis would go down the river to prison for the rest of her life? Like those slaves, sold down the wicked Mississippi river to a death sentence.

Is that me, Anth? Your beloved sister, is that what you're planning to do with me?

A Delicate Balance

'Hi,' said Anthea.

'Hi,' I said.

'How was your day?'

'Good. Yours?'

'Good.'

'Get everything done at uni?'

'Yeah. Thanks. Happy students.'

'That's what we like. Happy and content. Satisfied they're getting their money's worth. University's so expensive these days. And those student loans. Do your students have those terrible loans, the ones that they have to carry until they're middle-aged? Talk about a burden. A dreadful burden. Why the government doesn't just go back to the old days and make tertiary education a right, I don't know. I guess their hands are tied. Once you make a decision, it's almost impossible to shift it.'

—

She knew.

I saw it the moment I stepped into the lounge room, seeing her with the girls, the three of them on the couch, watching TV. Maxi and little Jen ran to me, as they do every time I come home and hugged me and asked if I'd let them have ice-cream after dinner. Jen just stayed on the couch, staring ahead at the TV screen. Ignoring me. Only for about five seconds, but that was ample time for me to figure it out and, when she did turn to me, her smile was forced and tight and she was play-acting. And now she's rambling. And look at her hands: they're trembling. Poor Jen.

I should have noticed it this morning. I thought she was a bit off but just put it down to the anxieties of the previous day.

And of course, there were the three knives. A childish display, which I noticed after I registered Jen on the couch.

'Did you go out?' I asked.

'No. Stayed inside all day. It rained a little bit,' said Jen.

'Did it?' I asked.

'Yeah. This morning and then about four this afternoon. I gave the girls some heated-up spag bol like you said.'

'Oh, great. Thanks for that.'

——

FOR THE FIRST time in my life I actually did want to commit murder. A blood-rush of anger swept through me and, without thinking, I thought I *had* to kill her. She took twenty years away from me. She killed me, so I had to kill her.

I had gone past the questioning. The doubt. The disbelief. It was her. I knew it. It all fitted into perfect, twisted, fucked-up, ridiculous logic. But for the why. I couldn't get that, but I knew it was her. She did it and led the trail to me. And because at school I was the dark bitch who made threats and lashed out after years of being bullied, the trail made sense. Anthea, on the other hand, had a loyal group. Her friends from then are still her friends now. If I close my eyes I can see her, standing at the edge of the kitchen door, the first time the police came. I can see her, standing at the front door stoop as Lara gripped my arm and led me down to the waiting police car. I can see her, standing in the rain, on the same door stoop, as the other police officers came back to arrest me and take me to the Valley to be charged.

She can't have meant for it to happen. Me going down for the crimes she committed. But I did.

And you couldn't speak up, could you? The Slayer had been caught. If it wasn't me, they would have had to keep looking. Everyone agreed that it was me, even Lara, even she testified to the knife. Everyone said it was me.

But for you. You stayed quiet.

And now here we are. The girls have given their mum a hug and she has said they can have ice-cream after dinner and suggested that maybe we could all go out to the upmarket burger place down on Racecourse Road, as a special treat, because Aunty Jen is here. And they shouted, as they always do when excited, *Yay!*

—

I PLACED THE knives on the dining table. Unmistakable. Unmissable. A fucking *cleaver*. No need for a highly awkward, 'Guess what I found in your office today?' moment. The defiant approach. Hey, look at this. Got an answer for this? Nothing said, the blades say it for me. Now, bitch, you fucking speak. Because I have nothing to say.

Then I thought of the girls and how they were due home from school before Anthea was due home from work. That wouldn't do. I couldn't bring them into this. Jesus, Anthea, did you fucking-think about the ramifications of what you did? Aside from me and twenty years gone. What about a future? Like, kids? Like, a career?

I picked up the knives, careful not to cut myself, and put them on her desk in her office. There I stood. Staring at them. Then I picked them up and walked downstairs and into her bedroom and placed them neatly on her pillow. There I stood. Then I picked them up and walked back upstairs and placed them on the breakfast bar in the kitchen, where the girls wouldn't pay close attention to them because they were just big knives, among the other kitchen knives. There I stood. Waiting.

The girls came home. Then, later, Anthea came home and walked into the kitchen, as she always did, to place her bag and briefcase on the breakfast bar, and as I was rambling about the high and unfair cost of tertiary education, I watched as she calmly took them and placed them in a drawer. Then suggested we all go out for burgers. She couldn't help a sideways glance at her trophies. The five teeth.

Five. Who are the other two victims, Anthea?

Not I

I HAD A DREAM. I HAD INVADED A DREAM. WE HAD, THE girls, my sister and I, gone to the burger place. We sat outside, on the footpath, under the sloping branches of jacaranda trees which hung low, so low that Maxi could jump up and touch some of them, little Jen trying but not reaching. A shower of rain swept along the street, coming in off the river nearby, where the old wharves used to be, where Anthea and I would play sometimes, creeping in through the wire fence.

She and I did not speak. The girls did not notice. Little Jen never got to touch the low branches of the tree.

I had a dream. I had invaded a dream. I was lying in a soft, warm ocean, at the edge of the water. My arms were splayed out and I was a starfish. The tips of my fingers trailed through the surface of the water. I heard the door to my room open and I felt the press of a person on the edge of my bed.

Listen, she whispered and I thought I could feel a tear-stained face upon mine. Is it you, Rosie?

Listen:

It was accidental, the first kill. I didn't mean to do it.

It was her fault.

She was in the scrub, across the road from the Sea World resort on the Gold Coast, that time mum and dad had sent us there on our own. The second time, or was it the third time? You were sleeping. I got up, left our bed, our room and went along the corridor and down in the lift and out through the foyer. Before dawn. I couldn't sleep. The people at the desk were worried that I was alone. I was twelve. You were thirteen. You were sleeping. I said: I'm okay, I like to get up really early and have a walk before dawn. They smiled and laughed, the people at the desk, as I walked out through the revolving front doors. I jogged along the road, turning into the bush and scrub of dry tea-tree. No butterflies. I was looking for butterflies. How can it be that, a hundred metres from the Sheraton and the Versace, there is a wasteland of scrub and sand. *C'est la vie. Sayonara, bonsoir.*

Little hills. Scrub in the sand, the sound of the waves on the beach nearby, and there she was.

She had long grey hair tied into a pony tail and she was sitting cross-legged with her back to me. Meditating. I guess. The dawn was far away but I could hear the sounds of barking. Dogs. Somewhere off. Along with the sounds of the waves crashing onto the sand.

I crept up behind her. Sat behind her. Watched her. Thinking:

She doesn't know I'm behind her.

Nobody knows.

I have total power. She has no idea I'm behind her, watching her. I can strike any time.

And I did. There was a tree branch next to me. Not too big, not too small. Big enough to hurt and small enough for me to wield. I cannot tell you why I did it. I just did. I picked up the branch and struck her, on the back of the neck, as hard as I could. She fell, of course, to the ground, sideways, and lay with her eyes fluttering like a butterfly in its death moment. Staring up at me as I stood over her and brought the tree branch down on her head.

And then another. And then another. By the time I finished, her head was a smashed, pulpy mess of blood and gore. With every blow, as her head got flatter and flatter, I got more and more excited. I just wanted to pummel it. There might have been thirty or forty blows to her head before it was just mush. There was a tooth. The daylight came and I could hear the sounds of birds, loud, from all around me.

I stepped into the ocean. In my clothes, I strode out into the surf. No-one was on the beach. No-one saw me. It had begun to rain. The wind was hard and strong.

I came out of the water and sat on the sand and dried off, which took a little time. Some blood and gristle had lodged in my hair, and some of her spray, blood and gunk had splashed across my face and seeped into my mouth. I swallowed some of her mushed head. Don't be disgusted, big sister, because it tasted like power and strength. I had tasted life. It tasted good.

While you and I went to Sea World and screamed on all the rides and ate too many chicken nuggets, I saw the police arrive and then an ambulance and saw her body being carried out of the scrub, all covered up. The police were there for days. They were still there after we left a week later. I read they arrested a man, sent him to jail. I didn't know it at the time but the area of scrub across the road from the resort was a famous gay hangout. So, the cops got a gay guy. They would never have considered me. I was too young and I was a girl.

Being a girl was the best disguise.

—

I WAKE UP early. That's prison for you. I got out of bed and walked upstairs, softly. It was Saturday. The girls get to sleep in.

As I made coffee, I tried to order my thoughts. My memories. Did Anthea come into my room last night, talk to me? Did she confess to a killing when she was twelve? Or was that a dream?

I looked across to the wall of butterflies. The box of teeth, the trophy box; in its place was another cabinet of butterflies. The blades were also gone. Not in the drawer and not back in her study.

The killer had covered her tracks.

What was I to do?

Be silent, acquiescent, say nothing, do nothing. That she knew I knew would keep her compliant. That she knew I knew would keep her from committing another murder.

I was certain she had planned another murder. Because she could. Because I was free, the perfect fall-woman, the last hit of an addiction strong but put on hold. Our secret, my sister's and mine. Never spoken of. But ours.

I would leave. I would go back to Southport and the job at Bunnings and just shy my eyes away as the throngs tried to capture me with their phones and viral me on social media. Those eyes would keep me safe: the killer would not kill again because I knew her secret and I would be in the spotlight of social media, my every move followed, recorded. My notoriety would be my alibi.

I wasn't sure what to do about the Attorney-General and his campaign to put me back inside. There wasn't anything I really could do but hope the #JenIsInnocent movement gathered enough momentum to turn public opinion. Maybe I should start a YouTube channel.

Gelignite

OVER THE YEARS I HAD BECOME A CAUSE-CÉLÈBRE FOR A number of well-meaning but strident women, and some men, who supported my innocence and opposed my long stay in prison. #JenIsInnocent. I figured that any prisoner with a profile would get that sort of attention while incarcerated, especially a woman and when the case was as salacious as mine, so I had mostly ignored it. I was not allowed internet while inside, so most of the flames blew past me. But I knew it was there. Just like I was aware of the TV shows about me. I knew there was a small band of followers, agitating for my release, convinced of my innocence.

But I was not prepared for the storm that would follow once I got out.

—

On November 18 1999 James Gibney was murdered in Brisbane. Shortly after, two more men were killed. By the same person, who became known as The Slayer. Very recently I, in my capacity as the president of the parole board, allowed the release of the person known as The Slayer.

Her name is Jennifer White and I believe she is innocent.

I do not believe she committed these crimes. Our Attorney-General, Ray Conway, is determined to put Ms White back in prison, for the rest of her life. He is wrong. He is acting illegally, and while he stokes the fires of public anger – a public that has not been fully informed – an innocent person is being threatened.

Nobody wants to hear that a person who has been demonised is innocent.

She is.

The Slayer is still at large.

I am writing this to inform the public that Ms White was wrongly convicted and that our Attorney-General is acting outside the law.

Yes, I was removed from the office of president of the parole board. No, I am not writing this out of anger. All I care about is honesty. Truth. Justice. My record speaks for itself. I have always spoken out for truth and justice, no matter how inconvenient it may be.

—

AND ON IT went.

Thanks, Ms Jones, but I think my life just got a lot more complex because of you. Thanks, *Courier Mail*, yet again, for poking another knife into my life, with your front page Saturday news story. Along with the headline: *Calls for a New Inquiry into the identity of The Slayer.*

Twenty years after baying for my blood, which they got, the media is now baying for the blood of the *real* Slayer and feasting on a new story: *Is Jen Innocent?*

Shot of Love

NILS WAS ALREADY ANGRY. HIS SIXTEEN-YEAR-OLD girlfriend, Iris, had left him overnight, run away. He'd thrown her to the floor, towered over her and pulled off his clothes and invoked one of his mad bullshit Celtic rants which freaked her out. She kicked him in the dick and skedaddled quick smart out of the grimy apartment, ignoring his wails.

And then he saw the front page news from the *Courier Mail* and, tucked into the two-page spread on pages seven and eight was a photo of him then, leaving court and a photo of him now, lizard man. Do the math. Nils was, he knew, going down.

He knew where Lara lived; he knew she hadn't moved out of the small house in Hendra, close to the racecourse. There had been a profile on her, after she became the first Asian woman police commissioner in the country. In the anywhere. Except for Asia. She was special, she was unique, a trail-blazer and, after the detritus of Iris and this new media gaze, she was in his sights to cut and kill.

Remembering his promise, that he would stick his knife into her and slice her to the neck or do to her what the Japanese soldiers did in China, in that competition between the two swordsmen, cutting Chinese men and women in half in one fierce swift blow to the head, down to the waist.

He put his sword – his favourite – into a sling, on his back. He admired himself in the mirror. He was the illustrated man. On his forehead was Ogmios. On his tongue was a bolt of thunder. On his left eyebrow were drops of blood. On his right eyebrow was a vagina. On his nose was a clitoris. On his chin was an AK-47. On his left cheek was a bleeding corpse, a woman whose chest had been ripped open, blood falling to his neck. On his right cheek were four blades, crossed over, forming a swastika. He sucked in his breath and remembered back to when he, another Nils, and Lara, lived in the caravan, when he was scared and confused and she gave him solace, lifting him away from the abuse of his father and mother who would stick pins into him. And then more. And more, until he ran.

Running still, as he stepped out of the apartment above the motorcycle shop and rode up to Brisbane.

In anger.

He didn't get far.

—

BILLY HAD TASKED Ranger Paul, an old mate from CIB back in the nineties, to stay close to Nils. Ranger Paul was driving a Subaru and pulled out of the kerb as the illustrated man rode off, sword slung over his back as if he didn't give a shit about anything.

Nils rode his Harley too fast. But that was how he liked it. He always thought he'd go out in a James Dean burst of flame. The end befitting the life.

Nils gunned the ton.

The last snapshot Ranger Paul saw of Nils's life was a Harley careening off the side of the highway, a few kilometres south of the Logan turn-off. The last snapshot Nils saw, as he lost control of his 750, as he hurtled towards the barriers along the highway, gripped with anger and having been distracted by an incoming call from Iris, was water. The creek below, as he smashed through the barrier and sailed to his death, the inky brown of the creek rising up to greet him.

He sank. The bike on top of him. Unable to wrestle himself out of its metal grip, he sank. The sword came loose and floated to the surface.

The Tensile Grip

SIMON WAS SHOWING IN THE MEDIA LIAISON TEAM WHEN I received the call from Billy telling me that Nils was finally on his way to eternally meet his god of thunder.

I had called a crisis meeting for six a.m. to discuss my strategy in response to Karin Jones's explosive newspaper piece.

To add further inconvenience to an already-irritating situation, Nils, the second serious suspect in the case, has just died. Once the media got hold of Nils's death, a new burst of energy would hit the story. Media stories like this are like fires: they need oxygen. I fully understood this and it was my job to take control and manage it. Like a firefighter, get ahead of the flames.

'Okay, this is the press release,' I told them. Recent grads from the Griffith University course in Media, they each had a tablet, hands poised, waiting for the spiel, staring at me. Anxious but determined to prove their worth. Just as I had been when I stood in the same spot, on the other side of the desk between Kristo and Billy as The Dutchman told us to get our goddamned acts together and find The Slayer who, in a turn of unexpected (or was it, I wondered, remembering back to the knife and its sudden discovery) events, is back in the headlines after twenty years.

'Following recent commentary in the media regarding a twenty-year-old case involving the tragic murder of three men in the Brisbane area, the Commissioner of Police has today ordered that a new investigation be opened to analyse whether any new evidence has come to hand which may lead to further action. Queensland Police asks that the privacy of the families involved be respected and that unwarranted media speculation be avoided, particularly if this case is to return to the courts.'

In Billy's day, media liaison was done with a fist or a beer.

'That's good,' said Samuel. 'Send?'

I nodded. 'Send. And, in response to all the calls, just remind them of the inappropriateness of comment regarding an ongoing investigation.'

'What if they ask who's leading the investigation?'

That was the next item on the agenda, but I needed some clean time to think. I was more rattled than I cared to admit. Not by Karin Jones's piece in the newspaper; I'd dealt with firestorms before, that was part of my job.

It was Nils's death.

—

TWENTY-FIVE YEARS LATER and he still had a grip on me. I never imagined that news of his death would affect me. But guys like Nils, they never completely go away, not even in death. I ran from him, twice, but it was I, in the first instance, who followed him. He was my first lover and my first real teacher. If it hadn't been for Nils and his abuse, I might never have stood up to find the woman I had now become.

—

SINCE 1999 WHEN Damon had last texted me, I have had many different phones with many different numbers. And none of those numbers had I given to Damon.

So, it was both a surprise and not a little eerie when I got a text from him after the media team left the office to spread the good word of the Commissioner's control of the Slayer situation. The text simply read:

Would you like to explain?

And, attached was a photo. Of Billy. In Damon's house, last night, after he had broken in. Clearly Damon had security cameras in his house and clearly Billy had not spotted them.

Why is it I keep stumbling with this guy? It's not as awkward as pretending I was gay, which he obviously knew was a lie, but it was awkward and here am I, forty-six years old and the person in charge of the entire police department, yet again caught out and feeling defensive.

I texted him back.

The Long Goodbye

'I THOUGHT I'D GO DOWN TO THE GOLD COAST, BACK TO Westaway House and the job at Bunnings,' I said to Anthea. It was early, the girls were still asleep. 'It was good of you to come and rescue me but, you know, I've got to stand on my own two feet. Can't go crying off to my little sister every time there's an issue.'

I couldn't stand the sight of her, and though I wanted to stay a part of my nieces' lives, I wanted nothing more to do with my sister. I would never forgive her. I would stay quiet, erase her from my life and build anew. I would never speak to her again. Maybe the girls would come to see me when they were older, when they could do things on their own.

I had wondered about the safety of the girls. After all, they were living with a serial killer, albeit one who had last killed when she was a teenager. I assumed. But Anthea appeared to genuinely love them and I remembered, when I became her, the killer, The Slayer, about the serial killers I'd studied who loved their kids: BTK (ten kills) or The Happy Face Killer (eight kills) or The Green River Killer (forty to seventy kills). All happy dads. All monster killers. Empathy this direction. None the other.

'Oh no, don't do that,' Anthea replied. 'I thought we'd all go out for lunch. And I was talking to Robbie last night, and he's going to organise a lawyer to come to see you here, to discuss all this crazy stuff that the Attorney-General is on about. Robbie says you can take legal action against them because what they're saying is illegal.'

I wonder if my sister read this morning's newspaper. I wonder if she might be a little anxious that a new investigation will be mounted and that she might actually become a suspect. Does she think I might tell? She's hidden, possibly destroyed, the evidence of the teeth, but what would happen if I told Lara Ocean what I saw?

Well, to be honest, most likely nothing. Because no-one would believe me. But if I were the killer, I would be a little nervous having someone aware of the truth.

'Just stay one more day. The girls would be crushed if you left again, so soon.'

Saturday lunch with the girls, maybe a movie and then some homemade pizza for dinner.

'Just one more day,' she implored.

———

BECAUSE I NEED you to stay one more day and night so that I can do what has to be done. The story in today's newspaper, Karin's little anthem to truth and justice, made it clear I was in danger. If the police re-open the case, they will ask questions. *The* question: Did we go after the wrong sister all those years ago?

And then there's Jen. For the moment she and I are dancing the dance of silence. But how long can that last? Once you have a valuable piece of information, it's just a matter of time before you release it, on purpose or not. And I do not want to be beholden to an angry, resentful sister for the rest of my life. Like dad's cancer, her feelings for me will fester.

Before, when I was planning the new kill, after the self-doubt, it was for fun, a return to the glory of the blood-lust. But now, the new killing will be for self-preservation.

Who Are You?

'WHAT'S HAPPENING? HAS THIS GOT TO DO WITH THOSE three guys who almost had their heads cut off?'

'What?' asked Jen, in a total daze, sitting on the end of her bed, staring out to space, staring out through the window at the rain. All the footpaths on the hill had flooded. It was three in the afternoon and cars had their headlights on and had to drive slowly so as not to slide away in a cascade of water.

'What are you *talking* about?' she said.

'Don't you read the newspapers or watch the news?'

'No. What three guys?'

'One in the Kangaroo Point Cliffs and two in the Gardens. Someone killed them by sawing into their necks and almost decapitating them.'

'Are you fucking kidding me?'

'Nup.'

I was freaking out.

'Why would they think it's you?' I asked Jen.

She had just come back from being dragged out of the house by those two cops. The tall Asian woman with dyed blonde hair, in black jeans, t-shirt and Docs, with a pistol tucked into a holster like Lara Croft and this stumpy old guy in a spick-suit with patent leather shoes had come to the house and I'd watched them, from the edge of the kitchen, as they asked Jen and mum a few questions before they took her away.

Now she's back.

She reached out and held my foot and began to cry.

'Is this really happening?' she asked me.

When I first saw them, the cops, in the house, I started to shut down. They think Jen had something to do with the killings? How did they get here? Why is it her they're talking to?

I'd seen these two cops when I was hiding in the shadows at the first crime scene, after I had realised that I'd dropped one of those weird daisy flowers that I had kept from the school trip to Stradbroke Island, out of my backpack where I kept the blades.

Now they were here.

I didn't mean it to be her. You have the wrong fucking sister! I wanted to shout.

But. Of course I did not. I remained silent. Doing nothing, saying nothing, was easier.

Then they took her and mum away, in the rain, leaving me alone in the house and I just stood there, in the living room, staring out into the backyard. I think I stood there, like that and without moving, for about two or three hours. Aside from figuring out – after I killed that first fear, which was totally spontaneous; he was just walking in a drunk walk along the jogging track at Kangaroo Point and as I got closer to him on my skateboard, realising that it was just him and me and nobody else, I took off my backpack, pulled out my cleaver blade and chopped him, on the back of the neck as soon as I skated past him, leaping off the board and chopped him and he fell to the ground under a very tall bougainvillea bush which was convenient because I could then straddle him as I cut into his neck and face, all of this, the tooth and the carving on his chest, done on the fly, me thinking after I pulled out the tooth, hooray! and then immediately wondering how I could keep on mutilating him, hearing the words of Taranis and Ogmios, who were my gods, as I rode the dying fear like a cowgirl would ride a dying horse – aside from figuring out as I stood, having finished with him and his blood, which was beginning to wash off me as rain came to reward me, aside from figuring out how to ensure I left no traces of me behind and that nobody had seen me kill him, which nobody had, I had not contemplated *at all* that the cops might find a trace which could lead them to my sister.

I hadn't thought at all about the possibility of another person becoming a suspect. I'd just been thinking about me and ensuring that it wasn't me who the cops came looking for.

Well, I was successful there. It's just that they came after the one person who mattered more to me than anyone.

As I stood in the living room, by the stupid white Christmas tree and its flashing lights which kept blinking at me, as I stood and stared out through the big French windows into the back yard, focussing on how all the trees seemed to be heavy with the deluge of rain, like they were weighted down, slumped towards the grass, I thought:

I must confess.

Save my big sis; release her from the horror, and I decided I would and then, after a few hours, she came home. By then I'd gone back upstairs to my room and fallen asleep. I think it was her crying, the sound of her tears through the adjoining wall, that woke me.

I comforted her. She had no idea that three men had been brutally and spectacularly killed by the river. Fuck knows what planet she'd been living on. I thought mum was the only space cadet in the house.

And then, I just decided not to. While I was comforting her. That was my opening and I let it slide to another world. The world gone wrong.

I guess I didn't really think through the ramifications of that decision either. I didn't imagine she would go to jail for Life, like for almost twenty years but, as it became more and more clear that she was the number one suspect for the cops, helped no end by those horrid not-friends of hers from school (Donna, are you listening, bitch?) I started to feel okay about it.

At first it was serious big-time guilt but that ebbed after a little while and I actually felt good, like I had gotten away with these amazing murders, which would go down in the history of Brisbane and I began to feel really buoyed about people starting to understand the power of Taranis and Ogmios; I was their ambassador and that made me feel very good, very strong. I was like a butterfly, free from its cocoon.

I loved my sister and I still do but I love me more.

It's not like I meant it to happen.

It tore me up when she got Life. For a couple of days I was a mess and I vowed to visit her and stay loyal to her. I vowed, after I killed the aoife down by the river, rolling her into the water, that I would not kill again, to ensure that I stayed free until Jen's release. I was an addict but I was strong enough to wait and back then, after I decided not to confess, to let her take the fall for me, I was only caring about me. Everything was about me, the world circled around me. Ogmios and Taranis, silly teenage fantasies that they were, a child's attempt at identity, circled around me.

Me, me, me.

And then Maxi. And then little Jen, named after my rising guilt and confirmation that life was not just me, my life; life was about others as well. The lives that I had brought into the world.

It wasn't so easy for me, after Jen went to jail. The whole Sister Death thing, the parents-collapse thing, losing all their money and moving to Bald Hills. Fighting the addiction of killing. The butterflies helped. Hunting them, killing them, mounting them in my never-ending collections. I love them like I love my sister. I can't help killing them although I would never use that word with my students or in any of my lectures or academic papers. I am preserving them.

I am, I have to confess, excited about killing again.

It's planned. Everything is planned.

To be honest, I won't actually be that sorry to see her go. Jen. Back to jail. I enjoyed it when she was in prison and she depended on me and I think I'd like that through to the end of her life and I think it would be good for the girls too, to be caring towards their auntie Jen, as I have been over the last two decades. It makes you feel good about yourself. I know how that sounds but there's no point in saying something unless I am totally honest.

I sometimes think about eviscerating Robbie. While he lies next to me. I have fantasies of taking out the cleaver and straddling him and digging into his pubic bone, like I did to Miss Homeless and cutting him up, up to his neck and then doing the swish across the neck and folding his head onto the pillow and grooming his smile so he and I could look at one another, lovers in death. I don't love him and never have. I couldn't give a rats if he died tomorrow. I love the girls.

It will be good, this last kill, the kill that will put sis back behind bars forever and will free me forever. It's better this way.

Mea Culpa

'HE'S HERE,' SAID SIMON.

Seeing Damon was not a priority and certainly not on a hectic day such as this, Karin's letter sending the government into a tailspin of crisis when the Attorney-General had been planning on defending his decision to sack the parole board with a press conference, with the Premier forced to stand behind him for the sake of the law-and-order votes, not to mention the increasingly popular mooted new act in parliament to put ex-cons like Jen away for the rest of their days. Now everything was in turmoil with the suggestion we had got it wrong twenty years ago.

I was confident I'd ride it out, having announced a new inquiry. But the phones were ringing non-stop and both the Premier and the Police Minister and the Attorney-General wanted the time of my assurances to ensure that any bad press would be sheeted away from them to me.

However, we all knew but did not say that the public trust a police commissioner a lot faster than they trust a politician. Thus, they had to tread carefully around me. Every politician wants one of two things: a front page photo of themselves and a Hollywood movie star and the steadfast assurance that their police will not attack them. I had the upper hand. I would never say it out loud, but as long as I had the complete support of the rank and file, I was the most powerful person in the state.

I got up from my desk and walked out of the office, down a plush carpeted corridor and into the boardroom. Closing the door behind me.

Damon, twenty years older, balding and pudgy, rose from his chair. I didn't even get a look-in with a hello or a thanks-for-coming-in or a this-has-to-be-quick; he just unleashed:

'Sorry, I don't get it. Have I done something to offend you? Like, is it your life's journey to make me some sort of joke? Twenty years' ago, telling me you're gay. Okay, fine, whatever. Did I try to come onto you? I don't think so. Did I try to harass you back to dinner again after it was very patently clear that you didn't want anything to do with me? I don't think so. Which is why I told your mother that the casino date was not going to happen. I stayed clear, gave you space, let you get on with your life. But now, after twenty years, after I send you a text, you respond by getting someone to break into my house. What? You think I am a person of interest? That's what you call them, right?'

And on it went. There was a clock on the wall behind him. I stared at the second hand as it registered one minute, twenty-six and then he stopped.

—

HEY MUM, DAMON came by the office today. He spoke at me for one minute and twenty-six seconds about what a bad person I am for not treating him with respect and for allowing Billy to break into his house. Remember Billy, mum? The old copper who spoke with the funny accent? You met him at the Christmas party I dragged you along to. When was that? Was that back in 1999? I think it was. When I was investigating my first big killer, you remember, you loved talking about her, saying she drank the blood of her victims. Remember I escorted you up to the Homicide office where all the blokes had their wives and girlfriends and Billy came directly over to you and like Michael Caine in a movie, reached down, took your hand and kissed it. And you blushed. Remember that night? The Christmas tree which almost fell over because our boss Kristo got a bit drunk and fell backwards into it. My first big case after my first big year in the big league. Homicide. My partner being the oldest and most experienced and he kissed your hand. Later he told me he thought you had all the elegance of the Orient.

I'm sorry about Damon, mum. He is an okay guy. Just weird. I guess I did abuse him but you know what they say about an investigation, don't you? You told me, when I was a kid, reflecting on your years as a cop in Hong Kong, before you got the horrors after I said I was going into Homicide and not Fraud: eliminate everyone and leave no stone unturned and don't judge a book by its cover and even a nasty killer can help a little old lady cross the road.

I'm sorry mum. I'm forty-six and left over. No-one's coming for me now mum. I have a confession: I am okay with that. I'll die alone mum, in another forty years' or so, listening to the sounds of the clack-clack of the horses out the front of my little house.

While we're on the mea culpas, I'm sorry I bombed you with the flakes of my fucked-up life, the moonage daydream of an angry teen. I didn't mean to hurt you.

我爱你妈妈。

Hey, I can write some Mandarin now. Is this good enough, mum?

The Fire Next Time

DARKNESS FELL SWIFTLY.

I was in the mind of the killer. I *was* her. Lying in bed, on edge, knowing what she had planned for the night.

She had forgotten that over my years in prison I had plenty of time to step inside the mind of the murderer. Be him. Be *her*. Think like her. Act like her. Understand her every move. I knew what she would do. From the moment, early this morning, imploring me to stay for just one more day, one more night. Using the girls as cover. *They really want to spend all of Saturday with their aunty.* Using the bogus excuse of the lawyer who could help mount a legal challenge to the Attorney-General's proposed new law, the Jen White law. The lawyer didn't turn up. *So sorry, Jen, he's been called away on last-minute business.*

She was acting to the script I had written. This morning, before the girls finally emerged from their sleep, I had returned to the killer, stepped inside her dark and twisted mind.

Now I was waiting.

—

OUR BIGGEST CHALLENGE will be the CCTV, won't it, little sis? Not like twenty years ago, when Brisbane had hardly any cameras in parks and on city streets and we could skate to the Botanic Gardens and not be filmed. Now there are cameras on every street corner. We have to find somewhere less visible and somewhere close, because we can't use the car – it might wake me up, and having big sis asleep in her room is part of the plan. I will have no alibi, so we have to find a park close by. We can't afford to rely on a random victim walking along a footpath on the hill because it's

391

very quiet up here on the hill, after about eight p.m., after the last
of the dog-walkers have returned home. And we have a timeframe
issue. Our kill has to be tonight because I'm going back to the Gold
Coast tomorrow. Tonight has to be it. But that's okay because there
are a few parks nearby and one of them is just perfect, isn't it? I
know our first inclination is Oriel Park, which is very close, only
four streets away and there is no CCTV there and some of its areas
are perfect. The massive bamboo thicket. The brick toilet block.
The towering Norfolk Island pine trees. The ring of houses where
everyone goes to bed early. But it's too uncertain. We could wait in
Oriel Park for eighteen nights before a possible victim strolled in.
We need a bit more flash and zap. We need a pub that closes at two
or three a.m. and disgorges the drunk and the young into its dark
streets. The Breakfast Creek Hotel, a magnet for all ages, especially
on a Saturday night. Great for food. Great for live music. Great to
pick up a fuck for the night. Great to get smashed with the boys or
the girls. Five bars, a restaurant, a steak-house, a beer garden. And
what is it about the Breakfast Creek Hotel, that old, huge rambling
complex of a pub built well over a hundred years ago in that creepy
faux French Renaissance style of architecture, that makes it so
perfect a target? Out the front is your Brisbane River but right
behind it is a racecourse. Where the greyhounds and harness racing
happens, once or twice a week. And all those narrow, dingy little
streets around the racecourse is where the drunks have parked
their cars. Lots of trees and shadows. A mangrove-infested creek,
running off the river, close by. It's a no-brainer for us. Ten minutes
to get down there, ten to wait and strike, three minutes to head-
fold, cut the sides of his mouth and extract the tooth. Ten back
home. All done, in well under an hour.

———

I HEARD THE stirrings at 2.15 a.m. The soft touch of her feet on
the floor in the room next to mine. She was moving quietly. Tiptoeing. I heard the door softly open and feet scurry up the stairs.

I was ready. Fully dressed, as she would be, in black tights,
black sweatshirt and a peaked cap. Black runners. Her clothes. She

had opened her wardrobe to me and told me to borrow anything I wanted. We were the same size. I waited until I heard her upstairs then got up and waited in the corridor downstairs. When I heard the front door open, I moved quickly up into the darkened lounge area.

As I stepped out the front door I saw her, ahead, as she jogged out of the driveway and onto the footpath. I followed.

There was a moon but the sky was dense with fast-moving black rain clouds. Every now and then another dark cloud would pass in the sky and reveal a burst of moonlight. The weather bureau had forecast no more rain for the weeks ahead. Even at this hour, it was hot. Anthea was jogging in her black outfit, along the footpaths that wound down the hill to the creek and our target location. Old trees hung from either side of the narrow streets. All was quiet. No-one driving.

—

AFTER THE MEDIA release went out and after the news of Nils hit the airwaves and after I tasked the Officer-In-Charge of Homicide to re-open the Slayer case so, in media-speak, *we could all move forward with confidence*, I got a text message.

I have two phones. One is my business number, which seems to buzz day and night. The other is personal and hardly ever rings, because hardly anyone has the number. Not even Damon could get this one. Mum had it. Billy does. Jen White does.

Jen sent me a photo she said she'd taken from the day before. A string of human teeth. Five teeth, maxillary canine teeth. The trophies. The elusive hard evidence that pinned the victims' DNA to the killer.

Her sister.

The second photo was a wider shot, of the cabinet in which the teeth were mounted, at the bottom of a wall of cabinets, the rest all filled with butterflies.

At first I thought it was a pathetic joke. Then I was shocked into disbelief. Then it slowly began to make sense. Right house, wrong sister. I didn't bother with the why. Like the drum-chested little Irish prosecutor twenty years ago, all that mattered was that she did it, not why she did it. Right now I couldn't care less about the why. Maybe, after the killer has gone down and I have some time, I'll consider the psychology, the black hole of a serial killer's mind, but for now, as I stared at the photo, I had only one objective.

And then a third text. *She is going to try to kill again tonight. Be at the back of the Breakfast Creek Hotel from 2am. I'll meet you there.*

So, here I am, at two in the morning, in a side street behind the hotel, music thumping out over the din of drunken laughter.

———

BY TWO-FORTY WE had arrived. Fifty metres ahead of me, Anthea had melted into the dark shadow of a laneway that ran off a street behind the hotel. The street was full of parked cars, on both sides. The racecourse was on the other side. I could hear the shouts and bombast yells of guys, the laughter and screeches of girls, all pouring out of the hotel as they made their way through the car park, onto the dark streets and up towards us.

I texted Lara and, hearing the shuffle of feet, realised that she was behind me. She'd been waiting in the shadows of the same street, where the roots of large jacaranda trees had cracked through the concrete of the footpath. The moon snuck in a short burst of white light every few minutes.

'She's there,' I whispered.

'I know. I saw her arrive. She's standing at the corner of the street and the laneway. It's a good place for a kill.'

We heard someone approach, feet dragging and an unsteady step. A drunk man.

Here he came, around the corner from the hotel car park, fumbling with his car keys, pressing the zap release to get a bead on where he had parked. Pointing his keylock in both directions and swaying on his feet. Well past the legal limit. He was in his thirties and wore a dishevelled suit with a white shirt hanging out. He would have looked business-like in the morning. Now he was a scruffy pisshead.

A car, parked just beyond where Anthea was waiting, beeped and its orange lights blinked. As the man began to shuffle past the entrance to the laneway, he stopped and looked in.

She stepped out and walked up to him. In her hand, by her side, was the long, wide blade.

Blood River

'YOU'RE DEAD,' HE SAID, MY DAD.

He didn't mean to hurt me. He was just being a dad, sitting at the end of my bed, telling me a story and all kids like to hear spooky stories, don't they?

I was four and I know, from the experiences with my girls, that all memories are erased, but for the occasional, indistinct and hazy image, when a child turns five. There's a switch which gets turned on. Erase, delete.

But not to me, not when I turned five. The story of Blood River, which he told me at the age of four, sitting in the dark, on the end of my bed, stayed with me forevermore.

Haunted me then. Haunts me now.

'I'm not dead,' I told my dad, starting to cry. 'I'm here, in bed!'

He laughed, but not, as it seemed to me then and now, at a little girl's innocent protestations but at her foolishness.

I see it now, I saw it then.

'And being dead,' he continued, 'you'll have to cross the Blood River, to get to the world of the dead; is it heaven or is it hell? Only once you cross the river, the ferryman's journey, will you know what your destiny is. Where are you going, Anthea? To heaven or to hell?'

'I don't like this story, dad.'

'Nor did your older sister but she never complained.'

No. Jen never complained. And, being the older of us, she had already forged what was acceptable. If she hadn't complained about anything then I had no right to either. Jen was the precedent and I was the follower.

Dad's journey, from the land of the living to the land of the dead, crossing the Blood River. He places me in a small wooden

396

boat, pushes me away from the edge of the river. It's night and a storm is raging all around me. Hail, rain, bolts of lightning, but not over me; I am protected, in a calm, as I am rowed across the river. I am four. I am five. Six. Sixteen. I am seventeen. Twenty. I am now as I was always then, being rowed across the dark river while a tempest raged around me, protected from the winds and the rain. There are no lights. There is no city. There are no people, but for the ferryman who rows me towards the other side, its shore seeming to recede as I grow closer. The ferryman has no eyes. In their place are two silver coins. That's the price of the trip, that's what I paid him as dad placed me into the little boat and gave it a push, on the edge of the river, casting me across the black water.

'Don't look down,' he said.

'Why not?' I asked.

'Because that's where they are.'

'Who?' I asked.

'The tormented souls of the dead. The river bed is writhing with their entwined bodies. They have not made it to the other side of the river or, if they did, they were cast back into the blood waters of hell, disallowed from travelling any further. Can you hear them?' he asked.

I could. I still can.

Thousands of slithering bodies held down to the bottom of the river, groaning in torment as they try to get away. Get free. They have been lashed to the river bed, the mud oozing over them under them through them. Naked, writhing bodies. Sea-snakes burrowing inside them, sliding into their eye-sockets, into their mouths, wriggling into the vaginas of the women and into the penis-eyes of the men. Sea-snakes the colour of red and orange, roiling inside the bodies of the damned as they try to escape the agonies of being bitten and eaten from inside, as the snakes enjoy their prey. The water is so heavy they cannot rise to the surface but, says dad:

Look, look at that.

What, dad? I asked in tears.

The surface of the river as you are rowed across it.

And I did what he said and looked down. All around me on the surface of the Blood River were the ears and tongues and the lips of the men and women and children and babies, which had been sliced off. Floating on the gentle swell of the river. As the cries of torment and agony rose from below, through the press of water.

They were screaming at me.

Stop! Help! Reach down to release me, little girl. Save us!

But they are chained to the riverbed. Their arms are locked around one another and the devil's force plays with them as he holds them down, sometimes dragging them deeper under the mud, sometimes gorging them up, like volcanoes. But they are never released from the limbs of the others which form the chain that binds them.

Can you hear them, Anthea?

Yes dad, I can hear them.

I still do.

I hear the dreadful scent of decay.

This is the Blood River, this is what my father led me to at the age of four and smiled as he placed me into the little wooden boat, placing the silver coins into the empty sockets of the ferryman.

You never reach the other side. The journey never ends. You never feel the rain, nor the wind. The tempest never touches you.

But you hear what is below you and you can smell what is below you and if you lean over and look down, you can see it because even though the water is blood-red and black, you can see right down to the bottom as if it were clear. You can see them, the tormented souls, staring up at you.

They are there, my fears and aoifes. I put them there. I can hear them wailing in pain, calling my name. I told them my name, I whispered my name as I rode them to death, I told them who I was and that they were about to cross the river of blood but that they would not make the other side because you can't. You never will. It keeps on receding. I told them they would be dropped into the river and sink to the end, where waiting arms, outstretched by the thousands upon thousands of God's children were waiting to embrace them into the mud and the blood, locking them into the inferno of my hell.

You're dead, I said, to them.

The Life of Butterflies

'HEY,' WE HEARD HER SAY, AND AS THE DRUNK MAN TOOK A step towards her, as she retreated a step back into the dark of the laneway as if to entice him in, Lara bolted across the street, with a 'Police! Don't move!'

In her hand was a gun. Shocked, the drunk would-be victim spun around, lost his balance and fell to the ground.

Anthea didn't move.

'Drop the knife,' said Lara. At that moment I realised she had not come alone – three other officers, all in uniform and carrying firearms, stepped out of the dark, just up from where we had been waiting, and then, in a daze of confusion, I heard the sound of a police siren coming at me from one direction and a second one from the opposite direction. Anthea had not moved. Lara stepped up to her, turned her around and handcuffed her as the two police cars converged on them.

Suddenly the street was crawling with police. And the snap snap of the red and blue lights had lit up the entire area of small houses and narrow streets at the bottom of the hill.

The drunk guy was totally confused as he was led away by a cop.

Another cop picked up Anthea's backpack and another bagged her knife into an evidence container. Someone was telling Anthea that she was being arrested for an attempted murder and was the subject of further investigations relating to three homicides in Brisbane in 1999 and that she would be driven to the city watch house and brought before a magistrate later this Sunday morning, in an emergency sitting. Did she understand?

She nodded. There was not a fraction of emotion on her face. It was like she had shut down. Maybe she had.

As they led my sister to one of the cars, pushing her into the back seat, she looked across the street and I stepped out, holding her gaze. For just a moment the moon appeared, casting a white glow across us, and then was hidden again.

—

THIS CANNOT BE happening. I planned this meticulously. How the fuck did Jen know what I was going to do? I cannot *believe* the betrayal. This is not happening. It's a mix-up. They've got nothing on me. I didn't slash him. No blood. How can they even imagine they can charge me with attempted murder? They cannot. I'm a respectable person, a professor at the most prestigious university in Queensland – people respect me, look up to me, I walk along the streets with my head held high – and they think they can pin an attempted murder on me? It's a joke. And if they think they can get anywhere near me with the killings of 1999, they're living in an altered universe. Robbie will hire a tribe of lawyers and they will decimate the police and then we'll sue them, sue their sorry arses from one side of the city to the other. Wrongful arrest, defamation. I'll write a book about it. And what was the Police Commissioner doing there? She belongs at a desk, not on the street. It's absurd. That has to be a sackable offence, leaving your desk and being on the street in a so-called operation in the middle of the night. I need to contact the Police Minister. Robbie knows the Premier. She will not be happy. That Asian bitch is going down. I'm going to make her life a misery. They can't touch me. Is it a crime to be walking along the street at night with a backpack and a knife inside it? And a pair of pliers? No. No, it is not. Is it a crime to whisper to a drunken guy at the end of a laneway, asking him if he could join me? No. No, it is not. I might have been lost. I might have been distressed, in need of aid. I wasn't going to kill him. I am not The Slayer. They have nothing on me. They are so going down. This is going to be the end of careers.

—

ANTHEA HAD NEVER been in a police car before. Most people haven't. The police officer who was driving kept glancing at her, through the rear-view mirror. He was young. Which made her think of her girls.

—

THERE ARE FOUR stages to the life of a butterfly. The first is, obviously, birth, when the butterfly is an egg. Eggs are laid in any of the seasons but rarely during winter. After four or five days, the egg will hatch in the second stage of what's known as metamorphosis and this stage is when it becomes a caterpillar. Not everybody knows that a caterpillar is a baby butterfly.

—

THE POLICE OFFICERS – the young driver and the other young officer sitting in the passenger seat – hadn't been told anything about the operation. They had no idea what was going down, and when this woman was thrust into the back of their cruiser, in handcuffs, amid a crazy melee out on the street, they hadn't been told who she was or what, indeed, was the charge against her. Just take her to the station at the Valley, put her in a holding cell until she's ready to be formally charged. So, that was their part in the capture of The Slayer. The real Slayer. Just a ferryman's journey, a ride across town of no more than ten minutes. Soon after they'd crossed the Breakfast Creek and were driving towards the station, the street lights buzzing over them with pockets of yellow-beam light, on an empty two-lane road, as a smatter of rain hit their windscreen, but no more than a smatter, all washed away with one swipe of the blades, their phones began to buzz with incoming texts. *u have the slayer in yr car*

—

SHE COULD SEE the look on the driver's face, as he looked up from his phone, to the mirror and stared at her in –

– in what? What was it she saw in his face?

Fear. Admiration. Respect.

She leaned back in the seat and held his gaze, as if daring him to keep a watch on The Slayer.

—

NOBODY REALLY KNOWS how many different types of butterflies there are in the world. Google will tell you there are approximately twenty thousand. Anthea, never one for approximates, believed, through her research and field work, that there were twenty-one thousand, three hundred and forty-six.

One of her most memorable sightings was of the incredibly rare *Ornithoptera alexandrae*, also called The Queen Alexandra Birdwing. Its wingspan can get up to nineteen centimetres long. This was when she went to Papua New Guinea, on a long and arduous field trip. With a long yellow and black-spotted body and wings that have pale green shapes and yellow spots with black circles, blue spots and a brilliant red heart-shaped area beneath its eyes. The female of the species has a wingspan that can reach up to twenty-eight centimetres. A sight, when she was stuck in a rain forest, she would never forget. She tried to catch one, for her wall at home, thinking how magnificent it would look in her lounge room. But it was too high off the ground, too far away. Too elusive.

—

WHAT WILL HAPPEN to the girls? She began to wonder. Who will tell them and what will they think? And, remembering how it was for her, when she was sixteen, when Jen was arrested, how she encountered walls of horror and incredulity at what people said her sister had done and how people stopped talking to her and walked on the other side of the street to avoid her, how the school suggested she should leave for the good of the others and how friend after friend peeled away until she was only left with a loyal group of girls who stayed in her circle, how her mum and dad lost their lives through grief and despair. Was this what was to befall the girls? Who would look after them? Fuck: Would they be put into care? Would Robbie handle it? No, he was weak. He would crumble with the pressure.

Guilt suddenly riding through her, she began to dread the inevitable confrontations with her husband, with her daughters. She wished she would die. Now. If only the police car drove off the side of the road, killing her. Then she wouldn't have to face them.

None of this was meant to happen.

She didn't want to see any of them. She vowed never to see them. She'll plead guilty, go straight to jail and never have to confront them, explain to them that she killed men by cutting across their necks, cutting open their mouths and ripping out a tooth, all the while adoring Him and where is He now? Not fucking here in the back seat of a police car, that's for sure. No, He's gone, like everyone has always gone.

Don't think about how the girls will feel when they discover what you did to the bodies. Remember when you used to smirk when another pedo would get done and you'd wonder how his wife and kids would respond when they knew that dad was wanking to the images of eight-year-olds? That's you Anthea. That's you and the girls and the Head Folds. Just put that out of your mind. It's okay, you won't have to see them ever again. Maybe it's better if they do go into care so they can forget about you like you're going to have to forget about them.

If you can.

—

THE THIRD STAGE in the life of a butterfly is when the caterpillar becomes a chrysalis, a wrapped-up cocoon which hangs under the branch of a tree. It may hang like this for two months, some even hanging for over a year and inside this cocoon, the butterfly is forming. Legs, head, wings.

Her students used to call this the womb-stage but, as she would point out in discussing the majesty of the butterfly and its ascent into life, this is the *third* stage.

It has already been born. It has already been a caterpillar crawling along twigs and grass.

When she was a little girl, Anthea used to put her head up close next to a chrysalis hanging from twigs or branches and try to hear whatever might be going on inside, perhaps the unfolding of a wing or the growth of a tail. As she imagined her dad did to her, when she was inside her mum's womb, trying to feel the kicks and listen to the hiccups.

She never could hear inside the chrysalis. Its magic was silent. Most times she would take a step back and stare at the green pupa or chrysalis, in wonderment. But sometimes anger would get the better of her and she would crush it in her hand.

——

JEN WAS LEFT standing in the middle of the road as many of the cops were dispersing as quickly as they had emerged. The laneway was full of light, from two kliegs, at both ends. As the crime scene was carefully examined by my forensics experts, I spoke to Jen.

'Thanks. You did well. Let's see how it goes down.' I couldn't offer her anything more.

It was unusual for me to be at a crime scene, but I needed to be front and centre, in command and in full control of the arrest of the real Slayer, not the one I helped send down the river twenty years ago. 'We'll need a record of interview with you,' I told Jen. 'I'll have some detectives come over in the morning.' I turned and walked away.

Before I climbed into my car, I texted Billy.

It's done.

All cops above the rank of Sergeant are politicians. At my rank, I was consummate. Billy, with his age and experience, was the same. Neither of us was going to be embarrassed by the discovery of the real Slayer. My media liaison people had already drafted the press release by five p.m. the previous day, after Jen had sent me the image of the teeth and well before the op went down.

Out of political courtesy, I rang the Police Minister. That it was three-thirty in the morning didn't matter. If it wasn't me, it would be Twitter and the mainstream media. The arrest of Anthea White was good for spin. A relentless police department, chasing justice even after twenty years; a sudden halt to the impending and very awkward Cowboy Ray law that was being drafted to go before parliament to put parolee Jen White behind bars for the rest of her life. That another person had been incarcerated for the crimes was gravely unfortunate and, by five a.m., the Premier had drafted a press release offering to compensate Jennifer White if indeed it was found, through the proper channels of the justice system, that another yet-to-be-formally-named person was responsible for the crimes.

That the yet-to-be-formally-named person whose face and bio was all over social media by four a.m. was Jen's sister made Jen's arrest and conviction a little less onerous. We just got the wrong sister. So close, almost nailed it. Right house. Wrong girl.

—

I WALKED BACK up the hill as the dawn began to appear. There had been a light rain that might have lasted for three minutes and with the heat of the morning, steam was rising off the black asphalt. It was Sunday. People were sleeping in. Somewhere, off in the distance, I heard the sound of church bells from below, perhaps from the other side of the river and, for a moment, I imagined the congregation, old and young, kids, at the beginning of life, some closing in to the end. Where had they come from and what would happen to them?

The house was silent and the girls asleep when I opened the front door. Lara had told me that Anthea's house would be impounded for any potential evidence. Meaning the teeth. Like me, Lara was intrigued by the additional two. Neither of us imagined that Anthea had destroyed them; she was too proud for that. They were her trophies.

I picked up the phone and dialled.

'Hello?' he said, answering after the third ring.

'Robbie. It's Jen. No-one is hurt but you need to come home immediately.'

'What are you talking about?' he demanded. 'Put Anthea on.'

I hung up. I didn't pick up when the landline went off straight after. I went downstairs and into Maxi's room, then into little Jen's room.

'Time to get up, girls.'

———

AND THEN, AFTER being wrapped in the chrysalis, the butterfly emerges. Unfurling its wings, tasting air for the first time since it was a caterpillar, reaching upwards, its wings in motion, perfect grace, it begins its ascent towards the sky.

Acknowledgements

THIS BOOK COULD NOT HAVE BEEN WRITTEN WITHOUT THE invaluable help and guidance from Lucio Rovis on just how the wheels of a Homicide investigation work. Lucio was tireless and generous in his feedback to me and in recounting his days as a rookie cop, working his way up into a long and distinguished career in Victoria Police.

Any errors are mine, not his.

I am blessed to have a brilliant editor, Claire de Medici. She and Rebecca Allen and my wonderful publisher Vanessa Radnidge at Hachette have been awesome in providing feedback on the story and the characters, not to mention the areas where I might go a little wayward. (The grammar stuff.) Again, any errors are mine, not theirs.

I would like to thank my Chinese friends and colleagues who have shared their experiences with me, as living betwixt two worlds, as Australians but with very Chinese parents, especially mums. I first encountered the left-over syndrome some years ago, when teaching some brilliant Chinese young women and this set off my interest in the difference between the two cultures, especially in the world of Millennials in C21. Without their insights, I could never have approached the character of Lara.

I'd also like to thank my mid-80s-year-old ex-gangster friend who grew up in the East End during the war, nicking a telly for his mum at the age of seven, for sharing his childhood experiences with me. Out of these stories came Billy and thanks to the real Bill W for allowing me to use his name. (And that's all they share.)

Thanks also to Donna Mex for allowing me to use her name. As with Bill, the real deal Donna and the fictional Donna are nothing alike.

Also from the greatest city in Australia (being Ararat) and mentioned in the text are Paul Leigh, being Ranger Paul, Annette, Annice and Jo.

Thanks to Dr Gordon Guymer, Director, Queensland Herbarium, Department of Environment and Science for his advice on the swamp daisy. Thanks to Professor Simon Lewis, Forensic and Analytical Chemistry in the School of Molecular and Life Sciences, Curtin University, for his advice on all things technical when it comes to forensics in an investigation.

I would also like to very much thank an ex-President of a parole board in Australia for sharing insight into how Karin would operate and how, generally, the board operates in some very tricky situations, especially with politicians.

Again, any errors, you know who to blame.

Thanks to Emilie Chetty for all the insight into the Seychelles, some of which ended up on the cutting room floor. Thanks to a circle of extremely talented writers who were terrific sounding-boards, Matt Ford, John Misto, Fleur Ferris, Martine Delaney, Rachael McGuirk, Scott Wilbanks, Louise Lee-Mei; thanks to Laura Franks for the info about how to get a job at Bunnings, Maggie Lamont on where Nils would probably have stayed in Port Moresby, 1990, to Ross Macrae for reading earlier drafts and for his memories of Bald Hills, to the anchors of Dela, Ruby and Scarlett and to Cassandra McGuinness, to whom this is dedicated, for putting up with a partner who exited life on planet earth for way too long while having embarked on this book and, with the best of grace, listened endlessly to the journeys of Lara and Billy, Anthea and Karin. Without her calm and love, I'd still be writing this in 2023.

This is my fifth novel. Never imagined I would write one and, with all of them, as I reach the end, I imagine there will be no more. But here we are; as always, I am in your debt, Dear Reader, whoever you are and wherever you may be.

I am honoured to have had the company of you and your precious time.

Tony Cavanaugh is an Australian crime novelist, screenwriter and film and television producer. He has over thirty years' experience in the film industry, has lectured at several prestigious universities and has been a regular guest on radio commenting on the film and television industry. His Darian Richards novels, which include *Promise, Dead Girl Sing, The Train Rider* and *Kingdom of the Strong*, have been highly praised and critically acclaimed in both Australia and in France. *Blood River* is a standalone thriller that demonstrates the master of crime Tony Cavanaugh has become.

For more information about Tony Cavanaugh visit his Facebook page (/tonycavanaugh888) or follow him on Twitter (@TonyCavanaugh1).

hachette
AUSTRALIA

If you would like to find out more about Hachette Australia,
our authors, upcoming events and new releases you can visit
our website or our social media channels:

hachette.com.au
 HachetteAustralia
HachetteAus